THE
REVOLUTION

Alicia Michaels

Crimson Tree Publishing

THE REVOLUTION
Printed in the United States of America
Crimson Tree Publishing

SUMMARY: Blythe Sol has an unusual New Year's Resolution…she wants to end the conflict between the government and the Resistance—by sneaking into Washington D.C. and putting a bullet in President Drummond's skull. If she can cut the head off the snake, the genocide of the Bionics might finally end. But if she fails, she will surely bring retaliation crushing down upon the entire Resistance…

ISBN: 978-1-63422-296-9 (paperback)
ISBN: 978-1-63422-297-6 (e-book)
Cover Design by: Marya Heidel
Typography by: Courtney Knight
Editing by: Cynthia Shepp

Fiction / Science Fiction / Apocalyptic & Post-Apocalyptic
Fiction / Science Fiction / Genetic Engineering
Fiction / African American / Urban
Fiction / Science Fiction / Cyberpunk

PART ONE: AFTERSHOCK
(Blythe Sol)

ONE

My hair clings to my face and neck, the wet strands curling as water washes over me in a deluge. A crack of thunder precedes the flash of lightning, but I keep walking, unperturbed by the manufactured storm. I know the Professor's weather program is created by machines, connected to a series of sensors and simulators built into the dome encasing Resistance Headquarters. Even though a computer randomly chooses our weather while keeping track of the seasons, it seems as if this storm has been selected just for this day. A sense of normality is what he was going for when he created the system—something to keep us from remembering we are trapped underground and hiding to preserve our lives.

Yet, today we said good-bye to one of our own—something we seem to be doing a lot of lately.

Sayer Strom. Yasmine. Trista.

Gage.

If this is normal, then the future seems pretty fucking hopeless.

Hunching my shoulders, I ignore the freezing temperature seeping through the soaked clothes adhering to my body. I pay no attention to the puddles causing my socks to grow wet inside my shoes, and keep trudging toward the sprawling green arcade at the center of the dome. Swiping my arm across my eyes, I clear it of the water destroying my vision and blink, finally seeing the reason I crossed the dome in the rain and cold without a coat on to keep me warm.

Not far from the playground, Dax kneels in the grass, his broad shoulders slumped, head lowered. He seems oblivious to the rain, to the lightning flashing overhead, and the wind battering him without mercy. In the midst of it all he sits unmoving, a six-foot-two, two-hundred-and-sixty-five-pound hunk of concrete. At his side sits Dog, a figure as forlorn as his master, his ginger-colored fur hopelessly matted and dripping wet. His ears are drooping, his tail the stillest I've ever seen it, as if he understands Dax's grief.

Pausing just behind him, I reach out but halt just short of placing my hand on his shoulder. Would he even want me here while he grieves? Should I have stayed in my room and left him where he's been kneeling since Yasmine's memorial service ended two hours ago?

Lowering my arm, I take a step backward and make up my mind to go inside. It was stupid of me to come out here to disturb him, especially after I'd closeted myself away in my room in the days following Gage's death, refusing to see or speak to anyone. But, eventually, Dax and Yasmine had forced me to let them in. They wouldn't allow me to grieve alone.

Just when I have decided to approach him after all, he turns his head and swivels his gaze toward me.

"I don't intend to stay out here all day, in case you were wondering," he mumbles before turning to face forward again.

It has stopped surprising me that he seems to always know when I'm close—as if he can *feel* my presence. I've stopped questioning our connection, because trying to figure it out has left me with more questions than answers.

Stepping up beside him, I kneel, joining him on the sopping grass. I glance over and notice he cradles Yasmine's urn in his large hands, its gleaming silver contrasting sharply with Dax's dark skin.

For a long while, I simply sit with him and Dog while the rain and wind continue to slam into us. A few hours ago, beneath an overcast sky, many of us stood in this exact spot while the Professor guided us through a funeral of sorts. It mainly consisted of us trying not to cry while people took turns saying nice things about Yasmine. Despite having known her better than the rest of us, Dax refused to speak.

I can't say I blame him. What he had with Yasmine is for him to remember in private, just as I have mourned Gage behind closed doors. Speaking of them to others feels like betrayal—it feels like giving away the only pieces of them we have left.

"It's been two hours," I say, raising my voice to be heard over the rain. "It's cold out today. Come inside before you make yourself sick."

The rain begins to slow a bit, signaling an end to the storm. Turning his head toward me again, he stares at me with his dark, glittering eyes. His face seems stuck in a permanent scowl, causing his forehead to crease and his mouth to pinch at the corners.

"Why?"

I raise my eyebrows. "Why what?"

He sighs. "Why come inside or care about getting sick? Why anything? What's the fucking point, B?"

Apathy. I know the feeling well.

"What happened to fighting?" I say, reminding him of his words the day Yasmine died in his arms. "I thought you said it was time for us to start winning for once."

He shakes his head and snorts. The last of the rain has fallen, leaving the sky overcast. The scent of the air after a real storm is missing, and it leaves a pit of longing in my gut. I've forgotten that smell, just as I've forgotten how to function like a normal person. All I know is death and loss.

"What are we even doing here?" he replies. "I'm tired. I don't have anything left to fight for. Yasmine was what I had decided to fight for—the chance to have something of my own when this was all over."

"You can still have that."

Setting the urn aside, he unfolds his long legs to stand, towering over me with his hands braced on his narrow hips. "Don't you get it? There *is* no end … not for us! We are going to fight until we die, and that's all there will ever be. And what the hell are we trying to gain anyway? A chance to live in fear, cowering underground?"

Standing to face him, I clench my hands into fists at my sides. "A chance to have a life out there when this war is over!"

I raise my hand and point toward the hovercraft hangar, which opens into a tunnel leading to the outside. "That world is just as much ours as it is theirs," I tell him. "Don't you want it back? Don't you want to crawl out of this hole, step into the light, and stop running? We have to fight!"

Bending to pick up Yasmine's urn, he tucks it under one arm. "I don't have to do a goddamn thing but be black and die. I got the first part covered, and the second is coming any day now if President Drummond follows through on his warning."

He starts to walk away from me, but I follow, trotting to keep up with his long strides. "What about me?"

Pausing, he swivels to face me. "What?"

I draw up short before I slam into him, the momentum of my fast pace almost causing us to collide. Swallowing past the lump of grief in my throat, I wrap my arms around myself. "I don't have anybody else," I whisper. "My family is dead; Gage is gone. Yasmine became like a sister to me, and I know her death hurt you more than anyone here, but I lost her, too. But before Gage or Yasmine ... before the Resistance ... we had each other."

Snorting, Dax rolls his eyes. "So, this is about you?"

Grinding my teeth, I fight the urge to punch him in the face. Could I have been this much of a bitch after Gage died?

"Of course not! This is about *us*. I will never stop fighting for you, because the man who saved my life deserves a chance to redeem his. And if I'm going to fight for you, then you have to do the same. I can't do this alone."

His jaw flexes as he looks away, staring off across the quad. "You aren't alone. You have the Professor, Olivia, Laura, and Alec. You have hundreds of people who would follow you into hell, and thousands more out there rooting for you even though they can't actually fight with you."

I curse under my breath as a tear slips free of my human eye. "What about Agata, huh? You gonna give up on her, too?"

Dax's eyes glimmer with tears when he looks at me and shakes his head. "I couldn't save Yasmine. What makes you think I can protect that girl?"

"It doesn't matter if you can or not," I insist. "It doesn't matter if you try and fail, or if you fall short. All that matters is that you fight. It's okay to be sad right now. Hell, I'm sad, too. But when we're done being sad, we have to keep moving forward. She would have wanted us to keep going, and you know it."

Nodding, he sniffs while a few tears track down his chiseled face. "I had stopped hoping, B. She made me hope again, and now she's gone. It hurts so much."

Reaching out, I take his face in my hands and pull him toward me, resting his head on my shoulder. He hunches from his massive height and leans into me, wrapping one arm around my waist and holding on as if his life depends on it. His hold is painful, but I endure it, hugging him and holding on just as tight. Loving Dax has always hurt; I am used to this.

"I know," I whisper, closing my eyes. "But the pain is a good thing. If we can feel the pain, it means we're still alive. We're healing."

He nods, the stubble on his jaw stinging my neck. "I'm sorry."

Forcing him to look at me, I give him a smile. "No apologies needed. We're allowed to be assholes to each other during hard times. We always forgive each other. It's part of our friend code."

Laughing, he reaches up and swipes his tears away. "We have a code?"

I nod, then wrap one arm around his waist, guiding him back toward Mosley Hall. "Oh, yeah. It's a standard friendship contract that doesn't end until we're both dead."

Arching an eyebrow, he purses his lips. "Standard contract, huh? Does that mean we can't do each other's exes?"

"Definitely not," I reply.

"Damn it," he grumbles. "You and Olivia ... that would be hot as hell."

Elbowing him in the ribs, I scowl, but then burst into laughter when he starts to chuckle. Just before we step into the dorm, the clouds part to allow the sun to shine. Pausing, I turn my face up to catch the warmth, holding tight to the best friend I've ever known—the best I'm likely to ever have.

It's a small moment, but within that span of a few seconds, I allow myself to feel normal. Maybe—just maybe—we will be okay.

Someday.

TWO

BLYTHE SOL, DAX JANNER, OLIVIA MCNABB, ALEC KINNEAR, LAURA
ROSENBERG, PROFESSOR NEVILLE HINKLEY, AND SENATOR ALEXIS DAVIS
RESTORATION RESISTANCE HEADQUARTERS
DECEMBER 26, 4010
8:00 A.M.

THE NEXT MORNING, DAX AND I ENTER THE CONFERENCE ROOM TO FIND ALEC AND
Olivia already there, sucking face and groping each other. I falter in the
doorway, causing Dax to barrel into me. The two remain oblivious, kissing
while Olivia straddles Alec with her arms wrapped around his neck. Alec's
titanium hand gleams in the overhead lights as he uses it to get a handful
of her ass.

"Are these two for real?" Dax mumbles, pushing past me to get into
the room. "Hey, knock it off!"

Breaking their kiss, Olivia remains in Alec's lap, but glances over her
shoulder. "Jealous?"

Rolling his eyes, Dax drops into his chair and slouches. "Not even.
Save that shit for the bedroom."

Joining them at the table, I take my place next to Dax and try not to
stare at the empty seat on his other side—Yasmine's seat. "He's right,
guys. The Professor will be here any minute, and we don't have time to
screw around."

"Speak for yourselves," Alec murmurs, still nuzzling Olivia's neck. "I
always have time to screw around."

Those two have been inseparable since Alec stepped in to help
Olivia recover from her traumatic imprisonment at Stonehead. She'd
been returned to us in pieces, a shadow of her former self. No one knows

exactly what he did, but it worked. She's mostly her old self again, though a harsh glimmer still lingers in her eyes. She still talks about finding the man responsible for her torture and killing him. Not that anyone blames her. Captain Rodney Jones, commander of the Restoration Enforcers Squadron arm of the Military Police, has destroyed many lives, including mine. The same man who ordered his guards to rape, beat, and torture Olivia also put a gun to my father's head and pulled the trigger, before doing the same to my mother. He'd stood by while one of his cronies shot my baby sister. The only person I want dead as much as President Drummond is him.

Reluctantly, Olivia stands and finds her own chair just as the Professor and Laura Rosenberg join us. Dressed in his usual lab coat, the Professor looks haggard and drawn, as if he hasn't slept in days. Laura isn't much better, her hair a messy ponytail with several strands hanging into eyes sporting dark circles. They both carry a lot of guilt concerning Yasmine's death—Laura, because the two of them had been together and she'd been unable to save Yasmine, and the Professor because his technology had been the weapon used to kill her.

Still, life goes on and the revolution stalls for no man.

"Good, everyone is here," the Professor says as he drops into his chair. "We'll just wait for the senator to arrive before we begin."

Clearing my throat, I sit up straighter in my chair. "Any word from Jenica yet?"

Sighing, he shakes his head. "Nothing yet, which could be either a good sign or a bad one. Either she's finally figured out what the Rejects are up to and is formulating a plan to stop them, or..."

He trails off and runs a hand through his messy curls. We all know the truth of what he doesn't say. If we don't hear from Jenica soon, it means the Rejects have likely found out she and several others infiltrated their ranks in order to gather intel. Should that turn out to be true, it means she might already be dead.

"Jenica is too smart to get caught," I assure him. "I'm sure she'll send word soon. She's probably just waiting until she can transmit a message to us safely."

The Professor nods, but his mouth is pinched and his eyes watery. Few people know he and Jenica are in a relationship, because the two decided to keep it a secret. I witnessed his tenderness and care with her firsthand, and know in my heart her loss would destroy him. I hope my words are more than just meaningless platitudes, and she really will make her way back to us.

The door to the office opens, and Senator Alexis Davis appears. It has taken some time to grow used to seeing her out of her usual white suits and sleek, blonde bun. She's taken to wearing the same clothes as the rest of us—flight suits and thermal tops with leather or suede pants. Always, the symbol of the Resistance can be seen on her person. Today, she's chosen to wear her armband, a black swatch of cloth wrapped around her bicep with the cog symbol standing out in white.

"Good morning, everyone," she says, assuming her place where Jenica usually sits at the foot of the table, across from the Professor. "Thank you for waiting."

"No problem," the Professor replies. "I was just telling everyone that we still have no word from Jenica concerning the Rejects, or the reason behind their presence in Des Moines. Perhaps we should discuss our next move on that front."

Alec clears his throat. "I'm still searching for answers, combing the internet for any whisper of what might be happening there. Unfortunately, there's very little coming out of the city itself. The Rejects have the people on lockdown, and all the news outlets are reporting that things have been mostly quiet. Whatever they're planning, it's going down soon."

"I say we send someone else in," Laura chimes in. "I know Swan told us to wait, but she could be in trouble and unable to send us her orders."

"She has a point," Dax says.

I shake my head. "It's too dangerous. The city is overrun with them. Baron is protecting whatever it is they're after, which means it's important enough for them to die for. They won't hesitate to go balls to the wall in taking us out if we go on the offensive."

"I'm not suggesting an attack," Laura argues. "Just a little recon mission. Maybe a few more of us can pretend to defect to their side like Jenica did. Alec has some black-market contacts who could even load us up with extra parts ... make us look freakish like them. The parts can always come off later, but they would get us in."

"I do not like the idea of risking more members of our team," Senator Davis says. "Jenica took people with her, and we lost many in the skirmish during the D.C. protest."

"And you all saw the video from the chip President Drummond delivered via Yasmine," the Professor says. "He has officially declared war on the Bionics, which means more people will be coming here to escape his reach."

Olivia shakes her head. "They can't all come here. We're stuffed to the rafters as it is. The dorms are overflowing—even the new one. We're two and three to a room already."

"No one will be turned away," the Professor insists. "Many of the hideouts are having to be cleared as the MPs uncover more of our bases. There is nowhere else for them to go."

"Which is why it's time to go on the offensive," Alec declares.

Every head in the room swivels toward him, and he stands with his hands braced behind his back.

"Look, I know this resistance began as a peaceful one," he continues. "But we're past that now. They are going to kill us, no questions asked. That wasn't a threat—it was a promise. Few of the hideouts have the fortifications and resources we have, which means hiding isn't going to be an option much longer. Yes, they can come here, but for how long? We can't keep living on top of each other and waiting for the president to stop being a piece of shit."

Dax snorts. "Not gonna happen."

"Exactly," Alec agrees. "Which is why it's time to start really fighting back. Our polls indicate several developments. The first is the American people want Drummond out. The only thing keeping him in the White House is martial law. His move in extending himself into another term has wound them up, and the people aren't having it. There are protests happening outside the White House daily ... people calling for Drummond to resign."

"That's a good thing," Olivia says. "They are waking up and realizing they've let him get away with too much for too long."

Alec nods. "Right. The second development we've seen is the people have spoken and declared they would rather have Senator Davis here leading the country. Yet, many of them don't see how we can make this happen. The senator is in hiding, here with us, and Drummond has the Senate and House in his pockets. This has made the people angry, and they are crying for new leadership altogether ... a complete purging of the political system."

"That'll never happen," Dax counters. "Politicians are scumbags who don't like to relinquish power. No offense, Senator."

Alexis shrugs. "None taken. And he's right. The current political climate is one of corruption and greed. The government profits off fear and propaganda. We need to start using those two things against them. The people have feared the Bionics for too long ... it's time they started fearing what their government has been doing. If they don't fight back, soon it won't just be our liberties being stomped on ... theirs will be, too."

"What do you suggest?" the Professor asks. "We can't ask them to fight our battle."

"No," Alexis agrees. "But we can open their eyes to the notion that it's just as much their fight as ours. Alec, can you fit our team members with body cameras?"

He nodded. "That's too easy. I can throw a few together today if you give me a few hours. They'll be waterproof and able to withstand a great amount of force. Blythe won't really need one since her bionic eye has recording capabilities."

"Good," Alexis says. "We are going to send our teams out as usual, to help rescue those who are trapped in their hideouts and need to get here. You will offer them an armed escort and shelter at Resistance Headquarters. Our intelligence indicates at least five hideouts the MPs are closing in on. Those people need to be extracted and brought here."

"That's a given," I say, turning to look at her. "But what are the cameras for?"

She raises her eyebrows. "You can count on the Military Police to show up ... especially in the places where our hideouts have already been sniffed out. They'll have surveillance watching for a rescue party. When it arrives, they will attack. The cameras are so people in the field can get footage of the officers' actions. Americans need to see what happens when the people—women and children—come face to face with our militarized police force."

Dax widens his eyes. "You want us to make snuff films of them murdering innocent people?"

The senator sighs. "Listen, I don't like it any more than you do. But I'm telling you, it's going to happen whether we record it or not. We're talking about moving hundreds of people—in some cases across the country, and under new laws proclaiming Bionics are to be executed on sight. You are all skilled fighters and good at what you do. However, we need to be realistic here. There *will* be casualties, and some of them will be innocent women, children, and elderly. The people need to witness what you all have suffered... They need to have it blown up and put on their televisions, so they can sit on their cushy couches and be forced to witness it. Alec can interrupt the airwaves at any time to run our videos, which he has done. It's time to turn up the heat, people. Americans need to see the truth, no matter how ugly."

Nodding, Dax glances at the gleaming table in front of him. "I'm in. When can we leave?"

"You can leave as soon as supplies and hovercrafts can be prepared," the professor declares. "Tomorrow if you like, once supplies are gathered and hovercrafts have been fueled."

Alec raises his hand for attention. "Um, if I can make another suggestion..."

The Professor inclines his head. "Alec, you have been a valuable member of this team. You are free to speak your mind."

He nods, seemingly flattered by the Professor's praise. "Thank you, sir. I'm all for going toe to toe with the Military Police, but if we're going to do that, we need to arm up."

"I thought weapons were recovered in Leesburg?" the Professor points out.

Alec shakes his head. "That stuff didn't go very far. As of now, we're about five to six men for every gun. With all due respect, sir, those are shitty numbers going up against the MPs who have body armor and an endless supply of weapons. We need to be more like two guns to every man, if not more."

"Weapons are scarce," Laura says. "The gun ban ensured even recreational weapons were outlawed. The only people with guns are the military and the government."

"I know where you can get weapons, and possibly even armored vehicles," he says.

"That's what I'm talking about," Dax says. "Details, man."

"I'm getting there," Alec says with a chuckle. "When the government decided to militarize the police force, it pretty much did away with our armed forces. They're all combined into one organization, which means less money to go around. They consolidated and closed about half the nation's bases. However, when they shut down, they left behind a butt load of supplies—armor, weapons, ammo, vehicles, and probably even some food."

"Just like Leesburg," I say, remembering how we helped him break into the old Marine base to grab weapons to use against the Rejects in their attack on the Virginia city. "You're right; there was a shit ton of stuff left behind. I always felt so stupid for not taking more."

Dax shrugs. "There wasn't time. We were in a hurry to get back to the city and help Jenica fight them off. Are they all just abandoned like that? I have a hard time believing the government would just leave millions of dollars in equipment sitting around, unguarded."

"It's not exactly unguarded," Alec says. "But the guards aren't human. All the bases have some sort of electronic security system that should be easy enough to disarm. If you can get in, you can take your time loading up on weapons and whatever else you need. While you're at it, you should probably grab any food you scrounge up. You'll be bringing back hundreds of extra mouths, and we need to be able to feed them all."

"Figuring out a new system of rationing is at the top of my priority list," the Professor says. "While you're gone, Alec and I will prepare to receive the refugees."

Alec nods in agreement, but I can see he'd rather be doing anything other than helping the Professor count bags of instant potatoes. The truth is we need him here even though he's a badass in the field. He's a tech genius, and the one who has kept our videos on the airwaves. While he would probably rather join us in the fight, he's more valuable here.

"I will assist as well," the senator offers.

"This will give us something to do while we wait for word from Jenica," the Professor adds. "Make sure you take our best COMM devices into the field. We'll need to make contact the moment we receive word from her."

I stand, stretching my arms over my head. "Sounds like a plan. Dax, you and Olivia can help me assemble our teams and divide up supplies while we wait for Alec to get those cameras ready."

Dax joins me on his feet. "All right then ... let's go give 'em hell."

THREE

DAX AND I RETURN TO MOSLEY HALL AFTER A LONG DAY OF PREPARING FOR tomorrow's mission, both exhausted and hungry. While I worked with the mechanics to ensure *Icarus* is ready for both flight and a possible fight, Dax teamed up with Laura to make sure we are ready to take on hundreds of refugees. With only a quick break to scarf down some beef jerky—which isn't made with actual beef, but beggars can't be choosers—we push through the day to make sure we leave no contingency unplanned for. *Icarus* has a full tank, with extra fuel on board, and each of its weapons systems have been tested and found to be fully functional. Stored in every available compartment are food and water rations, along with materials for starting fires, first aid supplies, blankets, and every weapon we can spare that won't be carried by the members of my crew.

We're wheels up at six, leaving us with nothing left to do but try to rest.

Entering the room we now share with Agata—due to the overcrowding caused by an influx of new residents—we find Gage's niece seated at the little desk in the corner, Dog curled up at her feet. Instead of the stacks of books usually littering any surface near her, she's got a set of tools and a hodgepodge of metal parts. Her bionic cerebrum has made her smarter than any eight-year-old I've ever met. She's basically a walking computer, and now that she's been spending so much time in the lab with the Professor and his apprentices, she's turned into quite the little inventor.

We've given up asking her what she's working on, since the string of complicated words she uses to try to explain only makes our heads hurt. All we know is, tinkering at this little desk after she returns from the lab seems to be helping her cope with the deaths of her mother and uncle.

No one could have imagined Trista would show up here with several children rescued from a Resistance hideout, but when she had, it had been too late to save her. She gave her life to save those children, and I hope Agata can find comfort in such a selfless act. Perhaps knowing Gage and Trista died to protect people like us stops their loss from feeling pointless. History may never remember them for the things they've done, but damn it, we will never forget.

"Hey, Gidget," Dax murmurs as he pauses near the desk, placing an affectionate hand on Agata's head. He leans down to pet Dog—a wiry red-brown terrier mix—who raises his furry head and whines for attention.

Gidget is the nickname he gave her once she became a tinkerer—a play on the word 'gadget', but with a feminine twist, according to him. Who knows how he came up with it, but Agata seems to like it. The two have grown close since Gage's death. Dax has made it his personal mission to look out for her after we lost her uncle.

"Hi," she replies without looking up from her work. "When do you leave?"

Taking off the thermal shirt I'm wearing over a tank top, I laugh. "How do you know we're leaving?"

"You smell like fuel, and Dax has ink on his hands, like he's been doing inventory," she says, barely sparing us a glance before going back to work.

It doesn't surprise me she notices these things; Agata perceives everything. Those piercing blue eyes only need a few seconds to pick something apart in that brilliant mind of hers and then put it back together.

I exchange glances with Dax, who simply smirks and stares at her with so much pride you'd think she was his by blood. And maybe she is. We are all connected by blood and loss ... by death.

Dropping onto the cot on my side of the room, I pull off my boots, wiggling my toes with a groan once they're free. "First thing in the morning...

at six."

Agata mutters something imperceptible and continues tinkering, while Dax ducks into the bathroom we share with the people on the other side of it. The room that was once his now belongs to four others. Things are getting crowded in Resistance Headquarters, but this is the most secure place for the Bionics to hide with nearly all of our safehouses now compromised.

After a few minutes, the toilet flushes and Dax reappears from the bathroom. After saying he's going to run downstairs and grab dinner for us, he leaves. With so many people now living here, the dining hall usually overflows during mealtimes. This late, it might not be so bad, but neither of us is good company lately—preferring to hole up in this room with Agata and each other whenever we aren't working or in meetings with the Professor. This mission will be a nice change of pace, giving us something to do other than sit around and wallow in our grief.

While Dax is gone, I prepare for bed—taking a quick shower and changing into soft shorts and a clean top. I carefully store my dirty clothes in the bag we carry down to the laundry when it's time to wash. Everything must be meticulously stored to keep our already-cramped space from being overrun. We let Agata leave her books and gadgets wherever she drops them, because even though she's a genius, she's still just a kid. To compensate, Dax and I keep our things stored, with only a few allowances made for certain personal effects.

For Dax, this means Yasmine's urn, a piece of shrapnel he once dug out of his shoulder—no idea why he insists on keeping it—and a scrap of pillowcase he swears still smells like Yasmine's hair. I catch him holding it sometimes, running his thumb over the fabric before lifting it to his nose to inhale the scent still clinging to the cotton.

On my side of the room are the photo of my father I received for my birthday, along with one of the sketches Gage drew of me—the one of my face in profile with the inside of my head exposed to show the wires and machinery attached to my bionic eye. In the corner of the drawing is his signature, along with the little cog symbol he created, which we've turned into the badge of the Resistance. Folded and stuffed in its envelope is the letter Gage wrote me before being forced to leave Resistance Headquarters—the one where he encouraged me to become the spark our movement needed in order to catch fire.

These are the only pieces of him I have left—a folded letter, the sketch he left behind with it, and my guilt over having been a part of voting to send him away in the first place. By casting the deciding vote, I sent him to his death, and I will never forgive myself for that. Perhaps by being there for Agata now, I can right that wrong. It was what he would have wanted, regardless of what I did to him, of the lies that had once stood between us, of the fact that even though I loved him, a part of me always has, and always will, belong to Dax.

On a shelf between both pictures rests the rank pin my father once wore on his uniform. On any given mission, it can be found somewhere on my person. It always serves as a reminder of my shattered dreams and the family I lost ... a token to help me never forget why I fight.

Soon, Dax comes back with three trays, one of which he places in my hands. While I sink onto my bed with my dinner, he gently pushes Agata's project and tools aside to place one in front of her.

"Eat," he commands in a firm tone that never ceases to make me smile. He tries to be so tough, but there's no disguising how much he loves this little girl.

He catches the grin as he sinks onto his own bed with the third tray and frowns. "What?"

Shaking my head, I lower my gaze to the tray in my lap. "Nothing ... just thinking you'll be a great father someday."

Taking a bite of genetically engineered chicken, Dax grunts and shrugs one big shoulder.

"Would have been," he mumbles with his mouth full. "Maybe."

I force myself to start eating even though I'm not hungry, and try not to dwell on Dax's newfound disdain for the future. He truly does not expect to live through this, and has let go of all dreams regarding any type of future he might have had. Those things lay inside that urn, mingled with

Yasmine's ashes.

We finish eating in silence, and Dax gathers our trays, then deposits them in the hall. Since more of us have started eating in our dorms, someone always comes to collect the trays.

While Dax takes his turn in the shower, I sit on my bed and glance over at Agata, who went back to working as soon as she had finished eating.

Inclining my head, I squint, recognizing the shape her project has begun to take. "A helmet?"

She nods and holds it up, so I can get a better look at it. "It looks a bit rough, but it'll function the way I need it to."

I wrinkle my brow and watch as she goes back to fiddling around with the parts inside it—various panels line the interior, which look as if they'll light up once activated. The helmet is small, likely made to fit her head.

"What's it for?" I ask, both curiosity and dread blossoming in my gut. I have a feeling I know where this is going.

"When Uncle Gage took me on that rescue mission to Stonehead, the MPs were prepared," she replies, as if that is explanation enough.

"Your bionic cerebrum emits an EMP," I recall. "You were supposed to use it to shut down the electricity at the prison and the night-vision capabilities of the Military Police armor."

"Right," she replies. "Only as soon as I emitted the pulse, they retaliated. Some sort of signal producing a high-pitched screech only I could hear. It made me unable to do what I'd been brought to do. So, I created this helmet … which will help to block out anything that would interfere with my EMP."

Thinking of the last time we used her EMP to shut down an MP hovercraft, I smile. She did her work from the safety of our hangar, and once she'd destroyed the electrical systems, we'd found Laura, Yasmine, Trista, and the rescued kids inside instead of the enemy.

"I don't think you're going to need that here," I reply, even though I can't be sure. If Headquarters is ever found and we're attacked, it will be a bloodbath—but first, they'll do everything they can to make sure we can't fight back.

Putting down one of her tools, she swivels in the chair to face me, the helmet clutched between both hands. "I know ... but it's not for me to wear here."

A cold stone of dread settles in my gut as I realize what she means. "Agata, you aren't a soldier, you're a child. A smart one, granted, but still ... we should never have sent you on the mission to Stonehead to begin with. You could have been captured or killed, and that's a risk we aren't willing to take."

I don't say out loud what losing her would do to Dax and me. What it would do to the members of this Resistance to watch her murdered by those sadistic MPs. On every mission we set out on since losing Gage in D.C., I expect to come home at least one man short. Things are too volatile, and we are now in the midst of an all-out war. Agata will not become a casualty of that. Dax and I promised each other, as well as Gage and Trista, that we would look out for her.

"May I ask you something?" she asks, her tone remaining even and calm.

Unlike most children, Agata doesn't become angry when adults tell her she can't do something. She simply tries to rationalize all the reasons she should be allowed to. Damned smarty-pants.

"Sure," I reply, deciding to humor her.

"How old was your sister when the MPs murdered her?"

The question is unexpected. For a moment, I feel as if I've been punched in the gut. My chest aches as I relive watching a bullet tear through Skyye's back and explode out through her stomach, her blood and intestines strewn across the front lawn.

Taking a deep breath, I blink the images away. "She would be your age by now," I tell her.

Agata nods, as if she'd already known the answer. She only asked me to make a point.

"If she could have saved herself—fought back somehow—wouldn't you have wanted her to try?"

I reach out to stroke Agata's hair with a smile. "Maybe. I think it's hard, wanting you kids to have some sense of a normal life, but still needing you to understand the reality of the world we live in. If Skyye was still here, I'd protect her with everything I have. She wouldn't have to know how to fight, because I would fight for her."

"Why give a man a fish so he can eat for a day, when you can teach a man to fish so he can feed himself for a lifetime?" Agata counters.

Damn. The girl has a point. I was only eighteen when I was forced to go into hiding. Soon after, I joined the Resistance, where I learned to fight, shoot, and fly hovercrafts. I had lost everything, and was determined to fight, to find something to put my hope in so I wouldn't fall apart completely.

This little girl has lost just as much as I have. Who am I to tell her she shouldn't fight?

I reach out to take the helmet from her and inspect it, turning it over to peer inside. Her work is immaculate, as if she's been inventing and tinkering her entire life. If someone had handed me this helmet and told me the Professor had made it, and I didn't know Agata actually had, I would believe them.

"This is good work," I say, handing it back.

She grins, showcasing the gap where a recently lost tooth used to be. "Thank you."

Sighing, I run a hand through my hair. "Let me talk to Dax about this, okay? He and I decided to take care of you together, so I won't make this decision without him."

Agata's smile widens as she nods. "That's fair."

"In the meantime, keep working on your helmet, but don't tell anyone what it's for," I warn.

Setting the helmet aside, she launches herself against me, wrapping her arms around my neck. I hold her and close my eyes, reveling in the sort of contact I used to shun. Before she and Gage came into my life, I didn't like to be touched. Now, it's all I have to remind me of my humanity. Clinging to the people I love who are left is the only thing keeping me alive anymore, and I love this girl as much as I loved her brother.

The door of the bathroom swings open, and Dax appears dressed for bed.

"Hey," he rumbles as he stashes his dirty clothes in the laundry bag. "Where's *my* hug?"

Agata bounces off me and into Dax's arms, giggling as he lifts her and spins her in circles before crushing her against him. They lock gazes and smile at each other, and I wonder if Dax can see Gage in her eyes the way I can.

"Love you, Gidget," he says.

"Love you too, Dax," she replies.

Kissing her cheek, he puts her back on her feet and gives her a nudge toward the bathroom.

"Shower and get ready for bed," he tells her. "No late-night tinkering, okay?"

She agrees and collects her pajamas before disappearing into the bathroom. Once she's gone, we fall into our bedtime routine mechanically—the same ritual we complete every night.

Dax pulls my bed to the other side of the room until it touches his, while I push the desk aside to make room. Together, we adjust the covers until the two beds look like one.

It isn't a very efficient setup, which is why we never leave it this way. Each morning, we get up and put things back the way they are, but at night, we need the closeness—all three of us.

Dax takes up the only other possession he keeps out in the open—an old, worn-out copy of the Bible. I was shocked when I first noticed him reading it, both because it's rare to see many religious texts in print anymore, and because he swore off all belief in a higher power years ago.

But Yasmine believed in God, and the goodness of most people. She was filled with faith and light. In her absence, I think he's searching for a little of that—the sort of hope he lost when she died. I don't know if he believes, but I do know he doesn't pass a day without opening that book.

I cross to the trunk I keep under my bed, now in the open with the cot moved to his side of the room. Reaching inside, I pull out the little kit the

Professor gave me for the care of my titanium arm. Sitting on top of the trunk, I oil the joints of my elbow, wrist, and fingers, then use a microfiber cloth to polish the surface. I drop a special solution into my bionic eye to keep it lubricated, and rub it in through my closed eyelid.

By the time I finish, Agata emerges from the bathroom dressed for bed, and Dax has closed his book. Silently, he lays on his side of the bed, and turns the covers down for Agata. She climbs in next, taking her place in the middle, followed by me.

She lays with her back against my front, and her face close to Dax's chest. Once we're settled in, he pulls the blankets around us, and drapes one long, heavy arm across both our bodies. I think it's more than a comfort thing. He needs to know we're safe before he can close his eyes. We are, after all, the only family he has left.

Sure, we have the other members of The Resistance, but Agata and I represent so much more to him—just as he and Agata mean more to me.

Tonight, I might dream of the accident that caused me to lose my arm and eye, of watching Gage being stabbed through the heart, or Trista drowning in her own blood. But should I open my eyes at any time during the night, I'll see the back of Agata's blonde head and feel her breathing against me. I'll see Dax's face and sense his arm around me.

And despite all I have lost, I will find the only peace there is left for me in this world.

FOUR

BLYTHE SOL AND DAX JANNER
ICARUS HOVERCRAFT
DECEMBER 27, 4010
7:00 A.M.

WE'VE BEEN IN THE AIR FOR ABOUT AN HOUR WHEN I BROACH THE SUBJECT OF AGATA with Dax. We're alone in the cockpit, with a team of fifteen seated in the passenger area. Heading to some base in California—with a name I can never remember, but don't need to because we have the coordinates plugged in—we are on a mission to collect supplies. Weapons, mostly, but Alec has instructed us to grab anything else that can be of use. The cargo hold is empty and ready to be filled with whatever we can scavenge. Then, we'll be heading to Gage's old safe house—the place he hid people when operating as The Patriot. To keep his legacy alive after his death, we tattooed Wes Graydon with an eagle similar to the one that had become Gage's calling card. We put him in charge of the operation so the media and the government would not be able to tell the public The Patriot had died. Gage might have been killed, but his legacy is alive and well.

However, since things have reached a boiling point, we have no choice but to bring Wes and the people he's hiding to Resistance Headquarters.

Olivia and Laura are simultaneously leading a mission to another base to scavenge for more supplies before stopping off to pick up more refugees from an old hideout. We're working with skeleton crews, since Jenica took a lot of people with her to Des Moines. The Resistance has been stretched thin, but everyone does their part.

It promises to be a long day, with lots of time spent flying from place to place. We have about another half hour before we reach the military base, so now's a good time to talk to Dax about my conversation with Agata last night.

"So," I begin, turning to him after switching on autopilot. "Agata finally told me what she's been working on."

Dax glances away from the radar screens, where he's been watching for any approaching crafts. So far, our flight has been uneventful, and we've gone undetected.

"Oh, yeah?" he replies.

"Yeah," I say. "It's a helmet ... created to keep anyone or anything from interfering with the EMP her cerebrum can emit."

He scowls, the expression putting deep lines and furrows in his dark face. "Why the hell would she make something like that?"

Sighing, I run a hand over my face. "She's got it in her head she needs to be ready to help us fight."

Dax's confusion melts into horror, then anger. "No. *Fuck* no!"

That was pretty much the response I expected.

"Look—"

"No, you look," he interrupts. "That little girl has lost her father, her mother, and her uncle. To top it all off, her grandfather is a psychopath who wants to kill us all, and I doubt she's excluded. We said we would protect her from any more pain or loss, and it's exactly what we're going to do."

"What good has protecting her done?" I counter. "While she was safe at Headquarters, both Gage and Trista were killed. And you heard Alec ... hiding isn't going to be an option for much longer. At some point, the MPs could come banging down our door any day, and then what point will us coddling her have served?"

"She's a kid, Blythe!"

"So was Skyye!"

I take a deep breath and try to calm down, aware our raised voices have caught the attention of some of the crew in the passenger area.

"My little sister was only five years old when they shot her," I add, my voice now at a whisper.

"I know," Dax replies through clenched teeth. "I was there, remember?"

"Being a kid didn't save her ... but maybe being prepared to at least defend herself could have. Agata has a unique gift that could be used to help so many people. If that hovercraft Yasmine was brought home in had turned out to be an MP vehicle, then the men inside would have been disarmed and at our mercy. Now, imagine that times one hundred—hell, times one thousand. That kind of power, focused on anyone who tries to storm her home and kill her. If it were your daughter, would you want her to cower and cry while someone invades her home ... or would you want her to fuck them up and make them pay?"

Dax doesn't reply, and I can tell by the look on his face he's thinking about what I've said. I didn't realize how badly I wanted this for Agata until it was time for me to plead her case. The feeling of helplessness that had overwhelmed me when I was forced to watch my entire family be executed is something I never want Agata to have to go through. I want her to be stronger and more capable than I ever was at her age.

"If she's smart enough to build the helmet, she's smart enough to be able to use it," I continue when Dax remains silent. "We can protect her anywhere she goes, and she never even has to handle a weapon."

"Screw that," he says. "If we let her do this, you're going to teach her how to shoot ... and I want to see her at the target range with my own eyes, proving she knows how to handle it."

I raise my eyebrows, surprised he so readily went along with it. "You're seriously cool with this?"

With a frustrated huff, he turns back to the radar screens. "Not really, but I know you, B. You'll go behind my back and do it anyway."

"No, I wouldn't," I reply, annoyed he'd think that of me. "Not when it comes to Agata. We decided to take care of her together, and that's how things will be. If you say no, it means no, and I respect that."

Silence stretches between us for a while, and I take _Icarus_ off autopilot since it's almost time to land. The muted conversations of the people behind us filter through the opening to the cockpit, but aside from that, only the low hum of our engines can be heard as we concentrate on our tasks.

Dax doesn't speak until the base comes into view, sprawling in neat rows of stark, efficient buildings below us.

"Watching Skyye die still haunts me, just like I know it does you," he murmurs. "And I know neither of us never wants to see something like that happen again—especially not to Agata. So, I'm with you on this one, okay? You teach her how to shoot, and I'll teach her how to shove a guy's balls up through his throat until they come out of his mouth. No one will ever lay a hand on her or take her away from us."

The resolution in his voice makes me confident we've made the right decision. I don't know if Gage would have agreed with our decision, but he trusted us with her, and so did his sister. We are doing the best we can, and I like to think they would be happy enough with that.

WE FIND THE OLD ARMY BASE DESERTED. THANKS TO SOME OF ALEC'S BRILLIANTLY invented technology, we are able to break in without being detected. I guide *Icarus* to the very center of the compound and lower him down. Then, I let down the gangplank and open the cargo hold. Our crew leaves the hovercraft, parting into groups of two and three to cover as much ground as possible. No orders need to be given, since everyone was briefed before we left Headquarters. They know what to do, and I trust them enough not to feel the need to micromanage.

Dax, a young man Gage had recruited during his time as The Patriot named Mohinder Baharani, and I locate a building marked 'Armory'. Together, we load the backs of several large trucks with every weapon our hands fall on—guns, grenades, rocket launchers, knives, brass knuckles. There's even an Annihilator—a weapon capable of melting the flesh off the bones of anything within range. Even though I hate that weapon with every fiber of my being, and think it's the most inhumane way to lash out at an enemy, we take it. Most of our weapons are chargeable and fire lasers, but among them are the old-fashioned kind that shoot bullets; so when we find crates of ammunition, we take those, too.

When it comes to this war, there's nothing I wouldn't do to keep the rest of my Resistance family safe. This is war, and sometimes that means doing things you wouldn't ordinarily do. It means necessary cruelty and uncharacteristic ferocity.

We drive the trucks back to the center of the base, and find members of our team already loading the cargo hold with marked crates. Dax and I stand at the foot of the gangplank and inventory the boxes of batteries, food, clothing, and other necessities as they're loaded. It takes two hours, but by the time we're finished, the cargo hold is crammed full of the supplies. Even still, we haven't made a dent in the cache of things stored on this base.

"We should come back on another supply run," Dax says as we scarf down a quick lunch of beef jerky and dried fruit before getting ready to leave on the second part of our mission. "This base alone has enough supplies to sustain Headquarters for six months at least."

"Agreed," I murmur between bites of jerky. "And who knows what Olivia and Laura will find. Coming to these bases was a good call."

"Kinnear turned out to be a good addition to the team," he replies. "I don't think we'd be so well off without him."

I nod my agreement and polish off my lunch. He's right about Alec, and just thinking about all the good he's done for the Resistance makes me grateful we convinced Jenica to let him join us. He might have a titanium hand now, but when he first joined, he wasn't one of us. Still, he reminded me so much of Gage, who didn't have a bionic organ, but felt so passionately about fighting injustice.

Once everyone has eaten, we take to the air again for the flight to what used to be Chicago. In the overgrown area that once housed the big city, an abandoned warehouse shields the underground hideout of The Patriot. In the distance, New Chicago stretches up toward the sky—gleaming white and silver buildings overshadowing the broken shells of businesses, shops, and homes destroyed in the 4006 nuclear blasts. Overgrown foliage creates a mixture of nature and desolation, while the smog from the factories beyond overhangs it all in a gray haze.

As we exit the craft, Dax pulls out a radiation meter to measure the millirems in the area. Anything above two hundred could be dangerous to our health, and I don't want anyone on my team to find themselves in need of bionic adrenal glands like Olivia. Cancer from radiation took as many limbs and organs from victims of the nukes as the actual blasts did.

"Weapons out, and switched to kill," I command the team as we lead them from the craft and into the woods surrounding Old Chicago. "If you see movement of any kind in the trees, be prepared to shoot."

"Watch out for the dogs," Dax chimes in, reminding us of the wild packs roaming a lot of the overgrown cities. Many of them are feral, and shooting them would probably just put them out of their misery.

We fall into a formation, and somehow, I find myself in the center. It seems everyone has silently agreed to put me in the middle to protect me from outside threats. It's something I've been forced to get used to since becoming the face of the Resistance. I'm not an ordinary soldier anymore, and even though everyone else has starred in the promo videos Alec runs on television, mine was the first. My speech at the D.C. protest where Gage was killed is still one of the most watched videos online. The people around me would give their lives to protect their symbol, and while I've become used to it, I'm still not sure I like it.

But there's never time to question it, or make my discomfort with the idea known. Like everyone else, I have my part to play in this war, and I will be whatever the Resistance needs me to be.

The radiation meter in Dax's hand beeps every few minutes, updating him as we make progress. He doesn't look concerned, so we press forward, making our way toward the old warehouse.

From where we stand on the outside, the building appears abandoned, its windows shattered, and large sliding doors broken away from their frames. Climbing plants cover the outer walls, and I can see why this is such a good hiding place. No one would think the Resistance would be ballsy enough to hide in plain sight—not with New Chicago a stone's throw away. But then, the Resistance isn't that ballsy—Gage was. I smile at the thought, exchanging a look with Dax, who seems to understand. He puts a hand on my shoulder and shows me the monitor—we're still within a safe range, though we're cutting it close.

I nod to acknowledge the readings, then pull out my COMM device. After quickly locating Wes' frequency, I call him and hold the device up to my mouth.

"Graydon, this is Sol, here and ready for transport."

There's no immediate answer. For a moment, I exchange nervous glances with Dax. There's no sign that this hideout has been attacked, but we've learned to keep our guards up when it comes to the Military Police.

After about a minute, the COMM crackles, and Wes responds.

"Sol, this is Graydon. Everyone here is packed and ready to roll. Sending someone to escort you down right now."

"Copy, Graydon," I reply. "Standing by for your escort."

Putting the COMM away, I keep a tight hold on the laser rifle that's become my go-to weapon. There's a smaller CBX holstered on my thigh, but the massive ARX rifle allows me to operate as a sniper from a distance, but is also capable of striking five different targets simultaneously at close range.

It doesn't take long for the promised escort to arrive, a young man sporting one of the black Resistance armbands. He's holding a weapon and looking at us with wide eyes, as if he's afraid. I'm not sure if it's the prospect of our transport being intercepted by the MPs that has him shaken, or what, but he looks like he's seen a ghost.

"W-Wes sent me up to lead you down," he stammers.

I smile to try to put him at ease, and reach out to offer him my hand. "Great. Lead the way."

He shakes my hand. His grip is limper than a dead fish, but I maintain the smile. The anxiety radiating off him seems odd to me, and makes my stomach churn as we step into the shadowed warehouse. A square hatch in the floor leads the way underground, and I can see that before our escort came up, various pieces of debris kept it camouflaged. The unease tickling the back of my neck continues as we navigate a set of rickety steps, then follow the young man down a tunnel tall enough for me to stand straight up—though Dax has to duck a bit—and wide enough for us to walk in twos. Little lanterns hanging from the walls of the tunnel light our way, eventually illuminating a steel door leading into the hideout. Pausing with one hand on the knob, the boy turns to me and sucks in a deep breath.

"Ms. Sol ... it's been an honor meeting you."

This time, I can't conjure a smile. His words don't line up with his expression. He looks like a man walking into the gas chamber, not someone being rescued.

That's when it hits me.

I know exactly what we'll find when he opens the door, but before I can stop him, he's pushing the steel slab inward. Turning to those behind me, I grab Dax and drop toward the ground.

"Get down!" I scream, just before the whiz of bullets arcs over my head.

Dax stumbles to one knee beside me, grasping my shoulders and forcing me facedown before climbing practically on top of me. He's protecting me from the gunfire with his body, but he's also crushing me, suffocating me in his panic. I lay still and concentrate on breathing, but the breaths are harsh and spasmodic, my heart thundering like a jackhammer against my sternum.

After what feels like an hour, but must only be a minute, the gunfire ceases, and Dax's weight slowly eases a bit. He's still on top of me, but I can now lift my head. What I find causes nausea to well in my throat.

Our escort lays a few feet in front of me in the open doorway, his eye obliterated by the bullet that tore through it and out the back of his head. The socket is nonexistent, and I can see clear through to his brain. I can smell the blood mingling with chunks of flesh strewn on the ground between us.

A shadow falls over the boy, and I raise my gun just as two MPs appear in the doorway, weapons leveled at us. I shoot one in the leg, taking him down. Someone from my team fires. The laser goes over my head and takes out the second man, but not before he fires his own weapon. I hear a body drop, but before I can look back to see who's been hit, the pounding

THE REVOLUTION

of boots precedes the appearance of men in white armor and helmets. I struggle to my feet as fast as I can before all hell breaks loose.

FIVE

CROUCHING BEHIND AN OVERTURNED TABLE, I POISE MY RIFLE OVER THE TOP AND TAKE aim. At my side, Dax is pointing twin CBX pistols over the table, rapidly shooting lasers at the MPs returning fire from the other side of the room. That's his style. Flash ... bang ... fire until nothing in his line of sight is moving.

Me?

I prefer the patience and steadiness of the rifle. I like homing in on a target while they remain oblivious they're even in my sights. Then ... lights out. A laser through the neck or the chest ... sometimes the head if they aren't wearing a helmet. They drop like stones with the most surprised looks on their faces.

I don't know if the boy sent to escort us did so to lure us into the MPs' trap, or if he was simply a pawn and the others were dead long before we ever got here. But then, I'd heard Wes' voice over my COMM device. He must be alive.

There's no time to think about that, not with the entire main room of the hideout erupting into havoc. The moment we stepped through the door, we were met with gunfire. Before long, we'd overturned the tables where the refugees must have taken their meals. We hide behind them now, trading gunfire with the men who want us dead.

As I close my human eye and use my bionic one to zoom in on a target, President Drummond's warning remains at the forefront of my mind.

33

Bionics are now to be killed on sight, no questions asked.

I pull the trigger, sending a laser at an MP poking his head out of his hiding place. It strikes him right in the vulnerable opening between his helmet and his body armor. He drops out of sight and doesn't get back up.

A hand appears from an open doorway on the other side of the room—it's the kitchen, I think. It tosses a round object toward us, and I don't think twice. Swiveling my rifle toward it, I fire, causing the sphere to explode on impact.

A grenade.

The detonation booms and echoes through the room, but because it didn't land, no one is hurt. The other members of my team trade fire with the MPs. Between bursts from my rifle, I scan the room for any sign of Wes or the others. There are several steel doors like the one we came through, but each one is closed with the MPs blocking them.

Glancing over at Dax, I jerk my head toward the doors. "We need to determine if our people are in here somewhere. Otherwise, we're trading fire for no reason."

Dax grunts between squeezes of his triggers and scowls. "These assholes will kill any Bionic they get their hands on; that's a good enough reason for me."

"You know what I mean," I counter. "Our mission is to get Wes and the others out of here, but we don't even know if they're alive. Give me cover fire so I can make a run for one of those doors."

Before I can stand, his heavy hand drops onto my shoulder to keep me in place. "Not without me, you don't."

He turns to the guy closest to him on the left, who's knelt behind a stack of crates, and yells to be heard over the gunfire. The guy glances over at me, then back at Dax. He nods and then turns to pass the message on to the person sharing his hiding place.

Dax keeps a hold of my shoulder while the word is passed down. Once he's certain we'll have adequate cover, he gives me a tug. We're on our feet in an instant, leaping over the table and charging toward the enemy. The footsteps behind me bring comfort in the knowledge that we have backup.

Three of the MPs charge us. Dax shoots one through the open face shield of his helmet, then swings a roundhouse kick toward the other, catching him in the head and whipping him around so hard and fast he drops like a lead weight. Pretty sure he's unconscious.

I take the third, flipping my rifle around and using the butt to shatter his lowered face shield. Following it up with a punch from my titanium arm, I throw him to the ground and then stand over him, flipping the gun back around and taking aim. My laser finds its way through the opening in his helmet, and leaves a charred hole between his eyes.

Stepping over his prone form, I find another officer in his place, coming at me with an electrified baton. Blue lightning crackles along its black surface, sparking ominously when he smacks it against his armored hand. He's too close for me to shoot with the rifle. Before I know it, he's on me, swinging at me with the baton.

When I duck, the baton swipes over my head, the sizzling sound causing my pulse to race. I come upright and jam my elbow into his middle, earning a smack from the baton on my neck for my trouble. The voltage slams into me, causing my entire body to jolt, sending me to my knees. My teeth clack together and my skin burns where the baton made contact, but I recover quickly, slamming a fist between the guy's legs. The armor crunches beneath the strength of my titanium fist, and the man screams in agony, taking another swing with the baton as he crumbles to his knees.

It cracks across my face, and I can't hold back the cry of pain it causes as the impact sends me sprawling to my back. The guy crawls toward me, still grunting and whimpering after taking a bionic punch to the balls, and raises the baton again to strike. Before it can land, Dax is on him, appearing from behind and grabbing his head in an unbreakable hold. A swift twist, and the MP's neck is broken.

Throwing the body aside, Dax crouches and extends a hand to me. I accept it and let him pull me up, ignoring the persistent throb on my neck and face left by the burns. He winces at the sight of the injuries, but says nothing. Instead, he puts my rifle back into my hand, and then pulls me along beside him. We make a beeline for one of the doors.

MPs come at us from all sides, but we take them down, both of us fighting with a ferocity we've never before unleashed. We shoot to kill and fight to maim. We do this for Gage and Sayer Strom ... for Agata and Trista ... for Yasmine.

By the time we get to one of the doors, the room is filled with bodies—mostly those of the MPs.

The first room reveals itself to be a storage closet. I make a note to come back for whatever supplies might be filling the crates inside before we move on. We find hallways filled with dorm rooms, but they're all empty. If Wes and the others are alive, they aren't here.

We come back out of the last dorm hall to find another swarm of MPs coming in the same way we did.

"Shit," Dax grumbles as he takes aim with his pistols and joins the other members of our team in engaging the enemy.

"There are too many of them," I say as I lift my rifle and fire. "If we can't find Wes and his people, it's time to run!"

By the look on Dax's face, the idea doesn't sit right with him. But I'm not going to risk our team fighting for a hideout that's already compromised.

I search for doors we haven't checked behind yet, but find they've all been opened. It isn't until I trip over something and land on my ass I realize I was looking in the wrong places all along.

"Dax!" I call out, bringing his attention to the trapdoor—and the handle I just tripped over.

He glances at it, then turns his attention back to the fight. "Go check it out ... I'll cover you from up here."

Nodding, I pull the door open, finding a ladder leading into a dark hole. The night vision of my bionic eye kicks in as I begin to descend. Above me, the main room of the hideout becomes nothing more than a square of light. Gunfire and the call of voices ring out from above, echoing further and further away as I continue downward.

Once my feet hit the ground, I turn and find another series of doors.

But only one of them has a large padlock on it ... and my instincts are telling me it's the one to open.

I ball my bionic hand into a fist and smash it into the padlock—over and over again until it breaks and falls to the dirt floor with a thud. When I pull the door open, I find hundreds of bodies huddled inside an empty room, only a single yellow bulb overhead illuminating them.

Wes bounds toward me as others part to make room for him. He's a large man with bionic forearms, as well as two titanium legs. A sleeveless shirt shows the eagle tattoo on one of his human biceps—a replica of Gage's.

"Blythe," he says, his expression grave as we lock eyes. "They surprised us last night and locked us down here ... separated us from the children and warned me if I didn't tell them when you were coming and help get you into their trap, they'd kill them all."

A sour taste fills my mouth as I glance over his shoulder at the people crowded in the room. How many of them are parents to the children locked away in another room?

"Well, it worked," I tell him. "When they sent up your escort, the boy led us right in and took a bullet for his trouble."

"Oh, no!" cries a woman from the back of the crowd. "Peter!"

My heart sinks at the sounds of her sobs as I realize Peter must have been her son. But there was no easier way to relay the news of his death. The boy had been scared out of his wits, and likely did what he thought he had to in order to keep his family safe.

"Listen to me," I say, raising my voice so everyone can hear. "Our team is up there, and we are outnumbered. But there are weapons on board our hovercraft, and enough of us down here to help even the odds. Everyone who's even slightly capable of firing a gun, come with me now."

I turn to Wes. "Is there any other way to get back outside other than through the main room?"

He nods. "Yes. There's a tunnel down here that'll take us back up through the warehouse."

"Perfect," I reply. "Let's go."

"But the children!" someone calls out.

I turn to face the people looking to me for guidance, finding frightened faces among the determined. "Those of you who can't fight or don't know how to use a gun, stay down here with them. Do you know where they are?"

"Another room off the tunnel," Wes replies. "That's where they locked them before herding us in down here."

"Good," I reply. "If you can't fight, join the children and stay down here, out of the way. Someone will come get you when it's safe."

Without waiting for a response, I turn and leave the room, gesturing for Wes to show me the way. We locate the tunnel quickly and become swallowed up in darkness, this exit lacking the lanterns the entrance has. From there, I take the lead, guiding the way with night vision and moving as quickly as I can without losing the others, who cannot see as well as I can down here.

We eventually come to another ladder, and I scramble up it to find a trapdoor much like the one we used to gain entrance to the hideout. Pushing it up, I shove aside the debris covering it and crawl out. The warehouse remains empty, and our hovercraft appears undisturbed outside. Apparently, the MPs were salivating at the thought of being the ones to take us down, so they didn't give any thought to guarding the perimeter or destroying our only method of escape.

Not for the first time, I find myself grateful for the incompetence of the Military Police.

We run for the hovercraft, and I dash inside to get the cargo hold open as fast as I can. Wes helps me hand out weapons. As quickly as we can manage, we're running back toward the entrance. I'd rather take them from behind than go back the way we came.

Now fully armed, we rush back in, dashing through the dimly lit tunnel toward the entrance where my team was ambushed.

As we enter the main room, guns blazing, I do my best not to glance down at the unmoving body of Peter and the open socket of his obliterated eye staring accusingly up at me.

BY THE TIME THE GUNFIRE DIES DOWN, EVERY MP WHO ATTACKED THE PATRIOT'S hideout lays dead. Strewn out among the bodies of our attackers are a few of our own. Dax leads some of the others in retrieving the bodies—reverently carrying them out to store in the cargo hold of *Icarus*. The sons of bitches who attacked the hideout will stay right where they are—in the underground shelter that will now serve as their tomb. I can conjure no sympathy for them—even the young ones who look like fresh recruits. If you knowingly sign up to serve a government that kills human beings hiding underground, then you deserve whatever you get.

Assholes.

While Dax tends to the dead, Wes takes over loading any supplies that haven't been damaged in the fight. As it turns out, the closet I discovered is full of freeze-dried meal rations, so I'm glad it went untouched.

With those things taken care of, I make my way back down to where I found Wes and the others. I'll lead the few non-fighters and children out the back tunnel and to the outside, so they can begin boarding the hovercraft. This time, I accept a flashlight from Wes, so I don't have to rely on night vision to guide me in the dark.

The moment I get to the bottom of the tunnel, voices reach out to me. I pause, one foot still on the bottom rung of the ladder, my heart sinking into my gut as I realize the voices are moaning and crying in grief.

I know what I will find before I take a single step toward the tunnel, and it makes me want to retreat—climb back up the ladder and let someone else deal with the horrors I will inevitably find.

But I need to see this... to be reminded of what I'm dealing with when it comes to my enemy. Sayer Strom taught me to never forget ... and I promised myself and him I wouldn't.

The door to the room the children had been herded into lays open now, its lock broken and on the ground. Dim light doesn't reveal much—mostly the shadows of people hunched over smaller forms on the floor.

The bodies of dead children.

Bile rises in my throat and my stomach lurches, but I force myself to swing the beam of the flashlight toward the room and confront the truth.

I pinch my lips together to stifle a sob, and tears fill my human eye as I look at them—children as young as three and no older than fifteen. All of them dead. I cannot see bullet holes or the marks of laser fire. There is no blood. If I didn't know my enemy as well as I do, I might have assumed they simply slept.

But the angles of their limbs and the horrors of their ashen faces, still twisted into expressions of terror, make it impossible to ignore.

Here and there, those who couldn't fight cradle the bodies of their children, brothers and sisters, and grandchildren. They glance up and meet my gaze with tears in their eyes. One woman sobs as if her heart has been torn from her chest, and it only makes my tears flow with a vengeance.

"How?" I choke out once I find my voice.

"Gas, we think," says one of the men cradling a small girl against his chest. He's too old to be her father, so I'm thinking he's an uncle or grandpa. His eyes are bloodshot, and he looks like he's aged ten years in the half hour since I went upstairs to finish off the fight.

"We found them like this," he adds. "While we were locked in the other room, they ... they were dying ... alone."

He lowers his head with a sob, and I turn away. His grief is too much for me ... the small body in his arms too similar to my sister's in size. But remembering the senator's words, I turn back and make myself look at them.

The American people need to know the truth. They need to see what the government and our president are capable of. Closing my eyes, I stare at the numbers and blips flashing across one lid—the readings from my bionic eye. Quickly switching on the recording mechanism, I open my eyes and take a good, long look around the room. My eye is recording and storing everything—the crumbled bodies in the darkened room with only a single bulb and my flashlight breaking through the darkness. The adults kneeling among the dead children, their sobs, and their tears.

I stand there for as long as I can, taking in every detail. Once I'm confident I have the sort of footage she will need, I end the recording and enter the room. Kneeling beside the old man, I reach out to touch his shoulder. I quickly swipe away my tears before he looks up at me, because I am the leader here. I am the one the Resistance chose as their symbol, and I will not let this man down. I will keep it together until I can find the privacy and time to weep for these children.

"Let me help you carry her up to the hovercraft," I say. "Once we're at Resistance Headquarters, we'll have a memorial for her ... have her cremated."

He sniffles and turns his head to dry his face on his shirt, then nods. "Okay. Thank you."

I take the body into my arms, avoiding looking at the face. If I look at her, I will think of Skyye and fall apart.

The man follows me from the room, and I lead him to the ladder stretching to the opening in the warehouse. He climbs up first, then I follow with the girl slung over one shoulder. Once I'm out, he helps me get her through the hole, then lets me take over again.

I carry her to the craft and pause, meeting Dax's gaze as he appears from the cargo hold. He's just stored yet another body there, and I can see by how tight his face has become it's getting to him. Neither of us will sleep tonight.

We pass each other—me on my way to the ship with the girl, him heading back inside to pick up more bodies. And we continue that way until the last corpse has been stowed. Then we lead our people and the refugees of the hideout onto *Icarus*, and ensure no man is left behind.

With the passenger hold and the cargo space filled to the brim with people, supplies, and the dead, we lift off and head for home, leaving Old Chicago behind us.

It isn't until we've been in the air long enough for me to feel confident we aren't being followed that I put the craft in autopilot and burst into tears. Without a word, Dax reaches across the space between us and takes my hand. I glance over to find no tears on his face, but then, I don't think he has any left to cry. He simply sits there and squeezes my hand, his face set in the hard expression of grief and rage he's worn since Yasmine died. Beside him, I lower my head and weep.

I don't stop until we're home.

SIX

BLYTHE SOL, DAX JANNER, AND ALEC KINNEAR
RESTORATION RESISTANCE HEADQUARTERS
DECEMBER 29, 4010
9:00 A.M.

TAKING A SIP OF LUKEWARM COFFEE, I STARE BLANKLY AT THE NEWS BROADCAST BEING projected into the room. The rec room of the main building of Resistance Headquarters is more crowded than ever—many of the refugees brought from The Patriot's hideout mingling with those Olivia and Laura retrieved from a hideout in Oregon. Usually, this room is buzzing with conversation and activity while people talk, drink coffee, watch TV, or play cards. Today, there's a morbid silence hanging thick in the air like a gray cloud. From time to time, I meet the gaze of someone with tears in their eyes and grief slashing across their faces like physical scars. They mourn their children, lost forever.

Laura and Olivia, along with their team, faced similar circumstances in Oregon, returning to Headquarters with a cargo hold full of corpses— many of them young or elderly.

"I understand the need to protect U.S. citizens from the threat of the Bionics," a news commentator says, her eyes filling with tears as she talks to her fellow reporter. *"But children locked in dark rooms and gassed ... left for dead? This is where I draw the line!"*

I lower my gaze into the dark contents of my tin mug as the video I captured in Old Chicago appears beside her in a picture-in-picture display. Seeing it once was more than enough for me.

"What threat?" argues the red-faced man in response to the woman beside him. *"The Bionics are no more dangerous than any other citizen.*

I've said this from the beginning—by chasing them down and arresting or killing them, we are committing genocide."

"I wouldn't go that far," argues the female reporter. *"We've seen several instances of the sort of violence the Bionics are capable of, and I agree with President Drummond ... the American people must be protected from such violence at all costs. However, I do not believe these children deserved to be killed. Look, they didn't choose this. Becoming enhanced by these ... these machines was a decision made by their parents—"*

"And the federal government, which sanctioned the use of the bionic prosthetics after the nuclear attacks," the man interjects. *"You can't offer people something like that, and then punish them for accepting it! That's not how this works. If a few of the Bionics are dangerous, then we go after them as we would any other criminal and punish them according to the law. Forcing them into hiding and hunting them like animals is not only unconstitutional, it is inhumane. And if you're angry about these slaughtered children, but turned a blind eye to the many atrocities committed against Bionics of all ages, then you are a hypocrite."*

"Turn that shit off," grumbles Dax as he enters the room, his own steaming coffee cup in hand.

No one responds right away. The media nowadays is rife with these sorts of arguments—the commentators taking sides publicly in the fight between the Resistance and the government, as well as the Rejects. It can be hard to watch, and is especially difficult today as they continually play the video footage of dead children on a loop.

"It's outrageous," the male analyst continues. *"And I'll say it here and now—the Drummond administration must be held accountable for this. Should it come to light that the president himself sanctioned these killings, he must be taken out of power."*

"Surely you aren't suggesting this is President Drummond's fault?" the woman contends. *"The man has had to lead our nation through some of its most difficult times in recent history."*

"He's a murderer and a coward."

"I said turn this shit off!" Dax yells, the vein in his neck starting to protrude.

Someone quickly does what he says, because when Dax raises his voice, something inside the people listening tells them going against him will be dangerous to their health. When Dax speaks, you fucking listen.

"They've been playing it all morning," I say, turning to face him as he perches on the arm of my chair. "Over and over again."

He curls his upper lip in disgust. "The people need to see it, but that doesn't mean those stuck in here have to. Those are their children ... their loved ones being used for propaganda."

"It's what needs to be done," I retort, even though I agree with him.

Having to use the story of losing my own family in the video promos the Resistance put out felt like exploitation, but it helped gain more people to our cause. Maybe the deaths of innocent children will shake things up even more. At the same time, I'm not naïve enough to think there won't be retaliation for this. President Drummond promised he'd bring the heat, and I believed him. We will pay for what we've just done.

A moment later, Alec appears, making a beeline toward us from the doorway. His mouth is a thin line, his brow furrowed. Since he's usually so easygoing, he can't have good news.

"Come with me," he says once he reaches us. "Now."

Exchanging a glance with Dax, I frown, wondering what this could be about. I stand and drain what's left of my mug, and leave it in one of the basins used for collecting dirty dishes on our way through the dining hall.

Today was supposed to be about resting after our mission, before having to head back out. We have four more hideouts to get to, and several more of the closed military bases to hit. The supplies we found will go a long way toward making sure everyone is clothed and fed, but it won't be enough for the long run. We need to stockpile, and the bases are our only hope of achieving that.

"What's going on?" Dax asks as Alec leads us across the quad toward the science and technology building—where his work area is located.

Alec waits until we're inside the building to answer. He turns to us while we wait for the elevator to come down.

"I received a message from a COMM in the field while you guys were gone," he says, his expression grim. "It came from an old device ... a real piece of shit. Because of that, it took me ages to download and unencrypt, and once I did... Well, you'll just have to see for yourselves."

We ride the elevator to Alec's floor, and he leads us past several labs and other work areas where the Professor's apprentices create new bionic organs and limbs. Sometimes, one of us has a malfunction, or loses a body part in the fight. Thanks to these guys, there are always spare parts when we need them. It's how Alec ended up with a new hand after Baron, the Rejects' leader, chopped his off in the same fight Gage was killed in.

Once inside, Alec sits in his rolling chair and swivels toward one of the several screens surrounding his workspace. Tapping a few keys, he causes one of the dark monitors to light up. Coming up behind him, I draw up short, the air forced from my lungs by what I'm seeing. The video has been paused. It's a bit dark and grainy, but there's no mistaking the face staring into the camera. The piercing blue eyes strike me in the gut, and pain radiates out to every region of my body.

Dax's hands come up to my shoulders in a comforting hold as he looks over my shoulder to see what I am seeing.

"Gage?" he murmurs. "What is this?"

Alec turns to glance at us over his shoulder. "I can't really put this into words, so I'll just play the video. There's a goldmine of information here ... everything we've ever wanted to know."

I press a hand over my mouth, keeping quiet as he presses play on the video. For a moment, I fear my ears won't work, that my eyes will take over for all my senses so I can drink him in. It is nighttime wherever he shot this video, and a dim beam—maybe from a flashlight—is the only thing illuminating his face. He doesn't look like the boy I met ... he looks more like the man who boldly landed his hovercraft on the lawn stretching out before the Washington Memorial, and strode up to me to steal a kiss. His hair is longer, hanging into his eyes, and his jaw is sprinkled with at least a week's worth of stubble. There's a scar along one cheek, and a harder look in his eye. As if fighting the good fight has altered him in the same ways it has altered me. He looks exhausted and worn out, but the electric crackle still lives in his eyes. That fire and passion for the cause. It was there in those beautiful blue eyes right up until the moment he died.

But then, he opens his mouth to speak, and the sound of his voice brings me sweet relief. I never thought I'd hear it again.

"This is Gage Bronson," he says. *"If you are watching this, then I am probably dead and was unable to get this to you in person. Please listen carefully to everything I have to say. What I am about to tell you flies in the face of what we know to be true, but it has to be told. This is the real story of the dawning of the Bionics..."*

HALF AN HOUR AFTER MEETING WITH ALEC TO WATCH THE VIDEO OF GAGE, I AM SEATED in the Professor's conference room, waiting for everyone to arrive. After the explosive information revealed by the message, there's so much to discuss. Nothing will be the same for any of us after this. Our entire mission, our focus, will have to shift. Nothing is what we thought it was.

My mind is still reeling as I sit next to Dax at the long, steel conference table. He seems content to leave me alone with my thoughts. Knowing me as well as he does, he understands I am still processing all that Gage revealed in his message.

My father was killed because he knew too much. His top-secret military security clearance allowed him to dig into matters kept hidden from the public. He'd learned the truth about it all ... just like Gage had.

The technology used to create Bionics was born during Project CyGen. Using the Professor's technology, they pushed Project CyGen to its limits, creating technology that made us seem superior—stronger, faster, able to do things like see through walls. The Professor, being the inquisitive scientist he was, went along with it for the sake of discovering what human beings could be capable of. He could never have known his inventions would someday be used for evil.

After the bombings, Project CyGen became Project BioCrisis—a secret initiative with one purpose—make the American public afraid of us. Once those injured in the blasts had been outfitted with prosthetic parts, the propaganda began.

Baron Helsing is a direct product of Project BioCrisis, and it shouldn't surprise me he's been in league with the president from day one. A former Marine, he signed up for the project and willingly allowed his heart to be replaced by a bionic one, along with his many other prosthetics. The Rejects are all Drummond's idea ... just another way to use fear to control the people and unite them against us.

My father knew this, and was on the verge of exposing the entire thing. It is no coincidence that shortly after his discoveries, our neighborhood was raided and all the Bionics who could not escape were taken away in chains. My father was murdered. My mother and sister are seen only as collateral damage—killed because they might have known something valuable. The truth is even if I'd never became a public figurehead of the Resistance, the president would still want me dead because my father dared to try to stand up for what was right.

Now I understand why he looked Captain Rodney Jones in the eye that day and confessed he'd been hiding me, even as he faced the barrel of a gun. I'd always wondered why he wouldn't lie to at least save my mother and Skyye. But he had to have known what I was ignorant to. They would have killed us all anyway.

As if this isn't enough to digest, Gage's video also revealed the true purpose behind The Rejects' occupation of Des Moines, Iowa. Beneath the capital building lies an old underground nuclear site, where weapons were made and stored in the event of an attack on US soil. Now in control of the site, Baron will carry out the president's plan of nuking Washington D.C., an act that will surely be pinned on The Resistance. Of course, the president will conveniently find himself someplace safe, so he can return and bemoan the evil deed and remind the people he was right about those violent, dangerous Bionics all along.

It would be a death sentence for the Resistance. If the people become angry with us, if they become afraid again, they will stop caring about the bodies of dead children strewn over the floors in dark rooms. They will stop caring about the deaths of my family, or the hardships we have faced. They will want us all wiped off the face of the earth, and the president will be able to do it with impunity.

After finishing the video, Alec had turned to us with that grim expression still on his face.

"I'm not sure when he sent this," he'd said. "But I'm glad he did. He might have just saved us all."

That was Gage, a fighter to the end. Maybe he had known his time was short. Acting as The Patriot put him in danger, but he never stopped wanting to do what was right. Things like this make me think *he* would have been more suited to this role of being the Resistance's symbol than I am ... even though he had no bionic parts. He embodied the spirit of the Resistance with every breath he took.

My biggest regret is not being able to tell him so to his face.

And as the others enter the conference room and begin to talk about how we must go about stopping Baron and The Rejects from launching the nukes from Des Moines, I tune it all out.

Yes, Baron must be stopped ... but I cannot stop thinking about another man who must be stopped.

The man who took my family from me. The man who forced Gage and Agata to flee their home, putting him in a position to die and her to lose her mother. The man responsible for every bad thing that has ever happened to anyone I ever cared about.

When I watched Yasmine die in Dax's arms, I vowed I would be the one to kill President Drummond. All this talk of finding supplies and taking in the refugees from our various hideouts had stolen my focus.

But not anymore.

With every breath I take, the need for vengeance fills my lungs. The rage burns in my veins, and my heart beats a war drum's cadence.

The first chance I get, I am going to slip away and undergo a mission of my own—the assassination of the president of the United States.

SEVEN

BLYTHE SOL AND DAX JANNER
MOSLEY HALL
DECEMBER 29, 4010
9:00 P.M.

I AM KNEELING BESIDE MY BED, ENSURING I HAVE ALL THE PROVISIONS I'LL NEED FOR MY little side mission, when Dax enters our room. Despite hearing his heavy footsteps stop directly behind me, and feeling his stare on the back of my neck, I don't turn around. If I look at him, the truth of what I'm doing will be in my eyes, and he will want to come with me. But I can't let him ... because the moment I go rogue, there's no guarantee I'll come back. And someone has to be here for Agata. Between the two of us, he's the best at this whole parenting thing, and she needs him. I have to do this alone.

Water? *Check.* Beef jerky and dried-food rations? *Check.* Clothes for every crazy weather change I might encounter? *Check.*

My weapons are waiting for me on board *Icarus*, along with a hover bike I stowed in the cargo hold. In the morning, four of our biggest crafts will be dispatched to the last remaining hideouts. It's risky, sending out our best and biggest vehicles all at once, but the last of our people need to be brought to Headquarters. Then, we can focus on Iowa and the threat of the Rejects. With all hands on deck and the weapons we've gathered, we definitely stand a chance of bringing them down.

And by we, I mean the Resistance. I will either be in handcuffs or dead after assassinating the president. Will it have been worth it, to be able to take him with me when I die?

You better fucking believe it.

As I zip the big duffel bag holding my supplies, Dax clears his throat.

I glance at him over my shoulder. "Hey."

Inclining his head, he gives me a look I am all-too familiar with. He knows I'm up to something.

Crap.

"What's up, B?" he asks, raising one eyebrow. "You cut out early on the supply inventory. Everything okay?"

I nod, standing and turning to face him with my hands braced on my hips. "Yeah ... I just wanted to make sure I had my personal effects in order. No telling if we might get stuck out there, and I want to be prepared."

He nods, but continues watching me as if trying to peel back all my layers. As much as I hate to admit it, no one does that better than Dax. He knows me like no one else. Dog gets up from where he's been sleeping at the foot of my bed. Trotting over, he nudges my hand with his wet nose, and then licks it.

"Look, I don't want to state the obvious here, but that video of Gage couldn't have been easy for you to watch," he says. "We're alone now, so if you need to have some feelings about it, now's the time."

Sighing, I cross my arms over my chest. "Of course I have feelings about it. It hurt to see him again, but at the same time, it felt good. Knowing he fought for truth and justice right until the end ... that he tried to find some way of making sure we knew how to carry on the fight after he was gone, it feels good."

He smirks. "Looks like someone has moved on to the acceptance phase."

I giggle. "Join me, won't you?"

It would have been a terrible joke with anyone else, especially with Yasmine's death being so fresh, but Dax simply smiles.

"I'm accepting it," he says. "Doesn't mean I have to like it."

Crossing the space between us, I wrap my arms around his waist and lay my head against his chest. He returns the embrace, his chin resting on the top of my head. Dog sinks to his haunches beside us, his tongue hanging out as he watches us embrace.

"We still have each other," I remind him.

Giving me a squeeze, he kisses my forehead. "Always."

We separate, and I turn to begin our ritual of preparing the beds for the night. Agata is likely having a nighttime tinkering session with the Professor—the only reason she wouldn't be here with us this late. But as I glance up with a blanket held in my hands, Dax is still standing there watching me. I raise my eyebrows at him, waiting for whatever's coming.

"So," he says, pursing his lips. "Where are we going?"

I frown. "Um .... Mississippi, I think? I've got the hideout coordinates waiting for us on *Icarus*."

"Nice try," he counters. "I mean, where do *you* think you're going without me?"

Crap. Shit. Crap.

I knew he would see through me, but I was hoping he'd just let it go so I could do what I need to do.

"Dax, leave it alone," I warn.

Snatching the blanket from my hands, he tosses it onto his bed and narrows his eyes. "No, I will not leave it alone. I know you, B. I knew that video got to you, and you'd have it in your head to do something about all the information Gage gave us. A huge piece of it involved your father and the reason your family was killed. So I want to know where you're going."

I shake my head. "It's better if I don't tell you. That way, if someone asks, you can honestly say you don't know."

"That's now how this works," he argues. "Start talking. Now."

Grunting in frustration, I run a hand through my hair. "I said let it go. This is my mission, Dax. I need to do this on my own, and I won't drag anyone down with me."

His eyes widen. For a long moment, he simply stares at me in silence. When he finally speaks, there is both determination and accusation in his tone.

"You're going after Drummond."

I'm not even going to try to deny it. "He has to pay."

Dax nods. "He does, but you won't come back alive."

Squaring my shoulders, I lift my chin. "We're at war here. That could mean death any day, any time. If I have to die, I want to choose how. This way, I get to take him with me."

"What about all the bullshit you said after Yasmine died, about me and you? You told me I had to fight for you and Agata. Now you're giving up?"

"I'm going down fighting!" I insist. "If I can take him out, he can't give the order to nuke D.C. He can't sic the Military Police on us. He can't keep terrorizing us! Maybe if he's gone, his entire regime will collapse from the top down. I have to do something, Dax! I have to try. He murdered my father, my mother, and my sister ... maybe not directly, but we both know he gave the order. I can't let that slide!"

Despite my outburst, he remains calm. His brow is furrowed, his jaw hardened as he grasps my shoulders. I see in his eyes he's resolved, just as I am. And I know I cannot talk him out of what he's just decided.

"Okay, B," he murmurs. "If you want to do this, I'm coming with you."

I shake my head. "You can't. Agata needs you."

"She does," he agrees. "But she needs you, too. If I come with you, we stand a better chance together. We can come up with a plan en route, and when shit hits the fan, you stand a better chance of escape with me watching your back."

I bite my lower lip, still uncertain. I'll feel better with him at my side, and I know he'd give his life to save mine. But that's the problem. I don't ever want someone to die for me again. I've had enough of that.

"Either we do this my way, or I'll tell on you," Dax threatens. "Don't turn me in to a little snitch bitch."

That gets a laugh out of me, knowing the old street thug Dax used to be would rather die than snitch. These days, he'd do it if he thought it would save my life.

Taking a deep breath, I let it out on a sigh. "Okay. We do it together. I've got a hover bike stowed in the cargo hold. I plan to slip away once we've secured the refugees at the hideout. Laura will be along for the ride, and she can take over once we're gone."

"Laura will understand," he reassures me. "She'll cover for us as best she can ... give us a chance to get a good head start. They can't spare the manpower to come after us."

We fall silent and stare at each other, both thinking about what this all will mean. We will be seen as abandoning the Resistance. It will hurt our friends. But if we can pull this off, maybe it'll mean some peace for us all. They'll have to understand, right?

"You know what this means," Dax says, as if reading my mind. "They'll be hurt we're going off mission ... and they'll have to handle Des Moines without us."

"I like to think of this as helping them," I offer. "While they use one path to get to the Rejects and stop the bombings, we'll use another. If one fails, the other is still in play."

Dax nods in agreement. "You're right."

Part of me feels I am. I know this needs to be done. But another part—the one that has become so deeply intertwined with the Resistance—needed to hear Dax say it.

"I'll pack my stuff," he says, before turning away to do just that.

Our night passes much like the ones before it, except for a quiet sense of purpose that seems to have fallen over us. After Agata returns from her tinkering, we put her to bed, then join her—me on one side and Dax on the other like always.

However, as she lays sleeping between us, neither of us closes our eyes. We stare at each other in silence, the sounds of our breathing cutting through the quiet. His arm crosses Agata's body and reaches for my hand, grabbing on and holding tight.

After this, there can be no turning back. We will never be the same again. But then, we've both gone so far beyond who we used to be. There's nothing left to do but hold on to each other as we continue to evolve and adapt in order to survive ... in the hopes that someday, we can emerge from the shadows and live.

DAX AND I HAVE NO PROBLEMS SNEAKING AWAY THE NEXT DAY. AFTER A LONG FLIGHT to Mississippi, we were fortunate to find the hideout untouched. Unlike the last mission, no MPs lie in wait for us, meaning we have nothing left to do but make sure the refugees are packed up and ready to move before bedding down for the night. By the time we're done, it's nine o'clock, and dark enough for us to make our getaway.

We find Laura in one of the beds in a room with about four other women. This place is one of our smallest hideouts, and all the rooms are tiny with bunks built into the walls. She's sitting on one of the bottom ones, cleaning her favorite CBX handgun. Glancing up when she sees me lingering in the doorway with Dax looming behind me, she stands.

"Everything all right, boss one and boss two?" she asks.

"We need a word, if you have a sec," I reply, nodding to the curious women staring at me.

They've been hiding here for a while, and look as if they haven't been eating much. We're getting them to Headquarters just in time, it seems.

"Sure thing," Laura replies, finishing the job before standing and slipping her pistol back into its holster.

She follows me out into the hall, and I close the door, leaving a crack so only a sliver of light illuminates us. The hallway lights have been killed so we aren't visible from the outside, just in case the MPs come snooping around. We'd rather not fight them when we don't have to.

Laura's face is just visible in the little beam of light—a face I've come to count among those I consider my family. With her thick New Jersey accent and no-bullshit personality, she fits right in. It doesn't matter she's Italian and I'm black ... or she's a Yankee and I'm from the South. The gleaming titanium chest plate concealing a bionic heart makes her my sister.

"We need your help," I say. "Dax and I need to slip away without anyone knowing where we're going or what we're doing."

She grins, probably thinking this is like all the other times we went rogue—like going after those weapons in Leesburg. "Going off to raise some hell?"

Dax runs a hand over his short hair. "Kind of. But we can't let you in on the details this time, Rosenberg. It's better if you don't know."

Her smile dies once she hears the grave tone of Dax's voice. "Jenica isn't going to like this, is she?"

"Jenica's not here," I remind her. "And by the time she is, we hope to be finished with what we need to do."

She raises an eyebrow. "So, you *are* coming back?"

Reaching out, I pull her into a hug. "Of course we are."

Nodding, she pats my shoulder with a strong hand. "Okay, then. I've got your backs. When do you leave?"

"Now," Dax answers. "While it's still dark. We'll tell the guys on security detail we're just going out to prep *Icarus* for tomorrow's flight. We have a hovercraft and some supplies stored there."

Laura glances back and forth between us, her expression grim. "I'll do what I can to make excuses for you guys ... keep them from going after you. Which should be pretty easy since I have no way of knowing where you're going."

"That's the way we want it," I tell her. "Tomorrow, you lead everyone back to Resistance Headquarters. Pilot *Icarus* to Des Moines and lead the team in my place. We'll meet you there when we're done."

She nods. "Will do. Won't be the same knocking heads together without you two."

Dax chuckles. "Knock a few for me, will you?"

The two bump fists and grin. "You got it."

Grabbing my hand so I can lead him back through the dark, Dax takes one last look at Laura.

"Keep your head down," he says, before we disappear down the hallway.

Within minutes, we're outside, giving our planned excuses to the guards watching the front and back entrances. We take our time walking to the hovercraft so we don't seem to be in a hurry.

Once the hover bike is free from the cargo hold, we load our things into its side compartments, along with a few extra fuel cells. By my calculations, we have more than enough to reach D.C., and then meet up with our people either in Des Moines, or back home at Headquarters.

We put on matching helmets—which contain night-vision capabilities and a system we can use to communicate with each other. Dax volunteers to drive first, and swings one long leg over the bike, settling on the front of the seat while I climb on behind him. Wrapping my arms around his waist, I hold on tight as we hurtle out into the night.

Trees zip past as Dax carefully navigates the thickly wooded area surrounding the hideout. Along with night vision, the face shields of our helmets offer navigation, so Dax gets turn-by-turn directions along with the ability to see in the dark.

Despite knowing I can talk to him through the helmet, I remain silent, and he seems content to do the same. I keep my eyes peeled for movement in the trees, but find our route surprisingly undisturbed. I set the helmet navigation to guide us along unbeaten paths, even taking us near some zones with levels of high radiation—all so we can avoid detection.

The trip won't be short—a hover bike is faster than a car, but much slower than a hovercraft—and with all the detours we'll have to make to keep away from large cities, I'm estimating it'll take us almost a week to get there. And that's only if we don't run into any delays or trouble and are able to ride for at least eight hours a day.

Once we start getting close, we'll still need to formulate a plan. How will we get to the president? How will we assassinate him and still escape with our lives?

I don't know all the answers, but not doing this will mean accepting what he has done to me ... what he did to my family. I no longer have that sort of passiveness inside of me. Anger and rage have mingled with loss until I exist with one singular focus—bring down President Drummond and everything he has ever built.

EIGHT

BLYTHE SOL AND DAX JANNER
UNKNOWN LOCATION
JANUARY 1, 4011
7:00 A.M.

OUR FIRST FEW DAYS OF TRAVEL PASS UNEVENTFULLY—WITH DAX AND ME TAKING turns driving the hover bike through the night. During the day, we stop to eat and rest, one of us standing watch while the other sleeps, then switching places. It's a grueling pace, but I don't let myself feel the fatigue. I don't let myself feel anything except the resolve I left Headquarters with. The path before me will end in death—for the president, and maybe even for Dax and me. It's all I let myself think about.

Dax makes it easy to stay focused. He's quiet most of the time, but silence between us has always been comfortable. After years of hashing things out and laying all our secrets bare, there seems to be nothing left for us to say. If we die, it won't be with regrets over words unsaid. We've said all the important ones.

New Year's comes with a bleak gray sky and a chill in the air. We don't wish each other a happy anything. Just like Christmas, the day seems meaningless. Maybe because in the years since going into hiding, the holidays brought us hope—hope that we would get to celebrate our freedom the following year. When a year would pass with us still in hiding, we'd tell ourselves it would happen the next year, or the next. There's no false comfort on the hidden paths in the woods. We know not to get our hopes up.

Stopping to rest on the third day, I finally break the silence. I sit across from him in a small space between trees, perched on a fallen, rotting log.

My rifle rests across my thighs—the weapon I will use to assassinate the president. Each day, I take it out and ensure all its parts are in working order—that it's charged and ready for use. After I've finished, I set it back inside its black case and lay it beside my duffel bag. Reaching in to grab my canteen and a packaged food ration, I glance over to find him completing his own morning ritual.

The worn Bible looks as if it'll fall apart any moment in Dax's large hands. The black piece of cloth he keeps the book wrapped in is draped over his knee while he reads. When he's finished, he will wrap it up before carefully stashing it back among his belongings.

"Does it help?" I ask. When he glances up, I indicate the book. "Reading that, I mean."

He inclines his head, glancing down at the Bible, then back up at me. "I don't know yet. I just ... this was Yasmine's."

I nod in understanding. He doesn't have to say anything else. I still keep Gage's letter and drawing in the same place I keep the photo of my father. They're the only pieces I have left of him, and for that reason, I read the letter often. I brought it with me, tucked into the original envelope, in case I find myself in need of a reminder. All it takes it glancing at the letter again, and it all comes back to me ... why I'm doing this.

"She believed so strongly," he continues when I don't respond. "And no matter what happened, no matter how bad it was, she never stopped believing. She told me everything had a purpose and a reason ... that we lived when others died because we were meant to be here for something."

Taking a bite of dried fruit, I ponder what he's said for a moment. If what Yasmine believed was true, my family was meant to die. In some twisted way, maybe their deaths had been necessary to propel me to this place. The thought of their losses acting as some sort of stepping stone for me leaves a bitter taste in my mouth. Appetite suddenly gone, I put my breakfast aside and take a little sip from my canteen. We only drink a little at a time since finding fresh, uncontaminated water sources out here is like finding a lake in the middle of the desert.

"Let me hear some of it," I say, if for no other reason than to fill the silence and distract me from such depressing thoughts.

Dax looks back down at the book a moment before reading out loud from the page he'd left off on.

"To everything there is a season, and a time to every purpose under the heaven," he reads. "A time to be born, and a time to die; a time to plant, and a time to pluck up that which has been planted. A time to kill..."

His gaze finds mine, and he trails off for a moment. How ironic. Even when seeking some sort of escape, the gravity of what we're doing keeps coming back to me.

"A time to kill," I repeat, looking over at the rifle nestled inside its case. "Do you think that means we're doing the right thing?"

Dax studies the Bible again, but doesn't seem to be reading. He collects his thoughts before answering.

"There's a lot of talk in here about destroying the enemies of God," he muses. "And it also says God is about love and peace. So, if President Drummond's agenda is about hate and war ... that makes him God's enemy, right? It goes against everything this book stands for."

I nod in agreement, taking another drink from my canteen before closing it. "We're doing the right thing, then. I'm convinced he's the Antichrist."

Dax chuckles. "Wouldn't surprise me in the least."

Standing, I stretch, groaning as my tense joints crackle and pop. "Think we can find some fresh water nearby?"

He joins me on his feet and shrugs. "Can't hurt to look around. I could use a bath."

Wrinkling my nose, I nod. "Yeah, you could."

Reaching out, he pulls me against him and puts me in a headlock. "What about you, stinky?"

"Stinky?" I scoff. "I happen to smell like roses, you big ape."

"Roses planted in manure," he quips as we set off away from our campsite.

Releasing me, he puts one hand on the butt of the CBX holstered at his hip. I've got a smaller model in my ankle holster, in case we run into any trouble out there. With the Bionics now being hunted and our hideouts being sniffed out and raided, we can't be too careful. Even out here in the middle of nowhere, we might encounter MPs.

We return to silence while we walk, mostly so we can listen for the gurgle of water or the crunch of footsteps approaching over the underbrush. My bionic eye can usually spot movement for a wide radius. So far, everything seems quiet.

About five minutes after we've left our camp, we come upon a dried-up riverbed. The wide crack stretches on in either direction, winding through the trees.

"Shit," Dax mutters. "That would have been the only water source for miles. We might not find water again for another day or two."

Huffing a sigh, I run a hand over my frizzy ponytail. Despite teasing Dax about the way he smells, I'm not much better. We've got enough drinking water to last another day or two, though, so I guess it's better than nothing.

"There might be a dam," I suggest, glancing left, then right down the naked riverbed. "If I can figure out where we are, I could look to see how close we might be to civilization."

"It's too dangerous," Dax argues with a shake of his head. "We can't risk going too close to any cities."

"We can if it's one of the old abandoned ones," I remind him. "If this river was damned off near one of those towns, there might be a reservoir or something. The city would be abandoned, and we could safely gather drinking water and bathe."

Furrowing his brow, Dax follows my gaze down the little canal. He rubs his chin thoughtfully, then sighs as if resigned. He knows I'm right, and the idea of a bath has him ready to risk it.

"Fine," he agrees. "We'll go back to the bike and check things out on the navigation panel. If it looks like we're close to something, we'll wait until it gets dark, and then go check it out before we get on our way."

"Sounds like a plan."

We turn to go back the way we came, and find our campsite

undisturbed. It's my turn to take the first watch, so Dax pulls out his bedroll and climbs in. Sitting on my log, I settle in for a few hours of guard duty.

THE SUN HAS JUST BEGUN TO SET WHEN DAX ROUSES ME. THE MINUTE HE WOKE UP TO take over keeping watch, I crashed in his bedroll. I was too tired to get my own. Plus, the sleeping bag smells like Dax, bringing me comfort even while I'm asleep. His dark face is framed in orange light, the treetops wavering above him as he looms over me, gently shaking me awake.

"Time to move, B," he murmurs.

Groaning, I rub my human eye—still bleary from sleep. My muscles ache from so many hours sitting on the bike, and I'm so tired. But we have to keep pressing forward. Being in one place too long puts us at risk for getting caught.

Dax offers me half the beef jerky from a pouch he's holding, and we eat it quickly before taking a few swigs from our canteens before packing up. He climbs on the bike first. Once I'm on behind him, we're off toward the empty riverbed.

"I checked navigation while you were sleeping," Dax says through the speaker inside my helmet. "You were right ... there's an old abandoned MP outpost up the river, and what looks like a dam. The chances we'll find a reservoir are high."

I'm glad about being right, but even happier about getting to wash my hair and scrub down with soap. The drive is uneventful. About ten miles down the riverbed, we find it—a gleaming steel dam encasing a water reservoir. The lake is small, but even in the moonlight, I can see it's clean and drinkable.

"Thank God," I mutter as Dax kills the engine.

"That must be the outpost," he says, pointing to a small cluster of buildings on the other side of the lake.

They look like nothing more than shadows against the midnight-blue sky and black splotches of trees. There aren't any lights on, and the place looks completely dead—proving Dax's assertion it's abandoned true.

"Should we raid it for supplies?" I offer as we unload our own from the bike.

"After our baths," he counters. "I can't go on smelling like this another second."

With a laugh, I fish a small zip-up pouch from my duffel bag, along with clean clothes. "Can't argue with that."

Before hopping into the reservoir, we pull our canteens from among our belongings and approach the water to fill them. Once all six canteens have been filled, we stow them away with our food rations.

Then, armed with soap and changes of clothes, we head back to the lake. The little reservoir is too small for us to really avoid each other, and we know there can be no splitting up. Turning our backs on each other for a split second could give someone the chance to sneak up on us. Besides, there isn't an inch of me Dax hasn't seen. We shared a bathroom for years in Mosley Hall, for one thing. Add to that an awkwardly botched, almost-sexual encounter, and the bizarre time he and Yasmine helped me shower Gage's blood off my hands and body, and I'm reminded he's seen it all.

Yet, out here under the moonlight, things seem different. While we undress, our movements are slow and stiff—as if the awkwardness we shouldn't be feeling has now come back into play. I cut my eyes at him, finding him stripped to the waist with his boots haphazardly tossed aside, and his hands on his belt buckle. He pauses, clearly avoiding my gaze, but not making any moves to take off his last few pieces of clothing. I've unhooked my bra, but it hangs from my shoulders, the cups still settled over my breasts.

The stillness around us has become unsettling—a reminder that the distractions typically surrounding us are absent. There's no Agata to take care of, no pressing mission other than the one we're heading toward. And hanging in the air is the one thought I've avoided until now.

In all the years Dax has been in love with me, something has always stood between us. My issues over the death of my family and the walls I built around myself. Gage. Yasmine. Agata, who needs our attention and care and happens to share our room.

Now, none of those things are here. I still carry the burden of anger over my family's murders, but the walls have come down. He punched a hole through them, then Gage obliterated them completely.

There is nothing between us now but open air and the realization that no matter how messy and complicated our feelings for each other are, they are very real.

Dax breaks the spell first, the sound of his belt hitting the ground snapping me out of my reverie. I drop my bra and quickly yank off my boots. He's in the water before me, submerging himself to the waist before I've even finished getting undressed. I hear him cursing and muttering to himself about how cold the water is, and I cringe. I'm not looking forward to that, but the scented antibacterial soap in my hand reminds me I haven't been able to wash in days.

"Holy shit," I grumble as I step in, the frigid water stinging the surface of my skin.

"Right?" Dax agrees. "My balls are in my chest, it's so cold."

I laugh, and our familiar comfort with each other eases the situation a bit. He ducks under the water and then comes back up, starting to scrub the lump of soap in his hand over his skin. I follow suit, sighing with relief when I emerge, my hair soaked and hanging over my shoulders. The different scents of our soaps mingle in the air—sandalwood and sage. Dax's splashing to rinse off draws my eye to him again. As always, I can't help but notice how humongous he is. His dark shadow dwarfs mine by at least a hundred pounds of solid muscle. The moonlight shines off his black-as-night skin, illuminating the ridges in his chest and abdomen. His tattoo isn't visible when it's this dark, but I know it's there—the same cog symbol of the Resistances that is etched onto the back of my neck.

"B?"

His voice jerks me back to reality, and I feel my face flush as I realize he's caught me staring.

I clear my throat. "Yeah?"

"Swim?"

He grins and jerks his head toward the rest of the lake stretching out beyond us. Returning his smile, I toss my soap back toward the shore. It lands on the bank beside my clothes and towel.

"Hell yeah."

I dive and take off before him, swimming toward the center of the lake and resurfacing several feet way. He cuts through the water toward me, and I take back off, preceding him toward the other side.

We go on that way for what feels like an hour, swimming back and forth, chasing each other from one bank to the other ... simply existing as if only this lake and the stars above us exist.

Really, it wouldn't be a bad way to live. Out here in the abandoned outpost, we might even be able to go unfound for a long time. I let myself think it could really happen during our little swimming session. But by the time we emerge and trudge toward our clothes, the moment has passed. There's nothing left for us but the mission we've claimed and the people waiting for us to come back home. Hiding isn't an option.

"I miss that," Dax says as we quickly dry off and start to get dressed.

"Miss what?" I ask.

"Swimming just for fun," he replies, still in his underwear as he bends to make sure his titanium legs are completely dry. They're waterproof, but letting water sit in the grooves and pockets can cause rust.

Pulling on clean cargo pants, I smile. "Me too. We had a pool at home, and Skyye and I would spend hours out there on weekends and in the summer. Having contests to see who could hold their breath the longest."

"And who would win?" he asks, closing his belt before reaching for a clean undershirt.

"Skyye, always," I say with a little laugh. "The girl was a freak of nature. I'm convinced she was part mermaid or something."

Dax laughs, too, pulling on a thermal top over the first. I do the same, and we sit on the ground to pull on our boots.

"You know what I miss?" I say. "Restaurants. Sitting down in a place where I can order whatever I want, and someone else brings it to me."

"Man, that was great," he agrees. "If I never see a dried hunk of beef jerky again, I'll die happy."

"Don't die yet," I tease. "We've got about two pounds of it in our rations."

We continue that way as we return to the bike, talking about the things we miss about living free—the everyday things we took for granted. Closets full of clothes that aren't flight suits or cargo pants and thermal tops. Being able to cook in our own kitchens. Grocery stores.

By the time we make it back to the bike, the nostalgia of it all has me smiling. This is what we've been fighting for—a chance to go back to all those little things that seemed so mundane at the time.

While Dax packs up, I pull a comb from my bag and work it through my hair, which has started to curl a bit from being wet. There's no time for anything like conditioner or moisturizer, so I pull it back into a ponytail, then wind it into a bun before pitching the comb into my bag.

I'm just about to pull my helmet back on when the sound of a woman screaming rips through the silent night. The helmet falls from my hands, and I glance over at Dax, who's looking around with wide eyes as if trying to find the source of the sound. It comes again, and there's no mistaking the panic in it.

Light flares near the compound, the headlights of what appear to be MP hover bikes.

"Fuck," Dax growls, the muscles in his neck going tense. "We don't need this right now."

Crouching to take my pistol from the holster lying on the ground, I peer into the distance, counting glowing bodies dismounting from bikes— the MP armor lighting up in the dark.

"Whoever is screaming needs help," I argue. "We may not need this, but neither does she."

Dax runs a hand over his face and huffs, even though he knows I'm right. "I'm counting about six of them."

"Same," I agree. "We can take them."

Reaching for his own weapon, he flips a switch on the side—one I know sets the weapon's function to kill. These days, it's always set to kill, not stun.

"Yeah, only if they don't have an annihilator or some shit."

Despite his bitching and moaning, he takes the lead. We head toward the lights and the sounds of a woman crying out in what sounds like either fear, pain, or a combination of both.

We stick to the shadows, sinking into the line of trees surrounding the reservoir and compound. As we get closer, we slow down to get the lay of the land. There are two MPs holding a woman between them, attempting to drag her into one of the buildings. Four others stand around as if they don't have a care in the world, while the woman kicks, flails, and screams in the holds of the other two men. A titanium hand catches the light, glowing on the end of one of her arms. She tries to use it to punch through the face shield of one of the MPs helmets, but the second man stuns her with a blow to the back of the head.

Dax makes a sound like a growl beside me, echoing my rage at what I'm seeing. I don't even want to think about what's going to happen to that woman once they get her inside.

"Let's go," Dax commands before stomping out from between the trees.

I follow, trotting to keep up with his long strides as he advances on the four men standing guard with his gun raised.

NINE

BLYTHE SOL AND DAX JANNER
UNKNOWN LOCATION
JANUARY 1, 4011
10:00 P.M.

THE ASSHOLES HARDLY KNOW WHAT HIT THEM AT FIRST. DAX COMES AT THEM, KICKING one of the MPs in the face, shattering his face shield and knocking him out cold. A primal roar tears from his chest—the anger over what we've witnessed sparking the dynamite stick of rage constantly sitting in his belly, just waiting to be ignited. The second guard raises his gun in reaction, but before he can shoot Dax, I send my fist flying into the opening of his helmet. The idiot left his face shield up, and I crush his nose inward and send him sprawling to the ground. As he squirms and moans in pain with blood gushing from his wound, I stand over him and give a swift kick to his jaw. His head snaps to the side, and he goes motionless—out cold.

The four men wrestling with their defenseless prey drop the woman to converge on us. While she screams and backpedals into the dark structure, Dax and I jump into action. Our pistols fire rapidly, quickly taking them out. Two bodies go down, then two more ... and I lower my weapon, sighing with relief.

Glancing into the little structure—which I realize is part of a row of barracks, I meet the gaze of the woman we just saved. She stares at me with wide eyes, then she takes in Dax. Her lips part as if she's about to say something, but before she can, an arm comes around my neck and pulls me up against a male body encased in armor.

The jerking motion sends my gun flying from my hand, and the arm tightening around me cuts off my air supply. Beside me, Dax grunts and falls facedown onto the ground. The pungent scent of blood tells me he's been injured. I kick and fight against the body dragging me backward, but I'm whipped around so hard and fast the world spins.

I'm now facing three more MPs, who must have snuck up on us. One approaches and backhands me across the face, the hard fiberglass of his armor striking me with the force of a brick. Blood and spit go flying, and the world around me spins dizzily again. The man approaches me again, his hand raised as if to strike me once more. Before the blow can fall, a red laser zips past me and strikes him, throwing him to his back, dead.

Dax's voice comes at me, rough and thick. "Son of a bitch."

Then, the hold on me slackens, and I fall to my knees, sucking in mouthfuls of precious oxygen. While Dax fights the man he just pulled off me, I struggle to my feet just in time to face another attacker. This MP is a woman and isn't wearing her helmet … I don't hesitate to take a handful of her blonde ponytail when she gets close. I yank hard enough to make her yelp, and she falls to her knees, tears welling in her eyes as I slam my titanium fist into her face. Blood goes flying, and my second blow knocks her out cold.

Dax snaps my first attacker's neck, his chest heaving with barely controlled fury as he looks me over, a scowl furrowing his brow.

"You good, B?"

The entire left side of my face is throbbing like crazy, but I nod anyway. It could have been much worse.

"Fine." I frown and turn in a slow circle, checking my surroundings. "Wasn't there another guy?"

"There," says the woman we rescued, appearing between us with my gun in her hand.

She must have been the one to shoot the man who hit me, and by the way she's pointing that thing, she knows how to use it. Dax and I follow the direction she's pointing with the gun, and spot the last remaining MP. He's running as if his ass is on fire, his body armor lighting up against the dark night like a beacon.

Pulling the trigger, our new companion doesn't bat an eyelash when she hits her target, sending him sprawling facedown onto the ground. Then, she points the gun at one of the MPs I knocked out with my fist. She pulls the trigger, and the body jerks before returning to its motionless state. I want to feel bad for standing by while the mysterious stranger shoots the unconscious MPs one by one. But she seems to know as well as I do what needs to be done. I stand by silently and wait until she's finished picking off the rest of them.

While she does this, I study her closely. She's tall and willowy, with inky black hair cut into a pageboy style, and narrow black eyes. Her clothes are dirty and travel worn, and she's sporting a black eye—likely from one of the jackass MPs who was just handling her.

Her smile is friendly as she flips my gun around and offers it to me. "Thanks for the save. I'm Lila."

Accepting the weapon from her, I give her a nod. "It was no trouble. I'm—"

"Blythe Sol," she finishes. "I know who you are. *Everyone* knows who you are."

Right. This whole 'face of the Resistance' thing is going to take some getting used to.

"Looks like your guy here isn't doing too well," she adds, inclining her head toward Dax.

She's right. Blood trickles down his neck and stains his shirt, and his skin has gone ashen. I rush toward him just as his eyelids grow heavy and his knees buckle. I take one of his arms over my shoulder and try to support his weight, but I can barely remain on my feet with two hundred and sixty pounds of solid male resting on me.

"Help me with him, please," I plead.

Lila jumps into action quickly, moving to Dax's other side and helping me take on some of his weight. Together, we start forward, though it's slow going with Dax so weak and sluggish. His feet drag against the ground, and his head lolls forward on his shoulders.

"Dax, you might have a concussion," I state as we drag him into the barracks room. "I need you to stay awake for me. Okay? Don't go to sleep."

He murmurs something in return, and shakes his head as if to clear it. Faint light streaming through the windows reveal rows of cots lining the walls. We drop him onto one, and I turn to Lila.

"I have supplies," I say. "I can patch him up and offer you food if you need it."

I'm hoping this woman can be trusted. Yes, we saved her life, and yes, she's one of the Bionics, but I have no way of knowing who she is or what she might do if I leave her alone with Dax. I'm not willing to risk his life, but I also don't want to chance telling her where our supplies are. She could take off on our bike with all our shit, and we'd be out to dry.

Seeming to understand my hesitation, Lila gives me another smile. "Listen, I'm with you guys. I'm actually on my way to Headquarters. At least, I *was* on my way with a group from a safe house in South Carolina. The MPs chased us down, and we all got separated. I turned back to distract them so my sister and a few of the others could have a chance. Those assholes caught me, and decided they could bring me here for a little fun. I heard one of them say President Drummond has given them free rein to do whatever they want with us."

My jaw clenches as I remember Drummond's threatening message, delivered to us by a video chip hidden inside the thing that killed Yasmine.

"Do you think your sister got away okay?" I ask.

She shrugs. "I hope so. Now that you saved me, I plan to push forward toward Headquarters. Maybe I'll find her along the way. Anyway ... I just wanted you to know you can trust me. I won't hurt your friend, and I won't steal your supplies. Though, the offer of food sounds great."

Nodding decisively, I incline my head toward the open door of the barracks. "You know how to drive a hover bike?"

When she confirms she can, I tell her where we left our stuff, and she leaves to go retrieve it. I turn to Dax, who's sitting on the bed fighting to remain awake. His sleepy eyes are fixed on me, and he sways a bit as if dizzy.

"I want to lay down," he grumbles as I circle to the other side of the bed and attempt to inspect the wound on the back of his head.

It looks nasty, but needs cleaning. I can't do anything until Lila returns with our stuff. Plus, my night vision only allows me to see so much in the dark, and I need a flashlight.

"I know," I tell him, sinking on the bed at his side. "But you need to stay awake for me ... just until I can make sure your head wound is taken care of, and you have something to drink."

He nods, but winces and groans, bringing one hand up to his forehead. "That asshole clobbered me good."

"I actually thought you were out cold," I say. I need him to keep talking so he won't drift off to sleep.

He slowly turns his head to look at me, bringing one hand up toward my face. I wince when his knuckles brush my sore cheekbone. I can already feel it beginning to swell, the throbbing more acute than ever now that I'm sitting still.

"I saw that guy hit you, and I wanted to fucking murder him," he murmurs. "No way I was going to pass out before I got the chance."

I want to smile, but the blood drying on the collar of his shirt—almost black now in the faint moonlight—is worrying me.

A moment later, the sound of the hover bike outside launches me into action. I leap to my feet and rush outside just as Lila stops near the door. As she dismounts, I pull my duffel bag from one of the storage compartments. I head inside and drop it near the front door, where the moon can shine on it enough for me to see what's inside. I unzip it, then retrieve my flashlight and a med kit.

"His bag is in the other storage space," I tell Lila before rushing back to Dax. "He'll need a clean shirt to put on."

"I'm on it," Lila replies.

I can hear her moving around, grunting as she retrieves Dax's heavy bag, but I concentrate on him. Flicking on the flashlight, I shine it at the wound on the back of his head. It's not terribly deep, but it looks like it hurts. The blood trickling from it is caking up in his hair and staining his skin.

Lila joins me. Together, we strip off Dax's shirt while he groans and curses under his breath.

"That's right," I say as I hand Lila the flashlight. "You curse and yell as much as you need to … as long as you stay awake."

"Fuck, shit, fuck," he growls, causing Lila to snort in an attempt at holding back a laugh.

"Shine the light on his wound, so I can clean it," I instruct her.

She does what I ask, while I retrieve a canteen and some clean gauze. I use the water from the canteen to wash the wound clean. Thankfully, it doesn't look like it'll need stitches—I'm terrible at them, and would have probably warped the back of his head. I clean his neck and shoulders of the blood, then set the canteen aside so I can douse the wound with antiseptic. This prompts another roar and a round of curses from Dax, which I take to be a good sign. After the wound is clean, I find sterile bandages and wrap one of them around his head, keeping a patch of gauze pressed over the wound to soak up any residual blood.

Then, I help him into a clean tank top before thrusting a canteen into his hands.

"I feel like I'm going to puke," he announces, scowling at the water container.

"Then I won't make you eat," I assure him. "But you have to drink water. If you drink the water for me, I'll let you go to sleep."

He nods sleepily and tips the canteen, chugging about half in one go. Satisfied, I pull a syringe out of the med kit—an anti-inflammatory painkiller. He doesn't flinch when I plunge the needle in, the sting no contest for the pain in his head.

Lila helps me pull off his boots, and we stretch him out on one of the cots. Once I've covered him with coarse blanket, I sit on the edge of the little bed and stare at him. He's not quite asleep yet, his dark eyes peering at me from beneath lowered eyelids.

"I have to wake you up every few hours to make sure you don't have any screws loose," I tease.

"You mean no more than usual, right?" he quips.

I smile. "Right. I'll ask you your name, your age, and something about you we both know to be true."

"My name is Dax Janner, I'm twenty-two, and I'm from Brooklyn, New York," he replies.

I nod. "Good. Check back in a few hours, okay? Go to sleep now."

Sighing with relief, he closes his eyes. It only seems to take seconds before he's out like a light. I pause to run a hand over his forehead, now smooth in sleep without worry to wrinkle the skin. Most people look harmless in their sleep, but not Dax. If anything, he looks even more formidable, his chest rising and falling rhythmically, the pulse thundering at the juncture of his throat and shoulder seeming as fast and wild as the rest of him. One massive fist bunches the covers, reminding me of his strength ... of the way he snapped that MP's neck like a twig. Even when he's sleeping, there's no mistaking Dax for anything other than what he is—a fighter ... a warrior. My protector, always.

I stand and find Lila waiting nearby, the flashlight now off but still clutched in her hand. Collecting all the medical supplies, I neatly arrange them in the kit and put it back in my bag. Then, I retrieve another canteen and food ration pouch for Lila.

"Thank you," she says when I hand her the water and small portions of beef jerky and dried fruit.

"It's not much," I say apologetically. "But we're traveling light."

"I haven't eaten in two days, so this is great," she assures me before taking a huge bite of the jerky.

She groans in satisfaction and chews, sighing and sitting on one of the empty beds. I sit on one close to Dax and take a sip of water from the canteen I offered him. I'm too worried about him to eat, but know I need to stay hydrated.

"I'd offer to get you to Headquarters safely," I say. "But we're headed in a completely different direction."

Lila shakes her head. "It's okay. I can make my own way. I'm thinking this base has to have some supplies left behind ... food and weapons, maybe even a vehicle."

"That's what we were thinking. We'd stopped to get water from the reservoir, and had planned to search the place for supplies afterward. But then we found you."

"I'm grateful you intervened," she says, wrinkling her nose and staring across the room. "If you hadn't…"

I lower my eyes at the thought of what she doesn't say. Just the idea of it makes me think of Olivia and the atrocities committed against her at Stonehead. She seems to have made a comeback now, stronger than ever … but sometimes, she gets this look in her eye. This faraway gaze that tells me she's remembering everything they did to her. I know she has not forgotten … will never forget.

"I'll help you look in the morning," I say. "I don't think I'm going to be able to move him for a few days, so we'll have to hunker down here. You take any supplies you need, and we'll keep the rest. If we're lucky enough to find a functioning vehicle, it's yours."

Nodding, she pops some of the dried fruit into her mouth. "I appreciate your help. What's the mission, if you don't mind me asking?"

I do mind, so I mumble something about it being top secret before changing the subject. We engage in small talk for a little while, but Lila seems to sense I'm not in the mood, because she eventually says goodnight and offers to take the first watch. I accept, but I don't sleep.

I sit at Dax's bedside and count the hours, waking him up every two to make sure he's still coherent. He answers my questions with ease each time. His name is Dax Janner, and he's twenty-two. Each time, the detail each of us knows to be true is different.

His mother's name was Moriah. He never knew his deadbeat father. He used to be a heroin addict and drug dealer, but hasn't touched the stuff since getting his bionic prosthetics and being put through rehab. He loves apple pie but hates peach.

Just as the sun rises and shines its rays through the windows, I pull my cot close to his and stretch out. Lila is waking for another turn on watch, and has urged me to sleep at least an hour or two before we go searching for supplies.

I wake Dax one last time, because even though he seems to be in the clear, I can't close my eyes without reassuring myself yet again. I reach out and stroke his face, then gently shake his shoulder. With a groan, he pries his eyes open, squinting as the sun seems to sting them. He sighs when he locks gazes with me, relaxing a bit beneath my hand on his shoulder.

"Dax Janner," he murmurs sleepily. "Age twenty-two."

I nod and smile. "Good. And one thing we both know to be true?"

Placing his hand over mine against his face, he closes his eyes again. "I love you."

TEN

BLYTHE SOL AND DAX JANNER
UNKNOWN LOCATION
JANUARY 2, 4011
12:00 P.M.

WHEN I RETURN FROM HELPING LILA SCROUNGE FOR SUPPLIES, I FIND DAX AWAKE AND sitting up in bed. He still looks exhausted, and I'm sure it's as much from my constantly having to wake him through the night as from the pain in his head. I'm holding a crate full of items I pilfered from the buildings around us. After making sure Lila had food and water, as well as a weapon to defend herself, I helped her search for a working vehicle. We struck gold, finding a few abandoned hover bikes parked behind the armory. I wish we would have found some more weapons and ammo, but the MPs seem to have completely cleaned it out.

"Keep your head down," I'd said to Lila as she'd swung one leg over the loaded bike. "The MPs are out in full force, as I'm sure you know. Stick to the woods and abandoned areas. I hope you find your sister and friends."

Reaching out to offer me a hand, she'd nodded and smiled. "Thank you for everything … and I don't just mean the rescue and the food. I mean everything you have done for the Resistance."

I'd accepted her thanks and seen her off, watching as her bike zipped away and disappeared into the trees.

"Hey, you're up," I say, leaving the door hanging open to let some light in and dropping the crate onto one of the empty cots. "How do you feel?"

"Like I got hit by a truck," he grumbles, struggling to his feet. "And I would know, having been hit by one before."

"At least you walked away with your head still on your shoulders," I say, reminding him when he'd gotten hit by a truck, he had to be surgically enhanced with bionic technology from the pelvis down.

"True," he replies, running a hand over the rough stubble growing along his jaw. "Where's Lila?"

"Gone," I reply, rifling through the crate. "She and I searched the other buildings for supplies, and I found her a hover bike. She wanted to try to catch up with her sister."

He nods, rubbing his close-shaven head. "Find anything good?"

Holding up the pack of MREs I found in the abandoned chow hall, I grin. "Oh, yeah. Ready-to-eat meals in about eight different flavors."

Coming toward me, he peers down into the box at the packaged meals left behind by its former occupants.

"Hell yeah," he says, reaching in to pull one out and read its label. "Chicken curry ... one of my favorites."

"Me too," I agree. "Remember when the pantry at Headquarters used to be filled to the rafters with these things?"

Sighing, he goes back to looking through the box. "Those were the good ol' days."

At least, as good as they could have been with us having to run and hide underground after losing our families. Neither of us says it, but the thought hangs in the air between us.

"There's a latrine next door to this building," I say, tossing the MREs back into the box. "There are urinals, toilets, and showers with running water. There's an armory, but it's empty. An outdoor target range, and a building that looks like it was meant for training. There isn't much here, but aside from the meals, I also found some flares, matches, two med kits, and solar-powered lights."

"Better than nothing," Dax says. "Good job. When do you want to head out?"

Shaking my head, I pull out the matches and start for the door. "Not until you're up to it. You'll be too weak if we get attacked while you're still in pain."

"I'm fine," he protests.

I purse my lips. "You can't stop squinting because the light is bothering your eyes, and you're still looking a little gray. You are not fine."

"B, we have a plan—"

"Which we can't execute when one of us is injured," I interject. "A day or two holed up here won't be so bad. We'll make up for it once we're back on the road. Now quit being a jackass and sit down so I can change your bandage."

Brushing past me, he slides his pistol into the waistband of his pants. "Gotta take a leak first."

I roll my eyes but let him go, preparing the medical supplies while he's gone. When he gets back, he sits still and lets me change his bandage. The gauze is bloody, but there doesn't seem to be any more oozing from the wound. I give him another shot for the pain, happy to be liberal with the drug since we found med kits with six more syringes inside each one.

Dax is hungry, and now I'm relieved enough to also feel pangs of hunger. Out front of our little hideout, I make a quick fire and heat up two of the chicken curry dinners over it. We sit outside and eat mostly in silence, sharing water from a canteen.

The outpost is tranquil, aside from the dead MPs where we left them last night. I want to bury them at least, but Dax will insist on helping me do it. He needs to take it easy, so I simply suggest dragging their bodies into the empty armory and abandoning them there. It'll be weeks before anyone realizes what's happened to them. By then, we'll be long gone. Dax puts up a fuss when I try to do it all myself, and ends up helping me.

By the time the last one has been hauled away, he's drenched in sweat and looking like he might pass out. I urge him back to bed, and make sure he stays there for the rest of the afternoon.

We pass forty-eight hours at the outpost, spending our days recovering from our attack, and our nights taking turn on watch. The working toilet and showers next door are nice, and we make use of those with enthusiasm. Neither of us wants to think about returning to the road and the uncertainty of when we might find another latrine or shower facility.

We decide to leave on the evening of the third day, with Dax insisting he's better and up for the ride. He looks good—his coloring back to normal and the wound on his head beginning to heal.

While the sun is setting on our last night, we share a meal over our fire, and try to turn in early. I take first watch, but Dax seems restless. After he tosses and turns for a while, he twists toward me on his cot, which is pushed up against the one I'm reclining on.

Reaching for me, he pulls me close, so I'm lying on my side facing him. He reaches up to stroke my cheekbone, where an ugly bruise has begun to form. I saw it in the mirror over the sinks in the latrine—a mottling of purple and green spreading over most of the right side of my face.

"Does it still hurt?" he murmurs, his voice low as the light of the day fades and darkness begins to approach. It's almost like he doesn't want to disturb the stillness around us.

I shrug one shoulder. "Yes, but it looks worse than it feels."

Giving me a half-smile, he runs his thumb over my jawline. "You're still beautiful."

In the past, words like that coming from him would make my throat swell until I couldn't breathe. They would fill me with the urge to flee, to erect stone walls to protect my heart. Because if I didn't let him love me, or let myself love him back, I didn't have to be devastated when he died. Or crushed when fate somehow took him away from me.

But now, all his words do is fill me with warmth and hope. Because out of all the people I've ever loved, Dax has been the most constant. He's always been there, has never lied, and in the few instances that he hurt me, it was unintentional. He is the one person I've always trusted without question.

So, when the hand on my face moves to cup the back of my neck, I don't fight it. I don't let myself feel fear. In a few days, one or both of us might be dead, and moments like this might be all we have left.

He's pulling me toward him, soft and slow. So unlike the Dax I know. Kissing him before was like standing in the middle of a hurricane—like being battered by rain, but soothed by the wind at the same time. This time, his kiss is soft and feather light, tentative as if he isn't quite certain what he's doing.

Our mouths touch and brush against each other, testing and exploring. Dax is tense, his hand cupping my face a heavy comfort. I shift closer and close my eyes, letting him know it's okay for us to do this, to find comfort in a kiss. He grows bolder then, seeming to take my closed eyes as a signal that this is acceptable.

Maybe we should feel guilt or shame. For a time, we loved other people. But those people are dead, along with others we once loved. Yet, here we are, the two of us, still together through it all.

My mouth opens under his, and he plunders the inside with his tongue. The hand against my face moves down my body—over my shoulder and arm, then clutching my waist. I cling to him, gripping the front of his shirt in my fist as I answer each movement of his lips and tongue with my own. Our breaths mingle, swift and harsh in the quiet room, and for the first time since we met, being with Dax this way feels right. It feels like being home.

We still cling to each other after breaking the kiss, only our breaths rasping through the silence. Dax nuzzles the top of my head, his arms tight around me. Having Agata between us feels familial. This feels like something else altogether. Lifting my head, I search for his eyes in the dark. I can feel the moment our gazes connect, the shockwaves of it rippling through my entire body.

"Blythe Sol," I whisper. "Twenty years old."

A flash of white teeth in the dark—Dax smiling. His arms tighten around me.

"And one thing we both know is true?" he prods.

In his voice lays years' worth of hope and pain—lust and longing and promise. The words fall off my tongue easily, because they've sat perched there for a long time.

"I love you, too."

ELEVEN

BLYTHE SOL AND DAX JANNER
WASHINGTON D.C.
JANUARY 7, 4011
1:00 A.M.

THE NEXT FEW DAYS OF OUR JOURNEY TOWARD D.C. PASS WITH SURPRISING uneventfulness. We made up for our two-day stop by covering a lot of ground. For reasons I can't guess at, we find surprisingly few MPs on the rest of our route. Typically, coming closer to the capital means a thicker concentration of peace officers. This time, however, there's an odd sort of stillness in the air, and despite being grateful we haven't run into any more trouble, I'm also a little on edge.

"What do you think is going on in D.C.?" I ask once we've reached the outskirts of the city.

Hidden by the thick overgrowth of the surrounding area, with the sparsest light from the moon filtering between the tree boughs, we are changing into the body armor we pulled off a couple of MP corpses before leaving the outpost.

"What makes you think anything is going on?" he asks as he closes the front zipper of the skintight black bodysuit that goes on beneath the armor.

The disguises should help us get into the capital without being accosted—but only if we can avoid the scanners. We saw the news after they were installed in the city on every traffic light, every lamppost, and even mounted on several buildings—after Drummond sent us the video message warning us that all Bionics would be killed on sight from now on. After he declared all-out war against us.

Keeping our eyes out for scanners and sticking to the shadows will be tedious, but worth the effort once we've infiltrated D.C.

"It's too quiet out here," I reply, working to get the various panels of the armor on over my own bodysuit. "Which means something is happening in the capital ... something requiring all hands on deck."

"Chaos," Dax agrees with a nod. "Could be good for us. If the MPs are busy dealing with some other threat, they won't be expecting us."

We finish dressing in silence, and I silently pray things will go in our favor. Unlike Dax, who seems to have changed his mind about the existence of God, I am still a bit dubious. However, if he's out there and he's listening, I figure he owes me one after all the hell I've been through. If he ever decides to start caring, now would be a great time.

Re-mounting our hover bike, we take our time riding into the city—Dax taking control with me behind him, arms around his waist. We enter in the factory district, which has gone mostly dark for the night. The employees of the various plants will be coming in for the shifts in a few hours, but for now, the area is completely dead.

After the neat rows of factories and warehouses have fallen behind us, we find ourselves in a residential area—one where the poor live on the fringes of society. Dax sticks to the alleyways between deprecated apartment buildings with crumbling facades. Glancing left and right as we navigate the narrow lanes, I spot scanners here and there, their red lights sweeping the streets in half-circles. The red lights don't touch the shadows, so we press on until we find a dilapidated hotel advertising hour-by-hour rentals. Neither of us has any money, but we don't need it when we're dressed like this.

Parking along the side of the building, we retrieve our duffel bags and approach the attendant—who sits staring at us through a pane of glass. A speaker system allows us to hear her bored, monotone voice as she flicks a disinterested gaze over our uniforms.

"How many rooms?"

"One," Dax replies, his voice clipped and authoritative. "Twenty-four hours."

Nodding, she reaches for one of the round disks hanging on the wall behind her. "Got your government credentials on you?"

Reaching for the badge of the officer whose uniform he stole, Dax presents it to the attendant. She gives it a cursory glance. To my relief, she doesn't ask either of us to lift our face shields. The badges ensure we won't be asked for money to cover the room, and by the time the government realizes an officer who checked into a motel on the edge of town has gone missing, our work will be done here.

The woman slides the key into the slot beneath her window, and Dax grabs it. She goes back to staring at the small television set resting on her desk, the 3D projection showing some sort of late-night soap opera.

We find our room quickly. Once Dax presses our circular key against the panel built into the door, we're inside. The room is dark and smells musty, but it's cleaner than some of the other places we've been forced to sleep. There's one bed just big enough for the two of us to squeeze onto, along with an old glass bedside table with a lamp resting on it. An ancient television has been mounted on the wall. A sliding door leads into a cramped bathroom with a toilet and shower.

Dropping our bags onto the floor in front of the bed, Dax removes his helmet. "We should rest up, and then spend whatever time we have left in this room coming up with some kind of plan. The longer we're here, the greater our chances of being found."

Shaking my hair free of the helmet, I set it on the floor in the corner and start the process of removing the cumbersome armor.

"Sounds like a good plan," I agree. "With there being only two of us, I think decision-making should be fairly easy."

He smirks, dropping the two panels that had caged in his torso to rest beside his helmet. "That's because you've gotten smart enough to realize I'm always right."

I scrunch my nose up at him, and throw the last of my armor to the side. "Or maybe it's because you're so big and dumb I can convince you to go along with just about anything."

"Including taking part in a suicide mission?" he jokes, rolling his eyes.

"Sounds about right."

We laugh together, and I cross toward my bag to pull out two of our remaining MREs. With this room holding only the basic amenities, there's no flash heating unit, so we'll have to eat our food cold. Dax doesn't seem to mind as he accepts his ration from me and tears it open before sitting on the edge of the bed.

I reach for the remote before opening my own MRE and turning on the television. While Dax digs in to beef stew, a newscast blares into the room.

"The streets of Washington D.C. have been flooded with demonstrators this evening, as they have been every night since footage and images depicting murdered Bionic children were released to the public. Despite President Drummond's speech Wednesday morning calling for order, the protests continue ... many ending in violence between citizens and the Military Police."

I pause in the middle of freeing the little metal spoon from its package, the MRE resting in my lap. My eyes go wide as footage fills the screen—people in the streets, going toe to toe with the MPs. Their raised voices fill the room in a cacophony of sound, with one clear message coming through—they are mad as hell about what's happening, and they will no longer remain silent.

Through the chaos, I can hear an officer commanding everyone in the street to return home in an orderly fashion, reminding them of the ten o'clock curfew that's been implemented nationwide as part of the president's martial law.

A petite woman holds up a picket sign reading 'No More Slaughter of the Innocent,' marches forward, and screams at the MP that she knows her rights. Following her verbal abuse with a swing of her picket sign, she earns a fist in the face for her trouble. Enraged by the brutality, two men standing nearby attack the officer, taking him down in a flurry of kicks and punches.

Rioting breaks out in an instant, but doesn't last long once the Military Police reinforcements arrive. I watch in openmouthed shock as armored tanks appear, rolling down the street and firing projectiles into the crowd. The projectiles aren't deadly, but they do hurt, and before long, the throng begins to disperse as screams of outrage melt into cries of pain.

"While Military Police work to maintain order, questions have now arisen as the entire world seems to look on and wonder just what the president intends to do going forward about the Bionics crisis. Drummond himself plans to address the nation from the White House lawn tomorrow evening, and hopes are high that his speech will bring solutions and hope instead of more gaslighting rhetoric."

I turn to Dax, who's looking at me with raised eyebrows.

"Gaslighting rhetoric?" he murmurs. "You know things are bad when the media start calling Drummond out on his bullshit."

Digging into my stew, I take a bite and nod. "It's about time. I'm glad this is happening, because it means we have a better chance of the people being on our side once Drummond is gone. But it also makes me nervous. We need to get this done quickly. With everyone turning against him, now is the perfect time to pull the trigger on his little plan."

Dax sighs, but doesn't reply with words ... probably because we're thinking the same thing. If the president and the Rejects follow through on their plot to nuke Washington D.C., the people will stop protesting and speaking up. All their anger will be turned toward us.

We finish our dinner in silence, watching more of the footage from the city play out. Crowds have gathered at major monuments, their shouts and signs speaking out against the evil that has persisted in this country for too long. Part of me bitterly wonders what took them so long to wake up. The hopeful part of me is just glad to have them on our side.

Dax finishes eating before me, and disposes of his food wrappers before calling dibs on the first shower. Despite nerves turning my stomach into a maelstrom, I force myself to eat every bite of my meal. MREs are loaded with thousands of calories, which can fuel my energy for prolonged periods between meals. Once we set our plan in motion, I can't be sure how long it'll be before we eat again. We'll be on the run, without much time to stop without risking being caught.

Once I scarf down the last bite, I turn the channel away from the news. Everything else being reported are things I already know about—things I live every day. I find a channel that plays old movies, and toss the remove aside, pulling out clean leggings and a tank top just as Dax emerges from the shower.

"Water's nice and hot," he reports, using a towel to dry his hair as he plops onto the bed.

So is he, stripped to the waist, droplets of water still trickling from his hair and down his neck. Tearing my gaze away from him, I trudge to the bathroom, trying to get my galloping heart under control. Things haven't changed much since our kiss at the outpost. We still ride the hover bike in silence. We take turns on watch when we stop for the night. We engage in small talk over dinner.

And yet, *everything* has changed. I can't stop thinking about that kiss and all the others that have come before it. About how much being so close to him soothes the pain throbbing deep in my chest every time I think about Gage. About how finally allowing things to happen between us doesn't seem so scary now. It seems right ... like a reckoning long overdue.

As I strip down and step into the shower, I try to think about something else—anything other than Dax sitting half-naked on the bed we are going to share. Anything other than how many months it's been since I've been touched, or how good it felt to kiss him without fighting to keep my walls erected at the same time. The hot water running over my body makes me think of his hands and the times he's touched me ... the times I urged him to stop, even when I didn't really want to.

What is there to hold me back now, other than my own hang-ups? Which, honestly, no longer mean shit. I could be dead as early as tomorrow, and I'd go with so many regrets. But tonight, right now, I can do something to make at least one of those regrets go away. Turn one of those 'should haves' into 'have dones'.

I stay in the shower until the water turns cold, then quickly get out, dry off, and dress. Wiping away the steam clouding the mirror, I confront my reflection. My hair is wet and curling around my face and neck, my skin still bruised from where that MP hit me. There are puffy circles beneath my eyes, and I look as exhausted as I feel. But Dax will look at me and see what I never can ... some*thing* that draws him to me in ways neither of us really understands.

Leaving the bathroom, I find him seated against the headboard, his gaze fixated on the television. A movie I remember loving when I was in high school is playing on the screen, and I wonder if it's an old favorite of his, too. We rarely talk about life before we met, because nothing else has existed for us outside of the Resistance. It's as if once we became Bionics, our old lives ceased to be. There is only us, the way we exist in the present, and the war waging around us, seeming to never end.

He glances up as I approach and smiles, patting the mattress beside him. It's an invitation to snuggle and watch the movie, to relax in a way we've never gotten to before. But I can't relax, and I can't stop thinking about what I want.

Dax seems to sense my hesitancy, but says nothing. He simply sits and watches me stand on the side of the bed, wrestling inwardly with myself over whether to make the move I've already decided needs to be made. There's an invisible line separating me from this bed. Once I cross over it, everything will change.

But there can be no going back. Nothing can be the same it was, for either of us, ever again. There can only be the here and now, and a future I'm not even certain about.

And so, I cross the line by climbing onto the bed. Instead of settling at Dax's side, I crawl toward him, brace my hands against his chest, and straddle him. His eyes widen in surprise as I sink onto his lap, and despite his relaxed posture, I can feel his muscles going tense. His eyelids lower a bit, and a familiar heat begins simmering in the dark depths of his irises, causing them to gleam like hot coals.

His chest heaves against my palms, his breath growing harsher right along with mine. My blood races in my veins, causing a tingling sensation over the surface of my skin. It never takes much for me to respond to Dax this way. It seems primal ... elemental ... the way a part of me seems to know it belongs to him. It's the deepest, most visceral part—the part driven by pure instinct and need.

He inclines his head and continues holding my gaze, almost in a silent challenge. The last time this almost happened between us, he initiated it. I was drunk and angry at Gage, and things didn't end well. This time, he's putting the ball in my court, letting me take the lead. I can't say I blame the guy. After all the times I've pushed him away, I can't fault him for wanting to protect himself a bit ... for wanting to be absolutely certain this is what I really want.

I move my hands up to cup his face, smoothing my fingertips over the rough stubble growing there. He hasn't shaved in days, but I like the way the dark hair shadows the lower half of his face. If I'd thought he couldn't look any darker or more dangerous, I would have been wrong. He tips his head back just as I lean down to kiss him, parting his lips the moment my mouth connects with his.

Our kiss is languid and slow—tentative. We've kissed at least half a dozen times by now, but this feels different. It feels like something breaking apart to make room so something else can fall into place. It feels like the end of one thing and the beginning of another. It feels like surrender.

Dax leans back after a moment to meet my gaze, his brow slightly furrowed. I can see the tension in his neck and shoulders, the way he's holding himself back.

"I've loved you for a long time, B," he whispers, his voice barely discernible over the movie. "Even when I loved her ... I still loved you so much it hurt. Sometimes, I think that must make me the worst person on the planet because both you and Yasmine deserved better than that."

Pity and understanding twinge deep in my chest for him, because I know all-too well how he feels.

"I love you," I tell him, with a freedom I never thought I'd be capable of. "But I also loved him. So, if you're a bad person, then so am I ... because you and Gage deserved better, too."

Giving me a soft smile, he reaches up to stroke my cheek. "It's always been you and me, hasn't it?"

I nod. "From the beginning."

"Until the end," he agrees, cupping my neck to pull me to him for another kiss.

This time, he's in control, dominating the kiss in the way only Dax can. My head spins as he nibbles my lower lip, invades my mouth with his taste, and drinks from me as if he's never tasted me before. I grip his shoulders and settle closer to him, while one of his arms come around me, his hand slipping beneath my shirt to rest against my bare back.

His stubble scratches against my skin as he kisses his way across my jaw and down to my neck, the sharp pricks at odds with the softness of his lips. Cool air whispers across my skin as he lifts my shirt over my head and tosses it away, but then his mouth is on me, and I'm burning up with need, on fire from the things he seems to know I want. It shouldn't surprise me that Dax is in my head as much as he's in my heart, in my veins, swimming around and lodging himself in places I could never pry him from.

The world tilts and shifts as he reverses our positions, turning me so I lay on my back beneath him. It doesn't take long for the last layers of our clothes to be removed—not much of a milestone considering how close we've come to this before.

But this next part ... the part where Dax's body becomes a part of mine ... it changes me in ways I couldn't have expected. His weight is both solid and protective on top of me, his scent invading my nostrils, his voice in my ear whispering how much he loves me, how beautiful I am to him ... it's nothing like I dreamed, yet it's everything I could have wanted.

I close my eyes and wrap my arms around him, then my legs, taking him in, keeping him close. And without reservations or guilt, without a second thought, I give myself over to the moment and to Dax. And as sure as I know my own name, I know nothing can undo what's been done tonight, in this room, in this bed.

I am Dax's, and he is mine. That's how it's always been, and that's the way it will always be.

TWELVE

BLYTHE SOL AND DAX JANNER
WASHINGTON, D.C.
JANUARY 8, 4011
9:00 A.M.

I AWAKEN THE NEXT MORNING TO FIND DAX GONE. A SINKING FEELING DROPS INTO THE pit of my gut as I sit up and look around, blinking against the brightness of the sun filtering through the metal slats of the blinds on the room's only window. Holding the sheet over my naked chest, I peer into the bathroom, seeing through the open door that he isn't in there.

He wouldn't just leave without telling me … unless for some reason, he felt like he needed space. Noticing his body armor is missing, I assume he's gone for a walk, and maybe to get the lay of the land. With riots and protests breaking out all over the city, it might be a good idea to see how lax security is on the streets. With all the MPs focused on crowd control, they won't bother themselves worrying about whether any of us are in the mix.

Still, knowing he's left without me stings, and I wonder where his head is at after waking up beside me naked in bed. I had fallen asleep with a smile on my face, at peace for the first time in a long time. Dax had seemed content as well, his arms tight around me as we lay in silence in the dark, our breaths meeting and mingling in the air as we drifted off to sleep. Maybe he regrets it now in the harsh light of day. Or maybe guilt over moving on so quickly after Yasmine is nipping at his heels.

If he were here, I'd tell him it's okay he loves us both … okay for him to mourn her while wanting to take his solace in me. It's okay, because I'm guilty of the same need, the same confused emotions.

But he's not here.

Standing from the bed, I quickly pull on my discarded clothes and pad into the bathroom. While brushing my teeth and splashing cold water on my face, I wonder how long I should wait before going after him. Even disguised as an MP, he could be discovered, and I don't think I could finish this mission without him. I'd been determined to come on my own, but now that he's here, I need him.

Cringing at the sight of my hair—a frizzy mess after I washed it last night and climbed into bed with Dax without conditioner or moisturizer—I run my hands over it and try to gather it into a braid. It still looks a hot mess, but at least it's not hanging in my eyes.

I've just left the bathroom when the telltale click of the key disk pressing against the door panel sounds through the room. I pause just within the bathroom, frozen in place as Dax walks in, his hulking figure made even more intimidating by the gleaming white plates of his body armor. He's holding a small box in one hand as he kicks the door shut behind him.

After setting the box onto the bedside table, he reaches up to whip off his helmet. The moment our gazes meet, relief floods me in a rush. They're bright and clear, shining with the same contentment I felt last night. His mouth curves slightly at one corner, and he crosses the room toward me in three impossibly long strides.

His arm comes around my waist, and he lifts me until we're at eye level. I sink into him despite the hardness of the body armor and the steel cage of his arm clenching my waist. We kiss, and all my uncertainty melts away. There are no regrets or second thoughts ... no fears or guilt. There is only the two of us, the way it's always been when the world around us continues to evolve and change.

He sets me back on my feet once he's done, and inclines his head to study me pensively. "I thought you'd still be asleep. I didn't want to wake you, but I'm sick of MREs. I know you are, too. It's insane what a government badge can get you ... the MPs, apparently, don't have to pay for shit out of pocket."

Crossing to the little box sitting on the nightstand, I open it to find two cups of coffee and a bag of pastries. The smell coming from the box makes my stomach quiver and my mouth water. I can't remember the last time I had a fresh-baked pastry.

"Sex and pastries ... what a guy," I tease, reaching into the box and retrieving a scone.

Dax chuckles. "I'm the full package, baby."

I hand him the other cup, and we sit on the bed with the bag between us. The scone is moist and chewy, and I moan in downright ecstasy as I chew the first bite.

"Damn, girl," Dax quips from my side. "Even I can't make you moan like that."

I cut my eyes at him and shrug. "*You* don't taste like lemon and blueberry."

Leaning close, he nibbles the shell of my ear. "I'm one hundred percent pure dark chocolate, B."

My eyes practically roll back into my head as he kisses the patch of skin behind my ear, moving down toward my neck. God, yes ... the man is definitely like a hunk of dark chocolate—decadent, delicious, and bad for me ... but so damn good I can't help but want to go back for more.

Leaning away from him reluctantly, I reach for the remote. "If you don't stop, we're going to spend all day in this bed, and we have work to do."

With a sigh, Dax puts a bit more distance between us and reaches for a second scone. "You're right. Let's see what President DoucheFace is up to today."

I click away from the movie channel we watched last night and back to the news. We sit and eat our breakfast in silence as replays of clashes between citizens and the Military Police flash across the screen. Nothing seems to have changed overnight.

"*Stay tuned for more commentary on the Bionics crisis, as well as live coverage of President Drummond's planned speech. Join us as we watch the presidential address, live from the White House lawn, at seven PM*

Eastern."

Turning to Dax as the screen displays a shot of the podium set up on the sprawling arcade of the White House, I kill off the last of my coffee.

"This might be our only chance," I tell him, glancing back at the television. "These days, Drummond doesn't leave the White House much ... mostly because of all the violence happening at these protests. He only steps out when it's time to address the people. He'll be out in the open, and if I can get a clear shot—"

"Have you lost your goddamn mind?" he interrupts, his expression hardening in an instant. "B, it's a presidential address. The secret service and Military Police will be out in full force—probably in double the usual numbers, because I doubt the people will simply sit at home and stay quiet. They'll probably assemble outside the gates, and the MPs will have increased numbers for crowd control."

"Don't you see that's why it's the perfect opportunity?" I reply. "Their focus will be on crowd control, like you said. I don't need to get close ... I just need a clear line of sight, which I can get from high ground. We have all day to find out where MP patrols will be, and search for a place to take the shot from."

Nodding slowly, he narrows his eyes and rubs his chin while thinking. "Once the shit hits the fan, all the focus will be looking through the crowd to find the shooter. No one will think to look to the rooftops right away."

"Right," I agree. "By then, it'll be too late ... we'll be long gone."

Sighing, he runs a hand over his face. I can tell he isn't completely on board with this plan. But he also knows we won't have many more opportunities like this.

"If we do this, we need to bring someone else in on it," he says, the firm tone of his voice telling me he isn't in the mood to fight me on this. "Someone who can help us get the lay of the land first, so we aren't going in blind."

"Alec," I say without hesitation. "He can hack the government systems and find out when and where we can expect MP patrols ... and then help us map out some locations with clear line of sight to the White House lawn."

"He's not going to be happy about us going rogue."

"Maybe not," I reply. "But we're already out here, and there's no stopping us. He'll help, if for no other reason than to keep us safe."

"All right," he relents. "Make the call."

I stand and approach my duffel bag, kneeling beside it to rifle around for the COMM device I stashed inside. I've left it turned off so Alec can't use it to track our location, but I switch it on now so I can make contact. It won't matter now if he knows where we are ... he's too far away to stop us.

I call up the frequency for the Headquarters control room, where Alec practically lives. It only takes a moment before I get an answer.

"Kinnear here," his voice says over the line.

"It's me, Kinnear ... it's Sol," I reply.

Silence crackles over the frequency so loud it's deafening. I can imagine Alec's look of shock as he realizes he's talking to me, which would then melt into anger over what I've done.

"Sol, what the fuck?" he explodes after a moment. "Where are you, and is Janner all right?"

"We're fine," I assure him. "Janner's right here with me, and we're both fine."

"Am I reading this right?" he asks, his voice rising as concern and confusion start to creep in. "Your frequency is coming out of D.C.? What the hell are you doing there? The senator and the Professor are both worried sick, and I'm not gonna lie, we're all a little pissed."

Nodding, I steal a glance at Dax, who's listening in silence, his mouth a tight, firm line. "Look, I understand all that. I can't tell you what we're doing, but if we succeed, you'll know soon enough. I just ... I called because we need your help."

Alec sighs, and I can practically hear the wheels in his head turning—calculating the benefits of helping us secretly, versus running to the Professor to tell him where we are.

"It's important, Alec," I urge him. "If you don't help us, we might not make it out of here alive. And we *want* to get back to the Resistance alive."

"All right," he concedes after a moment. "What do you need?"

"Information on tonight's MP patrol schedules in the city," I say. "As well as a grid map of D.C., showing buildings with a clear line of sight to the White House lawn. The higher we can get, the better."

The sound of computer keys clicking comes over the frequency as Alec gets straight to work on my requests.

"Also," Dax adds, speaking up to be heard over the line. "If there are any ways to avoid or deflect the Bio scanners, it could come in handy."

I nod in approval. If we can walk right under the scanners without setting them off with our prosthetics, it'll make our mission that much easier.

He starts taking off his body armor, quietly setting the pieces aside as I continue with my call.

"That one might be a little trickier to pull off," Alec replies. "But those other requests are no-brainers. Give me about half an hour, and I'll send you everything I can find."

"Perfect," I say. "Thank you. How are things there?"

"Still clearing safehouses," he replies, while his fingers continue steadily pounding over the keyboard. "We're full to the rafters with refugees, but there are also supplies and ammo brought in from a few more of the military bases. Soon, we'll be ready to move on to Des Moines."

I exchange a glance with Dax, and he seems to be thinking the same thing as me. If we succeed in our own mission tonight, it may not be necessary for them to travel to Des Moines. At least, going there for the purpose of stopping the nuclear launch won't be necessary. Taking the fight to the Rejects, however, might be something that still needs to happen. If it comes down to it, I'd like to be there for the battle if we can.

"If we'd had any other choice, we would be there," I tell Alec. "You know that, right?"

"I do," he replies. "But I can't say the same about the others. I won't lie, there's a lot of confusion here about why you left. A lot of questions being asked that we don't know how to answer. Laura's done her best to reassure everyone, but ... well, just get your asses back here as soon as you can."

"Understood," I murmur, my heart sinking at the thought of the people

I'm fighting to protect thinking me a coward. But this was what I knew would happen the moment I decided to go off on my own. I can only hope our actions will speak for themselves, and when we are finished—whether we are killed or are able to return home alive—they will know without a doubt that I did it for them.

"Keep your heads down," Alec says before ending the call. "And stand by for that info."

The frequency goes dead. I set the COMM aside, leaving it on so we can receive the Intel from Alec. With a sigh, I run a hand over my hair.

"I hate letting them think we've abandoned them," I whisper, lowering my eyes. "But it's not as if we could tell them why we were leaving."

Now completely stripped of his armor, Dax comes to sit beside me on the floor, reaching out to take my hand.

"We did the right thing," he assures me. "The fewer people who know what we're doing, the better. If things go according to plan and we're able to make a clean getaway tonight, we can head straight for Des Moines."

I want to feel hope at his words, but a part of me still believes there can be no way out of this for us. I've made my peace with that, though, and all there is left to do now is what needs to be done.

Reaching for the carrying case for my rifle, I open it and stare down at the weapon inside. I retrieve the cleaning tools and spread them out on the floor in front of me. If I'm going to use this weapon to assassinate the president, I want it to be in tiptop shape.

"All right," I say, glancing back up at Dax as the COMM chirps to notify us of new messages from Alec. "Let's get to work."

THIRTEEN

BLYTHE SOL AND DAX JANNER
WASHINGTON, D.C.
JANUARY 8, 4011
6:00 P.M.

HOLDING MY HEAD HIGH, I KEEP MY GAZE FIXED STRAIGHT AHEAD AND DO MY BEST NOT to glance over at Dax. He marches at my side, his cadence ringing out in perfect harmony with mine, as well as the dozens of other boots surrounding us.

After spending hours going over Alec's Intel, we realized the easiest way to hide would be in plain sight. Locating an MP patrol on the edge of town scheduled to join a larger group for crowd control during the president's speech, we leave our hotel room to seek them out. First, we take our belongings back to our hover bike—which remains where we hid it deep in the woods. If we are able to make it back, we'll have enough supplies to get us home. If not … well, maybe it'll be of help to someone hiding out in these woods.

We carry only our weapons, dressed in our stolen Military Police armor. Alec sent us instructions on how to rig the little computer systems inside of them, so our helmets only communicate with each other. Walking down to a hardware store near our hotel, Dax used our government credentials to buy the tools we needed. They also come in handy for modifying our COMM devices so they send out a beacon deflecting the Bio scanners in the area. When that red light sweeps over us, the signal will scramble the reading, allowing us to walk around in the open.

Our plan is simple, which is why I have confidence it will work. March with this unit of MPs into the city, find a way to break away before reaching the White House, and get to the rooftop of a nearby museum, where I will set up to take my shot. A tripod built into my rifle will help me hold it steady. My bionic eye will work as a scope, allowing me to zoom in on my target. Dax will keep watch while I do what I have to. Then ... it'll be balls to the wall, run-for-the-hills escape time. If we are caught ... well, we'll have done our part for the cause. And maybe the people we care about won't have to fight anymore. Thinking of the Professor ... of Jenica, Alec, Olivia, and little Agata ... I decide it's worth it. They are the only family I have left, besides Dax, and I will lay down my life for them.

In the hours leading up to our departure from the little hotel room, Dax and I didn't talk much. We cleaned our weapons and made sure the joints of our Bionic limbs were all in working order. Dax forced me to sleep for a while, insisting I'd need all my wits about me when it came time to take my shot at Drummond.

I only relented once he agreed to lay beside me, though I'm not certain he slept. Waking up hours later, I found him sitting up in bed beside me, the remote in hand as some stupid game show played out on the screen. Glancing down to find me awake and watching him, he'd reached out to pull me into his arms. We spent the rest of our time left that way, talking in hushed tones about nothing in particular, kissing whenever the mood struck—which was often. It had been our last time to pretend to be normal ... to act as if we hadn't become assassins undertaking the deadliest mission of them all.

Now, marching side by side, the beauty of our stolen moments together have fallen behind us. I won't forget them, but I can't allow myself to examine the memories too closely right now. Doing that might make me want to go running back to the hotel room, or to the outpost beside the lake.

The tall, gleaming white buildings of the city center finally come into view. From the back of the formation, Dax and I begin searching for a way to leave the group. There are long, narrow alleyways stretching between office buildings, restaurants, and museums, but we can't risk slipping away too soon.

Suddenly, the perfect opening seems to come out of nowhere—a sure sign we are meant to be here, in the right place, at the right time.

An alarm blares nearby—a Bio scanner going off about one block over. The leader of our formation stops, holding up a fist to halt us. Turning in the direction of the sound, he points to the back of the cluster—where Dax and I stand with four others.

He gives a signal with his hand and then points down the alley to our left—an alarm for us to go investigate. The other two officers with us salute in response. Dax and I follow their lead, before turning to follow them away from the group.

We disappear into the alley, our footsteps ringing out over the concrete. The leader of our little group directs us to the right, and we follow, remaining silent as we wait for the perfect moment to slip away.

Taking a left down another alley, we spot them—two men running away from the sound of the alarm. They are wearing wide-eyed expressions as well as backpacks, which tells me they are on the run, likely trying to get out of the city and to one of the Resistance's many safe houses. I don't know how they've managed to stay hidden in D.C. for so long, but like the rest of our people, they've been flushed out. They duck through the back doorway of a building. As a group, we take off after them.

My heart thuds in my chest as I realize these men could die at any second. One of the officers with us could open fire and execute them on the spot.

We can't let that happen.

Following the men through the door, we find ourselves in the kitchen of a restaurant. Shouts and the crash of falling dishes mingle with the sounds of our MP companions yelling for the kitchen staff to get out of the way. The frightened cooks and dishwashers scramble to clear a path when we spot the two men disappearing through another door and out through the dining area.

I come up short as one of the MPs in front of me is thrown to his back, the clang of a frying pan bashing against his helmet echoing through the room. The second MP turns to raise his gun, but a cook comes up behind him with a rolling pin and cracks him in the head, too. The impact sends them both to the ground. The two cooks who attacked drop their cooking implements, retrieve the fallen weapons of the officers, and level them at us.

The MPs remain facedown on the ground, while Dax and I raise our hands along with our weapons.

"You don't want to do this," Dax warns, his voice coming out warbled and mechanical through the speaker system of his helmet.

The man who attacked with the rolling pin flips the switch on the CBX pistol from stun to kill, glaring at us as the red glow of the waiting laser fire appears ominously through the barrel.

"Yeah, we do," he replies in a low, raspy voice. "I'm done sittin' around and watching you assholes terrorize the innocent."

"Time to start fighting back," agrees the other cook, taking a step toward me. He places a foot on the fallen officer in front of me, and presses his weapon right up against the face shield of my helmet.

"It's not what you think," Dax says. "Just look ... and don't shoot me."

Keeping the hand holding his weapon raised, he reaches up with one hand to lift his face shield. I breathe as slowly and quiet as I can, knowing one false move will cause the gun in my face to go off.

The man facing Dax falters once the face shield comes up, and his jaw drops. "Holy shit! You're—"

Dax holds a hand up to cut the man off before he can say his name. Pointing down to the men still lying on the floor, he shakes his head.

The man nods in understanding ... we can't let them know who we are. The first cook motions for his friend to lower his weapon, which frees me to raise my face shield as well.

"Jesus, Mary, and Joseph," murmurs the man who almost shot me. "I'm sorry. We didn't know."

I shake my head. "It's okay. We appreciate you guys for wanting to contribute. You might have helped us save those men's lives."

Now pointing his gun down at the man beneath his boot, the second cook sneers. "We can save countless more if we waste these two."

As much as I want to argue it isn't necessary, we know that isn't the case. These officers have seen the faces of the men who attacked them. They know the location of the restaurant where their so-called justice was obstructed. So, I remain silent as the cooks pull the triggers on their weapons, rendering the officers motionless with quiet laser fire. The smell of charred flesh mingling with food turns my stomach.

"Keep the armor," Dax says. "It'll come in handy if you ever find yourselves needing to help others."

The first cook nods. "Good idea... Thanks."

"Anything else we can do to help?" the second asks. "What are you doing?"

"We aren't at liberty to say," I answer quickly. "But any help you can offer others like us is appreciated. Just ... try not to kill anymore MPs if you can. It won't be as easy to get away with next time."

Dax lowers his face shield, and I follow suit as we turn to leave the way we came.

"Ms. Sol," one of them calls before we are out the door.

I pause in the doorway and turn back to face the first cook. He rolls up the sleeve of his chef's jacket to reveal a black armband wrapped around his bicep. It's been hand sewn, and the symbol on it isn't perfect, but there's no mistaking what it is. Tears fill my eyes as I recognize the logo of the Resistance—something this man could be killed for wearing.

He gives me a smile and a thumbs-up. "We're with you, no matter what."

Nodding, I sniff and blink away the tears. "Thank you. Thank you so much."

The man nods and lowers his sleeve, turning to help his friend with the two bodies. Dax and I escape out the back door. I take a moment to compose myself, raising my face shield just long enough to dry my eyes before lowering it again.

I never would have imagined the same people who feared me just a few short years ago would now begin to fight for me. Not just with picket signs and protests, but with their own bodies and their own lives. As we set off down the alley, I find myself unable to squash the hope this time. It builds and swells in my chest, until I feel as if I might burst with it. Even if I cannot fight beyond this day, I know others will pick up where we have left off. The banner of the Resistance will never fall, because there will always be someone else there to hoist it, raise it, and declare war on injustice.

As we set off down the alley at a run, I whisper a silent prayer for the men who risked their lives for us. I find myself doing this more lately ... praying. And for once in my life, I feel as if God has actually heard me.

WE REACH THE AMERICAN TECHNOLOGIES & COMMUNICATION MUSEUM WITHOUT incident. Through the glass doors and windows of the first floor, I can see the place is pretty much empty—with everyone who's anyone gathering either near the White House or around a television set to hear the president's speech. The sun has begun to set, which means our escape will benefit from the cover of darkness.

We ignore the front entrance of the building and circle around to the back, where fire escape ladders offer a path to the roof. I strap my rifle to my back, while Dax holsters his weapons at his hip and ankle. We begin the climb without exchanging a single word, peering over our shoulders from time to time to ensure we aren't spotted. Not that too many citizens would question the actions of MPs ... but we can't be too careful here.

Once on the rooftop, twenty stories up, I turn in a slow circle to take in the landscape. Other buildings stretch up around us, taller than this one, but that doesn't matter. What does matter is the White House, which I can see from between two buildings—the sloping green of its east lawn pointing directly at us. News choppers hover overhead, while bright lights illuminate the podium where the president will stand to speak.

Removing my helmet, I suck in a deep breath, releasing it on a slow exhale. I turn to find Dax staring at me, his own helmet removed and held beneath one arm. We lock eyes for a long moment without words. Then, Dax sets his headgear aside and turns to face me.

"Let's get you ready," he says.

I nod and remain quiet as he begins unfastening pieces of my body armor. While they might protect us from anyone in pursuit who might think to shoot me, the heavy plates will also slow us down when it's time to run. The headgear will disturb my vision. I need to be free from it all in order to take this shot. The pieces fall away to reveal the flight suit I wear underneath. The cold evening air is held at bay by the thermal material, and it whips stray strands of hair around my face. Motioning for me to turn around, Dax takes hold of my ponytail and pulls it loose. Then, using his big hands to gather it all, he ensures each strand is smooth and pulled away from my face, before winding it into a bun so tight it makes my human eye water. But not a single strand will blow into my face or tickle my neck. Once he's finished, he offers me a pair of gloves to keep my hands warm. I accept them with a smile and slide them on.

Then, while he strips out of his own armor, I prepare my weapon for the kill. Crouching on the roof, I open the tripod and set the rifle up near the very edge. I lay on my belly and check all its settings, using my bionic eye to make sure I've got it pointed squarely at the podium.

After that, there's nothing left to do but wait.

We perch on the edge of the roof with our legs dangling off, staring out over the city. It would be a beautiful place if not for the corruption that goes on here. The pristine white façade of the buildings does nothing to hide the bloody foundations each one is built on. It will bring me nothing but pleasure to tear it all apart, starting with the man who rules it all from within like some sort of god.

Dax's hand comes down on my thigh, and I rest mine on top of it. He turns his over so our palms touch, and we intertwine our fingers. We don't speak. We don't look at each other much. There isn't anything left for us to say or do now, and that's the way I'd want it to be. If I'm going to die tonight, at least I will go having told Dax I love him ... having given him every part of me remaining after loss, death, and hate. The good parts of me are all his now, and nothing about that feels wrong.

A city-wide speaker system announces the speech, giving a

countdown update every few minutes. Thirty minutes turns into twenty, then ten. When there are only five minutes left, I turn to Dax.

"If I'm killed—"

"Over my dead body," he interjects.

"But if I am—"

"You won't be."

"Dax, shut up and listen, you stupid prick," I snap. "If I'm killed, promise me you'll survive. Don't give up, okay? Run ... fight ... do whatever you have to do to move forward. I can't do this unless you promise me."

At first, I'm afraid he won't answer. His gaze is defiant, and he doesn't have to say with words that he'd rather be the one who dies if it comes down to it. But Gage and Yasmine didn't get to choose when or how they died. Neither did his mother, or my parents and sister.

So, when he nods, I take his agreement at face value. I don't think about the fact that he might be lying to me ... that he might curl up and admit defeat if he has to watch me go down. But I don't question him.

Happy he at least cares enough to lie to me, I take my place at the rifle—lying on my belly with the buttstock pressed to my shoulder. Closing my human eye, I zoom in on the White House lawn just in time to spot President Drummond.

"We've got incoming," I announce.

Dax peers over my shoulder, even though he can't see much from this distance.

The president is flanked by his Vice President and an army of Secret Service agents. Lining the perimeter of the lawn, MPs stand at attention, their weapons ready. Outside the tall, black gates surrounding the structure, thousands have gathered. Fists are raised along with picket signs, and even though I can't hear their voices from here, I know those are raised, too. The MPs patrol along the outer edge of the crowd, prepared for mayhem to break out at any moment.

Rage overwhelms me as I watch Drummond take the podium, the realization I'm looking at Yasmine's murderer making me sick to my stomach. As he waves and smiles to the crowds and cameras, I grit my teeth and force my body to still. I fight against the tremors making me feel as if I'll fall apart at any moment. Another deep breath, and I'm calm again, cold and unfeeling. I feel nothing for this man ... nothing except the determination I need to end his life.

The city-wide speaker system flares to life again, and his voice echoes between the buildings, reaching out to us.

"*Citizens of the United States,*" he begins. "*I know many of you have questions ... you are angry and confused, and deserve the answers you seek. So, I will cut right to the chase and address the matter that seems most pressing: the videos and images of dead children being used as propaganda by the terrorist organization known as The Restoration Resistance. These disturbing images are never far from my mind. The deaths of children—whether they have bionic prosthetics or not—keeps me awake at night.*"

"Bull-fucking-shit," Dax grumbles from behind me.

"*The accusations aimed at the Military Police are currently being investigated,*" Drummond continues. "*Though I can assure you the execution of the innocent was not ordered by myself, or anyone else serving in my administration. Those in positions of leadership in the Military Police have been instructed, when they can, to use a minimum of force when engaging with the Bionics. However, as you well know, that is not always possible. These terrorists are walking weapons and considered extremely dangerous. When faced with the choice of death at the hands of one of these vicious killers, a Military Police officer might find himself forced to act with deadly force. While the loss of life is unfortunate, I do want to remind our law-abiding citizens that we now approach all-out war with this terrorist organization. And in war, there are casualties ... there is collateral damage.*"

Curling my finger around the trigger, I itch to pull it back. The crosshairs resting just over the American flag tiepin in Drummond's lapel show a clean shot.

Not yet, I tell myself. *Patience.*

The sniper rifle is all about restraint and control ... about waiting for the right shot, because I've only got one chance to get this right.

"*Make no mistake,*" Drummond goes on, his eyes lighting up as he engages his most powerful weapon—his charm and way with words. "*The Bionics have attacked you in your homes, over the airwaves, spreading malicious lies and trying to convince you to take up their cause. By spreading propaganda, they hope to turn the people against their government and assure the destruction of a society they hate. Given half the chance, they would tear your cities and homes apart brick by brick. And to drive home just how far they are willing to go in order to destroy the American way of life, I am going to go against the advice of my national security advisers and share something with you that up until now has remained classified.*"

Pulling back from the scope, I turn to glance at Dax, who's looking at me with his brow creased with bewilderment. Like me, he seems to be wondering where the hell this is all going. Despite still having a clear shot, I hold off, needing to hear what he's going to say.

"*I share this with you because I believe you have the right to know. As the American people, you need to understand what you are up against. By now, you must be privy to the news of a Resistance takeover and occupation taking place in Des Moines, Iowa. Despite our many efforts to ferret them out, they remain in control of the city, attacking and killing anyone who tries to approach from outside the barricades they have created. Weeks of gathering Intel have finally shed light on the reason for said occupation. It is our belief that the Resistance has taken control of a cache of nuclear weapons. As well, we've been informed they mean to use these weapons against you, the American public, in widespread attacks not unlike the nuclear blasts of 4006.*"

"What the fuck?" Dax growls. "He's telling them his own plan!"

"No," I whisper, my heart sinking into my gut. "He's making sure that when it happens, he can tell them 'I told you so.' He's blaming us before it even happens, so when he attacks—"

"It'll seem justified," he finishes. "Goddamn it!"

Swallowing the bile rising in the back of my throat, I close my human eye again and zoom in through the scope. I move the rifle until the crosshairs rest over Drummond's forehead.

"I'm taking the shot."

"Wait," Dax says. "Maybe you shouldn't."

Disbelief drops my jaw, but I don't take my eyes off the president. "What? Why the hell not?"

"Listen to me, B," he says, his voice sounding closer. I feel him crouching beside me. "If we kill him now, they'll just say we did it to silence him. Don't you understand? If we kill him now, he'll look like a martyr."

My palms break out in a sweat, and Drummond's voice fades to an unintelligible warble as my blood begins to rush so fast I can hear it roaring in my ears. Dax is right ... but Drummond is in my sights. The man who destroyed our lives and killed my family. The man who murdered Yasmine and threatened to come for the rest of us.

"I have to," I whisper, curling my finger around the trigger once more, shaking my head to clear it. "We came all this way."

"Undetected," Dax argues. "We can leave the same way. It's not too late."

"Yes, it is," I argue. "It's too late to go back! I won't get another shot like this."

"We'll find another way," he insists, his hand now on my shoulder. "A way that doesn't make us look like the terrorists he's making us out to be."

I jerk away from his hold and refocus through the scope. "You can only treat someone like shit for so long before they snap. You can't keep backing people into a corner without expecting them to eventually come out swinging. Drummond wants me to be a terrorist? Fine ... I'll earn my fucking spot on the FBI's Most Wanted list. I'm taking the goddamn shot."

Dax whispers a string of curses under his breath, but he doesn't physically try to stop me. He doesn't touch me again. I think it's because, deep down, he wants to see this fucker pay for what he did to Yasmine. He wants to see Drummond fall, even though he knows the consequences we'll face for it.

I zoom in a little closer ... so close it feels like I'm staring directly into his cold, dead eyes. Spittle gathers in the corners of his mouth as he gets really riled up, waving his hands and pointing as he raises his voice to rally the crowd to his side. All around the world, people are buying into this ... believing every poisonous word that comes from his mouth.

It's time to silence him once and for all.

Taking another deep breath, I hold it as I prepare for my moment of truth. I see my father falling to the ground with a bullet in his skull ... my mother sobbing hysterically as Skyye's insides paint our front lawn red. And the hot rage in my veins goes cold like ice, freezing there as the entire world around me goes still.

As I exhale, my finger squeezes the trigger.

FOURTEEN

BLYTHE SOL AND DAX JANNER
WASHINGTON D.C.
JANUARY 8, 4011
7:30 P.M.

THE RED LASER LEAVING MY RIFLE ZIPS ACROSS THE CITY, ITS TRAJECTORY PERFECTLY estimated. Sucking in another deep breath, I hold it and maintain my position, my bionic eye working to follow the little red laser ... the thing that will kill the man I hate more than I've ever hated anyone or anything in my life. Time seems to slow around me, and I can't even hear Dax breathing anymore, or register the feel of my own heart in my chest. The laser crosses the distance between the White House and me within the blink of an eye, but it seems to take an eternity. And when that eye's blink has passed, the laser careening toward the president...

Disintegrates into thin air.

Shock slams into me with the force of a ton of bricks, and my jaw drops as some unseen barrier absorbs the laser, sending its red light rippling along its surface. Then, spidery red lines glow through the air in front of Drummond, spreading like cracks in a pane of glass.

Glass!

The sound of it shattering carries all the way to where we stand on the rooftop, while shards of it rain down through the air, showering the president, his security, and the pristine lawn.

"No," I whisper as the realization of what has happened washes over me. "No!"

Screams ring out through the crowd, and bodies trample over others to scramble away from the unseen threat. Drummond crouches behind his podium, while the Secret Service jumps into action, yelling at each other through their earpieces. Some form up around Drummond, while others draw their weapons and disperse out into the crowd, likely to search for the unseen shooter.

"Fuck," Dax bellows. "B, come on. We have to go!"

I numbly register his words, as well as the blaring sirens whining over the citywide speaker system. Yet, my hands remained clutched tightly around the rifle, my heart thundering a deadly cadence of rage and revenge.

"No," I whisper, fitting my eye back to the scope and my finger to the trigger. "It's not too late. I can still take the shot."

"Are you fucking mental?" he roars, crouching beside me to grab my shoulder. "B, the MPs will be crawling all over the city within minutes. It's time to go ... right fucking now!"

Jerking my shoulder from his grasp, I swivel the rifle, searching for Drummond among the chaos. I spot a phalanx of Secret Service agents crowded around him, leading him back toward the security of the White House at a run. I clench my jaw, baring my teeth like the primitive animal that seems to have taken up residence in my body. My finger slams back on the trigger ... once, twice, a third time.

Agents fall like dominos, but my target remains out of my reach. I follow him all the way to an eastern door, pulling the trigger one last time.

"*Goddamn it,*" I screech as the laser makes impact with the smooth white siding of the building, missing Drummond altogether. He ducks through the door with the last two agents left hot on his heels. Before I can take another shot, a steel door slides over the wooden one, sealing him in. One by one, more of the doors slide over the windows and remaining doors, locking the White House down like a fortress.

"No!"

My voice carries out to rival the blaring sirens, which have now been joined with flashes of red light and a robotic voice.

Terror alert... Terror alert... All citizens, please take shelter and remain indoors. Terror alert... Terror alert...

Dax's hands grip beneath my armpits, and he hauls me backward, causing me to drop the rifle. The rage unfurls from my chest and out through the rest of my body, setting my blood on fire, making the surface of my skin burn.

"Let go," I cry, my throat burning from the force of my voice as I struggle in Dax's hold. "It's not too late... I can still... I can do it... Dax, please!"

He gives me a rough shake ... hard enough to rattle my teeth. "Blythe, I love you, but I swear to God if you don't get your shit together, I'll knock you the fuck out and carry you out of here myself. Now let's *go!*"

Sucking in a breath and choking down a sob, I nod, realizing just how close I am to getting us killed. There isn't time to dwell on the fact that I've failed ... that we came all this way to be thwarted by a pane of glass so clear and thin even my Bionic eye couldn't detect it.

Turning his back to me, Dax crouches. "Get on."

Nodding, I grab my rifle and strap it over my shoulder before climbing on. I wrap my arms around his neck and my legs around his waist, clenching tight, as if my life depends on it ... because it kind of does. He pauses a second to make sure my grip is secure.

Then, he takes a running leap off the building we're on. The pistons in his legs work overtime to propel us, and we're flying toward the next building. The impact of his landing jolts me, but I maintain my tight grip on him as we leap from rooftop to rooftop, heading toward the city's edge.

After about the fifth building, they appear—MP hover bikes rising to search the streets from above. Spotlights swivel from the noses of the vehicles, and it doesn't take long for one of them to find us. Voices call out for us to halt and surrender, but Dax takes another leap. When we land this time, he lets me off his back. We run for the fire escape leading down the side of the building. I go down first, and Dax follows, the bright beams of light searching for us, slicing through the dark and arcing through the various streets and alleys surrounding us.

The moment my feet hit the ground, the light falls on me. Dax jumps down to land beside me, and we take off together, three hover bikes in hot pursuit. Mechanical-sounding voices command us to stop and put our hands up. Not one gunshot rings out, leading me to believe they mean to take us alive.

I don't know whether to be relieved or terrified.

We duck in and out of alleys, only to come up against more of the bikes. They multiply in a swarm too large to escape—three turning into six, then ten, and now fifteen.

Pausing in a narrow space between office buildings, I flatten my body against it beside Dax and glance around. To my left on the ground, there's a manhole cover laying just slightly off balance. The dark crack leading underground catches my eye, and I realize I know exactly where we can go to escape.

"Dax, down there," I hiss, grabbing on to his sleeve and pointing toward the manhole cover.

He cringes, but glances back up at the lights, which are circling closer and closer to us now. In a second, we'll have to start running again.

"Trust me," I urge him. "I know where it leads."

And if I'm lucky, the place I'm thinking of is deserted—giving us the perfect place to lay low, as well as an escape route.

He agrees with a nod, and we dash toward the round metal covering. My bionic arm makes easy work of pulling it aside and revealing the deep, dark hole. I drop down into it first, blinking as my night vision kicks in. Dax follows, his heavy body echoing down the tunnel stretching in front of us with a resounding thud. He grabs me by the waist and lifts me, so I can pull the cover back in place. I manage to ease it over the hole just as one of the lights sweeps past the place we'd just stood.

Cloaked in darkness, with night vision revealing only Dax's face and the dark tunnel I know leads to the city's old underground train system, an odd sort of calm washes over me. The blaring of the sirens is nonexistent down here, and the flashing lights proclaiming to the world that I am a terrorist have been blotted out.

Taking Dax's hand, I propel him along beside me as I follow the tunnel. It winds and twists left and right, then left again … but I don't bother to memorize the pattern. All these tunnels converge in the same area.

Only my breathing mingling with Dax's fills the silence, and I think we both prefer it that way as we work to digest what just happened and what it'll mean for us, as well as the Resistance, going forward.

The tunnel eventually guides us onto monorail tracks, which I follow in the direction I'm fairly certain I went the last time I took this escape route ... with Gage. After what feels like hours, we finally reach the end of the line—and just a few feet beyond it, the entrance to the Rejects' hideout.

"Get your weapon ready," I warn Dax, pulling my own rifle free from its place over my shoulder. "If I'm right, this place is deserted ... but just in case..."

Nodding, he pulls both of his guns free from the holsters at his hip and ankle and raises them. I pry open the secret opening, remembering the way I once stood here and watched Baron reveal the entrance to the underground hideout.

Thankfully, the lighting I remember being down here still works, flipping on automatically in response to our movement. The common room is empty and stripped of a lot of the equipment I remember being here—the makeshift barbeque grills, televisions, and stereo equipment ... all gone. Couches and chairs remain scattered here and there. There are a series of more tunnels leading out into the rest of the hideout—rooms where the Rejects slept and lived, as well as a workshop for creating their freakish bionic parts.

"Where are we?" Dax asks, furrowing his brow and gazing around the space.

"The Rejects' main hideout," I reply, pointing my gun at one of the tunnel openings. "I'm assuming they abandoned it when they headed for Des Moines, but we should probably clear it just to be sure."

With another nod, Dax takes the lead. Together, we move down each tunnel and painstakingly clear each room. Even when the first tunnel proves to be empty, we keep going, not stopping until we see for ourselves that each area is vacant.

Once back in the common room, Dax tosses his guns aside and runs both hands over his hair. Sighing, he closes his eyes and seems to try to pull himself together.

Me? I'm unravelling. Now that the adrenaline from our escape has worn off, all the feelings I tamped down in order to make this escape are bearing down on me. My breath speeds up and my chest heaves as I fight to contain it, but I quickly lose the battle.

It unfurls from me in a scream of rage and anger, my ears ringing and my entire body vibrating from the force of it. And then I'm moving, the vibrations becoming too much for me to stand still. I'm pacing, sobbing, fighting to breathe, my heart plummeting into my gut as I am forced to accept I have failed.

Failed to avenge my family … to end this war. Failed to do the one thing I promised myself I would do the day I had to watch Dax hold Yasmine in his arms as she died.

I scream again, this time throwing a punch with my titanium fist … needing some sort of release, an outlet for the emotions threatening to cripple me. It makes contact with the wall and cracks the concrete with the most satisfying sound. But the cracks in the stone remind me of those ones in the glass protecting the president—red, glowing, and mocking me with the evidence of my ineptitude. I grunt and take another swing, this time creating a crater in the concrete.

And on and on it goes until I've drilled a hole into the stone and then collapsed to the ground in a fatigued heap. Pulling my knees up to my chest, I fight to reel it in—to close myself off to these feelings. I let them back in because I didn't want to forget, and dropped the walls I'd erected because I thought it would make me stronger. But all its done is increase this feeling of helplessness and remind me of just how futile it all is.

Dax approaches me now, kneeling in front of me and taking my shoulders in his hands. His brow is creased, his mouth pinched at the corners as he shakes his head at me.

"Don't you dare," he growls from between clenched teeth. "Don't you close me out … not again. I need you, B. The Resistance needs you. Don't close yourself off."

A tremor rocks me to the core with the impact of his words … and damn it, it's so hard to erect my walls again. Because I love him. Because I loved Gage before he died, and his niece has her own place in my heart as well. Because I told myself I'd fight for them, and I can't forget that. I can't go back to being the selfish bitch who kept people at arm's length, no matter how badly I might want to right now.

Shaking my head, I blink, causing tears to stream from my human eye. "I wasn't prepared to fail. To die, yes ... but not to fail."

Cupping my face, he swipes away the tears with his thumb. "I know. But we've failed before... We've lost before. And we're still here, B. Me and you ... we're still here. As long as we're here, we have to fight, remember? We have to go on fighting. We did what we had to do, and failed. But there's so much more work to be done. We'll be needed in Des Moines ... and after that, there will be more missions, more chances to take a stand. And I need you with me, okay? I need you to stay with me."

Closing my eyes, I choke back a sob and try to keep myself together. But when Dax pulls me into his arms and stands, I lose it. This was what I feared about letting myself be vulnerable to him—moments like this, where his strength would allow me to be weak. And now might be the weakest I've ever been since Gage's death, the knowledge of what just slipped through my fingers yet another bitter reminder that the man who killed my family and the man I loved is still out there. He's living and breathing while Gage's corpse rots away more and more each day.

Sitting on one of the worn couches, Dax holds me, his arms a fortress around my pain. I bury my face in his chest and purge it all out of my system—my anger, my tears, my regrets. Soon, it will be time to press forward, and I have to leave it all behind in order to survive.

Dax is patient, something he seems to have mastered when it comes to me. He waits until I've cried the last of my tears. Then, dragging me to one of the rooms—similar to the one I spent the night with Gage in—he sits me on the cot in the corner and helps me out of my boots. Tossing them aside, he arranges me on the cot, shifting my limbs around like I'm a rag doll. Then, he pulls off his own boots and climbs in after me, pressing my body against the wall, and closing me in from behind. I should feel trapped and confined. Instead, I feel safe and protected. His warmth and the slow cadence of his heart beating against my back begins lulling me to sleep.

One last tear rolls down my cheek as I stare at the wall. "I wanted it so bad, Dax. For me, but for her, too ... for Yasmine."

He gives me a squeeze and buries his face against my shoulder. His voice is low and tortured when he answers.

"Me too, B ... me too."

FIFTEEN

BLYTHE SOL AND DAX JANNER
UNKNOWN LOCATION
JANUARY 12, 4011
10:30 AM

WE'VE BEEN TRAVELING AWAY FROM D.C. FOR FOUR DAYS WHEN THE MPs FIND US.

We had been lucky up until now—safely making it out of the city using the underground tunnels Baron had shown me and Gage during our time here. Then, we found our hover bike right where we'd left it, with all our supplies still loaded. Abandoning our former system of traveling only by night, we pushed through for twenty hours each day. We'd paused to take turns sleeping, though neither of us rested easy.

Dax and I rode as if hell itself was on our heels, eating when we could, but surviving mostly off sips of water. I was too afraid to take more than a few bites at a time anyway, my stomach quivering at the thought of being captured.

It is never far from my mind that we could be found at any moment, to be dragged back to Stonehead for a public execution. I am not delusional enough to think torture won't be on the menu as well. Dax and I know too much about the Resistance for them to just kill us without trying to extract information.

By the time the Military Police find us, we've made it almost across the country, and are making our way between the trees in the wildlands between Iowa and South Dakota. We have no way of knowing what the news is saying about the assassination attempt, or whether our people have been dispatched to Des Moines yet, so our destination is Resistance Headquarters ... the only place we can truly feel safe.

They converge on us from between the trees, blindsiding us with a blitz attack. Dax pulls up too hard on the bike, and it careens from beneath us, sending us skidding to the ground. I barely have time to recover from the pain of rocks and tree branches scratching my skin through my clothes before they're on me—two MPs hauling me to my feet to put me in shackles.

Dax roars and thrashes in the hold of four men, and each struggles to hold him down. One of his legs lashes out in a kick, and the unfortunate bastard trying to hold said leg gets hit square in the face, his helmet shattering as he falls to his back on the ground, unconscious.

I lose sight of him as I'm thrown to my face, my hands pulled behind my back and secured with ionized cuffs. A booted foot crushes between my shoulder blades, stealing my breath, and a malicious twist of that foot causes a cry of agony to become lodged in my throat. I feel as if all my ribs are about to snap, the burning in my lungs excruciating as I try to fight for breath.

Dax is calling my name, the sounds of his grunts and the thuds of fists hitting flesh telling me he's trying to get to me. And I know if he succeeds, only one of us can break free to run, and he'll want it to be me. Tears fill my eyes, and I vow not to leave him. We came on this mission together, and if we die, we die together.

After what feels like an eternity, I'm hauled to my feet. I cough as I try to suck in mouthfuls of clean, pure air. Even the taste of dirt in my mouth can't spoil the relief of oxygen hitting the back of my throat and cooling my chest.

Dax is on his knees in front of me, shackles binding his wrist and ankles. A device I've never seen before is clenched over his head—covering his mouth and jaw to keep it closed like a muzzle. Blood stains his chest and hands, and judging by the corpse lying a few feet away, they muzzled him because he bit someone ... to death. I try not to heave at the sight of chunks of flesh littering the ground and the blood staining the grass, as well as the gaping hole in the side of the man's neck.

I am left reeling at the evidence of what Dax is willing to do to protect me. He meets my gaze before lowering his head in shame. I want to tell him it's all right ... that I failed, too, and that's why we're in this mess. But he won't look at me.

Someone behind me hauls me to my feet, and Dax is lifted to his. MPs surround us, weapons trained on us, even though our steps are shortened by the shackles and they've taken our guns. A large hovercraft is hidden by the trees, and lies waiting for us with its hatch open. An MP craft prepared to take us back to D.C.

We pause just in front of the gangplank, while two of the officers stand looking down at a tablet and punching in some information. I can imagine what they're typing.

Blythe Sol. America's Most Wanted. Twenty years old. Terrorist.

A sudden flash of movement to the left catches my attention, and I frown, trying to follow it with my eyes. I see it again, this time behind a tree. Zooming in with my bionic eye, I spot it ... a person peering at me from behind a huge tree trunk. It's a woman I've never seen before, but the gleam of her own bionic eye is unmistakable. She is one of us.

Holding one finger to her lips, she shakes her head as if to warn me not to give her away. I raise my chin in acknowledgement. Then, she holds her hand up and eases it down in a motion for me to hit the ground.

I turn to Dax and catch his gaze, before holding my shackled hands up and repeating the woman's motion. His trust in me has never been clearer as he throws his weight against the MP guarding him, propelling the officer away, and dropping to his belly on the ground.

Following suit, I bring my shackled hands over my head just as gunfire explodes from among the trees in all directions. My veins rush with adrenaline, the need to stand and fight so overwhelming that remaining where I lay becomes harder by the second. But my hands are literally tied. So, I remain on the ground with my head down, listening to the pounding of boots over the ground, the trade of laser gunfire between the MPs and our rescuers, and the fall of bodies thumping in the dirt.

I'm not sure how much time has passed before everything goes quiet. Turning my head to look around, I see a pair of boots crunching toward me across the underbrush. Big feet ... likely a man. Someone grasps me from the other side, and lifts me quickly to my feet. The world around me tilts. As the blood rushes from my head, I grow a little dizzy. Lack of food and fatigue make matters worse, and my knees buckle under the strain.

A pair of arms catch me up, bracing me against a strong male body. A familiar male body that does not belong to Dax. His rough gray sweater abrades my cheek as he pulls me close ... far too close.

I stiffen against him, but then take a deep breath, inhaling a familiar scent. One I had almost forgotten when it wasn't around for me to smell anymore. A scent that brings tears to my eyes and a dozen beautifully painful memories to my mind.

I don't want to look up at him, because this can't be real. This man isn't who I think he is, and when I look up into his face, it's just going to hurt when it turns out to be someone else.

"Hey, it's okay," he murmurs, his voice a low, soothing baritone making the hairs on the back of my neck stand on end. "I've got you."

A lump lodges in my throat and I can't breathe, can't see as my human eye is blurred by tears. Even my bionic eye goes haywire, beeping and filling my vision with readings of both mine and his vital statistics.

My heart is racing. So is his.

It's far too fast ... an undeniably mechanical cadence. His heart is bionic. But before it was bionic, his heart was *mine*.

A hand touches my chin, strong and sure, the thumb caressing my lower lip. And then he's lifting my head, forcing me to confront him ... to see if this is real or not.

It can't be real. I must have been shot in the attack, and I'm dead ... or they knocked me out and I'm dreaming.

My gaze clashes with his, and the breath I've been holding escapes in a rush, my vision clearing as he peers at me with those beautiful blue eyes. I tremble in his arms, my knees giving out completely ... but he doesn't let go. He lifts me, my feet now dangling from the ground, and smiles.

He looks different, but the same. A scar running down one side of his face ... several days' worth of stubble sprouting along his jaw, a hardened expression that can only come from having experienced far too much death and trauma.

Yet, the eyes are like I remember—so crystal clear and blue I feel as if I'm drowning as I drink him in. His expression softens the longer we stare at each other, and his mouth curves into a smile.

"Blythe," he whispers.

His voice jars me back to reality ... to the realization that I am not dreaming. This is real. He's standing here with his arms around me, his scent and the feel of him invading all my senses.

But I have to be sure. I need confirmation.

"Gage?" I respond, narrowing my eyes and inclining my head ... as if changing the angle might make him disappear or morph into someone else.

Yet, he remains the same person he was from the moment I looked into his eyes. Unwavering. Unchanging. Alive!

He doesn't answer with words. Instead, he pulls me even closer, until not a breath of space exists between us. We exhale at the same time ... sighs of deep longing and relief.

And then, his lips are on mine ... hard, rough, and sweet. He drinks from my mouth as if he's crawled across a desert and I'm his oasis ... as if he's dying, and I hold his last breath.

The world around us fades away, and I bring my arms around his neck. Opening my mouth to him, I return the kiss.

PART TWO: IMPETUS
(Dax Janner)

SIXTEEN

DAX JANNER, BLYTHE SOL, AND GAGE BRONSON
SOUTH DAKOTA
JANUARY 12, 4011
12:30 P.M.

"YOU DIED," BLYTHE SAYS TO GAGE AS I LOOK ON IN SILENCE.

There isn't much a guy can say when a friend he thought was dead rises from the grave. Or when said friend strides up to the woman you've claimed as your own and kisses her full on the mouth while you are forced to watch—while wearing shackles and a muzzle to rub salt in the wound. Or when previously mentioned woman hasn't been able to take her eyes off said friend since he appeared—always her rescuer, always her hero.

I can practically *feel* her slipping through my goddamn fingers.

The sensation of loss is bitter, mingling with the sweetness of seeing with my own eyes that Gage is indeed alive. Somehow, he survived taking Baron's blade to the chest... He survived us walking away and leaving him on the battlefield, drowning in his own blood.

Now, he sits across from us with a crude fire pit crackling in the middle, the established camp shared by him and the people he's rescued from various places sprawling around us. Hidden away by the Black Hills of South Dakota, the camp is secured by a guard patrol. There are tents, crates of various supplies, and a hodgepodge of vehicles hidden among the thick line of trees skirting the mountain range.

There was a quick explanation given as Blythe and I were released from our bonds, and the dead MPs stripped of their weapons—something about Gage being on his way to Resistance Headquarters with every person he could save along the way. But there's still so much we don't know … still so many things we have to tell him. Like the fact that his sister is dead.

Gage has eyes only for Blythe when he answers her after a tense silence. "Yes. For a moment, I did die."

Blythe's throat bobs as she blinks back tears. I want to reach out and take her hand, consoling her the way I've been doing since we were both forced to watch the people we loved die. But will she let me, now that Gage is here?

"Your heart," Blythe continues. "It's bionic now."

I frown, glancing from her over to Gage—who still looks the same on the outside. But she can see things I can't, and her bionic eye is powerful enough to penetrate his clothing and flesh to see straight through to the organ beating in his chest.

Gage nods and rubs the center of his chest absently. Remembering how long it took me to get used to having metal legs, I can understand how he feels. Like a part of you is dead, and the new part doesn't fit … like you aren't completely you anymore.

"While I lay there bleeding to death, Baron and the Rejects found me," he says. "I woke up in their hideout with a fresh surgical scar and this bionic heart."

At first, it doesn't make sense, the Rejects helping Gage survive. But then, all the information from the video he sent us comes back to me. Drummond is in league with Baron, and the Rejects are his creation. If the president thought he could control his son by saving his life, then he would absolutely order the Rejects to save him.

"The Rejects," I say, finally finding my voice. "Then you must have seen Jenica?"

He nods. "She was there, and doing a damn good job of making them think she'd crossed over to their side. My father summoned me to the White House once I was strong enough, and that's where I learned … well, a hell of a lot of shit I didn't know. Did you get my video?"

Blythe nods. "A few days ago, Alec was able to open your encrypted file. We know everything. But we thought you'd created it before you died."

"Once I found out about the plan to nuke the capital, I knew I needed to escape. I managed to get away with Jenica's help, but from there, I was on my own. On my way out of town, I stopped at a hideout run by a man named Gio Arlotti. He runs a safe house I stayed in the first time I ran away with Agata. I had hoped my sister would be there, but she was gone before I arrived. With my dad threatening to order the MPs to execute Bionics on sight, I made it my mission to stop at every place I could think of along the way and collect anyone who needed refuge. I wanted to get them to Headquarters."

Right. Because of course his intentions are fucking honorable. They're always fucking honorable, which makes me hate the guy almost as much as I like him.

"You've done a good job of it from what I can see," Blythe replies, gazing around at the group of nearly one hundred people eating or resting around us.

Gage shrugs one shoulder. "I just wanted to do my part. I also figured you guys would be heading to Des Moines soon, and would need as much help as you could get."

Pausing as if just realizing something, he inclines his head and swivels his gaze to me, his eyes narrowing a bit.

"What are you two doing out here by yourself?" he asks. "Where's your team? What's going on?"

I exchange a glance with Blythe, and she shakes her head. Out here in the middle of nowhere, Gage can't possibly know about what we've done. I give her a little nod in response to let her know I'll keep our secret. We both know it won't stay a secret for long.

"It's a long story," she hedges, turning back to Gage. "But that can wait. There are things you need to know about ... things concerning your family."

Gage straightens a bit, his brow furrowing with concern. "Are Trista and Agata okay?"

Blythe lowers her head, and I can tell she won't be able to get through his. She can't hurt him this way. Now, I let myself reach out to take her hand. Squeezing it tight, I silently reassure her before taking over.

"Laura and Yasmine were taken prisoner at Stonehead and scheduled for execution," I begin, trying to find the best place to begin the story. No matter which way I slice it, it's still going to end with 'by the way, your sister's dead.'

"I know," he replies. "In order to get my father's guard down, I had to pretend to come to his side... In exchange, I bartered for their release."

My jaw clenches as I think of Yasmine stretched out on a lab table with a mechanical bug chewing through her insides. Laura hadn't been sure why she and Yasmine had been released and allowed to return to Headquarters. My gut becomes a maelstrom of anger as I realize Gage's interference likely caused her death. Bitter bile rises in the back of my throat, even as I try to remember he had good intentions. We were already in the process of planning a rescue mission, and he did what he thought was right. This rests on the shoulders of his father, who lashed out at us all by implanting Yasmine with the bug ... by sending her back to us a screaming, writhing mess as her organs were destroyed from inside her body.

I suck in a deep breath and push forward. "While they were traveling back to Headquarters, they came across your sister... She was traveling with a group of kids she'd rescued from a hideout."

He perks up, a wide smile crossing his face. "She did it. She got them to safety."

Shaking my head, I avoid his gaze. This shouldn't be so hard. I've lived through more pain and loss in twenty-two years than most people have in two or three lifetimes. I held the woman I loved in my arms, and watched her die. I felt the moment her heart stopped beating, her last breath a soft whisper against my skin.

Gage has it easy. He didn't have to watch his sister die ... won't have to help prepare her body to be cremated.

"When Laura and Yasmine found her, she'd been shot, her hovercraft attacked by MPs," I manage. Once I start, the rest of the words flow easily. "When they showed up at Headquarters, she was still alive ... and she lasted long enough to tell Blythe things weren't what they seemed in Des Moines ... that we needed to look underground."

His smile disappears, and shock ripples over his features. His entire body tenses as he looks from me to Blythe and back again.

"Trista is dead?"

I nod, my hand tightened around Blythe's. "She and Yasmine both died that day. By the time they got to Headquarters, they were too far gone to save."

Gage blinks rapidly, as if he's trying to come to terms with what he's hearing. His shoulders heave like he's fighting not to lose it in front of everyone.

"Yasmine can't be killed," he murmurs in disbelief. "How?"

My tone comes out rougher than I mean it to, my hands curling into fists in my lap. "Your father found a way."

A tear rolls down his cheek, but he remains silent, pressing his lips together and nodding absently. We all sit that way for a while—Gage staring out over the mountains, Blythe gazing down at her hands clenched together in her lap, and me wondering what the hell is going to happen now. Too much has take place in such a short time to be absorbed, but we won't have time to sit around and process. Now that Blythe and I have failed in our rogue mission, there's sure to be some sort of payback from Drummond. The repercussions of what we've done are coming—swiftly and harshly. Added on to what we're already dealing with, it's a heavy load.

Gage shoots to his feet suddenly, swiping the back of his hand across his face to get rid of the tears. Then, he's leaving camp, his long legs propelling him toward the trees where the vehicles are parked.

Beside me, Blythe deflates, her shoulders curling inward and her hands still in fists. I study her, but can't decide how I feel about all this. Part of me envies her, because if Yasmine appeared in front of me—alive and healthy—there isn't a force on earth that could stop me from taking her into my arms. Yet, another part of me wants to tear Gage's head off, stand between them, and remind Blythe she is *mine*. The paradox leaves me feeling turned inside out, all my nerves exposed to the elements.

The struggle of what she must be feeling isn't lost on me. We both know how it feels to love two people at the same time ... to get what we need to survive from two very different sources. We both know how it feels to watch one of those sources die right before our eyes.

Which leaves only one feeling unnamed. I know what it is, but I don't want to name it. The feeling of envy. What I wouldn't give to see Yasmine's smile even one last time.

With a sigh, I run a hand over my face and make my decision. "Go after him."

Her head jerks up and she eyes me in disbelief, her mouth dropping open. "What?"

I incline my head to where Gage has disappeared, swallowed up by the trees. "Go to him. He needs someone right now. He needs ... you."

She shakes her head slowly, but then pauses, furrowing her brow. "Dax..."

Reaching out for her, I cup her face and lift her chin. "It's a lot to digest, and I get it. We'll sort it all out later, but for right now ... he just found out his sister died. Just go, okay?"

She's looking at me as if she can't believe what she's hearing. Honestly, I can't believe I'm saying it. The primal animal inside me—the one driven by pure male instinct—wants to grab her and throw her over my shoulder, claim her as mine and make sure Gage knows it. But the part of me that loved Yasmine—the part that understands compassion and empathy—needs to let her go.

Whether or not it will be permanent is entirely up to Blythe.

Taking my hand, she kisses my palm and smiles. Then, she's on her feet and leaving me, trailing after Gage.

NOT LONG AFTER BLYTHE AND GAGE ARE GONE, I SIT WHERE THEY LEFT ME, FIGHTING the urge to go after them. I tell myself to stop being a moron. The guy is mourning his sister ... I doubt he's trying to take Blythe down in the middle of the woods to dry hump her.

Boy Scout Gage would at least wait until there was a bed around or something.

Burying my face in my hands, I try not to think about sex.

Sex with Yasmine, which I miss, in all of its sweetness and purity.

Sex with Blythe, which was mind-blowing and the most satisfying experience of my life after two long years of waiting for her to be mine.

Sex between her and Gage, which I know has happened before, and is likely to happen again now that he's back.

With a groan, I scrub my hands over my face and look up to find a girl coming toward me. Petite with olive skin and dark hair, she looks like she can hold her own in a fight. She reminds me of Olivia, who is also fiercer than her size would have people think. She's holding two bowls, one of which she offers to me. I accept it, giving her a nod as she sits across from me in the place Gage just occupied.

"Michela Arlotti," she says before digging into her bowl with a tin spoon.

I glance down to find some sort of stew in the bowl. On the other side of camp, someone is serving it up to those gathered and waiting around a solar-powered kettle. I don't know what's in this, but the smell of beef broth makes my stomach howl. Blythe and I have been on the run constantly, and haven't eaten much since leaving D.C.

"Dax Janner," I reply before digging in. "Thanks."

Then, remembering Gage's story, I glance back up at her. "You related to Gio Arlotti?"

She nods and swallows a mouthful of stew. "He's my cousin. I was helping him run the D.C. safe house when Gage stopped through. When I found out he was joining up with the Resistance, I begged him to bring me along."

Glancing over her shoulder to where Gage took off with Blythe hot on his heels, she frowns. "Everything okay with Gage?"

Shaking my head, I force myself to chew and swallow the stew, which has now turned to glue in my mouth at the mention of Gage.

"It's his sister."

Michela sighs, her shoulders slumping. "Oh, no. I had hoped she made it. He's been worried sick."

We return to eating in silence. Even though my appetite is gone, I finish every bite. Michela holds her empty bowl in both hands and studies me closely for a while before speaking.

"So," she says. "Is *everyone* in love with her?"

Frowning, I glance toward the trees. Blythe has yet to reappear. "I don't follow."

Michela snorts. "I think you do. Gage is a hero, and a sexy one to boot. He's got women throwing themselves at him out here, and he turns them all down. I'm the only one who knows why."

Judging by the look on her face, she's likely one of the women who tried to get in Gage's pants. It's definitely one of the perks of being considered a hero—there is no shortage of women willing to climb into your bed. Before Yasmine, I took advantage of that perk more times than I could count. Mostly to distract myself from my unreturned feelings for Blythe.

"No," I say in answer to her question. "Just two of the biggest idiots on the planet."

Michela laughs, but it's kind of true. Blythe is a mess, and people who get close enough to figure that out eventually learn how to deal with it. Gage and I just happen to be the two dopes who became obsessed with cracking the surface. Those cracks swallowed me whole, and now I can't find my way out of the maze. Most of the time, I don't want to.

"Well," she says, standing and holding a hand out to take my empty bowl. "Whatever the case, it's good to have you with us. We've all heard the stories ... apparently you and Gage are a badass fighting team."

Remembering taking down Reject hovercrafts with only guns and hover bikes, and tag-team fighting against Baron, I grin.

"The stories are true," I say. "And of the two of us, I'm the pretty one. Don't let him tell you otherwise."

With a laugh, she begins making her way back toward the cook and the pile of empty bowls beside her.

"He already has," she throws over her shoulder.

Left alone again, I can't help but watch the woods like a hawk, waiting for Blythe and Gage to reappear. The longer they're gone, the more I begin to feel as if they're both—metaphorically, at least—never coming back. And for the rest of their time alone, I wrestle with myself over whether to fight for her, or let her go.

Unable to sit still any longer, I rise and stretch, tramping off in search of a private place to piss. I purposely go in the opposite direction Blythe and Gage took, giving a friendly nod to the patrolling guard who walks past me, a lit cigarette dangling between his lips. Pausing on the edge of the clearing, I spot a bit of gleaming titanium in the dirt—the restraining muzzle the MPs put on me after I tore an officer's neck open with my teeth.

My upper lip peels back into a snarl as I crouch to pick up the device, which seems to mock me. A symbol of my place in this world—an animal ... hunted and feared. Caged. My blood starts boiling, and it all converges on me at once. The rage, the grief, the fear.

With a growl, I turn and take a swing with the muzzle, bashing it against the side of a tree. The titanium is strong, and doesn't give under my assault. So I keep going, slamming the insulting torture device against the trunk over and over. Until bits of bark and chips of metal go flying. Until it starts to fall apart in my hands with the most satisfying crunch and snap.

Until there's nothing left, and I'm standing there, snorting and panting like an enraged bull. Tossing the remains aside, I continue on my way, pausing to crunch the last bit of it beneath my boot.

SEVENTEEN

THAT NIGHT, SOMEONE SETS UP A TENT FOR BLYTHE AND ME AMONG THE OTHERS erected for Gage and his ragtag bunch of refugees. The plan is to push on first thing in the morning, making one last stop at a safe house before pressing on to Headquarters. Which gives Blythe and me forty-eight hours or so before the shit hits the fan. No way the Professor or the senator will watch the news and not realize we are the ones who tried to assassinate the president.

We offered to help with the nighttime guard rotation, but Michela—who, apparently, is in charge of the schedule—urged us to rest after our ordeal. We've seen very little of Gage since breaking the news of his sister's death, though I know he hasn't gone far. He'd never abandon the people he's risked his life to protect.

Blythe returned from the woods alone, arms wrapped tightly around herself, as if she was trying to keep her insides from spilling out. As if she was about to fall apart and those arms were the only thing keeping her together. Any other time I'd have went to her, added my arms to the strength, helped her keep herself in one piece. But my defenses are back up after Gage's sudden reappearance, because experience has taught me this is the part where Blythe rips out my heart. This is the part where she goes running back to Gage, leaving me behind.

After losing Blythe to him the first time, then finding Yasmine, only to have her ripped away from me, too, I don't think I could take another blow like that. Loving Blythe has always hurt, and a part of me—some deep-seated, sick fucking masochist—loves the pain and revels in it. But this time, I don't think I would survive it.

Blythe sits talking with a few people who fire questions at her about her life and heroic actions over the past few years. Some of them tried that with me, but soon realized I wasn't in the mood to talk. I've been left alone, so when I get up to enter our tent to find my pallet for the night, no one gets in my way.

I stretch out on the little bedroll, my calves and feet hanging off the edge because of my height, and stare at the canopy above me. Only a sliver of moonlight illuminates the space, and the pallet Blythe will sleep on—not even an arm's length away from me.

I hope to fall asleep before she comes to bed, but no such luck. My mind is twisting and turning in so many directions I can't seem to quiet it enough to fall asleep. I'm not sure how much time has passed when I finally hear her boots crunching over the ground toward our tent, but I'm not ready to look her in the eyes. I'm not ready for her to metaphorically slit my throat and watch me bleed out.

So, before she can duck into the enclosure, I turn onto my side, putting my back to her bedroll and closing my eyes. The energy that always seems to crackle between us whenever we're in the same room is even more potent in such a tight space, and my gut clenches from the force of it as she drops to her knees on the pallet. I force myself to breathe, to hold still, to not roll over and pin her onto my bedroll so I can remind her she was mine first.

"Dax," she whispers, going still behind me. "Dax, are you awake?"

Now I'm holding my breath, waiting for her to touch me or shake me to see for herself I'm not asleep. If she touches me, I'm done for.

But she keeps her hands to herself. After a few seconds of silence, she sighs heavily before letting it go. I don't know if she can tell I'm faking being asleep, but I don't care. I need time to get a handle on my emotions … to prepare myself for what life is going to be like back at Headquarters now that Gage is back.

I'll probably have to move out of our room and sleep somewhere else. No doubt, Gage will want to move in with Blythe and Agata.

The perfect little family.

My family for the past few months.

But the truth is I've just been a placeholder for someone else ... a man both the girls I've been caring for would prefer over me.

Blythe moves around a bit more—taking off her boots, unzipping her jacket and tossing it aside. Then, she's lying down, her back coming against mine as she wiggles to settle in. My entire body tenses at the contact, and I curl my fist around the thin blanket covering me. I've never felt so disconnected from someone while being so close. But maybe it's better this way. It's better for me to put some distance between us before she has a chance to toss me aside.

For a long while, we lay there in silence, our backs warming each other while the moonlight shines through the open tent flap.

A moment later, I hear a sound come from Blythe—a sob. Her body shudders, and it happens again. My fingernails bite into my palms from how hard I'm clenching my fists to keep from rolling over and taking her into my arms. That one part of me—the part that is all about self-preservation—won't allow me to do it. It won't allow me to stick my hand into a rosebush no matter how beautiful the blooms are. The thorns have now become hazardous to my existence.

So, I lay in the dark and pretend to sleep while Blythe cries as if she's just taken a knife to the heart.

TRAVEL TO HEADQUARTERS OVER THE NEXT FEW DAYS IS UNEVENTFUL. BLYTHE AND I join one of the hovercrafts that happen to have room for two extra bodies. We travel in a convoy under the cover of the woods. Sitting by a window in our craft, I keep my weapons ready, and help watch for any signs of ambush. Beside me, Blythe is stone-faced and silent ... withdrawn.

Our pickup at the final safe house goes smoothly, and we spend the night there before rising early the next morning to return to Headquarters. It only takes us a few hours. We arrive by noon, the familiar landscape of the red rocky canyon surrounding us as we get closer to home.

Once we've gotten within range, Blythe puts in a call to Alec, warning him we're returning with a convoy. The round metal doors slide open for us, and then the long tube leading into the hangar surrounds us.

Instead of feeling glad to be home, I'm on edge, my teeth clenched so hard my jaw aches, my hands balled into fists, my breathing shallow and swift. I half expect to be greeted by Senator Davis in the hangar, or even a projection of Jenica calling in to chew our asses out. She doesn't call into Headquarters often—it's too dangerous with her in Des Moines surrounded by Rejects. But she'd probably make an exception in light of me and Blythe's epic screw-up.

Instead, we find Alec and Olivia waiting, along with a crew of people who step in to help get the vehicles parked and the people and supplies unloaded.

Alec approaches us as we disembark, his mouth a grim line, his arms folded over his chest. "Welcome back."

"Thanks," I reply, extending a fist to him.

He frowns, but gives me a bump, while Olivia shakes her head at me as if in disbelief.

"Meeting in three hours in the Professor's quarters," Alec tells us. "I hope you guys are ready to explain yourselves."

"We will be," Blythe replies, her voice clipped and strained.

Olivia's eyes go wide as she glances at something over Blythe's shoulder. I turn to find Gage approaching us, a large backpack slung over one shoulder.

"Holy shit, you're alive," she blurts before clapping one hand over her mouth.

Gage gives her a tense smile as he comes up to stand on Blythe's other side, putting her between us. How fucking appropriate.

"So it would seem," he replies gruffly.

Olivia launches herself at him, squealing and wrapping him in a hug.

He chuckles, dropping his pack and using one arm to hug her back.

"Nice to see you too, Liv," he murmurs.

"Okay, after the meeting, you're gonna have to tell us how the hell you survived getting stabbed in the heart," Alec says, walking up to pound Gage's shoulder once Olivia has backed off. "Goddamn, it's good to see you, Bronson."

"Great to be back," Gage replies. "Can someone show me where to find my niece?"

"I'll take you to her," Blythe chimes in, though she doesn't look at him. She isn't making eye contact with anyone—pointedly staring at some fixed point across the hangar. "We'll have to talk to someone about finding a spare room for you guys ... things have gotten a bit crowded."

"We'll take whatever's open," Gage replies, turning to look at her.

He's staring at the side of her face, as if willing her to look at him, but she simply stares straight ahead. I remain where I'm standing, and watch the two of them cross the hangar, disappearing through the sliding metal doors. Bending to pick up my own bag, I turn to Alec.

"How bad is it?" I ask.

He sighs, running a hand over his buzz-cut blond hair. "You haven't been identified, if that's what you mean. But there's a lot of talk in the news about what it all means ... whether the Resistance is responsible for the attack in an effort to silence Drummond. Revealing his own plan and pinning it on us was a genius move. You guys taking that shot at him only validated his position in the eyes of the American people."

I bite back a string of curses as Alec confirms my worst fear. It was exactly what I tried to warn Blythe would happen. As always, our snake-in-the-grass president has found a way to turn us into the villains, ensuring the people will never want to stand up for us.

But I can't say I blame her for taking the shot. If I had stared down the barrel of a rifle, with the man who orchestrated Yasmine's murder in my sights, I can't say I would have been able to resist. I followed Blythe to keep her safe—that much is true. But I had my own selfish reasons ... reasons that had nothing to do with her and everything to do with watching the woman I'd planned to have a future with bleed out in my arms.

Olivia's hand settles on my arm, and I gaze down to find concern written all over her face. "You gonna be okay, D?"

Shrugging off her hand, I brush past her and head toward the doors. "Fine," I throw over my shoulder before putting her, and her pity, behind me.

I don't have the stomach for pity—not after weeks of people tiptoeing around me as if Yasmine's death turned me into a fucking snowflake.

Ignoring the stares and whispers of people who shuffle to get out of my way, I make my way toward Mosley Hall. Anyone who tries to confront me right now might just get punched in the face, because I'm not in the mood for bullshit. I don't have to explain myself to anyone except the Professor and Jenica, and anyone questioning my motives doesn't know me well enough to try to call me out for going rogue.

I take my time once I reach the dorm, taking the stairwell instead of the elevator. If Gage and Agata are in the middle of a reunion, I don't want to interrupt that. Besides, our room is entirely too small for both my and Gage's big bodies—especially with the girls squeezed in.

Once I reach our floor, I pause outside the room, hesitating with my hand on the knob. The panel isn't all the way shut. I lean forward and peer through the crack, seeing movement inside.

Holding my breath to keep from being heard, I watch as Blythe and Gage move around, putting odds and ends into boxes. Agata's things, I realize. They're preparing her to move out of the room, maybe.

Gage pauses in the middle of clearing the desk where Agata sits to tinker, and turns to Blythe. He grabs her arm and pulls her toward him, causing her to drop a handful of Agata's clothes.

"Come here," he murmurs, lowering his head as if to kiss her.

She gasps and rears back—a complete one-eighty from her response to his kiss in the woods. He frowns and tries to wrap his other arm around her, but she braces a hand against his chest and pushes him, dislodging herself from his hold.

"Gage, don't."

He runs a hand through his hair, his expression similar to a wounded puppy's. "You still mad at me? Look, I know we never really got a chance to talk about it, but I had my reasons for keeping my identity a secret. I was going to tell you, but the truth came out before I could and ... I regret it. Okay? I've regretted hurting you every minute of every day since I was forced to leave here."

"I'm not angry about that anymore," she whispers, lowering her gaze and shaking her head.

He takes her shoulders in a firm grip. "Then what is it? Blythe, I *missed* you ... so damn much. I came here wanting two things the second my feet hit the ground. One was to have Agata back, and the other was you. So, what's wrong? What do I have to do to make you understand that I'm not leaving you again ... that I won't hurt you ever again?"

This time when Blythe pushes him, it's with enough force to send him across the small room. He falls back against the desk, using his hands to brace himself as it trembles beneath the force of his body.

"You *died*," she screams, her entire body vibrating with the force of her anger and pain. "I had to sit there and watch you bleed to death ... watch you *die*! And you almost took me with you!"

He tries to advance on her again, but she lunges at him, pummeling his chest with her human fist as she sobs.

"I almost died, too," she cries. "I almost didn't survive it!"

My throat constricts at seeing her this way, knowing I can't do anything to fix it. As much as I don't like it, this is between her and Gage. Still, I can't seem to make myself move away from this door ... not when what happens next will clue me in on whether I need to be the one packing his shit to move.

"I'm *sorry*," Gage bellows, his voice rising to smother hers.

He grabs hold of her arm just as she takes another swing at him, catching her by the wrist and yanking her into his embrace again. Crushing her tight against him, he rests his chin on top of her head as she goes limps and closes her eyes, tears staining her cheek.

"I'm so sorry," he murmurs, lowering his voice now that she's silent. "I never would have left you if I could help it ... and if I was going to die, I wouldn't have wanted you to be there to see it. I fought with every breath in my body to get back to you. *You* were the reason I fought... You have always been my reason."

Blythe raises her head and looks him in the eye, shaking her head slowly. "I can't ... too much has changed."

"You've changed," he agrees. "So have I. But one thing that will always be the same is the way I feel about you. I love you."

My teeth grind together at his confession, even though I've always known how he feels about her. And despite knowing how she will reply, I can't bring myself to walk away.

Biting her lower lip, she sniffles, then uses her human hand to wipe her face dry. "I can't, Gage. Me and Dax..."

He scowls, his shoulders tensing. "You and Dax what? I don't care what happened while I was gone and you thought I was dead. But you love me, Blythe ... I know you do."

She shakes her head again. "It's not about whether I thought you were dead. I made a promise to Dax..."

"And what about me?" Gage interjects, his face reddening. "I'm just supposed to stand aside and let him have you?"

"*Let* him *have* me?" Blythe screeches, her hands coming to her hips.

Oh, shit. Gage has just achieved a fuck-up of epic proportions. This will not end well for him.

"I didn't mean it like that," he says, trying to backpedal.

But Blythe is on the warpath.

"No one is *letting* anyone *have* me! I am not a toy, or a gun, or a fucking hat. You don't own me, and neither does he."

"No," Gage agrees. "But *you* own *me*. You have since the first time I looked into your eyes. And you want to throw that away? For what ... because Dax lost his girlfriend and you think you need to take her place out of pity?"

My body shakes with fury, causing me to want to put my fist through a wall. Or through Gage's fucking mouth, pulling a few teeth out if I'm lucky. He doesn't know shit about Yasmine and me, or Blythe and me for that matter. They are, in no way, interchangeable to me.

"That's not fair," Blythe fires back. "You weren't here ... for months, you've been gone, and life has moved forward without you. Don't you get it, Gage? Life goes on without you... The *world* does not revolve around you!"

Shaking his head, Gage snorts as if disgusted. "You chose me. You looked in my eyes that night at the Rejects' hideout, and you said my name... You chose *me*. What's changed?"

Blythe squares her shoulders, the last of her tears having passed. The strength I've always loved about her has returned, and she's not about to stand there and let someone tell her the decisions she's made are wrong.

"I love him," she whispers. "I always have, even when I didn't want to admit it. Dax and me ... we're together. We've been together for a while now—maybe not in the way you're thinking, but ... we've had each other when there was no one else."

He sighs, his entire body deflating as his expressions softens. "I love the guy, too, Blythe. Like a brother. And I appreciate everything he did for you and Agata while I was gone. I really do. But that doesn't mean I intend to lose you without a fight, not out of a sense of gratitude."

"This isn't up to you," she counters. "I'm happy you're alive, Gage. God, you have no idea how glad I am that Baron didn't kill you. That little girl needs her uncle, and now she has you back. The Resistance needs The Patriot, and now you can take up the mantle again and help us fight."

He reaches for her again, cupping her face this time. "And what about you? What do you need?"

She doesn't try to move away from him, but keeps her hands passively at her sides. "I won't abandon Dax. Do you understand what I'm saying? It's me and him now, and that's the way it's going to be."

For a long while, neither of them speaks. Gage keeps his grip on Blythe's face, his expression shifting with about half a dozen emotions in the span of a minute. I am certain my face is executing the same gymnastics as I try to process what I'm seeing and hearing. On a surface level, I'm aware Blythe is still mine. But deep down, I can't accept it. I can't be certain she's doing it for the right reasons. At the same time, I can't really say I'd be willing to let her go either. Call me selfish, but I've waited too long and fought too hard for Blythe to let her go now. After everything else has been snatched from me, she's the last thing I have left to cling to.

Finally, he lets her go and steps back, crossing his arms over his chest. "Just tell me one thing. Did you, or do you still, love me?"

She sinks onto one of the beds, burying her face in her hands. "Please don't do this to me."

He slams one hand down onto the desk, rattling a collection of gears and cogs. "What about what you're doing to me, huh? I need an answer... You owe me at least that much. The other day when we rescued you and Dax, and I laid eyes on you for the first time in months ... the way I felt... God, you have no idea how long I waited for that. And you can tell me you love Dax, and I believe you, because I know you guys' history. But the way you looked at me ... the way you kissed me when you realized who I was... It didn't mean nothing, Blythe. It meant something... It meant everything."

Groaning as if in pain, she lowers her head, running her hands through her hair and giving it a little pull.

"Gage—"

"Just say it," he urges. "I need to know I didn't fight my way across the entire country for nothing. That I didn't hold you up like some sort of beacon in my mind for feelings that are one-sided."

Her voice is weak and tortured this time when she replies. "Gage, please."

"Say it," he snaps, glaring at her as if she's snatched his heart out and thrown it across the room. "I love you, Gage. Something! Give me something!"

With a frustrated growl, she's on her feet again, facing him. "Yes! Okay? Yes, I loved you. Even when I was pissed at you for lying to me, I loved you. But you died, and I had to survive. I had to move on with my life."

He stares at his feet in silence for a moment before nodding decisively. "You're mine. You understand that, right? Say what you want ... be with Dax ... I don't care. You've been mine from the first time I touched you, and someday, you're going to realize it."

Picking up the box he was working on, he swipes the rest of the contents of Agata's desk inside, then lifts the bag Blythe was filling with clothes and settles it on top.

"I'll be back for the rest," he says before turning to walk out.

I back up from the door, but I'm not in a rush to be out of his way. At this point, I don't give a flying fuck if he sees me, or knows I've heard every word they've said. Crossing my arms over my chest, I raise an eyebrow at him as he explodes from the room, throwing the door open with one arm while cradling Agata's stuff in the other.

He pauses on the threshold and falters, his gaze narrowing when he sees me. I hold his stare and refuse to look away, even when I feel Blythe watching us from inside. His jaw ticks, his nostrils flaring as if he's working to contain his anger. I ball up one fist, my cracking knuckles echoing down the empty hallway. As jacked up as I am after all that's happened, I'm ready to break some bones. If he wants to go, we can go right now.

But he doesn't say a word, or—to my disappointment—try to hit me. Instead, he shakes his head. With a sneer, he turns to leave. Once he's disappeared around the corner, I step through the open doorway and slam the door behind me.

Blythe remains on one of the beds, hands folded in her lap, gaze cast downward. I drop my bag onto the other bed, my gaze never wavering from hers. I'm searching her face for any sign of the truth—any indication she wants to follow Gage from this room and down the hall. If I let my guard down before I know for sure, it'll end me.

She remains silent, so I collect clean clothes and prepare for a shower. Days camping in the woods don't have me smelling my best, and I need a clear head before this meeting with the Professor.

Pausing in the doorway of the bathroom, I turn to look at her. "If you want to go with him, just go. Do it now while I'm expecting it, and not later when my back is turned." My voice comes out harsher than I'd intended, but maybe I need her to get it ... to understand I can't let her put me through this shit again.

I let the door close behind me and toss my clothes onto the counter.

Pushing the shower on and cranking it as hot as it'll go, I start to strip. As steam starts filling the small space, I step into the stall, lowering my head and allowing the hot water to cascade over me. The heat melts my muscles, and the tension slowly abates as I stare at the white tiles, watching the water sluice down the drain.

A few minutes later, the glass door opens and Blythe appears. She's undressed with her hair piled on top of her head, her expression solemn. I stand back to let her into the shower with me, and lean against the tiles, watching her with as neutral an expression as I can manage. Her nudity is pushing all the right buttons, and the typical guy response has all the blood draining away from my head and going straight to my groin.

But I simply stand there and study her, waiting for her to push me, pull me, throw me in whatever direction she wants. Like a piece of glass she shatters and then puts back together, I am in her hands, always.

Coming toward me, she puts her hands on my chest and then presses her lips to the skin, right where the symbol of the Resistance is tattooed. I close my eyes as she works her way up to my neck, then let my head drop so our lips brush. She sighs against my mouth, wrapping her arms around me. Her wet body is against mine now, and I can't think past the primal responses making me want to physically lay claim to what's mine.

"I love you," she whispers. "Do you hear me? I love *you*. That doesn't change."

I nod, resting my forehead against hers and opening my eyes, drinking in the sight of her face framed by steam. Water droplets run down her face, washing away her tears, while a few beads cling to her eyelashes.

Taking her waist in my hands, I lift her and turn, pressing her back against the tiles and pinning her there with my body. Keeping her braced there, I cup her face in my hands and kiss her. She gasps at the rough invasion of my mouth and tongue, but melts against the onslaught. I'm not gentle, because I need her to know the depth of my need, the truth of my passion for her and only her. She returns the kiss with equal vehemence, her fingernails digging into the back of my neck as she tightens her legs around my waist.

Drawing back a bit, I take her hair in my fist and pull, tilting her head so she's looking me in the eye. Her lips are parted, the lower one trembling a bit as she stares at me, at the naked intensity I allow her to see for the first time in so long. I need her to know this is it for me. If she's mine, she's going to be until the day I kick the bucket. I don't give a fuck who came back from the dead or why.

"Yours," she whispers, as if knowing it's what I need to hear.

With a growl, I lower my head toward her throat. "Mine," I rasp, just before sinking my teeth into her shoulder.

Her cry of pleasure echoes from the tiled walls, mingling with the steam in a wordless plea for more.

Eighteen

Dax Janner, Blythe Sol, Gage Bronson, Alec Kinnear, Olivia McNabb, Laura Rosenberg, Professor Neville Hinkley, and Senator Alexis Davis
Restoration Resistance Headquarters
January 15, 4011
9:00 PM

"*What the fuck, Sol?*" screeches Jenica's agitated voice through the speaker sitting in the middle of the conference table.

Settled in chairs around the table, we all stare at her hologram. She's called in from Des Moines, where she and the squad she took with her are working undercover among the Rejects. It had been their mission to find out what they were up to ... and now that we know the truth, the mission has changed to putting a stop to it.

But not before she's gotten a chance to chew Blythe and me out for what we did.

"*I have to say, I've gotten used to you and Janner going rogue when it suits you,*" Jenica continues when Blythe merely stares silently at the projection without speaking. "*But this goes beyond the usual, dim-witted fuckery you two usually engage in! What the hell were you thinking? You could have been caught, tortured, and killed. You could have actually succeeded in your little side mission, turning our organization into the terrorists we're accused of being. And, Rosenberg, don't think I'll forget you had a hand in helping them.*"

From her place at the foot of the table, Laura opens her mouth to object, but Blythe cuts in.

"Don't blame Laura," she insists. "We would have done what we did with or without her help. She had no idea what we were up to, and we only told her we were leaving so she wasn't blindsided."

Laura nods her thanks to Blythe, but stays quiet.

"We did what we thought needed to be done," I add. I'm not about to sit here and let Blythe take all the heat for this. Not when I stood in a position to stop her, but chose to go along for the ride as well. "Drummond is the root of our problems, and we all know it. Taking him out would have destroyed his entire administration from the top down."

"Yeah, except you botched it, genius," Olivia grumbles from where she sits on my left.

"No one expected Drummond to suddenly start giving his speeches from inside a gigantic fishbowl," Blythe snaps. "It was a contingency we weren't prepared for. If it weren't for that sheet of glass, he'd be dead right now."

"Then I say thank goodness for that pane of glass," Senator Davis chimes in. She's standing behind the Professor, who sits at the head of the table. "While I understand your reasoning, assassinating the president would have done more harm to the Resistance than good."

Blyth shoots to her feet, fists clenched at her sides. "No, you *don't* understand!"

The room falls silent, and even Jenica doesn't interrupt as Blythe continues.

"With all due respect, Senator, you couldn't possibly understand. That man ordered my entire family executed ... including my *five-year-old sister.* He has allowed his MPs to get away with rape and torture of people like us ... the murder of defenseless *children*. He promised Gage he would let Laura and Yasmine go as part of a bargain, then double-crossed him by sending Yasmine home with a flesh-eating mechanical bug in her stomach that ate her from the inside out! He would have his own granddaughter murdered just because she's one of us. For three years, the Bionics have run from him... We've cowered and lived in fear, waiting for the people to fight for us. I'm done waiting, and I'm done asking nicely for people to accept me for who I am. This is war, in case you've all forgotten, and in war, it's kill or be killed. Even though I failed, I'm not sorry for what I did. Given half the chance, I'd pull the trigger again."

The room falls silent again. For a long while, no one says anything. I glance around the room, observing the people seated at the table. In the hologram, Jenica looks nothing like the commander I remember. She's chopped off her long hair, and it frames her face in a spiky bob streaked with blue highlights. Makeup leaves dark circles around her eyes and a red stain on her lips. There's a tattoo on her neck ... something in a foreign language that I can't make out. It seems she's done whatever it takes to fit in with the Rejects ... to assimilate with them and make them think she's actually turned on us. She doesn't call us often, in an effort to keep Baron from finding out she's a double agent. Which means she's really ticked off about what we did, if she's willing to risk getting caught. It's been weeks since we heard from her, and her last communication was brief, rushed in effort to keep her cover.

The Professor sits with his head is in his hands, and he looks even more haggard than usual—the stress of everything that's happened causing a few more gray hairs and lines around his mouth that weren't there before.

The senator stands at his back, arms folded over her chest. Even in the faded worn sweater and leggings—the uniform of most women here during the colder months—she carries the same sophisticated bearing she's always had. She might as well be wearing a three-piece suit and heels.

At my side, Olivia has her head lowered to hide the fact that Blythe's speech got to her. I might not be screwing her anymore, but I know her well enough to know she's thinking about Officer Rodney Jones and the torture and rape Blythe mentioned. She speaks often of vengeance against the men who did those things to her, so I know she is on our side here, even if she doesn't say so out loud.

Laura is wearing her usual white tank top, the metal plate covering her chest gleaming in the overhead lights. She keeps casting supportive glances at me, and I know that, as always, she has my back.

Alec and Gage have been silent through the entire exchange, seated side by side across the table from Blythe and me. Alec appears indifferent, but I know better. The guy's mind is like a machine—always working and processing information. I can't get a read on what he's thinking.

Gage, on the other hand, looks like shit. His face is haggard, causing the scar going down one side to stand out more prominently. There are dark circles beneath his eyes, which appear haunted and hollow. I can't tell if it's because of Blythe, or finding out about the death of his sister. I imagine it's both. A twinge of pity resounds through me, and I'm reminded that this guy is my friend, even while he's my enemy. If it weren't for Blythe, I'd probably be trying to think of ways to cheer him up ... but it's a line neither of us will likely cross. The line named Blythe will keep us on opposite sides of an emotional battlefield at all times.

"I understand as well as anyone the way you feel," Jenica says finally. *"Drummond and his administration have taken things from me, too... They've taken from all of us."*

Blythe sneers. "You know about that, don't you? You know every goddamn thing ... like the fact that Gage has been alive this whole time."

Gasps and murmurs ripple through the room, as the occupants stare from Blythe, to Jenica's projection, then to Gage.

Jenica scowls at Blythe. *"What I knew and when have no bearing on the present."*

"Doesn't it?" Blythe counters, slamming her fists on the table. "We've been mourning him for months... *Months!* And you knew the entire time where he'd been and that he was on his way to us. Instead of telling us, you let us go on thinking he was dead, and when he shows up like a fucking ghost, we were all *blindsided!*"

I reach out and place a hand on the small of her back to try to calm her. She's spinning out of control, her emotions still too raw after all that's happened. Despite the assurances she's given me, I understand she's still processing all this. Gage seemingly rising from the dead has impacted us all.

"I expected Bronson to get to you all far sooner than he did," Jenica

replies, her tone softening. "If I'd realized it would take so long, I might have tried to give you a head's up. But it doesn't change what you've done or how it will affect us all in the end. There's a way to do things, Sol, and you and Janner crossed the line. You endangered all of us with your little stunt, and it almost cost us everything."

I quickly cut in, hoping to give Blythe a moment to get herself together.

"Laying it on a little thick, aren't you?" I say with a snort. "Look, we get it. We fucked up, and you don't approve of what we did. But what's done is done. We're back now, and our focus should be on stopping the Rejects from blowing up D.C. Now that Drummond has made his little announcement, it'll be blamed on us, and we can't have that."

The senator nods and approaches the table, standing between the Professor and me, and resting her palms in the surface.

"Plans are already being made for a journey to Des Moines," she replies. "Kinnear is seeing to the logistics, and we should be ready to depart in about three days."

"*We?*" Alec speaks up. "Senator, you coming along isn't part of the plan."

The senator's mouth pinches at the corners, and she stabs Alec with a cool, level stare. "I have said it before, and I'll say it again … I would never ask another American to put their life on the line when I will not."

"That is understandable," Alec relents. "But for all intents and purposes, Senator, *you* are the next president of the United States. The people have spoken through voting, and will likely continue to support you once we get Drummond out of office. As a senator, it was okay for you to run around on the battlefield with a gun. As the future president, it just isn't smart. Protecting you is one of our top priorities."

"Young man—"

"*The senator stays,*" Jenica interrupts. "*And so do Dax and Blythe.*"

My jaw drops as I glance over at Blythe, who juts out her jaw in that stubborn way of her and shakes her head.

"No," she argues. "No way you're leaving us behind."

"After the shit you pulled in D.C., you're lucky I don't throw you out

altogether," Jenica snaps. *"You're on thin ice here, Sol... Don't push me."*

"Battling the Rejects with the possibility of the MPs showing up is an all-hands-on-deck situation," I remind her. "We are two of your strongest leaders, and she's one of your best pilots. Leaving us out of this mission is a mistake."

"One might argue trusting you again after what you did would be a mistake," the senator says, eyebrows raised.

"Precisely," Jenica agrees. *"If I can't trust you to follow orders or stick to a plan, then how can your fellow soldiers trust you with their lives on the battlefield?"*

Olivia perks up at this. "Wait a minute. I trust these two with my life, no matter what. And don't we usually put this sort of thing up to a vote? It's what we did after we found out prep-school jock boy over here was Drummond's son."

Despite the little jab, Gage remains silent, one hand balled into a fist on the table, his gaze focused someplace none of us can see.

"She's right," Laura adds, giving Olivia a nod of approval. "We should all have a say here."

"She's right," the Professor chimes in. "Jenica, a vote will only take a moment, and it's the way we've always done things."

Jenica seems annoyed by this, but for some reason, she always listens to the Professor. Even when none of us can reason with her, one word from him seems to balance her out. It's truly the oddest partnership I've ever witnessed.

"Fine," she relents. *"We'll put it to a vote. I say they remain behind. What say the rest of you?"*

"I agree with you, Ms. Swan," the senator says. "While Sol and Janner are both spearheads in this revolution, I fear they lack the qualities to effectively lead ... at least for the moment. I vote they remain behind for the safety of the entire team."

My jaw clenches as I glare at the woman who has become a symbol of hope for the Resistance. With her as president once Drummond is out of the way, we have a real chance at peace.

That doesn't mean I particularly like her right now.

Olivia stands and glares at everyone seated around the table, hands braced on her slender hips. "Are you fucking kidding me? These two have saved more lives than I can count, including mine. They're important to the Resistance, and it'll lift our soldiers' spirits to have them along for the ride. I don't care what they did ... I vote they get to come."

From across the table, Alec meets her gaze and nods. "I agree. Let them come."

Reaching for Blythe under the table, I find her hand already seeking mine. We intertwine fingers and hold on tight. I can feel the anxiety radiating from her at the prospect of being left behind while everyone else goes off to fight. It's the price we might have to pay for trying to take matters into our own hands ... but, damn, it feels unfair to be forced to pay it.

"Professor?" the senator prods.

Hinkley glances at me from over the rim of his glasses, his shoulders sagging as he sighs. "I'm sorry, son."

Knowing he's about to vote against me stings, but I understand his reasoning and love this man as if he were my own father. Nothing he does will change that.

"It's okay," I murmur with a nod. "Do what you have to do ... no hard feelings."

Nodding, he clears his throat and sits up a bit straight. "Perhaps just for the time being, having them on a probation of sorts will smooth things over. At least until we can be certain something like this doesn't happen again. I vote they stay behind."

Jenica glances toward Gage from her projection. *"Bronson?"*

Shifting a bit in his chair, he shakes his head, still avoiding looking at anyone. "Leave me out of this. Half of you voted to kick me out in the first damn place, which means I don't have much of a place here, do I?"

Everyone seems taken aback by his tone, this sort of insubordination being completely unlike him. He ignores the shocked glances and open mouths around the table, slouching in his chair.

Jenica sighs. *"Bronson, I can admit we were wrong about you. As The*

Patriot, you've proven to be a vital member of the Resistance, and a true freedom fighter. We want you along on this mission to Des Moines, and your input in this situation will be invaluable."

"Amen," Olivia agrees, clearly seeming to think Gage will side with us.

She has no idea how pissed off he is at us right now, and just like Blythe tipped the vote for sending him away, he could just as easily sway this one to keep us away from the mission.

With a heavy sigh, Gage sits up and rests his elbows on the table. "I'll go last."

All eyes swivel to Laura, who shrugs and leans casually back in her chair. "I wouldn't feel safe without Janner at my back and Sol at the helm of *Icarus*. So I say let them come... We need all hands, just like Janner said, and I trust no hands more than theirs."

I breathe a little sigh of relief, but remain very aware that the vote is now at a tie. Three to three, with Gage still holding the deciding vote. Blythe stares down at her lap, defeated. She knows as well as I do what's about to happen.

Standing, he braces his fists on the table, his arms flexing menacingly as he glances around the room. He meets everyone's gaze, stopping on me and holding. I cross my arms over my chest, inclining my head in an open challenge. He's already made up his mind... I can see that. I don't really care to beg or plead with him to play nice.

"They stay behind," he says, his voice clipped.

Then, without another word, he turns and leaves the conference room, slamming the door behind him.

NINETEEN

DAX JANNER AND GAGE BRONSON
RESTORATION RESISTANCE HEADQUARTERS
JANUARY 15, 4011
9:25 PM

ALLOWING THE DOOR TO THE CONFERENCE ROOM TO SLAM SHUT BEHIND ME, I PURSUE Gage as he strides down the hall toward the elevator. His shoulders and back are rigid, his strides long and determined. It doesn't take me long to catch up with him.

"Hey," I call, grabbing his shoulder and spinning him around to face me.

He jerks out of my hold, his expression melting into one of pure rage as he stares me down.

"What the fuck was that?" I snap. "If this is your idea of some sort of petty-ass retaliation, you need to remember what's at stake here."

Coming toward me until we're almost nose to nose, he snarls. "I know exactly what's at stake here, and this has nothing to do with you screwing me over. I happen to agree with Jenica, Senator Davis, and the Professor. You and Blythe risked everything to take out the president, without talking to anyone, without clearance from any Resistance leadership, and without any goddamn idea what you were up against!"

I scoff and shake my head. "So you're mad at us for trying to take out your daddy?"

"Please," Gage growls. "The only thing that would give me more satisfaction than watching someone murder him is being the one to pull the trigger myself. If you guys want back in on the next mission, then start acting like you're part of the team, instead of going off to do whatever the hell you want whenever the mood strikes."

"Part of the team," I repeat, rolling my eyes and folding my arms over my chest. "You've been back for, what, like thirty seconds? And you want to lecture me about being part of the team, Mr. Patriot?"

"Right, I just got back," he agrees. "And I'm sure you would have preferred things to happen differently."

"Come off it, man," I retort. "Why don't we just get down to what's really on your mind? You can't handle it that things changed after you left … after we literally watched you *die*."

His hands come up to my shoulders, and he shoves me back so hard I crash into the wall behind me. I rebound quickly, returning shove for shove, leaving a crack in the opposite wall when his body makes impact.

"You were supposed to be my *friend*," he roars, stomping back toward me and getting in my face.

"I *was* your friend," I reply, pointing a finger at myself.

"What's one of the biggest unspoken rules between men, huh?" Gage asks, lowering his voice. "What's the one thing you don't do?"

"That's bullshit, and you know it. First off, you lost any claim to Blythe when you lied to her and got yourself kicked out of Headquarters. Secondly, you fucking died right in front of her! Keeping your hands off your buddy's girl doesn't apply when your buddy is fucking worm food!"

"I'm sure you were all too happy to step up once I was gone," he grumbles.

Grunting, I clench my fists, but fight with all my might not to use them on his face. Regardless of all the shit that's going down right now, I *do* still consider him my friend. Despite his return worrying me in regard to Blythe, I'm glad he's still alive … even though at the moment, I kind of want to kill him.

"I was your friend, even when you had her," I remind him. "Even when I loved her, but she chose you … I was still your friend. I sucked that shit up and took it like a fucking man. Why the hell can't you now that the tables are turned?"

"Because she was mine," he snarls, his voice dropping lower as the others begin trailing from the conference room. "You had someone... You had Yasmine. But it wasn't enough for you, was it? The hundreds of women throwing themselves at the hero Dax Janner everywhere he goes just wasn't enough! You had to have her, too."

That did it. The second Yasmine's name came out of his mouth, the fragile thread of my control snapped. My hands whip out and close around his throat, then I propel him back against the wall, holding him there as I consider ripping his head off his shoulders.

He fights against me, but I tighten my grip until he's forced to hold still or pass out. Gasps and cries for me to let go ring out down the hall, and Blythe is running toward us, her eyes wide with panic.

"Dax, don't!"

Ignoring her, I lean in, my breaths coming short and fast like the huffs of a bull.

"Say her name again and I'll kill you with my bare hands," I threaten. "You don't know shit about her, or what she meant to me. As for Blythe ... she's made her choice. Grow some balls and accept it, and stop acting like a jackass."

Letting him go, I turn and stomp past the elevator, opting for the stairs. Hearing footsteps behind me, I swivel in the stairwell, a hand instinctively lashing out toward my pursuer. My galloping heart starts to slow as I realize it's Blythe. Releasing her arm, I take a deep breath and try to calm down.

"What the hell?" she explodes, looking at me as if I've lost my mind.

"Don't come at me," I warn her. "Your ex is the one who pulled out the cheap shots."

With a sigh, she rubs her temples, as if her head has started to pound. "You should have just left him alone."

"I think Daddy's boy can handle himself," I grumble, turning to continue down the stairs.

That she has decided to defend him has my hackles up, and I don't want to say anything I shouldn't. But Blythe never did know how to let matters go. She pursues me, her footsteps echoing on the steps behind me.

"Do you really think I'm taking his side here?"

Pausing on the bottom step, I clench my jaw. Turning to glance at her over my shoulder, I shrug.

"Wouldn't be the first time," I remind her. "If I'm going to be painted as the bad guy here, fine. Just remember, when I had the chance to vote him out of here before, I didn't. I was one of the people who voted for him to stay. He gets the chance to railroad us in there, and he takes it. Which of us is really the bad guy here?"

Without waiting for a response, I storm through the stairwell door and out through the lobby of the main building. The dome has gone dark for the night, with the twinkle of fake stars and a false half-moon guiding my path back to Hexley Hall.

In the back of my mind, I know I'm being an ass to Blythe, but I'm too pissed to go back and apologize to her right now. My skin feels too tight, as if I might burst out of it any second. My blood is rushing like molten fire in my veins, and my hands itch to hit something.

So, at the last second, I turn away from the dorm and head toward the training building. The gym is always open, and a few rounds with the heavy bag should help me get my head on straight.

The moment I'm inside, memories of Yasmine assault me. It was in this room she came to comfort me after we watched the St. Louis hideout get blown to smithereens with everyone still inside it. It was here I knelt on the mats in front of her, took her into my arms, and told her I loved her.

Stripping off my shirt, I toss it aside and attack the punching bag. My knuckles sting from the impact, and even though I don't have my hand wraps with me, I keep going full force. The pain keeps me grounded, keeps me from falling apart when everything around me seems to be crumbling.

I don't intend to let go of Blythe now that she's mine, but that doesn't stop me from wishing Yasmine had never died. That the sweetness and light she brought into my life hadn't evaporated into thin air along with her last breath. With her, there were no guessing games ... no doubts or fears. With Blythe, I feel like I'm always standing on the edge of a cliff—and while the feeling thrills me to the core, it also terrifies me. I never know when she might push me over the edge and turn away to run after something else.

Yet, as I collapse in a heap on the mats, my strength and anger finally sapped, I realize I have nothing to fear. Blythe and I have been to hell and back together. In the end, it's always come down to me and her. We turn to each other when others fail or leave us, because we know where home is. *I* am her home, and she is mine.

Rising from the mats, I pull my shirt back on and leave the gym, exhaustion now setting in after the long day. Tomorrow, I guess I can sleep in a bit, since Blythe and I won't be in on the preparations to leave for Des Moines. Maybe I'll go see what Alec might need help with, since he always stays behind to run things when we're out in the field.

Once back in our room, I am disappointed to find myself alone. She hasn't come back yet, and I'm not sure she'd want me to come looking for her after the way I acted. I take my time getting ready for bed—taking a shower and pushing our two little beds together to make one. Whether she's mad at me or not, I will not sleep without her at my side.

I settle into the bed with Yasmine's worn Bible, feeling contrite over neglecting to crack it open for days.

Blythe doesn't understand my need to read it, to discover the little passages Yasmine highlighted and take them in. But I need to understand her belief system... I want to believe there is something beyond this life. I need to be ready to die at any time without fear ... knowing there might just be something bigger and better waiting for me on the other side.

Blythe returns to find me thumbing through Song of Solomon, pausing in the doorway and casting me a nervous glance. Laying the open book gingerly in my lap so as not to disturb the already crumbling pages, I reach a hand out to her.

With a sigh, she closes the door and crosses the room, kicking off her shoes before climbing into bed with me. I pull her against my side, resting my chin on top of her head. She curls into me, nuzzling the side of my neck and resting a hand on my chest.

"I'm sorry," she whispers.

I shake my head. "No, I'm the one who's sorry. Gage pissed me off, and I took it out on you."

"But you were kind of right," she replies, sitting up a bit to look at me. "He was wrong for what he did, and you had every right to be mad at him. I just..."

When she trails off, I lift a hand to stroke the line of her jaw. "You don't have to explain. I know how hard this must be for you—twice as hard as it is for me or him. Just because you chose me doesn't mean you don't get to have your own feelings about him suddenly coming back into our lives. It's okay to need to work through those feelings, to try to wrap your head around it."

Giving me a soft smile, she runs her hand along my abdomen, trailing a heated path from my chest, down to my stomach, then back up again.

"Do you think it's always going to be this strained between us?" she murmurs.

I shake my head. "Nah. Gage just found out about his sister and ... well, he needs time and space to process, too. But in time, I think we'll be okay."

Her smile widens and she nods, settling back against me. "I hope so."

We sit that way for a while, before Blythe reaches out and gently touches the highlighted passage I'd just read. A note in ink in the margins reads 'Dax' with several hearts scrawled near it.

"Read some to me?" she whispers.

Picking up the book, I read the highlighted passage to her. "Place me like a seal over your heart, like a seal over your arm; for love is as strong as death, its jealousy unyielding as the grave. It burns like a blazing fire, like a mighty flame. Many waters cannot quench love; rivers cannot wash it away."

Her jaw drops as she gazes up to meet my eyes. "That's in the Bible?"

With a chuckle, I nod and hold it up to where she can see for herself. "Song of Solomon is, apparently, very romantic ... and downright sexy at certain points," I say.

"I like it," she decides, leaning back against my chest. "Read some more."

Scanning until I find something I know she'll like, I grin once I've found it. "Let him kiss me with the kisses of his mouth—"

"Now we're talking."

"Hush," I admonish with a laugh.

Silently, she curls up against me and rests. I read to her until she falls asleep. Then, setting the book aside, I settle her more comfortably beneath the covers, and lay beside her, pulling her against me. As always, having her safe beside me is enough to help me fall almost instantly asleep.

In the days following Gage's vote, Blythe and I throw ourselves into helping prepare for their departure. Yes, being voted off the team—even temporarily—hurts, but this is bigger than us. We are still part of the Resistance, and that means doing whatever is required of us. For now, it means ensuring weapons are charged and clean, first aid supplies are stored on hovercrafts, and other supplies are prepared for those going out to fight.

The day following Gage and my fight in the hallway, he approaches Blythe to ask her to teach Agata how to shoot. He's a fair hand with a pistol, but everyone knows she's one of the best with a gun in all of Headquarters. Despite the awkwardness of our situation, Blythe takes on the task, likely remembering that she and I had agreed to do what we could to make Agata battle ready in case of an attack. She won't be going to Des Moines, but when Gage feels she's ready, there might be some use for her. I wonder how he reacted when he learned what her latest science project was all about. If I know him, he was likely as pissed off as I was until Blythe helped me see the truth. Agata can die at any time, just like any other soldier of the Resistance. So, why shouldn't she learn to fight like one?

Each evening, Blythe works with Agata while I help Alec and Wes Graydon train some of our new recruits. With the new influx of bodies at Headquarters, we've got a fresh crop of soldiers to join the cause. The ones with actual fighting experience will be allowed on this mission—ex soldiers and government agents who can use weapons and know how to follow orders. Others with a willingness to join must learn basic self-defense first. Weapons training will come after they've learned to defend themselves with their hands.

Blythe and I collapse into bed together each night, exhausted but unable to sleep restfully. She's still beating herself up over what happened in D.C., and I'm worrying about how this mission to Des Moines might play out. There are any number of things that could go wrong, and I hate the idea of having to remain here while the others go off to fight. I find myself praying for a good outcome—something I've never done before. I'm used to taking things into my own hands—making things happen instead of waiting for someone to save me or show up with all the right answers. But with my hands tied like this, praying seems to be the only thing I can do.

On the morning the others are set to leave for Iowa, I come awake at four. Beside me, Blythe is alert, and I wonder if she ever even fell asleep the night before. I sit up and turn to put my feet on the floor, bracing my head in my hands.

"What time are they heading out?" she asks, her voice a quiet whisper.

"In one hour," I inform her.

She heaves a heavy sigh, but remains lying on her back, one arm thrown over her eyes. This is, perhaps, the worst consequence of our rash actions. Being made to ride the bench while everyone else goes out to fight leaves a bitter taste in my mouth, just as I know it does hers.

"Do you think Alec will let us into the control room?" she asks after a few minutes of silence. "So we can see what's going on? I'm sure some of our people will be outfitted with body cams."

I shrug. "He took our side in the vote, so I don't see why not."

Suddenly, a knock sounds at the door, propelling me to my feet in an instant. The hand knocking is heavy, the sharp sound making my heartbeat kick up a notch. There aren't too many people who would come knocking on our door this early in the morning.

I reach for a t-shirt and pull it on before padding barefoot to the door. Swinging it open, I find Gage standing on the other side. He's dressed for battle, a black flight suit stretched over his bulky frame, the little cog symbol of the Resistance sewn over his chest. A black armband sporting the same symbol wraps around one bicep.

Opening the door wider so Blythe can see it's him, I raise my eyebrow. Aside from him asking Blythe to train Agata on weapons, we have hardly seen him since the council meeting. His expression is flat, his gaze flicking past me to Blythe sitting on our joined beds, hair tousled from sleep. His jaw hardens a bit, but he simply looks back to me and inclines his head.

"Get dressed," he says. "If you want to sneak into the cargo hold of *Icarus* before everyone arrives in the hangar to form up, you need to hurry."

I frown, and can hear Blythe standing to join me by the door. "What?"

Gage rolls his eyes and releases a heavy breath. "You want me to say I was wrong? Fine ... I was wrong. Whatever. We don't have time for this. If you want a piece of the action, you have to sneak on when no one's around. The Professor and the senator will be joining Alec in the control room soon, and will be able to see the hangar's security-camera feed. We have a small window here. You coming or not?"

Glancing back at Blythe, I find her grinning.

"Fuck yeah," she says before quickly moving to the dresser and starting to rummage through the top drawer.

I turn back to Gage. "What she said. Give us five."

He doesn't reply with words, just gives a little nod before turning and disappearing down the hall. Closing the door, I join Blythe in quickly preparing to leave, stripping off my pajamas and trading them for a black flight suit and combat boots. We quickly talk it over and decide to pull on pants and jackets over our suits, and to carry our weapons in a duffel bag, so if anyone sees us walking toward the hangar, we can just tell them we're going to help prepare to departure.

Once we're ready, we leave the room together, hand in hand. I do my best to look casual and appear as if I'm doing what I'm supposed to be doing and not disobeying a direct order. Excitement hums through my veins, my fingers itching for some action. I've been walking around in a rage since I had to watch Yasmine killed, without having any real outlet for my pain. Doesn't matter that it was the president who had her killed. The Rejects are an extension of him. I can't wait to bash some heads together, shoot some people in the face, and crush some skulls with my titanium feet. Now that we've reach the war phase of this revolution, there can be no more peaceful resolution. It's kill or be killed, and I've got no bones about killing.

We reach the hangar and find it all but empty, just a handful of mechanics going over the pre-flight checks. Still holding tight to Blythe's hand, I pull her swiftly toward *Icarus*, skirting the room and sticking to the corners and shadows.

Inside the hovercraft's cargo hold, we find Laura and Olivia doing a last-minute inventory. Laura turns to us with a grin, while Olivia folds her arms over her chest and gives us a knowing smirk.

"I told him you guys would come if he asked," Laura says with a chuckle.

"Good thing prep-school jock boy came to his senses," Olivia adds. "I was beginning to think I was going to have to kick his ass."

The sound of footsteps up the gangplank alerts us to Gage's approach, and we turn just as he comes near, his face still as inscrutable as it had been upstairs. I don't know what caused him to change his mind, but I won't question it. Whether it had anything to do with Blythe doesn't matter in the grand scheme of things.

"This prep-school jock boy needs the inventory done," he says, his tone clipped and short.

"Geez, untwist your panties," Olivia teases. "It's all done, *sir.*"

"Don't call me sir," he snaps. "It's time to form up. I need to talk to these two, and then I'll meet you out there."

Olivia and Laura nod, handing Gage the small tablets holding their checklists before leaving the cargo hold. Holding them under one arm, he turns to us.

"I just want to make a few things clear before we roll out," he says. "Jenica put Laura and me at the head of Bravo team today. Just because I changed my mind about you coming along doesn't mean I'm going to let you run up and down my back. Stay out of sight until we get there, and then follow my orders. Don't make me regret this."

My spine bristles at his high-handed speech, but I clench my teeth to keep from saying anything. The fact of the matter is we're here on his mercy. If I piss him off, he could rat us out. I don't want that.

"Of course we'll follow orders," Blythe says, her tone soft and placating. "We aren't here to take over... We just want to fight."

Gage stares at her for a second before nodding and turning to leave without another word. Flipping a switch on his way out, he closes the cargo hatch, leaving us with meager light, alone with the supplies.

Picking up our duffel bag full of weapons, I lift it onto a stack of crates that stands as tall as my chest, then use my arms to haul my body onto them. Settling on top of the containers, I pop the top of one and find it full of food rations.

"Breakfast?" I offer, grabbing a few packets of dried beef jerky.

"Sure," she replies, reaching up for my hand.

I lift her easily and settle her beside me on the crate. We eat a quick breakfast, and share water from the canteen stashed with our weapons. After what feels like hours, the sound of the hovercraft engines being fired up echoes through the hold. Then, we're taking off, my stomach dropping as the hovercraft exits the hangar and begins its ascent. We should arrive within a few hours, which gives us nothing but time. Instead of filling the silence with small talk, Blythe and I simply sit together, waiting for our chance to make up for our past mistake. Glancing over at her, I wonder where her head is at, if she's as fired up for this fight as I am. If I had to guess, I'd say she probably is. The Rejects have stood in our way for too long, casting a shadow over our revolution by causing people to see us as being no better than them. They've taken things from us—specifically, they took Gage away from her. I feel sorry for Baron if she ever gets her hands on him again.

TWENTY

Dax Janner, Blythe Sol, Gage Bronson, Olivia McNabb, Michela Arlotti, and Laura Rosenberg
Des Moines, Iowa
January 18, 4011
8:05 AM

BY THE TIME *ICARUS* LANDS AND THE CARGO HOLD IS OPENED TO LET US OUT, I'VE grown restless. My pulse races and my skin feels too tight, the need for action making my limbs jumpy. Once Blythe and I felt the hovercraft coming in for a landing, we undressed down to our flight suits, then slipped on our holsters and armed ourselves. The second the gangplank drops, I'm barreling out of the space that had started feeling smaller and smaller with each passing minute. Blythe is hot on my heels, and we join the group of one hundred gathered in a neat formation in front of Gage.

He stands with Laura by his side, a COMM device in one hand. A few people at the back of the formation hear us come up to join them and turn, glancing at us with various degrees of shock. I simply face forward and wait for Gage to deliver our orders. A few of the others looking back at us don't seem surprised, which brings a little smirk to my face. It wouldn't be the first time Blythe and I have gone rogue, and I doubt it'll be the last.

Beyond Gage and Laura, the city of Des Moines, Iowa sprawls, the large dome-shaped roof of the capital building thrusting up toward the sky. Even from here, I can see the barricades made by the Rejects to keep people out—cars crushed and stacked on top of each other, just like they did in Leesburg. The news reported several failed raids on Des Moines, during which MPs attempted to infiltrate and were killed. Now knowing the truth about this little plan, I realize those attempts were half-assed to make the media and the American people think something was being done about the Rejects' occupation. The MPs could have made it through those barricades if they tried, but it doesn't matter now. *We* are going to get through them and into the city.

"Listen up, everyone," Gage calls. "As we speak, the other six teams are advancing on the city to try to infiltrate and clear a path for us to the capital building. Our mission is probably the most important out of all the teams. We are responsible for getting our technology team safely to the capital building and underground. We will guard them with our lives, because once we get there, they are the only people who can dismantle the bombs and keep them from being launched."

At the center of the formation, I spot Mohinder Baharani—the young kid with the titanium face who gave a group of us our Resistance tattoos. He's also a tech geek and an applied-sciences genius. Mohinder and Alec hit it off the moment we brought the young kid to Headquarters. He and the small crew of men holding what appear to be metal briefcases seem to be the technology team Gage refers to. In part of the group surrounding them, I find Olivia and Michela Arlotti, the girl Gage brought with him from D.C. She's armed to the teeth and looking fierce, her dark hair pulled into a high, tight ponytail. I've heard whispers at Headquarters that her father used to be a Navy admiral, and she can fight like no one's business. Today, I'll get to see her in action.

"I don't think I need to remind you we're past taking prisoners," Gage continues. "It's shoot to kill if you want to make it back home to Headquarters and your family. Keep your COMM devices on and tuned to the Bravo Team frequency. We've got three medics on our team, so they can only tend the most serious of injuries. If you scratch yourself or twist your ankle, suck it up. We have limited supplies and no time to hand out bandages."

I spot the three medics in question, recognizing them as former nurses and a doctor. They sport white armbands with red crosses to be identified.

Drawing his pistol, Gage hooks his COMM device onto his belt. I retrieve mine and find the frequency he referred to, while Blythe does the same. Turning to Laura, he murmurs something I can't here. She nods in response, and raises her COMM to her lips. She must be in a different frequency because I can't hear what she's saying through my own device, but a few moments later, a loud noise booms from behind us in response. A blast from *Icarus'* heavy artillery cannon, aimed and fired right at the barricade. The projectile slams into it, blowing a hole wide enough for us to get through.

Laura speaks into her COMM again, talking with the person working the controls inside the hovercraft. Another blast comes, widening the hole and sending cars flying in every direction. In the distance, the sound of more artillery fire resounds through the air—the other teams following our lead and preparing to converge on the city. The thin sounds of raised voices and crying out means the Rejects know we're here and are probably gathering forces to fight back.

Lifting a hand, Gage points it toward the opening in a silent order to move out. Everyone falls into step behind him and Laura, who lead us fearlessly forward. I draw a pair of twin CBX pistols from the holsters at my hips, and switch them on to 'kill'. They practically vibrate in my hands, as if they understand my need to use them as instruments of death—to bathe in the blood of the people intent on destroying our world.

Our pace picks up as we get closer, breaking into a trot, then a jog, then a full-fledged run once we spot the figures rushing at us with weapons raised. The Rejects are coming to meet us.

Gage shoots first, the laser shotgun in his hand booming like a cannon and dropping two men at once. The rest of us follow suit, spreading out and opening fire. A cluster of our soldiers surround Mohinder and his team, sticking close to keep them safe from the gunfire.

I slam my fingers back on the triggers of my handguns, the kickback hardly fazing me as the red lasers find their targets, dropping two of the Rejects in the blink of an eye. Blythe brushes past me, looking for a clear line of sight with her rifle. I keep shooting, but tail her, wanting to stay close so we don't get separated. Twisting a dial on her rifle, she aims and pulls the trigger, firing five lasers at once. Three of them make impact.

We converge in the middle, bodies clashing against bodies, weapons being knocked to the ground. I holster one of my pistols and pull a knife from my boot, using them simultaneously to cut or shoot through any Reject who crosses my path.

A man with face tattoos and a grenade launcher attached to his bionic arm comes at me through the crowd of fighting bodies. He raises the arm and fires at the same time I do. My laser takes him down, but his grenade sails through the air toward me. Reacting as swiftly as I can, I leap up and kick, using my titanium foot to bat the explosive away. It careens against the chest of another Reject and explodes, tearing him apart in a spray of blood and gore.

Another one comes at me, this one with long blades where his hands should be. He swings them at me with a swiftness that throw me into survival mode. I duck and dodge the blades, batting his arms aside and trying to get a clear shot at his chest. My laser fire misses three times before I give up and lodge my knife in his eye. Screaming, he backpedals, taking my knife with him, the blade still lodged in his socket and blood running down his face. I kick him in the chest and send him sprawling to his back, then go down on top of him before he can recover and attack me. Crouching over him, I pull my knife from his eye and jam it into his chest. He jerks and goes still beneath me, so I pull my knife free.

I stand and find the formation surrounding Mohinder and his team have moved forward, breaching the barricade. I run to catch up, falling in between Blythe and Olivia. We form a phalanx around them, fighting off anything that comes at us from any side. On my left, Olivia doesn't use a gun—choosing instead to rely on her superhuman speed and a set of knives she keeps sharp enough to butcher meat with. She *is* like a butcher, fighting with the sort of ferocity she didn't possess until after the MPs at Stonehead assaulted and terrorized her. She strikes to kill every time, aiming for faces, throats, and vital organs, her hands and neck splattered with blood. Blythe remains composed, firing at the enemy with cool detachment. On her other side, Michela holds her own, the shotgun in her hands deadly accurate. She's got a huge machete-style blade strapped to her back, but she hasn't pulled it yet. I wonder how many heads will roll once she does.

The other teams fight nearby, the streets filled with brawling bodies. I feel as if I'm being watched, and know the citizens of Des Moines must be peering at the violence through their windows. They've been held captive in their own homes by the Rejects, and I wonder if they believe we are here to liberate them, or capture them ourselves.

Bloodcurdling screams draw my gaze left, where several Resistance soldiers drop to the ground, twisting and writhing in agony as they go up in flames. Nearby, a Reject with a flamethrower surgically attached to his back grins and laughs as he spews another stream of fire from a bionic arm attached to the device.

Gage breaks away from the formation and catches my eye, and I already know what to do. I peel away from the group to join him, and we fall back into fighting together as if we were never separated. Charging him, we push him back from the rest of our fighters, Gage ducking to avoid the flames spewing from the weapon as I deliver a swift kick to the arm. The man whips around, more fire spraying from his arm as Gage discharges his shotgun at the bionic limb, detaching it from his body. I jam my knife into the back of his head and pull it free, then Gage shoots him in the face, sending him sprawling to his back between us.

Glancing up to meet his gaze, I can't help but grin. Goddamn it, the guy gets under my skin, but we make a good team. At first, I think he won't return my smile, but then he does, his eyes crinkling at the corners as he extends a fist to me. I bump it with mine, and we rejoin our formation. We might not ever get past this thing with Blythe, but on the battlefield, at least, he is still my brother. That becomes more and more apparent once we've joined the fight, picking up on the sense of camaraderie that made us a good team to begin with.

The Revolution

By the time we reach the capital building, we've left a miles-long trail of bodies in our wake. The city is literally going up in smoke, fires breaking between buildings. Blood trickles into gutters, its scent a heady, metallic tang in my nostrils. I see some have grown weary from the constant fighting it took for us to get this far, but my body trembles with the need for more blood, more death at my hands. It isn't enough for me—it won't be enough until they are all dead. Our team has been joined by two others, swelling our ranks, while three other teams sweep the city, picking off whatever Rejects might remain.

Pausing just before the beautiful capital building composed of silver metal and prisms of glass, we find it surrounded by reinforcements. The Rejects have formed a circle around it and stand five rows deep. The building isn't very tall, so when I crane my neck to gaze up toward its roof, I easily spot Baron, standing on a narrow balcony walkway that circles the entire building from the third floor. Flanking him are various other Rejects, all boasting upgraded bionic parts that are as deadly—or even more so— than the weapons we carry. Sprinkled among them, I recognize some of our soldiers, who have transformed themselves to fit in.

At his right stands Jenica. Seeing her projection during our conference calls hasn't prepared me to witness in person what she was forced to become in order to infiltrate their ranks. Her formerly waist-length jet black hair has been snipped to her chin in jagged layers that frame her face and make it look sharper, more angular. Blue and purple highlights streak through it, giving her a rebellious bad-girl edge. She's pierced the eyebrow over her human eye, as well as her septum. A black tattoo covers one side of her neck—a word in a foreign language I cannot read. She's traded in one human arm for a bionic one, though from here, I can't tell if it's been outfitted with any weaponry like the others. She's dressed like them, too— black leather and caked-on eye makeup making her look more like a biker chick than the leader of a resistance movement.

"Well, well, well, if it isn't our friends from the Resistance," Baron drawls, his deep voice booming out, his Aussie accent as thick as ever. His metal-domed head gleams in the sun, rivaling the shining building behind us. And the double blades connected to his bionic arm are protracted. "Doesn't surprise me that you ran right back to these idiots the moment you left your father, Drummond."

At my side, Gage flinches at being called by his father's name. Everyone knows he refuses to be associated with him, preferring to use his mother's maiden name. Still, he remains silent, his jaw clenched hard as he levels a murderous glare at Baron.

"You're only going to get one opportunity to turn around and walk away," Baron warns. "I'd take it if I were you."

"Not a chance," Gage retorts. "We aren't going to let you and my father paint us all as terrorists. Stand down and give us access to the nuclear site, or we will take it by force."

He knows as well as the rest of us that Baron will never step down, but the conditioning of at least attempting a peaceful resolution first is hard to shake off.

Baron chuckles, the sound grating in its mockery. "Me, stand down? Did you think I wasn't expecting you?"

Suddenly, his hand whips out and closes around Jenica's throat, quicker than a snake. On my right, Blythe gasps, and on her other side, Laura curses under her breath. Olivia elbows her way between Gage and me, her slender frame tense.

"You think I didn't know you sent this little bitch to spy on me?" he adds, giving Jenica a little shake when she begins to struggle.

He's holding her with his human hand, but he's strong—stronger than her. She goes still, her hands clutching his wrist. Turning her head to gaze at us, she appears eerily calm ... as if she'd expected this to happen all along. She gives a slight nod, the movement almost imperceptible. As if to reassure us that everything will be okay

"Don't be ridiculous," Gage deflects. "Everyone in the Resistance knows Jenica Swan is a traitor to our cause."

Baron scoffs, turning so Jenica is held in front of him. He detracts his arm blade and wraps the bionic arm around her waist, keeping a hold on her throat with his human hand.

"She almost had me fooled," he retorts, pressing his body against her from behind. Jenica looks as if being so close to him is enough to make her feel nauseous. "Especially when she climbed into my bed and offered me her sexy little body."

Her eyes lower as if in shame, but I know what she did was necessary. She might not have lived this long if not for the one act that could serve to earn Baron's trust. Only, it doesn't seem as if it worked for long.

"But then, all of a sudden, the president is announcing the nuclear attacks in advance, and not long after, you fuckers show up here," Baron continues. "So a man has to wonder just what might have set those things in motion. How about a clever little whore who worms her way into my organization with a sudden change of heart?"

He releases her waist and spins her, keeping a tight hold on her neck as he thrusts her away from him until she dangles precariously over the rail of the walkway. Gasps ripple through our ranks, though the Rejects separating us from the front steps and entrances remain still. They don't even look back to see what their leader is up to.

Jenica kicks and flails, but eventually goes still once she realizes the only thing keeping her from going over the side now is Baron's hand on her throat.

His grin is knowing, our reaction to the threat on Jenica's life telling him everything he needs to know.

"You want the nukes?" he taunts, tightening his hold on her throat until we can hear her struggling to breathe, choking and gasping for air. "Come get them."

What happens next occurs so quickly I might have missed it if I'd blinked. As callously as he might throw away a piece of trash, Baron flings Jenica away from him and over the banister. At that exact moment, something red appears from her new bionic arm—a laser, I realize. It sweeps outward toward Baron and across his neck just as she goes over the side of the walkway.

The other Rejects on the balcony gasp and watch in wide-eyed horror as Baron's body collapses, his head now detached by the laser. It tumbles over the rail along with Jenica, racing toward the ground. The head and Jenica fall onto the front steps of the capital building with a thud and sickening crunch.

Beside me, Blythe screams, an enraged cry from deep within her gut. Gage swears under his breath, Laura shrieks a string of curses, and Olivia simply looks on in openmouthed horror. Shock ripples through my body, paralyzing me. I can't make a sound, can't move as my eyes lock onto the mangled and twisted form of Jenica, sprawled out on the white stone steps as Baron's head tumbles and rolls, disappearing among the Rejects surrounding the building.

A war cry stuns me out of paralysis, and my legs begin to move as everyone around me springs into action. Above us, a Reject I assume must be second in command to Baron howls like a wolf, his anger propelling his soldiers toward us.

We are feral, snarling and crying out our own wrath as we run to meet them, guns blazing, while those of our people among the Rejects turn on the ones closest to them. Jenica might have been hard on me, and there might have been times I hated her guts, but she was our leader. They've just taken her from us, but they could never have counted on her being enough of a boss bitch to hide a secret laser in her arm. In death, she has taken Baron out with her, so now the rest is up to us.

We will not let her down.

I sheath my knife in my boot and put my CBX back in its place at my hip. Drawing the larger automatic rifle from over my shoulder, I open fire, spraying laser fire so rapidly that Rejects are falling in clusters of five at my hand. I grit my teeth, tightening my hold on the rifle to compensate for the kickback. Beside me, Blythe is alternating shots from her rifle with using it as a bludgeoning weapon. Skulls crack and blood flies, splattering her face, which is now a twisted mask of fury. On my other side, Michela has freed her machete from its sheath. She swings it with impressive speed and accuracy, sending bionic limbs flying and heads rolling.

We fight like berserkers, with no mercy and no reservations. I'm not sure about anyone else, but I don't feel an ounce of guilt as we battle our way through the Rejects, forging a path toward the steps. Once we've broken through, with a clear line of sight to Jenica's mangled body and the front doors of the capital building, Gage motions for his team to follow. The other teams have the situation outside handled, the Rejects' numbers dwindling by the minute. As much as I want to stay and fight until not one of them is left, I understand the sense in following Gage. He's got the strongest fighters on his team, and we still don't know what's waiting for us inside the capital.

We dash up the stairs, and I pause when we pass Baron's head, resting halfway down the steep climb. With a snarl of disgust and fury, I stomp on it, my titanium foot adding to the weight of my combat boots, causing his skull to cave.

Supposedly, his bionic heart means he can be brought back to life with a defibrillator. But no machine can bring him back from a severed head and crushed brain. Turning away from the blood, gore, and bits of brain matter splattered over the stairs, I join the others, who continue upward at a steady pace.

Further up, we find Jenica's body. We stutter to a stop, a collective silence falling over our group. My stomach turns at the sight of her, blood oozing from her nostrils and ears, limbs twisted at unnatural angles. Eyes closed, makeup smeared by tears shed as she stared death in the face ... she isn't a pretty sight.

Crouching onto one knee, Blythe reaches out to touch her, running an affectionate hand through Jenica's hair. The two of them were often at each other's throats, disagreeing over the way the Resistance should conduct itself. But at the end of the day, they were two sides to the same coin—broken, angry, and willing to give their lives for the cause.

"I'm so sorry," Blythe whispers, lowering her head and taking a deep breath as if trying to keep her composure. Then, turning to glance at Gage over her shoulder, she adds, "We should have someone carry her body back to one of the hovercrafts. The Professor will want to see her one last time."

The two trade long glances, and something passes between them—

something secret and understood only by them. Whatever it is causes Gage to agree with a nod. He turns to the two large men to his right.

"Get her to *Icarus* and store her in the cargo hold," he commands. "We have body bags in there for…"

He trails off, unable to say the words. When this day began, I doubt any of us thought we'd be using one to transport Jenica.

The two men jump into action, one crouching beside Blythe, the other pulling his weapon to cover the man who will carry her. Their bodies block Jenica from my view, but a long moment passes in silence, and I wonder what the holdup might be. Below us, the other teams fight against the Rejects, while inside, the pressing matter of the underground nuclear site demands our attention.

But then, Blythe gasps and I tense, my heart thundering as I wonder what could be the matter. One of the men speaks, his voice raised in shock as he stands and turns to face us.

"There's a pulse!"

My throat constricts to cut off my breath, and Gage and I both stumble forward, coming closer. Peering down, I find Blythe with one hand pressed to Jenica's throat. She turns to look up at us with tears in her eyes.

Her words slam into me hard and fast, like a fist to the gut.

"She's alive!"

TWENTY-ONE

Dax Janner, Blythe Sol, Gage Bronson, Olivia McNabb, Michela Arlotti, and Laura Rosenberg
Restoration Resistance Headquarters
January 18, 4011
9:25 AM

Everyone seems to jump into action at once. Gage screams for a medic, while Blythe grabs Jenica's head to hold it straight and steady. If she's injured her neck, jostling her will only make it worse. Laura and I run the rest of the way up the stairs to the front doors of the capital building. Two of our group's largest men join us, and once I've shot through the thick panes of glass, we run inside, searching for something sturdy we can carry her on to keep her body straight. We find a storage closet filled with large crates, one of which is long and rectangular, its top the perfect size. There are towels used for cleaning, and Laura grabs as many as she can carry while me and one of the men carry the large crate top between us.

By the time we get back to Jenica, a medic has joined us and begun rifling through the medical pouch attached at her hip, searching for anything she can use to help Jenica. She's in bad shape, so there isn't much to be done. Someone murmurs that her breathing is too shallow, and she might not be able to continue on her own much longer. A pocket knife is produced, a tiny slit cut into her throat so the medic can slide a tube in to get oxygen through her. The medic puts someone in charge of controlling a manual ventilator, urging them not to stop pumping air into her lungs for any reason other than death.

A shot of morphine for any pain she might be feeling, and then the medic is helping Blythe hold her head steady while we slide the wooden board beneath her. Laura, Olivia, and Michela quickly tie the towels together, end to end, making ropes that we use to secure her onto the board.

Another set of tied-together towels is used to create an improvised neck brace. Gage gathers more men—two to carry her, and four to surround them and provide cover fire. He sends the medic off with them, urging her to remain with Jenica on board *Icarus* with the men there for protection.

As they move quickly but carefully down the steps with Jenica between them, we continue our mission. None of us wants to think or talk about what just happened, or hope Jenica will survive even another hour. If we do, we'll fall apart, the familiar grief of losing yet another member of our family will make it difficult to carry on.

Gage takes the lead with Blythe and me on his heels and everyone else bringing up the rear. He's the only one among us who has seen the diagrams of this building and possesses the knowledge of where the underground nuclear site is located. It takes him mere minutes to find a door leading into a stairwell, which we take down to a basement-level parking garage accessible from a tunnel on the other end of the building. From there, a trap door opens to another set of stairs, which lead down to an underground tunnel stretching both left and right. Gage isn't certain which turn will lead us the right way, so we split in half and proceed down separate tunnels. Blythe and Gage take half the team left, while Laura pulls me along with her and the other half. There are several doors down our tunnel, most leading into rooms that look like laboratories. We don't have time to stop and try to figure out what's being tested down here—not when the nuclear launch could happen at any time.

We get a call over the COMM device from Gage, confirming his team has found the correct tunnel. So, we all turn back and run after them, finding them opening a section of the wall to reveal gleaming elevator doors. Mohinder and his technical team put away tools that look as if they were used to open the concealing wall and give us access to the elevators.

We can't all fit at once, so we crowd inside in small groups—me,

Blythe, Gage, and Michela squeezing in with the technical team. My stomach lurches as we drop swiftly, burrowing even further underground.

"Weapons ready," Gage says as we begin to slow. "The upper level was too quiet. I refuse to believe Baron would be stupid enough to leave the underground site unguarded."

Keeping hold of my assault rifle, I reach for one of the CBX handguns and prepare to fire from all cylinders.

The doors slide open and a flash of swift movement catches my eye. Grasping the collar of Blythe's flight suit in one hand, and Mohinder's in the other, I throw them to the floor of the elevator and drop beside them just before gunshots pop off from the room beyond. The impact of bullets striking the inside of the elevator echoes in the tight space, and around me, other bodies drop to avoid being shot. Someone is on top of me, but I hold still and wait for the smoke to clear.

The scent of blood fills the space, and a rough sound from Gage confirms what I've just heard. He's been hit.

"Goddamn it," he grumbles, groaning and slamming his fist against the elevator wall.

I lift my head just in time to see the people who fired at us coming close. "Heads up!"

I raise my gun at the same time Blythe braces her rifle against the floor. We open fire, each taking out a Reject—one with a gun mounted on a bionic arm, and another firing an automatic rifle. They fall, and I get to my feet as quickly as I can, realizing the person who fell on top of me is one of the guys from the technology team. There's a bullet clean through one of his eyes, and his limp body falls away with a thud as I go upright.

"Are you okay?" Michela asks Gage, concern creasing her brow as she reaches out to help him to his feet.

He grunts and nods, though the wound in his shoulder probably hurts like a bitch. He's bleeding slowly, and as I crane my neck, I notice there's no exit wound. Leave it to the Rejects to resort to using old-fashioned, inhumane, bullet-firing guns.

"We have to get that out of you," I tell him.

Shaking his head, he grits his teeth. "No time."

He steps out of the elevator, and we all follow. Blythe crouches to grab the body of the dead techie out of the space, lifting his briefcase into her own hand.

"There are still enough of us to get the job done," Mohinder tells her as he accepts the briefcase.

"Good to know," she replies. "But we're going to do our best not to lose any more of you."

The elevator closes, going back down to pick up the others, and the rest of us make our way forward.

The small alcove we're in opens into a massive room that seems to stretch on for miles. Rows of computers and machines fill one side of the room, while a queue of airplanes sit on the far end, pointed toward a round door I assume opens into a hangar or tunnel leading out.

In the center of it all, a cylindrical structure leads to an opening in the ceiling—and inside it sits the nuclear bomb.

Rejects appear from all sides—from between the computers and machines, and from doors leading into other rooms—weapons drawn. We duck behind the nearest structures we can find, returning fire while the guys on the technical team cower behind us. They're fixers, not fighters, and only Mohinder is competent with a gun. He surprises me, wedging between Blythe and me, pointing his gun over the table we've overturned and crouched behind. He remains calm, firing his weapon every few seconds and managing to pick them off.

"We have to get to the control panel of the launcher," he shouts in my ear after a few minutes of trading fire with the Rejects. "It is the only way to prevent a launch so we can disarm the nuke."

Following his gaze to the cylinder, I find a circular kiosk of desks around it, and several men in lab coats scrambling to the computers sitting on them. Some are typing madly at their keyboards, while one speaks frantically on a phone—likely calling for some sort of backup. I nudge Blythe and point to the one on the phone. She immediately swivels her rifle toward him and fires. Her laser tears through his forehead, sending him slumping on top of one of the computers.

Searching for Laura and Olivia, I find them nearby, hiding behind a large machine that looks as if it's made for creating parts of some kind. They are firing from behind it whenever they can, and are mostly covered. I gesture toward them to get their attention, then motion toward Mohinder and the two other guys with him. With two fingers, I motion toward the control panel. Laura nods her understanding, and I turn to Blythe, Mohinder, and the other techies.

"We're making a run for it," I say. "Tech team, stay to the center and try to keep up; we'll provide cover fire."

Blythe nods her understanding, and I grab Mohinder by the collar, pulling him along as I come out from behind the table. He stumbles to keep up, and the others dash along behind me, while Laura and Olivia rush to meet us in the middle. We box the guys in between us and start forward, guns blazing as we cut through the Rejects and try to make a beeline for the control panel. I don't know where Gage and the others might be positioned in the room, but I feel their presence. Their laser fire comes from all directions, helping cover us while we cover the team.

A slender metal disk comes whizzing at us through the air. It slices into Laura's bicep, causing her to go off balance, falling to one knee with a rough bellow.

"What the fuck?" Olivia cries, reaching out to help Laura to her feet.

Laura grits her teeth as Olivia helps her pull the hunk of metal out of her arm, sending blood trickling down toward her elbow. Another one flies from seemingly out of nowhere, this one almost taking Olivia's ear off. With a high-pitched cry, she turns and searches for the source of the attack.

"What the hell is that?"

"There!" Mohinder cries out, pointing toward a Reject who is advancing on us on double bionic legs.

She lifts one toward us, sweeping it through the air as if executing a roundhouse kick, and her prosthetic releases another disk toward us like an arrow being shot from a bow. I duck to avoid it, my pulse leaping as I realize it could have decapitated me. The Reject smiles and keeps coming, executing a somersault and causing her leg to fire another projectile. This one nicks my shoulder, slicing through the fabric of my uniform and breaking the skin. The aggravating sting and scent of my own blood enrages me. I want to rip her legs off and beat her with them.

Before I get the chance, Olivia is stepping up, twirling her twin knives with expert flair. "That bitch is mine," she growls before shooting forward, propelled toward the Reject in the blink of an eye.

"Save some for me!" Laura calls out, taking off after Olivia, cracking her neck with a wide grin.

While they converge on our attacker, Blythe and I start forward again, our path momentarily cleared. The room has gone quiet, but I doubt it will be for much longer.

Mohinder and his team stumble to a stop in front of the control panel, each taking up seats at different computers. Their fingers begin flying rapidly over the keys, while Blythe and I turn to guard them, guns ready.

Olivia attacks the double bio-leg chick with her knives, little cries of rage emitting from her with every swing. The Reject is lightning fast, deflecting each of Olivia's swings with kicks and punches from bionic hands. Seeming to be more machine than woman, the Reject fights off Olivia and manages to avoid blows from Laura, who tries to come at her from the other side.

The elevator doors open again, and more Rejects come spilling into the room. Gage and the others start shooting from their hiding places, and Blythe and I join in, taking down anyone who moves even one step toward the control panel.

A mechanical female voices rings out through the room, echoing from the walls.

"Five minutes until launch … five minutes until launch."

With wide eyes, I turn and glance at Mohinder, who is still pounding away at the keyboard along with his band of nerds.

"What the fuck, dude?"

"It was already set for launch," he replies without sparing me a glance.

His gaze is fixed on the screen, the sounds of his typing mingling with his words. "It takes time to stop it. We have to break into the—"

I fire my gun at an approaching Reject, the sound muffling the rest of Mohinder's words. "Save the geek speak and just stop the fucking thing!"

"I'm trying," he growls from between clenched teeth.

We go on shooting, protecting the only people in the room smart enough to stop Washington D.C. from becoming a smoking hole in the ground. If it were up to me, I'd be shooting at the panel with my gun, but apparently this is now how things are done. So I focus on the thing I'm good at so the eggheads can do the thing they're good at.

On the other side of the room, Olivia ducks to avoid another flying projectile while Laura bashes their opponent in the back of the head, sending her facedown on the floor. The two crouch over her, Laura pulling her head up by her hair to expose her neck, while Olivia slashes her throat open.

All the while, that ominous voice rings out, counting down the time.

Four minutes until launch.

Three minutes until launch.

Two minutes until launch.

"Any minute now would be great," I call out, turning to find Mohinder still furiously pounding at the keys.

Sweat has begun streaking across his forehead and soaking the back of his neck. His hair is plastered to his metal forehead.

"Almost there," he grunts, hunching his shoulders and going at it with renewed effort.

I turn and lock eyes with Blythe, who's worrying her lower lip between her teeth. If these guys can't disarm the bomb in time, then all we've gone through will be for nothing. The journey here, the lives lost ... Jenica.

It can't be all for nothing.

One minute until launch.

"Mohinder, I swear to fucking God," I warn, gripping the back of his chair.

"I'm in!" he cries out.

His tech partners all whoop for joy. Apparently, Mohinder breaking into the system has now given them all access. I'm sweating now, too, my brow damp and my knees weakening as the seconds tick by. I'm gripping the back of the chair so hard I'm surprised it doesn't break.

"There," Mohinder declares, pressing one last key on his keyboard.

The other two follow suit, and suddenly the lights on the panels around the cylinder change from green to blue.

System overridden ... launch aborted.

I pat Mohinder on the shoulder while the others cheer and clap. With the Rejects attack having ceased, the sound echoes through the room like sweet music. Holstering my guns, I reach out and pull Blythe into my arms, crushing her against me in relief.

"We'll need more time to completely destroy the program and dismantle the bomb so it cannot be used ever again," Mohinder informs us.

Ruffling his curly hair, I grin. "Take all the time you need, my man. Take all the time you need."

Blythe and I approach the others, who have come out of their hiding place. Olivia is cleaning the blood from her knives—the Reject she and Laura tag-teamed lying in a bloody heap at her feet. Laura sneers down at her in triumph, kicking her dead body in the ribs just for spite.

Gage comes staggering across the room with his COMM device in one hand, Michela at his side. The rest of our team surrounds us, waiting for orders.

"Looks like we've got a bit of a reprieve," Gage announces, his voice hoarse and strained. "Another team made contact to inform me that the remaining Rejects have retreated."

"Good riddance," Olivia grumbles, sliding her knives into the sheaths at her hips.

"Everything appears quiet for now," Gage continues. "We should be clear to go home as soon as these guys are done disarming the bomb."

"That could take hours," Michela argues, placing a hand on his uninjured shoulder. "Maybe one craft can go back with the wounded ... including you."

"I'm fine," he argues, just as he begins to sway on his feet.

I rush forward to catch him, looping one of his arms over my shoulders and bearing most of his weight. Blythe comes in and holds him up on the other side.

"You are *not* fine," Blythe snaps. "Michela's right ... we should get you, Jenica, and anyone else who has been seriously wounded out of here now. The others can stay behind to guard the capital building and the city while Mohinder and team finish their work. Once the president finds out we killed Baron and stopped the bomb, there will be retaliation... If he strikes us here, Jenica could die waiting for a safe transport."

Gage nods, his eyelids starting to droop. He's pale and shuddering, the pain likely setting in now that all the access adrenaline has worn off.

"Then that's what we'll do. Blythe, you pilot *Icarus* home with me, Jenica, and anyone else who needs transport out of here. Grab a few medics and the rest of Bravo team can come along. Dax, you and Laura stay here to oversee this. I'm leaving the safety of the technical team in your hands ... as well as Alpha and Charlie teams."

"We've got it, man," I assure him. "Get him out of here, B."

A few of our male soldiers step up to help relieve Blythe and me of Gage's weight. I reach for her, cupping the back of her neck and pulling her close, placing a tender kiss on her forehead.

"Be careful out there," I murmur.

I hate being separated from her at times like this, when anything can happen. I don't like not being close enough to put myself between her and anything that would hurt her.

"You too," she whispers, standing on tiptoe to give me a quick peck on the lips.

She turns to leave, falling in with Bravo team. Michela opts to go with them, her obvious concern for Gage gluing her to his side. Finding an empty rolling chair near one of the computers, I pull it close to Mohinder and sit, bracing my rifle across my thighs. Olivia and Laura follow suit. Together, we settle in for the long wait.

TWENTY-TWO

DAX JANNER, OLIVIA MCNABB, AND LAURA ROSENBERG
RESTORATION RESISTANCE HEADQUARTERS
JANUARY 18, 4011
4:00 PM

IT TAKES MOHINDER AND HIS TEAM THE REST OF THE AFTERNOON TO SUCCESSFULLY disarm the system. In that time, members of Alpha team arrive with water and food rations for us. I'm starving, so I scarf down two rations of jerky and one of dried fruit before chugging half a canteen. I'm restless to get going now, even being this deep underground not enough to make me feel safe. These days, no place is safe except for Headquarters, and the sooner I get there, the better I'll feel. Blythe is surely there by now, and since we haven't heard anything over our COMMs, I'm assuming they arrived unscathed. That's a relief, because Jenica and Gage needed medical attention, and it's best that Blythe is out of dodge. She's still sitting close to the top of the America's Most Wanted list, and her capture would devastate the Resistance ... and me.

Once the system was shut down, Mohinder and his guys opened the cylinder to retrieve the bomb, working with their tools to carefully separate the parts and destroy the ones they can dispose of safely. With the threat of a nuclear bomb now distinguished, it's time to go home.

"Great work," I say as Mohinder stretches, the sounds of his strained joints popping making me flinch. "And sorry for yelling at you earlier."

He smiles, the parts of his bionic face moving fluidly. That still takes some getting used to, but I try not to stare, knowing it makes the kid uncomfortable. There's a polyurethane mask he can wear over it to give himself a normal appearance, but I've noticed he doesn't wear it on

185

missions like these. It's almost as if he wants our enemies to be forced to look at him—to see him as a person instead of a freak.

"It's all right," he replies. "Heat of the moment ... I understand."

Clapping his shoulder, I nod. "But you got the job done. I never doubted you for a second."

He opens his mouth and replies, but falls silent when every computer screen in the room flickers, their images changing until each one portrays the face of President Drummond. It's a video feed, I realize as I take him in—carefully combed hair, smug expression, navy-blue suit. His icicle-blue eyes seem to bore into me as I stare at the feed, brow creased as I wonder just what the hell is going on now. A shiver runs down my spine when I remember Yasmine and the video message the president left on the microchip inside the weapon used to kill her. Any move by Drummond almost always ends in death.

"Well played, leaders of the Resistance," he says in that brusque ways of his, each word enunciated perfectly. *"You set out to stop my little plan, and, for now, it seems you have succeeded. But as I warned you before ... crossing me has consequences. As promised, I am delivering the war you people so badly wanted. You move, I counter. So, when my next play reveals itself ... just remember you started this. You sent your little assassin after me—oh, yes, I know it was one of you. Now, reap the consequences of what you've sowed."*

The president's smug face disappears from the screens, and they all go ominously dark. The chill of a premonition continues to nag me, and I can't shake the feeling that something is about to go down. Turning to Laura, I reach for my COMM

"It's time to leave," I say. "Now."

Nodding, she rounds up the tech team and Olivia while I put the COMM to my lips, putting in a call to everyone on the frequency.

"Alpha and Charlie teams, board the hovercrafts and prepare for immediate departure," I bark, bringing up the rear on the way to the elevator. "I repeat, Alpha and Charlie teams, get to the hovercrafts ASAP and prepare for takeoff."

My COMM crackles, the voices of first Charlie, then Alpha team leaders responding to my command. My hands are shaking with nervous energy, my breathing growing harsh and fast as the elevator carries us upward. It can't move fast enough, and by the time the doors slide open, I'm about ready to tear them apart with my bare hands. We explode from the elevator at a run, the others seeming to have caught on to my sense of urgency. Coming out on the front steps of the capital building, we dodge fallen bodies, which litter the sidewalk in huge piles. It looks like our guys have been busy while Mohinder disarmed the bomb, because none of the bodies left on the ground are our people.

Des Moines is starting to come to life again, citizens stirring from inside apartment buildings and businesses. The gravity of the situation hits me hard, and I cup my hands and scream to be heard as we run away from the capital building as quickly as we can.

"Run," I warn them. "Get away from the capital building! Take cover!"

My voice carries, and I know I've been heard when one person takes off to follow us, then another, and another. Laura and Olivia join me, urging the people to get to safety. I don't know if they trust me enough to have my back, or they feel the urgency of not knowing exactly what will happen, but still realizing something is coming.

Cars and bikes zip past us, citizens of Des Moines following our lead and getting the hell out of dodge. Ahead, I spot the barricade of cars we blew a hole through, as well as our hovercrafts beyond. Large clusters of Resistance soldiers scurry toward the planes, a few stopping to assist those who have been injured.

The sound of an explosion fills the sky, and the resulting blast seems to snatch the ground right out from under me. I'm thrown forward, while the cacophony of terrified screams and chunks of rock and stone making impact with cars and other structures barely registers through a ringing sound that seems to pierce straight through my ear drums. Shrapnel rains down from above, a few shards hitting my back as I curl my head down and cover it with my hands to protect it.

Once I'm certain no more chunks will come hurtling out of the sky, I lift my head, the ringing persisting in my ears. Glancing left and right, I find Laura and Olivia sprawled out on the ground, having been thrown in separate directions by the blast. They're banged up, but seem intact as they begin trying to struggle to their feet. Pulling up to my knees, I wince at the pain in my shoulder from where something slammed into it. A broken hunk of what looks like brick rests on the ground beside me—a likely reason for the pain I'm feeling. Once I'm standing, I turn in a slow circle to survey the damage. Beyond the barricade, the capital building has collapsed, blown to bits. From this distance I can't be sure, but it appears a few other buildings also suffered from the blast. As much as I'd like to think we warned people in time, the bitter reality is most of those in the surrounding structures are likely dead. The city had been under siege for so long with the Rejects here, most of them would have been too afraid to come out until we were all gone. Drummond had no qualms about taking them out to get to us. The capital must have been rigged with explosives in the event we showed up to interfere. I wonder if the explosion would have happened sooner if Jenica hadn't taken out Baron. The thought of him blowing it with everyone still inside, taking us and himself out at the same time, makes me shudder.

Glancing down, I find one of the tech guys struggling to his feet, his arm twisted at an unnatural angle. A dislocated shoulder most likely. Still lying on the ground are Mohinder and the third member of their team. The one whose name I never learned was crushed by a huge chunk of building propelled by the blast. Mohinder has been almost decapitated, a large piece of metal having pinned him to the ground by his neck, causing him to bleed out in what must have been a matter of seconds. Bile rises in the back of my throat at the sight, sorrow making my shoulders feel heavy. The boy was only seventeen, having been injured in the blast when he was thirteen. Touching the tattoo on my chest—the one he put there himself—I sigh.

"You did good, kid," I murmur, turning away from his corpse.

Laura and Olivia are at my side now, one sporting a nasty bruise across her forehead, the other bleeding from a cut beneath her eye.

"What do we do now?" Olivia asks, glancing from the hovercrafts, back to where the people of Des Moines are leaping into action.

After weeks of being held captive, they seem ready to leap into the fray. Some are already sifting through the wreckage, while in the distance, sirens tell me the hospital is back up and running, sending out ambulances for the wounded.

"If we stay, we risk bringing more firepower down on these people, and they don't deserve that," I say. "Let's get the fuck out of here."

We make our way to the waiting hovercrafts, sidestepping dead bodies and pieces of crumbled wreckage. It only takes minutes for us to go through pre-flight checks while a few soldiers go back with body bags for Mohinder and his teammate. I board the *Neville I* craft with Laura and Olivia, strapping in once we're sure everyone is on board. Breathing a sigh of relief, I rest my forehead against the window. As the craft ascends, circling over Des Moines before heading home, I gaze down at the mess left behind by the president's bomb. I wonder if, before long, our entire country will look like this—nothing more than a smoking crater in the ground, a wasteland of hatred and the bodies of the dead lying in pools of blood.

We arrive at Headquarters without incident, leaving me to wonder just what's coming next. I refuse to believe that little explosion in Des Moines will be the only payback for our interference. Something is coming, and soon. But, just now, all I can think about is getting Blythe in my arms, and a good night's sleep. Despite the fact that the sun has barely begun to set, I'm ready to sleep for the next twelve hours. My body aches from head to toe, even from my minor injuries, and I'm weak, probably still not fully recovered from the concussion I sustained on my rogue mission with Blythe.

She's waiting for me in the hangar, dressed in an oversized sweater and a pair of leggings, freshly showered. A sight for sore eyes, she brings a smile to my face, even though I'm still feeling heavy over the loss of Mohinder. He hadn't been with us long, but he was a good kid and a fighter.

"Hey, you," she says, returning my smile as she approaches, wrapping her arms around my neck.

And just like that, all my pain seems to fade away. Her body is soft and warm against me, her lips sweet as I dip my head for a kiss. She means for it to be a short peck, but I hold her closer and mash my lips against hers, taking comfort in her nearness and love. I pour all of my hurt into her, and because she's so goddamned strong, she takes it all, clinging to me and letting me kiss her for as long as I need to start feeling a little better. Not completely better, but enough that I now feel like I can make it through whatever is coming next.

"What's wrong?" she asks when we pull apart. "What happened, Dax?"

"Drummond," I reply gravely. "He got wind of what we did and blew the capital building. We managed to get out in time, but the blast killed others … including Mohinder."

Her face falls, her mouth falling open. "Oh, God … no. He was just a kid."

I nod. "Yeah … hadn't even had his eighteen birthday yet. But he was one of us … a fighter. And he died for the cause. He did a hell of a job under pressure. Because of him, the nuclear blast was prevented."

She nods, her eyes welling with tears, which she bravely manages to hold back. No one does that as well as she does.

"You're right," she whispers, her voice strained. "He was a hero."

I nod, taking her under one arm and holding her against me as we fall into the line of soldiers clamoring to get out of the hangar.

"Jenica?" I ask.

She sighs and shakes her head. "It's hard to explain, Dax. It … it isn't good. The Professor is with her now. We can go visit once you're cleaned up."

"Okay," I agree, glad to be able to have a moment of reprieve.

I can still see Jenica lying on those steps, her body broken and twisted. That she survived is a miracle, but I'm not sure if it's for the best.

If her injuries are permanent, her life will be a constant hell worse than the one we're already living in.

"How's Gage?" I ask as we near Hexley Hall.

"Fine," she replies. "He lost a lot of blood, and they had to dig the bullet out, but he'll be fine. They're keeping him in the infirmary for observation for a day or two to be sure he didn't sustain any significant nerve damage."

I chuckle, imagining Gage in a hospital gown and confined to a bed. He's probably as much fun to be around as I would be in that situation.

"I'm sure he's loving that," I joke.

She snorts a laugh. "Yeah, not really."

We finish the walk to our room in silence. Once we're there, Blythe goes into the bathroom to start the shower for me, hot water taking longer to reach us with so many people sharing the dorm now. I strip out of my boots and flight suit, then take my time in the shower. The hot water stings my cuts and scrapes, but helps relax my tense muscles. I wash from head to toe three times, until all the blood on my hands and neck are washed away, the pink-tinged water running clear.

After I dry off and pull on a pair of boxers, Blythe makes me sit for a minute so she can inspect my cuts and scrapes. She declares them minor, but when she pours antiseptic over them, they sting like a bitch. I laugh when she calls me a big baby, then smack her on the ass. She glares at me and calls me a caveman. I retort that she's not complaining when this caveman is rattling her headboard, which earns me another smile and a kiss.

I want to stay like this with her, shut away in our room where we can forget about everything. But trying to escape reality only makes it harder to bear once the things being outrun come knocking at your door. So, I reluctantly pull on a pair of pants and a sleeveless undershirt, then top it with a long-sleeved thermal. Leaving my titanium feet bare, I take Blythe's hand and we leave the room together.

The lightheartedness of our moments alone fade away the closer we come to the infirmary. Blythe's hand tightens around mine, as if she's trying to comfort me in advance. Whatever shape Jenica is in, it isn't going to be easy to confront.

Entering the infirmary, we dodge nurses and medics, most of them moving swiftly with harried looks on their faces. After Des Moines, I'm sure they have an unusually high number of patients to tend to. Reaching the area where the patients needing the most care are located, we pause at the second to last door. Taking a deep breath, Blythe reaches out for the knob, pausing to gather herself before pushing the panel open.

The first thing I notice is the number of people in the room. Not only is the Professor here, but Olivia and Laura have showered, changed, and joined the vigil. Alec has his arms around Olivia, who looks like she's been crying. Alec himself is stoic, but his eyes appear a bit haunted, so I wonder if she told him about Mohinder. He had taken the boy under his wing, hoping to teach him everything he knew about applied science and technology. The two had grown close during Mohinder's brief time here.

Gage and Michela are in the corner, him seated in a wheelchair with an IV bag attached to it, and her holding on to the chair's handles as if she pushed him in here herself. He's shirtless and wearing a pair of white scrub pants, a white bandage wrapped around his injured shoulder. I notice the puckered scar running down the center of his chest, leftover from the surgery that ended with him coming back to life with a bionic heart.

Everyone glances up to acknowledge our presence, but they remain mostly silent, turning back to the bed. At first, it's hard to make Jenica out. She's covered in blankets, surrounded by so many contraptions and attached to so many machines she almost disappears. Her face is as pale as the white sheets she lays on, her body stretched out vertically, a bunch of stuff I can't identify boxing her in and holding her steady. A halo surrounds her head, presumably to keep it still. It looks like a torture device, but then, nothing could feel worse than falling three stories onto hard stone steps.

Her eyes are open and sharp, glancing about the room. Despite having a tube down her throat held in place by a strip of tape, she appears alert, her gaze snapping to me and remaining there for a moment before going back to Professor Hinkley.

He's flitting about her bed, his hands steady as he checks various monitors and machines, pressing a few buttons, and then ensuring her tubes and cords are untangled. Turning his head, he spots us, and my chest feels as if it'll cave in from what I find on his face.

Even after all that's happened, I've never seen him like this. He appears as if he's been crying for hours, his eyes bloodshot, his face flushed. Yet, his voice is even when he speaks.

"Son," he says, reminding me that we are bonded by something deeper than blood. This man is my adoptive father.

"Is she..." I pause, my throat constricting as my gaze strays over to Jenica. "Is there anything you can do?"

Clearing his throat, he removes his glasses and presses his fingers against his eyes. He looks exhausted and wrung dry, and for once, older than his years. His hair seems to have grayed since yesterday, the lines in his face deeper and more pronounced.

"The fall injured her spinal cord," he says, his voice hollow and devoid of all emotion—as if he's repeated this several times already and the words have lost their ability to hurt him. "The cord was severed at the C-3 spine, which is high in the neck. Aside from now being a quadriplegic, she is no longer able to breathe on her own, and may never be able to. Even without the tube down her throat, her ability to speak is nonexistent. Aside from that, there is extensive internal bleeding. She's lucid and awake now, and has been communicating with us by blinking her eyes—once to answer yes, twice to answer no."

My frown deepens as I look back to Jenica. She's staring up at me, holding my gaze as if to confirm what I'm being told. Olivia sniffles, and I hear Alec soothing her as she begins to sob again.

"I don't understand," I say, turning back to the Professor. "We have the technology to help her, don't we? Agata has a bionic spinal cord, right? Why can't you make one of those for Jenica?"

His composed demeanor falters, and a tear escapes one eye, racing down his cheek. He swipes it away quickly and replaces his glasses.

"In order to get her back on her feet, I would literally have to rebuild her from the inside," he says. "She would need multiple surgeries, not just to repair her spine, but all her other injuries as well. The reality is she might not survive a single surgery, let alone three or four. As well, there is an extensive recovery and rehab process that must follow the operations, and with all that's happening out there..."

I close my eyes and inhale, trying to keep my shit together. I understand what's being said, as well as what he can't say. If we are attacked or it becomes time for us to run for the hills, she would have to be left behind. At that point, she'll wish she were dead.

"I could try to put her back together, but she might never speak again ... might never regain all of her strength. She'd be more machine than woman."

The words hit me in the gut. As I glance around at the others, I realize they've already been told. I'm the last to know.

"There's more," he adds. "I asked her myself if she wished for me to attempt to save her. She blinked twice."

Turning to glance at Jenica again, I meet her gaze just as she blinks once ... to confirm the Professor's words. Nodding, I take another deep breath and remind myself to keep it together. My father needs me to be strong for him. He seems okay now, but I want to be ready once the grief really hits him. He and Jenica worked together closely, forming the Resistance together. This loss will hit him harder than anyone else.

"So, what now?" I ask, feeling Blythe's hand slide into my palm and clutch it, holding on for dear life. "She just stays like this, hooked up to a machine?"

The Professor shakes his head, staring mournfully at the broken woman lying on the bed.

"No," he declares. "Now that everyone she would have wanted is here to say good-bye, we pull the plug."

TWENTY-THREE

Dax Janner, Blythe Sol, Olivia McNabb, Alec Kinnear, Laura
Rosenberg, Gage Bronson, Michela Arlotti, Jenica Swan, and
Professor Neville Hinkley
Restoration Resistance Headquarters
January 18, 4011
7:15 pm

It only takes the Professor a few minutes to prepare everything he'll need to ease Jenica from her fragile hold on life over into death. As everyone sits around, crying or staring numbly off into space, he works efficiently, spreading syringes out on a tray, and quietly paging a few nurses to assist him. I hold Blythe tight against my side, and she buries her face against my chest, her tears soaking my shirt.

Across the room, Gage is watching us, his face a stoic mask betraying nothing. But as he watches Blythe cry on my chest, his eyes give away everything. Watching us together hurts him. As much as I want to feel bad about it, I only hold Blythe tighter. We need each other right now, and I can't push her away just to make him feel better. If things were reversed, it would be me forced to watch him hold her while she cried, becoming her source of comfort.

Michela slips quietly back into the room, holding a few items Gage asked her to retrieve. One of them is a shirt, which she helps him put on while he winces and grunts from the pain in his shoulder. I notice how her hands linger, how she looks at him when his face shows the pain he's in. She likes him, probably more than he likes her. In fact, the way she looks at him is a lot like the way he was just looking at Blythe.

God, we're all so fucked up. Lost love, unrequited love, twisted love.

This is what war has made of us, winding us around each other like barbed wire. We tear each other apart, yet we are hopelessly linked. Gage doesn't see the hurt in Michela's eyes when he doesn't return those long glances ... though I'm sure Blythe is very much aware of the way he watches her, like a wounded puppy.

The other item turns out to be an envelope with a letter from Jenica inside. Apparently, when Gage was being held captive by the Rejects, Jenica slipped it to him and asked him to give it to Professor Hinkley if she didn't return. And while she is present, there's no way for her to vocalize the things she might have wanted to say. It seems fitting for Gage to give the letter to him now.

Now finished with his preparations, the Professor accepts the envelope when Michela extends it to him. His eyes grow misty as he opens it, unfolding two sheets of paper with Jenica's flawless, precise handwriting on it in neat rows. The paper isn't lined, but in true Jenica fashion, her words are straight and perfect. It strikes me as being in line with the way she did everything else—with care, perfectionism, and dedication.

His Adam's apple bobs in his throat as he swallows forcefully, blinking rapidly as if trying to hold back tears. His hands shake, and the papers flutter to the floor. Alec comes forward to pick them up, extending them back to the Professor, who seems to be in no condition to read them, his face soaked with tears. His entire body shakes, as if he's trying to contain his grief.

Alec clears his throat. "Should I read it out loud?"

The Professor looks to Jenica, whose watery eyes meet his before she blinks once.

Yes.

Alec sees the exchange and nods, holding the pages up and beginning to read the letter out loud.

"*My dearest Neville...*"

He trails off as varying degrees of shock ripple through the room. We're all looking from the Professor to Jenica and then at each other, wondering how we all missed the signs of a romance between our two leaders. I'd always known he had a bit of a crush on her, but to know she returned his feelings makes this moment even more heartbreaking. Like the rest of us, the Professor found love amid war and revolution, only to have it snatched cruelly away from him.

Alec clears his throat again and continues, his voice even and clear.

"If you are reading this, then I am dead. Forgive me, my love, for leaving you this way. When our world fell apart, and you approached me about beginning the Restoration Resistance, I pledged my life to you and to this cause, fully prepared to sacrifice myself for it. Yet, as I fell deeper and deeper in love with you, the thought of death became more and more unbearable. Being an outcast of society, hated because of circumstances outside my control, filled me with so much anger. Even after we had won this war, I could not fathom living happily in a place that despises and judges me. But then you made me see that none of it mattered. I did not have to worry about the world when you became the center of my existence. You were my world, and I didn't need anything or anyone else to love or accept me."

Alec pauses to turn to the next page, and I find the glimmer of tears in his eyes as well. Beside me, Blythe trembles like a leaf in the wind, clinging to me as if I'm the only thing keeping her grounded. The pain in my chest is becoming unbearable, the twisting in my gut causing me to feel sick.

"I'm writing this letter, Neville, to remind you not to give up. Please. I know my loss will hurt. And for a time, you might feel as if none of this has been worth it. But I promise you, my death will not be in vain. You taught me to hope, so I think it's fitting for me to remind you of that. This war will end someday, and you will be free to live the life we dreamt of. Perhaps that dream will change once I am gone, but you can have a new one. In time, you can find love and joy again. Until then, fight for our cause, fight for me, fight for the young people who stand beside us, the future of our world. Speaking of which, I want you to remind them that war has a cost. Tell them I am paying the price so they can carry on. They can win this fight … each

of them has what it takes. Tell Blythe to hold her head high, even when it seems life has done everything it can to beat her down. After everything she's been through, she's risen to become the face of our movement. Tell her how proud I am of the strong woman and fighter she has become. Tell Dax even though I gave him a hard time, I admired him for his loyalty and fierce protectiveness. Tell Olivia how inspiring she is to every woman in the Resistance, a lesson in courage and inner strength. Tell them all I go to my death secure in the knowledge that they will carry on just fine without me ... that they no longer need me as a leader, because they have everything they need to become the new leaders of the Resistance. And you, my love ... never forget that none of it would be possible without you. You saved us all, when the world was ready to turn their backs on us. And for that, we are forever in your debt.

Until we meet again,
All my love,
JENICA HINKLEY."

I release the breath I've been holding, the tears I've been fighting back heating my face. Beside me, Blythe begins to sob, along with Olivia, who collapses in the corner of the room, pulling her knees up to her chest and hugging them. Gage has his head lowered and buried in his hands, while Michela places a comforting hand on his shoulder. Laura has a hand clapped over her mouth, her eyes wide as she tries to digest what Jenica's signature at the bottom of the letter means.

Jenica Hinkley.

Not only was she the Professor's lover ... but she was also his wife. At some point, they had married, keeping it a secret from all of us. I can't think of anything more heart-wrenching than what we are about to witness—a man assisting his wife in crossing over from life into death.

Sniffling, the Professor accepts the letter from Alec, folding it neatly and replacing it inside its envelope before sliding it into the breast pocket of his lab coat.

"I am sorry we kept it from you all," he says, his voice a low whisper. "But we did not want our relationship to be a distraction. Our focus was always on the Resistance first."

Pulling away from me, Blythe stands up straight and reaches for his hand, giving it a squeeze. "You don't have to explain anything to us. You two were blessed to have each other."

Around the room, heads nod in agreement, while Alec crouches beside Olivia to comfort her. I swipe at my eyes and try to pull myself together. We still have to get through this next part.

"Come," the Professor urges, motioning for us to gather around the bed. "Now's the time for good-bye."

Collectively, we crowd in, Gage getting up from his chair and making his slow way to join us. He's moving around just fine, but he's sluggish from lack of blood and can't go far attached to his IV.

I grasp Blythe's hand in mine, holding it tight as I gaze down at the woman who launched a revolution. Tears are streaming from her human eye, falling back toward her hairline. Her eyes are darting as she tries to take us all in, her gaze meeting each person and holding for a moment.

I speak up first, because I need her to know something. "It isn't in vain," I tell her. "Your death. You took that asshole Baron with you. Your last act as our leader was the most selfless, courageous, and fucking badass thing I've ever seen."

Her chin trembles. She closes her eyes, more tears streaming from her human eye. I reach down and grasp her hand carefully, giving it a gentle squeeze even though I know she can't feel it.

Blythe is next.

"When I came here, I was broken," she says, her voice hoarse from crying. "I'd just lost my entire family, and I wanted to die. But you taught me how to stand up and fight ... how to fly hovercrafts and fire weapons. You molded me into a soldier, giving me the tools I needed to stop being so afraid. If I could trade places with you, I would in a heartbeat, because I feel as if you saved my life. You saved me, and I'm so sorry I can't return the favor."

Jenica blinks twice for no. As if trying to tell Blythe it's okay ... that there's no need for her to return a favor done selflessly. I raise Blythe's hand to my lips and kiss her knuckles reassuringly.

Everyone else takes a turn, Gage thanking her for inspiring him to become The Patriot; Olivia thanking her for making her strong enough to endure everything she went through at the hands of the MPs; Alec thanking her for giving him a chance to become part of the Resistance; Laura thanking her for giving us all a place to hide from the world, and a way to fight back against oppression; and Michela wishing she'd had more time to get to know Jenica the way the rest of us do.

Then, we stand back and let Hinkley have his time with her. Leaning over the bed, he cups her face and whispers to her—words none of us can hear. He strokes her hair and holds her hand before he presses one last kiss to her cheek, close to the corner of her mouth. It's as close as he can get with the tube down her throat.

Once he's finished, he turns to us and clears his throat, becoming a doctor once again.

"The nurses and I will administer some drugs to sedate and make her comfortable first," he tells us. "Then, I will remove the breathing tube. From there, it won't take long. Unable to breathe on her own, she'll drift away within seconds."

"Will it hurt?" Olivia asks in a meek voice. "Will she feel any pain?"

He shakes his head. "The drugs we'll give her will ensure she passes peacefully. It will be as if she fell asleep and simply never woke up."

Olivia nods as if satisfied, clinging to the front of Alec's shirt as if for dear life. The room falls silent, until all that can be heard is the blipping of various machines and monitors. The nurses approach the bed, assisting him with the syringes, then removing some of the padding and the halo attached to her head. She won't need them now that she's going.

"Don't be afraid," he whispers to her, his hand cupping her face, his thumb moving softly over her cheek. "It'll be just like going to sleep. I won't let go of you until it's over, I promise."

Seeming content with that, Jenica allows her eyes to drift closed.

She's asleep within seconds. For a long moment, nothing else happens. The nurses stand patiently by while the Professor continues to stroke her cheek, staring down at her in silence. I know what he's doing, because it's what I did after losing Yasmine. He's memorizing the contours of her face, remembering the way the eyelashes of her human eye rest against her cheekbone, the way her chest rises and falls, and counting the strands of hair spread out on the pillow.

Watching them this way is overwhelming, filling me with the urge to rush to a toilet and lose what little food there is in my gut. But I choke it down, determined to stand strong for the only man who's ever loved me as his son. He's strong now, but in the moment of his weakness, I need to be present and clearheaded.

After what feels like hours, Hinkley moves to take her hand instead, then nods at one of the nurses to proceed. She comes forward and gently pulls the tape holding the breathing tube in place away from Jenica's face. Then, with gloved hands, she slowly pulls the long tube out of Jenica's mouth.

The moment the tube is out, the machines start going haywire, beeping and blaring with all sorts of warnings. The numbers on the screen start plummeting, and Jenica's chest ceases to move.

It happens in seconds, just as he predicted. One moment, Jenica is here. The next, she is gone, the heart monitor filling the room with a persistent, high-pitched whine. The nurses quickly turn off the machines, and the room falls silent.

For a long moment, no one moves or speaks. There isn't a dry eye in the room, and Olivia is pressing both hands over her mouth as if to contain her sobs. Laura turns the face the wall, pounding one angry fist against it. Alec is holding Olivia as if he's afraid she'll fall into a million pieces if he lets go. Michela is stroking Gage's hair, but he seems oblivious to the affection, his head lowered as his shoulders shake with uncontained grief. Blythe leans against the wall behind me, staring numbly across the room.

The Professor lets go of Jenica's hand and takes a step away from the bed, then another. Instinct drives me forward just before he collapses, his legs giving out from under him in the blink of an eye. I catch him up beneath his armpits, wrapping my arms around him and sinking to one knee to ease him down. Seated on the floor, he leans back into me and starts to sob, each hoarse sound stabbing me in the chest like a sharp knife. Lowering my head so it rests on top of his, I hold on, lending him the last of my strength. I don't know what else I can do. Like any child, I have no notion of what to do when my father collapses in front of me. I can only hold him while he cries and pray it'll be enough.

How can I assure him everything will be all right, when it feels as if our entire world has been destroyed? How can I tell him it'll get better, when I still feel the visceral burn of pain caused by Yasmine's absence?

How are any of us supposed to find the strength to fight when the strongest of us all is now gone?

LATER THAT NIGHT, WE GATHER IN GAGE'S ROOM IN THE INFIRMARY. HE ISN'T CLEARED to leave for another day or two, and none of us wants to be alone right now.

After picking up the Professor from the floor, I carried him in my arms to his personal quarters. He was limp like a rag doll in my grip, drained by exhaustion and grief. Together, Blythe and I made him comfortable and offered to stay with him. But he urged us to leave and be with our friends, seeming to want his solitude. As much as it hurt me to leave him—his shoulders dejectedly slumped as he sat on the edge of his bed alone—I led Blythe from the room and closed the door. I understand the need for solitude in the moments following the death of the person you love.

Right now, medics are preparing Jenica's body for a memorial. The next time he sees her, she'll be free of all the tubes and wires, more closely resembling the woman he loved. He'll probably sit in that room with her for hours then, taking his last look at her and saying all the things he wishes he'd said before she was gone.

At least, that was what I did.

Because it seemed appropriate, Blythe finds a key to Jenica's quarters—which we realize now she likely never slept in since she was married to Hinkley. She returns with several bottles filled with liquor—a stash Jenica reserved for celebrations and special occasions. There aren't many bottles left, but we crack three open and share them, passing them around and numbing ourselves as much as we can from the grief.

For a long while, no one speaks. We simply drink, gazes meeting as we pass the bottle around. Gage is in his bed, the rest of us in chairs pulled from the hallway and other rooms. I've got Blythe in my lap, needing her closeness and the contact of her body to keep me grounded. One arm wrapped tight around her waist, I keep her balanced on my thigh while I take a long drink from a bottle, the liquor going straight to my head. I haven't eaten anything since Des Moines, and there's nothing to keep the buzz from racing through my system instantly. Handing the bottle off, I rest my head against Blythe's back and inhale her scent, closing my eyes.

I can feel Gage's eyes on us, piercing and accusing, but I don't care. I've had enough to drink that I don't give a flying fuck, the guilt I felt earlier now passed. Blythe is mine, and will be until I'm dead if I have anything to say about it.

I'm grateful when Alec breaks the silence.

"I remember the first time I saw Jenica," he says. "It was in Leesburg, not long after I approached Laura, recognizing her from our old Army unit."

Laura laughs, swiping the back of her hand over her mouth after a sip, then passing the bottle to Michela. "I remember that day. Blythe almost ripped your head off when you called her a little girl."

He and Blythe trade smiles over the memory, and Alec leans back in his chair, clasping his hands behind his head.

"You pissed me off, but I could see you were good people," Blythe recalls. "You convinced me to let you help us."

"Right," Alec says with a nod. "And you snuck me into you guys' formation, so I could go along and help you grab some weapons from the shutdown army base. That was the first time I saw her ... standing at the head of our formation, barking out orders. I remember thinking, 'if this is the woman I have to convince to let me join the Resistance, I am fucking screwed'."

We all burst out laughing, even Gage joining in.

"She was a hard one, for sure," Laura says. "A single look from her could cut you right in half."

I grin, thinking of her dark eyes, harsh and glittering with the rage she kept contained just beneath the surface of her skin. "Man, she gave me those looks so often I'm surprised I'm not as short as Olivia by now."

"Yeah, she fucking hated you, Janner," Olivia teases, even though her letter revealed the complete opposite. "Always going against the grain ... never knowing when to just shut up and follow orders."

"The Resistance needed her to be a hard bitch," I say with a shrug. "It needs me to be a badass motherfucker."

More laughter. The bottles make another pass through the room. And as the hours go by, we reminisce about Jenica. About her perfectly straight ponytail that was never out of place ... the way her flawless figure looked in those black flight suits ... the way she could make you feel two inches tall with just a look and a few words. We trade stories about the times she caught us doing things we shouldn't have, or reprimanded us for stepping out of line.

Each story is colored with admiration, because for all the time she busted our balls, there were twice as many times she fought for us. No matter what, we knew she had nothing but love for her people ... the Bionics.

By the time the bottles are drained, it's midnight. Fatigue from our mission, along with the heady feeling of the liquor clouding my brain, have me tired. Blythe, who is slightly less drunk, leads me back to the dorm by the hand. When we get there, she closes the door and turns to me, her eyes filled with concern.

"Hey," she says, grabbing my attention as I sway on my feet, eyes half closed from the urge to collapse and pass out.

"Yeah, B?" I mumble.

She approaches me, resting her hands on my waist and looking into my eyes. "I'm here if you need me. I know watching him say good-bye to

Jenica couldn't have been easy."

The look in her eyes tells me she's thinking of Yasmine and the downward spiral I experienced after she died in my arms. Cupping her face, I lower my head so my forehead rests against hers.

"You're always here when I need you," I whisper.

"Yes," she replies. "Just like you're always here for me. Are you going to be okay?"

I nod, brushing my lips against hers. "Losing her hurt me probably as much as it hurt you ... like it hurt everyone else here. But one thing I know I can count on, when everyone around me keeps dying or leaving ... is that there's always you, here with me. Even when we weren't together the way I wanted, you were here. I love you so much, B. I want you to know that while I still have time to say it."

Coming up onto her tiptoes, she wraps her arms tight around my waist and mashes her body against mine. "Don't say things like that. We have nothing left but time. I fully intend to hear you saying you love me fifty years from now. You understand me?"

Smiling against her lips, I reach down to grab the hem of her sweater. I pull it over her head, then she helps me out of my thermal. Dropping my pants, I kick them off before lifting her in my arms and carrying her to our beds, already pushed together for the night.

Usually, the sight of her in those tight leggings and form-fitting tank top get me cranked up so much I can't wait to tear them off her. But tonight, I just want to hold her and revel in the fact that she's mine. After so much pain and fighting and longing, Blythe is mine to love.

I put her on the bed, then join her, lying on my side to face her. Our hands clasp between our bodies. I can't seem to stop kissing her, drinking her into all of my senses—her feel, her scent, her taste, the sound of her slow breaths.

"Do you want to get married?" I ask, thinking of Jenica and the Professor. If they can get married during all this, why shouldn't we?

"Now?" she asks, wrinkling her brow.

I shrug one shoulder. "Whenever you want."

Closing her eyes, she smiles. "Not now ... after. Once this is all over. I don't want it to be a secret, or some rushed thing we do between missions. If we're going to get married, I want everyone we know to be there. I want to see you all dressed up in a suit... You'll be so sexy."

I can't help but grin at the picture she's painting. I *do* look damn good in a suit ... not that I've had the chance to wear one in years.

"You in a white dress, looking all innocent ... even though we both know you're anything but."

She slaps my shoulder and laughs, causing me to chuckle along with her. "You're the dirty one, remember? Or do I need to remind you about the other night ... or the night before that ... or last week?"

My grin widens as I think of each encounter and the various things I did to her. "I didn't hear you complaining."

"Not at all," she murmurs, nestling closer to me. "You'll be my rough-around-the-edges husband who all the neighbor ladies want. Those bitches will be so jealous of me."

"What about you?" I tease. "All the guys in the neighborhood are going to envy me. I'll have the hottest wife on the block. But, if any of them touches you, I'll be forced to break their necks."

"We'll have kids," she whispers

"One girl," I agree. "We'll name her Skyye, after your sister. And a boy... We'll name him Zion, after your dad."

"We have to have two girls," she argues. "So we can name one Moira."

My heart swells in my chest at the realization that she wants to name one of our kids after my mother.

"Okay," I agree. "Two girls and a boy."

We hold each other in the dark, another hour passing while we fantasize out loud about our future ... one we both know is all but impossible given the realities of our current situation. Yet, verbalizing all the things I want with Blythe makes me feel oddly at peace. Something about knowing she wants those things, too, brings me a sense of tranquility I've never felt in regard to her. I've always felt as if my hold on her was tenuous—as if I stood to lose her at any moment. Now, our bond seems solidified even more, in a way that makes me realize I have nothing to be afraid of.

Except, perhaps, losing her the way the Professor lost Jenica, or of me having to leave her before we've gotten to experience everything we just talked about.

As she falls asleep in my arms, I hold her tight and cling to her, as well as hope. I pray it'll be enough to carry us through ... that someday, our dream of marriage, kids, and a house in a nice neighborhood might just come true.

TWENTY-FOUR

THE DAY OF JENICA'S PLANNED MEMORIAL, I RISE EARLY AND SET OUT IN SEARCH OF THE Professor. He's been holed up in his quarters, leaving only to ensure that her body is being properly prepared for viewing. Because she was such an integral part of our movement, she will not be cremated until after everyone has gathered for a final viewing. We've taken turns checking on him for the past two days, bringing him food from the mess hall and trying to coax him to eat. He seems to make an effort to try for our sakes, but mostly stares off into space, his bloodshot eyes haunted and weary.

When I arrive, I find Olivia and Laura in his quarters, tidying up and preparing some of his best clothes for the service. They tell me he's in the infirmary, the room where Jenica's body has been stored to await the memorial. I go to him, needing to see for myself that he's all right ... wanting to be there for him if he is not.

Pausing outside the door of the small room, I peer into the little window carved into the steel. The sight of him sitting in a rolling chair beside a gleaming table holding her corpse hits far too close to home for me. It was in that same room, in that same chair, that I sat holding Yasmine's hand and telling her dead body how sorry I was for not being there to save her—how much loving her changed me for the better.

My blood runs cold. I am frozen, unable to move an inch. I feel as if my titanium legs are filled with lead, my heart sinking into my stomach. But then, he lifts his head and glances straight at the window, as if he senses someone watching him. Our eyes meet through the glass, and it is enough to get me moving again.

I take a deep breath and open the door, tamping down my own anxiety over being in this room again. I don't have time to get in my feelings over Yasmine on a day that is about Jenica and the man she loved.

Forcing a smile, I close the door behind me and approach the table. Standing on the other side of it, I gaze down at Jenica. She's been dressed as she would have wanted—in her black Resistance flight suit, the armband bearing the symbol of the Resistance wrapped around her bicep. Her best black boots cover her to the knees, while a pair of black gloves cover her hands. Hands that had shown defensive wounds from trying to fight off Baron before he tossed her over the balcony rail. Her short hair has been slicked back from her face, the dark blue strands almost imperceptible this way. It looks like someone polished the titanium part of her face, which covers only the upper left half like an opera mask. Makeup was applied so she'd look a little less battered. This close, though, I can see the bruising from her fall, the bluish undertones only partially hidden.

The acrid odor of strong antiseptic and other chemicals makes my eyes water, but was necessary to keep her body preserved long enough for the viewing today.

"Hello, son," the Professor murmurs.

"Hope I'm not intruding," I reply, folding my hands behind my back.

"Of course not," he replies with a little smile. It wobbles, his eyes watering a bit. But he keeps his composure. "I simply wanted one last moment alone with her. Once it's time for the memorial, she'll belong to everyone else—their symbol of hope, their leader. But behind closed doors, she was always mine."

The possessiveness of his words surprises me, as I'm still coming to terms with what we learned about their relationship. It's so hard to think of him attached to anyone or anything other than the Resistance. Seeing him mourn his wife drives home the heavy reality of his humanity. Even the man we have exulted as our idol, our father, our creator, can be hurt. Even he can suffer loss in the same way the rest of us have.

"The part of her that was yours will always be exclusive," I say. "No one else knew her like you, and that's something to cherish."

Nodding, he reaches out to rest a hand on her slicked hair. "That is very true. How are you holding up?"

That he can even think about my state of mind in his time of suffering shouldn't shock me. The Professor has always been a selfless person, a considerate one.

"As well as can be expected," I reply. "I've mostly tried to remember the good, you know? Focus on the impact she made on us all ... the way she motivated me to be better."

This time, his smile is genuine. "You're as good a man as any I've ever known."

I lower my head, having a tough time accepting his praise. I might be a freedom fighter now, but my past life as a drug dealer is never far from my mind. Perhaps losing Yasmine was some sort of punishment ... my penance for a life of crime and violence. If it is, then I hope God, the universe, or whatever, are done with me. Blythe is all I have left, and losing her now would literally kill me.

"I try to be," I reply, my voice low. "But trying to do the right thing in times like these is hard."

I think of the rogue mission Blythe and I undertook, and how close we came to our goal. Part of me regrets that Blythe missed her shot, and that the president is still alive. Another part wonders if it would have mattered in the end. Drummond is a corrupt politician surrounded by other corrupt politicians. Perhaps cutting the head off the snake would have killed the entire body ... but maybe another head would have simply grown in its place. That we will never know keeps me up some nights, the possibilities turning themselves over and over in my mind.

"Even when you make a mistake, your intentions are honorable," Hinkley argues. "That is all anyone can ask of you these days. Perhaps we did not take that into consideration when voting to keep you and Blythe off the last mission. For what it's worth, I'm glad you went against orders. If you hadn't, you might not have been there for Jenica and the others. They needed you."

"You don't owe me an apology for anything," I assure him. "You did what you thought was right. In truth, we probably deserved it. But I'm glad we were there, too."

Glancing down at Jenica again, I decide to leave, but the tattoo peeking out from the neckline of her flight suit catches my eye. I study it curiously, noticing it appears to be either Chinese or Japanese—the latter, I'm assuming, given Jenica's Japanese-American heritage.

"Did you ever figure out what this tattoo means?" I ask, gesturing toward her neck and the black lines scrawled there.

Hinkley reaches out to caress the tattoo with his fingertips, a tear rolling down his cheek. "It's Japanese for Neville."

I chuckle, and his confused expression prompts an explanation. "She was a fighter until the end... Even when conforming to the Rejects' way of life, she rebelled by tattooing your name on her body. Her own little silent protest against what was going on around her ... a reminder of the man she loved when she was forced to suck up to one she hated."

He smiles, a wide, genuine grin this time. "I hadn't thought of it that way... Thank you for that, son."

Rounding the table, I bend down to hug him. He feels so small to me, fragile and slender. Yet, he is the strongest of us all—the one who literally carries thousands of us on his back. His children, his creations, people worth defying the government and facing death for.

"I'll leave you alone now," I tell him when we pull apart. "We're all here, Professor, for whatever you might need."

He nods, removing his glasses to swipe at his damp eyes. "Thank you, son."

Pausing in the doorway, I take one last glance at him. He calls me 'son,' and I think of him as the father I never had—a replacement for the deadbeat who couldn't even bother to show up until I was on my deathbed following the nuclear blasts. But I've never done before what I do now, giving him a smile before slipping back out into the hall.

"You're welcome ... Dad."

I EXIT THE SCIENCE AND TECHNOLOGY BUILDING TO FIND THE GREEN ARCADE STRETCHING out across the dome all but empty. It's been this way since the day Jenica died, quiet and still. Classes have been suspended for the children, and only those chores and tasks that are vital to the smooth running of Headquarters are being tended to. It's as if everyone has collectively decided this death requires a timeout ... a moment of stillness and reflection.

Dog rushes up to me, and I pause to scratch the top of his head before striding across the grass, heading toward Hexley Hall. I've got a few hours before the memorial, and I plan to wake Blythe so we can get ahead of the long lines in the chow hall. With so many people here, it can often take hours to get a tray.

I come up short when I pass the park and find Blythe there with Agata. The two are dressed in sweatpants and t-shirts, circling each other with strategic steps. She's teaching the kid self-defense, I realize as I watch Agata attempts to strike Blythe, but throwing too much of her weight behind the swing and almost falling on her face. Blythe smiles patiently and corrects Agata's posture, encouraging her to try again.

On a nearby bench, Gage sits watching, his back to me, one arm braced on the seat back. Dog takes off toward them, tongue hanging out of his mouth and tail wagging once he spots Blythe. I approach the bench, pausing just beside it as Dog lumbers toward the girls, heedless to their training. Blythe laughs as he tackles Agata, covering her face in slobbery kisses while the girl squeals and giggles beneath him.

Blythe glances up at me and smiles, giving me a tentative little wave. I wave back, then turn to find Gage glancing at me from the corner of his eye. Without turning his head, he shifts across the bench to make room, gesturing for me to sit. I settle in, deciding my empty stomach can wait until Blythe is finished with Agata's training. Leaning back, I cross one leg over the other, ankle rested on my thigh, and watch as Blythe commands

Dog to sit before resuming her work with Agata.

"If she's going to learn to shoot, I figure she ought to know what to do if her gun gets knocked out of her hand," Gage says suddenly.

I glance over at him, but he's watching the girls, his gaze intent. I can't tell if he's just monitoring Agata's progress, or simply staring at Blythe.

"It's a good idea," I reply casually, deciding not to care if he eye-fucks my girl until the end of time. Doesn't change that she's mine. "With things heating up, it can't hurt for her to know how to defend herself if necessary."

A moment of silence passes before he speaks again.

"When I asked Blythe to teach her to shoot, she told me about Agata's helmet, and the decision you guys had made about her."

"Look, man, we were just doing what we thought was best for her," I say, running a hand over my hair. It's starting to get longer than I prefer it, meaning it's time to spend some time in the mirror with my clippers. "Without you here, we just wanted her to be strong and whole."

I feel his gaze on me when he turns his head, so I meet his stare head-on, finding no animosity there.

"I'm grateful," he says. "With all that's happened, I don't think I ever really got a chance to say this. Agata told me it was you who comforted her after she heard I'd died, and again when she lost her mother. That it was you who made sure she never fell behind on her studies, and was brushing her teeth, and getting a good night's sleep."

I straighten, putting both feet on the ground and bracing my elbows on my knees. For some reason, him being so friendly toward me all of a sudden makes me feel guilty ... as if I've done something to be sorry for. Which I certainly haven't. Quite the opposite, really. I've cared for his niece, helping her through the deaths of both him and her mother. That I just so happened to end up with Blythe in the end doesn't make me the bad guy here.

"I did it for you," I confess. "You were my friend, and she was the last piece of you we had left. Blythe and I would have killed for her... We still would."

He nods, running a hand over his face and scratching at a few days' worth of stubble. "Were, you say. Kind of sucks to hear you *used to* be someone's friend."

I shake my head. "Kind of hard to still be friends with someone who accuses you of stealing his girl when I thought you were dead."

Heaving a heavy sigh, he nods slowly as if to acknowledge my truth. "I know you didn't mean to steal her. It's just ... I love her. She makes it so hard *not* to love her."

My sarcastic laugh can't be held back as I realize just how ironic his statement is. No one knows better than me how hard it is to stop loving Blythe. Even when I fell for Yasmine, a huge part of me still belonged to her.

"I know," I reply. "And she loves you."

Those words taste bitter, but they *are* true. Gage's death didn't stop her from having feelings for him. Just because she chose me doesn't mean the parts of her that he owned aren't still his. Being with her means I have to swallow that shit and accept it ... something I've been doing when it comes to Blythe since the moment I met her. Sucking it up, swallowing the bad with the good. Taking the parts of her that she gives—the only parts she has left to give.

"But she also loves you," Gage says, lowering his head. "If I ever doubted it, watching her choose you over me proved it."

"Serves you right, you arrogant prick," I tease.

He glances up at me and smirks, shaking his head. "Stupid asshole."

"Preppy-jock boy."

"Good-for-nothing shithead."

We burst out laughing, the sounds seeming to startle Blythe. She stares at us with a furrowed brow, as if trying to figure out whether we've lost our minds. I reach over and clap Gage on the shoulder.

"Good to have you back, you dumb fuck."

He grins, and gives me a shove, almost throwing me off the bench. "It's nice to be back, you meat-headed ape."

And in that moment, Gage and I find firmer footing. It isn't our former friendship—we might never have that again—but it's something. With all the death and loss we've suffered lately, it doesn't make sense to be at each other's throats all the time. We've learned the hard way how quickly the regrets can pile up once the people you care most about are gone.

We sit together in silence while the girls finish up their lesson, then I collect Blythe to head off for breakfast, while Gage takes Agata to shower and change for the memorial. Before we separate, Agata hugs me and calls me Uncle Dax like she always does, reminding me that family doesn't break ... it simply evolves. But the people in it, the people who make life worth living ... those people are always a part of it.

THE EVENING OF THE MEMORIAL, A LARGE GROUP OF US GATHER IN THE ROOM ADJOINING the chow hall, filling up the couches and chairs surrounding the old television set. The service hit everyone a bit harder than we expected. Even after getting to say our good-byes in that hospital room, the core members of our team seem to still be processing everything. For what felt like hours, we stood in the hangar, Jenica's body displayed for viewing on a high platform, while the senator spoke a few words. The Professor, a man who always seems to know what to say, remained silent, often swiping at his tears with a handkerchief. More people stood up and spoke, including Blythe and Gage, words of comfort for everyone, words to remember Jenica by.

The cooks in the chow hall made a thick stew tonight, breaking out foods they usually don't spare—as if they knew we would need comfort food, the rich tastes and warmth in our bellies reminding us of our lost mothers and the homes we will never return to.

I'm slouched in an armchair with Blythe on my lap. She seems smaller today, curled against me with her head resting just beneath my chin. A massive sweater swallows her up—one of my old castoffs she likes to wear when she's cold. Her boots rest on the floor, her legging-covered legs and stockinged feet folded under her. I'm absently stroking her hair, staring blankly at the news broadcast someone turned on.

In a chair nearby, Laura sits staring off into space, while Olivia lays on a loveseat with her feet in Alec's lap. He's clasping one of her ankles, his tattooed fingers keeping a tight hold—as if reminding himself the woman he loves is safe with him.

Gage and Michela occupy a couch, crammed between a few other people. He hardly seems to notice her hand resting on top of his, her fingers absently stroking his knuckles. Or maybe he does. Maybe they're an item now, and he's trying to move on from Blythe. It's probably for the best. Maybe he can find with Michela the same sort of peace and affection I had with Yasmine.

We've been mostly ignoring the news, but when an aerial view from Des Moines flashes across the screen, I perk up.

"Hey, turn that up," I say to Alec, who's holding the remote,

Eyebrows knit together, he increases the volume, while the low hum of conversation in the room ceases.

"And some good news tonight out of Des Moines, Iowa," says the voice of the reporter over the video, which displays the smoking remains of the capital building just after the explosion that killed Mohinder and several others. *"The Military Police succeeded in eliminating the terrorist threat that's had the city on lockdown for weeks when a drone strike took out the capital building—which, we are told, had become the base of operations."*

Blythe snorts in annoyance. "Of course they find some way to spin the explosion in their favor. Fucking assholes."

"Reported to have been killed in the explosion is this man," the reporter continues as the screen changes to display an image of Baron. He looks downright feral, staring into the camera with deranged eyes, his metal-domed head shined and gleaming. *"Barony Helsing, a known associate of the Restoration Resistance movement, is no longer a threat according to White House officials, who say the MPs reported his body to be among those of the dead. Also found in the wreckage—evidence supporting President Drummond's speech a few weeks ago, during which he warned that the Restoration Resistance might be planning to hijack nuclear sites around the country."*

The camera cuts to footage from an earlier press conference, where Captain Rodney Jones, the leader of the Enforcers Squadron, stands surrounded by several of his men in uniform.

"We wholeheartedly believe the terrorists known as the Resistance planned to decimate our nation's capital using the weapons we found hidden underground in Des Moines," he says to the gathered reporters. *"That, in light of the recent attempt on President Drummond's life, leads us to believe more attacks could be in the works, with several other cities at risk. The president has personally charged me with increasing our efforts in taking down the various sects of the terrorist organization, the Restoration Resistance. What you saw in Des Moines is only the beginning. With threats such as these being made against the American people, we can no longer stand idly by. You can be sure we will do everything we can to eliminate the threat and restore order to our great nation."*

And just like that, the promised retribution begins. It comes as no surprise that Drummond would twist what happened in Des Moines to fit his narrative, once again stirring up mistrust among the American people toward us.

Alec hits the mute button, and we all exchange glances loaded with various degrees of outrage, anger, and despair.

"What the hell are we supposed to do now?" Olivia grumbles. "We saved D.C., but no one will ever know thanks to Drummond and Jones."

"Yes, they will," says an intruding voice.

We swivel our heads to find Senator Davis in our midst, a cup of coffee clutched between her slender fingers.

"We will ensure the people know the truth," she continues, her gaze connecting with each of us, one by one. "Because that is what we do, people. We fight for justice, and the truth. Kinnear, it's time to start reaching out to the residents of Des Moines via the internet. Encourage people to tell their own stories, to spread the word about what they saw that day. Jenica was not included in the broadcast, which means they may not know yet that she's dead. When news of her passing hits the airwaves, we get to control the narrative by telling the truth. By ensuring everyone knows Jenica Swan was a martyr for our cause, and took out a dangerous terrorist in the process."

Blythe perks up, bracing a hand against my chest to come upright. "I'll have to download the video files from my eye, but I'm pretty sure I've got the entire standoff in front of the capital building recorded." At my surprised glance, she grins. "It helps to get these things on video."

Nodding, I give her a little squeeze. "Good job, B."

"Excellent," the senator says with an approving nod. "We might be down right now, but we aren't out. We won't go down without a fight. This is what Swan would have wanted … for us to give it everything we have until the end."

"Senator, might I suggest a video from you as well?" Alec speaks up. "A show of support for the Resistance and a condemnation of the lies spread by Jones, as well as a reminder that Drummond still has not addressed the people's demand for him to call off martial law and allow the election. Our online polls show Drummond's lowest approval rating since he took office, which means more of the people are on our side than it may seem."

"A good idea," she agrees. "We can proceed with our plans first thing in the morning. For now, I believe everyone has earned an evening of rest."

"There's one other thing," Gage chimes in, standing to face the senator. "The video I sent … the one where I tell you about my father's plan to bomb D.C. and the truth about how the Bionics began. What about that?"

"It's too soon to use your video," Alec cuts in. "I'd rather keep it close to the chest until we have enough evidence gathered to back it up. Otherwise, it can be spun as propaganda and lies from a young man angry with his father. You've already been portrayed as unstable by the media."

"I concur with Kinnear on this one," Alexis replies. "Gage, your eye-opening video will be our ace in the hole… We won't play that card until we need it."

Leaving us, she takes her coffee and disappears. Someone changes the channel, the constant hatred of us on the news being something we can only take for so long. The atmosphere in the room changes, the mood lightening a bit. While it is easy to hope we can beat this, in the back of my mind, I remember the recording of Drummond I saw in Des Moines. I remember the vehemence with which he promised his revenge.

And I can't help but think that we are outnumbered and outgunned. Whatever Drummonds plans are, this is only the tip of the iceberg.

TWENTY-FIVE

DAX JANNER AND PROFESSOR NEVILLE HINKLEY
RESTORATION RESISTANCE HEADQUARTERS
FEBRUARY 4, 4011
9:00 P.M.

WE SPEND TWO WEEKS FIGHTING OUR BATTLE ON THE AIRWAVES WITH THE PRESIDENT and Jones. It begins with the footage of Jenica's death, downloaded from the files on Blythe's eye. Alec blasts it all over the internet, the clip of Jenica taking out Baron as she fell to her death spreading like wildfire. The video makes the news, where political pundits and newscasters argue with each other about what the video means. Some rightly argue that it shows the Resistance and the Rejects are not one and same—that Baron and his band of freaks are not, and never have been, a sect of our organization. Other say it simply illustrates a power struggle between different leaders of the same terrorist group, a fight ending in the deaths of two notorious terrorists.

All over the country, people hold candlelight vigils for Jenica, hailing her as a national hero. Black banners wave with the white symbol of the Resistance on them, while heads bow in prayer. The MPs raid them all, shutting them down and burning the flags. People are arrested for fighting back, and there are casualties on both sides.

The senator's national address comes next—a video of her taken inside the hangar, dressed in her Resistance uniform. She calls out the president for the lies he has told, as well as the unfounded accusation of the attacks we are supposedly planning. The senator also reminds the American public that the president has yet to respond to calls for the suspension of martial law, and that their elected officials have yet to act by voting it out. The media airwaves buzz even more, with arguments between journalists and interviews in which elected senators and congressmen make excuses for their failures to act.

The citizens of Des Moines begin coming forward, many sharing their accounts anonymously online to avoid backlash from the government. They report seeing Jenica take out Baron, and the Resistance rush the capital in order to take out the Rejects. They tell the story of how I did what I could to warn people away from the building just before it exploded. They expose the lie about the so-called drones, which were nowhere in the area when the building went down.

More demonstrations and marches are planned, while people take to the streets, converging on the homes and offices of their elected officials. Violence and riots break out, the people going toe to toe with the MPs. They improvise weapons and body armor, but most can't match the strength of the Military Police's technology. We watch it all from the safety of Headquarters, wanting to intervene and fight alongside the people, but knowing it is no longer safe for us to do so. The senator reminds us that the people must rise up even when we aren't around, and it seems they are doing that, even at great personal cost.

We venture out when there's word of refugees needing to be taken in, fighting off the MPs in a few skirmishes. Thankfully, everyone comes home alive after each trip, something we are grateful for. After Des Moines, we've had all the loss we can take for quite a while.

As the days pass, I notice a change in Blythe. She walks about like a zombie, her eyes unfocused and her reflexes a bit off. It could be exhaustion from all we've done over the past month or so, but she's worrying me. Waking her each morning gets harder and harder, and even after I make her go to bed early, she still wakes up tired. When I ask her if she's all right, she brushes it off, insisting she's just recovering from back-to-back missions.

Yet, I can't help but notice her sudden changes seem to align with the first time I realized Gage and Michela have become a couple. I discovered it by accident the first time, on my way back from training new recruits a bit later in the evening than usual. We don't know when we'll need the newbies to fight, so Wes Graydon and I have been pushing them extra hard, demanding time and energy of them after dinner to make sure they get into fighting shape.

I'd taken the dorm stairs up to our floor because the elevator was in the middle of repairs. It was there in the stairwell that I caught them, groping each other and making out. Gage seemed embarrassed when they pulled apart and stepped aside for me to pass, while Michela didn't really care. The stairwell was a sucky place to get it on, but with Gage bunking with his little niece, and Michela sharing a room with three other girls, there weren't too many other places for them to go.

I'd kept my mouth shut about the whole thing. If they wanted people to know they were together, then they wouldn't be sneaking around.

But then, about a week later, I saw them sitting together in the mess hall, laughing and leaning into each other. Everyone else noticed it to, and before long, the gossip spread like wildfire. It figured even during war, the latest rumors still found their way into everyone's ear.

Watching Blythe whenever they were around, I started to notice she wouldn't look their way ... as if she was pointedly doing her best not to confront that Gage has moved on. At first, I cut her some slack because it's an awkward situation, being in close quarters with your ex and his new girlfriend. But after a while, it starts to get to me, and I find myself watching her *not* watch them, the unease in my stomach growing worse by the second.

Is she pissed because Gage moved on? Does she regret choosing me now that he has someone else, and he's no longer available to sit around pining for her?

It gets so bad I can't sleep at night for wondering if I'm with someone who would rather be with someone else. If, once again, loving Blythe isn't going to lead to me having the rug pulled out from under me. Because—and I have to be straight up with myself here—if Blythe wanted Gage, she could take him from Michela in an instant. I couldn't stop it, and neither could the petite girl who has Gage's attention right now.

And so, a third week passes with me saying nothing, training our new recruits, and trying not to think about the certainty of losing Blythe to the Blond Wonder, yet again.

At the end of the third week, Blythe and I are coming back to the dorm after dinner, when we see them together—Gage and Michela pressed up against the side of one of the buildings. It's dark, but we can clearly tell it's them, his big body large enough to make hers nearly invisible to anyone who happens upon them. Her hands are tangled in his hair, and they're kissing. By the way she's pulling at his clothes, I'm thinking it won't be too much longer before they're looking for a place to get horizontal.

Blythe freezes in her tracks, pulling me up short because I'm holding her hand. The meager moonlight reveals her expression—her skin ashen, her lips pinched as if she's nauseous, her eyes wide.

Then, she releases my hand and runs, dashing into Hexley Hall and letting the door slam behind her. Hands balling into fists, I glance back at Gage and Michela—at the sight Blythe literally ran away from to escape. The evidence of what I suspected all along turns my blood into molten fire. Within seconds, I'm seeing red.

Stomping after her, I throw the door to the dorm open, taking the stairs two and time until I reach our floor. The rage boils in my gut, and I need to get it out, to take it out on the only person capable of literally tearing my heart in two.

I storm into our room and find her coming out of the bathroom, her face wet with tears and one hand pressed to her middle. She starts when I slam the door, eyes widening as she meets my gaze.

"Are you fucking kidding me?" I growl, my voice low and ominous through clenched teeth.

It's a struggle keeping my voice low when all I want to do is howl and scream and tear the room apart like a hurricane.

She frowns. "What?"

"Don't play stupid, Blythe," I snap, remaining on my side of the room, not trusting myself to get too close to her without dragging her against me, then throwing her on the bed so I can spend all night making her forget about Gage. "Just admit it ... admit that seeing them together bothers you."

Her frown deepens, and then her mouth drop opens as she glares at me accusingly. "Is that what you think?"

I snort, running a hand over my freshly cut hair. "It's what I see every time we're in the room with Michela and Gage. You can't even *look* at them! And don't get me started on how distant you've been the past few weeks... You barely let me touch you anymore."

"Dax," she says, her voice low and soft.

I close my eyes and shake my head, determined not to let her suck me back in, to draw me in with her sweet voice and those beautiful brown eyes, or the broken look on her face that makes me want to make everything right for her.

"Just say it, Blythe... I want to hear you say that you still want him, and that seeing him with her upsets you so much you literally just ran away from them in tears."

Her expression changes to disbelief, then anger as she advances on me, an accusing finger pointing in my face.

"Fuck *you*," she screeches. "If that's what you believe, then you must not think too highly of me. How can you claim to love me if you can't trust me?"

She's too close, and I give in to the urge to grab her, touch her, make some claim to her in any way I can. Grasping her shoulders, I haul her against me, trembling with the force of my need to keep her, to remind her who has always loved her when she had no one else.

"Because loving you is part of who I am," I tell her, my lips pressed against her forehead. "But you keep pushing me away. Just when I think you're finally ready to give me all of you, something happens, and you withdraw."

Staring up at me, she stiffens in my hold. "I came up here to puke, you idiot. I haven't been pushing you away; I've been feeling sick."

My grip on her shoulders loosens, my anger melting away in an instant, replaced with concern. "What? What's wrong?"

Shaking her head, she shrugs my hands off and backs away, crossing her arms over her chest. "Look, I get that you might not trust me when it comes to Gage, and maybe I understand why to a certain extent. And yes, seeing him with Michela is kind of awkward, but I *chose* you, Dax ... even though you can sometimes be the single most oblivious person on the planet. Haven't you noticed the signs? I'm tired all the time, I'm puking my guts out, and my boobs are huge!"

Wrinkling my brow, I look her over. Sure, she's looking a little chestier than usual now that I'm paying attention. I've been putting in a lot of time in training new recruits, so I haven't seen her vomiting. But I *have* noticed how tired she is all the time.

Alarm bells sound in my head as I realize what all these things add up to.

"Blythe..."

Tears fill her eyes. She swipes at them with the sleeve of her sweater, choking back a sob. "I'm pregnant, Dax."

"HOW LONG HAVE YOU BEEN HAVING THESE SYMPTOMS?" THE PROFESSOR ASKS BLYTHE the next morning.

I'd approached him at breakfast about discreetly running some tests. While there are plenty of other people in the infirmary we could go to, he's the only one I trust to keep this under wraps. I don't want everyone at Headquarters to know, especially when I still haven't fully wrapped my head around it yet.

I'm pregnant, Dax.

With those three words, my entire life has changed. Whether it's for the better—whether even thinking of the clump of cells growing in her body as an actual child is a good idea—I'm not sure about yet. It's ironic, considering our conversation a few weeks ago, where we laid in bed and fantasized about having a family someday. I want that with Blythe more than anything in the world ... but here, now?

"Just the past two weeks or so," Blythe answers, shifting uncomfortably in the chair beside mine. "But I haven't had a period in over a month. I had one just before..."

"Just before we went off to D.C.," I answer for her.

She'd told me all of this last night—how she had just come to realize she might be pregnant, how long it had been since her last period. It all adds up to me knocking her up in that hotel room where we were together for the first time. As a former man-whore, I have always been a stickler for protection and being careful. The infirmary keeps a room stocked with basic needs like aspirin and condoms—both of which I always grab handfuls of whenever I'm in the area. But that one night with Blythe caught me unprepared. It was the only time we've been together without protection. Of course, once is really all it takes.

The Professor nods, glancing down at the vial of Blythe's blood he's just drawn. "Everything adds up here, but the labs will confirm it for sure. I'll go run it myself to make sure no one else lays eyes on the results."

Standing, he tucks the vial into the pocket of his lab coat, then stares mournfully at us. There is no judgement in his eyes, but I notice the sadness. He knows this baby stands no chance. He knows what we are going to have to do.

"Have you discussed your options yet?" he asks, his voice low.

Blythe glances over at me and bites her bottom lip. I reach out and grab her human hand, gripping it tight.

"Not yet," I tell him. "But we will."

We could hardly get past the part where Blythe revealed her condition before we ended up sitting on the bed staring blankly off into space.

He nods and clears his throat, avoiding making eye contact with either of us. "Just know we have the equipment here for termination. It can be arranged as soon as you're ready, and carried out quickly and privately. Blythe, if you are uncomfortable with me doing it, then there are other capable doctors here who would do it. Patient confidentiality means no one would ever know, regardless of who performs the procedure. Should you decide to keep the baby, we'd need to do an exam and start you on some vitamins."

She nods, but keeps her gaze lowered to where our hands are connected and resting on my thigh. The Professor blushes and scrubs a hand over his jaw and the stubble growing there.

"I'll just go run this and come back in with the results," he mumbles. "It'll only take a moment."

"Thanks," I reply when Blythe still seems incapable of speech.

Once he's gone, I glance over at her. She's as implacable as ever, her face showing none of her emotions. Not that I expected her to show any. With Blythe, I can always anticipate the shit storm of feelings to come later, once holding it in has become too much for her.

Raising her hand to my lips, I kiss her knuckles in what I hope is soothing gesture. "Hey, it's going to be okay. We'll get through this."

She doesn't look at me, but her fingers tighten around my hand. "It's kind of ironic we're in this room, about to decide the fate of..."

Lowering her head, she pinches her mouth shut, stopping just short of saying something like 'our baby.' She doesn't want to think of it as a baby yet... doesn't want to give it humanity. If she does, then doing what needs to done will become that much harder for her.

"Why is that?" I ask, hoping the time will pass faster if I keep her talking.

"Because this is the room where Jenica had her abortion," she whispers.

I flinch in shock, my hand closing around hers so hard and fast that she cringes and pulls away. I can't say I blame her ... a few more seconds and I could have broken her hand.

"What?" I manage through a constricted throat, my voice coming out hoarse and strained. "What did you say?"

Still staring across the room, she sits back in her chair and folds her hands in her lap. "It was after the rescue mission at Stonehead—the one where we went to save Olivia and the others. Me and Gage had come to the infirmary to visit Olivia, and ended up in this exam room. We were just talking at first, then we started fooling around. We heard the door opening, and ducked into the observation room next door ... because we didn't want to be seen together yet."

I turn my head and glance over at the pane of glass that functions as a two-way mirror between this room and the other.

"It was Jenica and the Professor," she continues, her voice flat. "He asked her if she was sure about what they were doing, and she convinced him it had to be done. The world was too fucked up to bring an innocent life into it, she said. She couldn't imagine having to run and hide with a crying infant, or having to watch it snatched away by the MPs. The Professor did the procedure, even though he looked like the whole thing was tearing him apart."

She turns her head suddenly, her human eye brimming with tears, her voice becoming gruff as she tries to hold it all in.

"He had to destroy his own baby," she sobs. "That man had to ... and now we have to..."

She leans into me, closing her eyes and trembling as she does her best to pull herself together. I reach over and pull her out of her chair, settling her on my lap. As I wrap both arms around her, trying to give her all the strength I can, my mind whirls with everything she just revealed.

She has known about Jenica and the Professor for far longer than the rest of us. She'd witnessed Jenica having an abortion. The Professor had to perform the procedure on his own wife ... destroying the beginnings of what could have been his kid.

It's a lot to take in, so I simply sit in silence and hold Blythe. She's calming down now, but I don't want to let her go.

"We will win this war," I assure her, my hand absently rubbing her back. "And when it's over, we'll have as many babies as you want. They'll all be beautiful and tough like you."

She glances at me and tries to smile, but the expression only breaks my heart more. "What will they get from you?"

I smile back and chuckle. "My filthy mouth and quick reflexes."

This time when she laughs, it's genuine. "I'd be okay with that."

"We're going to have all the things we've ever wanted, me and you," I promise her, even as I realize it's a promise I'll never be able to keep.

Things are looking worse by the day out there, with no indication they'll ever improve. But we need something to fight for, something to press toward. A future with Blythe is a good a reason as any to fight like hell, and never stop fighting.

"And for what it's worth, I'm sorry," I add, my tone becoming serious.

"Why?" she asks, wrinkling her brow.

"Because I feel like this is my fault," I reply. "I'm usually more careful, but that night in the motel—"

Her finger falls against my lips, silencing me. She removes it, then replaces it with her lips, giving me a sweet, soft kiss. Then, she cups my jaw and stares into my eyes, holding my gaze.

"Don't apologize," she whispers. "I don't regret what happened that night, when I stopped being afraid of what we could be. I'm not sorry, Dax. I'll never be sorry."

That comes as a relief, because even though I know she loves me, I'm not going to pretend she also didn't love someone else—might still love him. If it ever turns out she regrets her choice, I don't think I could survive it. Losing her in any way isn't something I'm prepared to suffer through.

The Professor returns, and Blythe swiftly gets off my lap and back in her own chair. Being affectionate in front of him feels weird ... like being caught making out by your own father.

His eyes are solemn, his lips a firm line as he delivers the news.

"The test was positive," he says. "I estimate you to be about six weeks along."

Blythe nods resolutely; she's known the truth all along. The confirmation of it makes my heart sink with the knowledge that I'd be happy about this baby under any other circumstances. Hell, a part of me is happy knowing the woman I love is carrying a part of me inside her.

But that part of me will have to be destroyed, and I need to be strong for Blythe for what will come after. The guilt, the anger, the sadness.

"Okay," she says. "Let's schedule the procedure."

PART THREE:
FALLOUT
(Gage Bronson)

TWENTY-SIX

MICHELA ARLOTTI IS IN LOVE WITH ME.

It's something I've known for a while now, but tried not to think too much about. I do not think this out of some sense of arrogance or pride in my own magnetism. The truth is that she's shown me how she feels more times than I can count.

The night we camped out in a raided Ohio hideout, when she kissed me. All those times while we were on the road together, rescuing stranded and hunted Bionics, when she would look at me with long, drawn-out gazes. The way she comforted me after news of my sister's death was delivered.

She's a great girl, petite but strong, tough, loyal ... and yes, beautiful. Dark hair, darker eyes, pretty lips. If I'd met her during my prep-school days, I would have relished chasing her, charming her, getting under her skirt.

But these days, I've turned into a different man—a version of myself I don't even recognize. As I stare at my reflection in the bathroom mirror, I take inventory of all the things that have changed. I'm still six feet four inches of solid muscle, but the body that was once honed by athleticism is now jacked by constant fighting and running.

Down the center of my bare chest runs the scar from my transplant, the operation that traded my wounded human heart for a bionic one. The pink line has completely healed, though sometimes just thinking about the agony I woke up in after the operation causes echoes of the old pain to flare up.

There are other scars, too, so many I wonder how long before I'm more scar tissue than smooth skin. Puckered lines from stab wounds and the scratches of tree branches. A stripe beneath one armpit from a bullet graze, the now-closed hole in my shoulder where this time, the bullet had actually penetrated. And of course, there's the scar running down the right side of my face, cutting through one eyebrow, missing my eye and continuing to my cheekbone. A MP laid my face open during a fight, and the hasty suture job left me with a permanent souvenir.

My hair is longer than usual, falling into my eyes. I haven't shaved in days, and it seems to be something I forgo these days. There isn't time to be fastidious about my appearance, not even now that we are safe here at Headquarters. There's always something to be done, always a person who needs saving.

Over the past few weeks, while the Senator and Alec waged war with the president over media airwaves, I joined every available rescue mission I could. I need some distance from Headquarters, and being out on my own was something I'd grown used to while operating as The Patriot. Now part of the Resistance again, I've got all the weapons and manpower I was missing at my fingertips, but an actual chain of command to report to. It's going to take a bit of adjustment on my part.

Aside from the freedom leaving Headquarters gives me, it also provides a bit of distance from the people I try my best to avoid. Not that I'm still angry with Dax or hate Blythe for her decision. But seeing them together still cuts me, the knowledge that she was mine first never far from my mind.

I try not to stare when I'm in the room with her, but it's difficult. My eyes are drawn to her. *I* am always drawn to her … always wanting, needing any piece of herself she is willing to give.

Except now, all those pieces belong to Dax. When I look in her eyes, I don't see regret. Maybe a bit of sadness, some discomfort when Michela is being overly affectionate in front of everyone. Part of me wants to believe she's even jealous, and on some level, she might be. But I have no doubt in my mind she loves Dax as much as she claims. Kind of makes the whole jealousy thing feel like water under the bridge.

And me? Well, I'm in a relationship on unequal footing.

Michela is in love with me ... and I am still hopelessly in love with Blythe.

The first time she kissed me, I brushed her off. I told her the truth—that there was someone else. Even as lonely as I had been all those weeks and months without Blythe, I wouldn't let myself even think about being with her. Even from such a distance, every little piece of me belonged to Blythe.

The second time, I initiated the kiss. It was the night we returned to Headquarters with Jenica's broken body. The night we all stood by and watched the Professor pull the plug on the woman who had been his wife. I'd been stuck in the infirmary, recovering from taking a bullet to the shoulder. Not wanting me to be alone after an emotional night, Michela had arranged for Agata to sleep in a dorm with one of her friends, then returned to spend the night with me.

She'd fussed over me more than the nurses did, making sure I had water, checking my bandages, fluffing my pillows. After about the fourth time of suffering through this, I placed a hand over hers, pausing it before it could prod at my IV. She'd glanced up at me. For a long moment, we'd communicated without speaking.

Michela is new to the Resistance, and hardly knew Jenica. Hell, I barely got to know her before being forced to leave Headquarters. But even the brief time she was in my life left an impact, and her loss devastated me. Michaela seems to see this, understands I'm hurting. Coming home to death and loss has gutted me, and I'm rubbed raw and turned inside out, all my nerves exposed to the outside of my body.

It all hurt so damn much—fighting to get to my sister only to be told she was dead, watching Jenica fall from that balcony, losing Blythe.

That night, I was tired of hurting, tired of feeling so hopelessly alone. Yes, I have Agata, and will never cease being grateful she survived. But there's another need inside of me, a gaping hole that yawns and stretches more and more with each passing day.

So, I used Michela to fill it.

I'd given her hand a little tug until she perched on the edge of my infirmary bed. I sat up, ignoring the pain tearing through my shoulder, and slid my good arm around her waist, pulling her chest flush against mine.

She'd gasped, her eyes widening, then becoming heavy-lidded as she seemed to realize my intent. I paused, my lips hovering just over hers, my breath held and caught in my lungs as I waited—for her to push me away, to tell me she knew what I was doing, and refused to let herself be used.

Instead, she closed her eyes leaned in even closer, until her lips brushed mine.

Closing the distance between us, I'd kissed her with every ounce of pent-up anger and sadness I possessed. I kissed her the way I'd been wanting to kiss Blythe from the moment I saw her face again. Michela had whimpered against my lips, going slack in my arms and surrendering to me. It seemed to go on forever, and by the time I came back up for air, her lips had become red and bit a swollen.

Guilt had assailed me then, as I'd looked into her eyes and seen the depth of her feelings. But it wasn't enough to keep me away. She was willing, and I needed something to take comfort in, some outlet for my pain and grief.

One kiss turned into another, and before the night was over, she was taking her clothes off and climbing into my infirmary bed. I might have blamed it on grief or the combination of liquor and pain pills … if not for the fact that it happened again a few days later, then again, and again.

I wasn't romantic about it, looking for any place we could be alone, so I could indulge in a fleeting time of not feeling anything beyond the physical. But Michela didn't seem to mind, and as long as she didn't turn me away, I had no reason to stop. No reason to believe I could hope for Blythe to be mine ever again. The sooner I could come to terms with that, the better.

The Revolution

I come back to the present as Michela's petite form appears in the bathroom doorway. Beyond her, Agata is still sleeping, the covers pulled over her head and her body curled into a little ball. Michela still wears her pajamas—a pair of shorts that show off her toned legs, and a tank top that hugs her waist. Her hair frames her face messily, her eyelids still a bit heavy from sleep. She had to have just stumbled in from the room she shares with three other girls across the hall.

Our moments together are quick and stolen, worked in between missions or when everyone else is asleep. There isn't a lot of talking, which I appreciate. I'm all talked out at this point. I just need to feel something that isn't pain.

Coming away from the counter, I swiftly close the distance between us and grab her by the waist. She jumps into my arms as I lift her, wrapping her legs around me. Holding onto her with one arm, I reach out to close the door. Then, spinning back toward the counter, I plop her down onto its surface and brace my hands on either side of her, leaning in for a kiss.

She tips her head back to meet my mouth with hers, and the sharp edges of the daggers pointing in toward my soul become blunt. My blood heats as her hands come up against my naked chest, then slide down over my abs. It's happening so fast—her hands yanking at the waistband of my pajama pants, her lips kissing their way from my mouth to my chin, then my neck and shoulder. Grasping the bottom of her shirt, I swiftly yank it over her head and toss it aside.

Glancing up at the mirror, I catch a glimpse of myself ... and shame washes over me for a second. I know what I'm doing—using Michela to feel better—but I have nothing else. Nothing except my little niece, who can only fill so many of the voids in my life. Closing my eyes against the guilt, I concentrate on Michela, but even that's hard. I keep wishing her skin were darker, legs longer, that the hair I'm gripping in my fist was a bit thicker.

Don't think about Blythe.

That'll only taint the moment more, and I feel shitty enough as it is. I let my thoughts go blank and start to sink into the sensations of the moment, letting raw instinct take over. I sink so deep into that place I don't hear the alarms at first.

It isn't until Michela rears back and gives me a little shake that I register it—a loud, whining siren emanating from the dorm's hallway. Her eyes are wide with fear and concern, and the adrenaline the alarm sends through me kicks my bionic heart into high gear. The organ batters my sternum as I yank away from Michela and quickly retie the drawstring of my pants before crossing back to the door. Michela pulls her shirt back on while I throw the door open, finding Agata upright in the bed, her expression frantic as she glances around the room.

"What's going on, Uncle Gage?" she cries, clapping her hands over her ears to block out the sound.

Hastily throwing on a thermal and then shoving my feet into my boots, I try to remember being told what alarms in the dorms might mean.

"I don't know," I tell her. "Get dressed while I find out."

As I open the door to the room, I can hear Michela reassuring Agata and urging her from the bed. Doors are opening up and down the hall, and while some simply poke their heads out and look around in confusion, others dash down the hall with weapons in hand. Red lights mounted on the ceiling flash ominously in rhythm with the sirens.

Spotting Wes Graydon—the guy they passed off as me while I was presumed dead—barreling down the hall toward me, I reach out to grab his arm before he can get away.

"Hey, what the hell is going on?" I ask.

Wes' bicep is tense in my hold, his face white as a sheet as he meets my gaze and shakes his head in disbelief. "Code red ... possible invasion."

For a moment, I'm so stunned I can't move. My hold on his arm tightens, and my heart pumps so hard I'm surprised it doesn't leap up my throat and out through my mouth.

Then, the severity of the situation hits me, and pure instinct kicks in.

"I'm coming," I inform him before ducking back into the room.

"What is it?" Michela asks, keeping a tight hold on Agata's hand.

My niece appears calm now, her natural curiosity taking over as she searches my face for the answers.

"Something bad," she says as I kneel beside the bed and pull the container holding my weapons from beneath it.

"It's a code red," I inform them, quickly pulling on a shoulder holster before sliding a CBX into it beneath one arm. "Apparently, that means we might be getting invaded."

"Invaded!" Michela cries out, rushing forward to kneel at my side.

A second holster goes around my ankle, and a smaller version of the CBX goes in. Then, I grab a shotgun and my best knife.

"I'm coming with you," she announces.

"No," I snap, turning my head to look at her. "I need you to stay here and guard Agata."

"But—"

"If I don't come back, I *need* someone to be here to protect her!" I interrupt, my voice coming out harsher than I intend. There's no time for this. "Someone I trust. Do you understand? There is no one else; it has to be you."

Her lips pinch into an annoyed line, but she nods in agreement. She's a valuable fighter, but I know Blythe and Dax are already on their way to investigate, and I meant what I said ... Michela is the only other person I trust with my niece.

Pulling one last weapon out of the case, I hand it to her. Accepting it, she straightens her shoulders and holds my gaze.

"I'll protect her with my life."

Grasping the back of her neck, I give her a swift kiss. It feels like the right thing to do with her standing there looking as if she wants to follow me wherever I go.

"I know you will," I reply before turning to barrel from the room.

It doesn't take me long to get to the stairs, and I hurtle down each flight without missing a beat. The advantages of a bionic heart mean I don't tire as easily, and my heart can tolerate a lot more physical strain. I'm faster, my reflexes are sharper, and once I get pass the first initial kick of adrenaline, my heart rate remains low even when I'm going hell for leather.

I follow the running bodies toward the main building, where several have gathered around the front steps. The senator stands beside Alec on the fourth step, a bit elevated as they wait for everyone to converge. Lingering at the back of the crowd, I scan the ranks for familiar faces. I spot Olivia at the center beside Laura, while Blythe and Dax are—as expected—at the front of the mass of bodies.

"Listen up, everyone," Alec yells to be heard over the confused voices buzzing as everyone tries to figure out what's going on. As one, they fall silent, and he continues. "As you might know, we have a code red ... which means there's a possibility of invasion, and our secret location is at risk. For future reference, should the citadel itself come under attack, that would be a code black."

Good to know. I must have missed the different codes when first moving in, and will have to ask someone to let me in on what else I'm ignorant to.

"What we're looking at here is a caravan that appears to be too close for comfort," the senator chimes in. "The security drone system Kinnear put into place picked them up about thirty miles out, coming through the canyon. While there are vehicles, there are also others on foot, and they appear to be moving slowly."

"Is it the MPs?" someone asks from the front.

"We can't be certain," Alec replies. "My instincts say it isn't. The Military Police are flashier than that, and would probably drop bombs on us before they outright approached. Whoever this is, they seem to know where they're going... I'm positive they know where we're hidden."

"Then we need to take them out!" someone else exclaims.

"What we need to do is prepare to take them out, but also do a little recon," the senator interjects. "We cannot simply blow them sky high without knowing who they are and what they might be doing here."

"So, we're going to send out a recon team, and a demolition team,"

Alec adds. "The recon team will scout ahead with stealth, and try to determine what we're dealing with here. The demolition team will set up charges along the canyon walls between the recon team and the entrance of Headquarters. The moment recon gives the word, demolition will blow those fuckers sky high. The rest of you will remain in the hangar, weapons ready to defend our home. Should the recon and demo fail, then it's go time."

Nods of assent and murmurs ripple through the crowd, while the Professor and a handful of his lab aids appear toting boxes. While Alec begins assembling the teams, they start pulling various pieces of equipment out of the boxes, neatly arranging the items at the top of the steps.

"Leading the Demo team," Alec calls out. "Janner ... take Sol, Graydon, and McNabb with you."

Dax and Blythe start up the steps toward the Professor, while Wes and Olivia shoulder their way through the crowd to catch up. While they meet with the Professor and his aides to gather their equipment, Alec glances out at the crowd before locking eyes with me.

"Recon team will be Bronson and Rosenberg," he states. "Suit up, and move out. The rest of you, to the hangar."

While the other soldiers move out, I make my way to the steps, joined by Laura, who has her game face on, as usual. Once at the top of the steps, Alec directs us to pull on camouflage body suits made of stretchy fabric painted the same red, brown, and orange tones of the canyon. We pull them on over our clothes, the suits including hoods that cover our necks, hair, and faces. Only our eyes are left uncovered. We're both handed a pack, which contains tactical binoculars, a COMM device, and a set of antigravity gloves and boot covers for climbing.

"Keep your COMMs on," Alec tells us. "I'll be in the main control room giving you instructions on how far out to go before you start climbing. Once you're high enough to observe while staying hidden, use the binoculars to try to get a read on them. Janner will be waiting with his team for instructions."

"Got it," I reply, while Laura nods her understanding.

Slinging my pack over my shoulder, I lead her down the steps, with Dax and his team hot on our heels. They're wearing the same camouflage suits, and while their bags hold the same climbing equipment, they also contain several powerful explosive charges.

No one speaks as we march through the hangar, past the formed-up soldiers ready to fight if we should fail. Then, we're walking through the hovercraft tunnel. The only way in or out of the citadel. Our boots clank over the metal lining the tube, echoing beyond. Small lights guide our way, illuminating the hatch that opens when we approach it—operated by Alec in the control room.

We step out into the canyon, the bright light of the rising sun shining in our eyes and painting the rocky slit surrounding us in splashes of vibrant color.

Coming up beside me, Dax pauses, hands braced on his hips. "Well … it's a beautiful day to blow up some invaders."

I turn to glance at him with a grin. "Let's go fuck some shit up."

We fist bump, then lead the others down the canyon, the heavy hatch of the tunnel slamming shut behind us.

TWENTY-SEVEN

A TRICKLE OF SWEAT ROLLS DOWN MY FOREHEAD AND TOWARD THE BRIDGE OF MY NOSE, but I ignore it, my muscles straining as I make the climb up one side of the canyon. About halfway up, I am adhered to the wall like a spider, the antigravity equipment keeping me from plummeting to my death ... or least a few broken bones. The sun is rising quickly, the heat characteristic of the area making me feel as if I'm baking inside the camouflage suit, the clothes I'm wearing under it sticking to me like a second skin. The pack on my shoulders is light, at least.

I pause and glance over my shoulder at the other side of the canyon, where Laura shimmies up the wall at about the same pace as me.

"*Ten miles out*," Alec's voice calls through the COMM attached at my hip.

I'm almost to the top now, giving me plenty of time to take my position.

A few minutes later, I haul myself over the edge and roll onto my belly, then pull myself onto my knees. Taking the COMM off my belt, I respond to Alec, also noticing Laura is in position across the way.

"Rosenberg and I are in place," I tell him, then reach for the tactical binoculars.

Going belly down onto the ground, I prop myself up on my elbows and peer into the things. Over the COMM, I can hear Blythe, Dax, and the others checking in as they set up the charges along the canyon. Within a matter of minutes, they've finished and stand by to await our orders.

The binoculars allow me to see for miles, so I zoom in, searching for any sign of movement along the canyon. Overhead, I know one of Alec's security drones is circling the place, but they're quiet and made to blend in with the sky, keeping them from becoming obvious to anyone approaching. Alec Kinnear might have been one of the Resistance's best finds, his inventions and smart ideas keeping us safe and arming us for the fight.

"See anything, Rosenberg?" I ask Laura over the COMM

"Negative, Bronson … no movement that I can detect."

"Sit tight, they're coming," Alec chimes in over the line. *"Drone picked them up about six miles from your location a while ago … they're getting close."*

I lay there in silence and study the bend in the canyon, from around which our enemy is approaching. Or, maybe not. Maybe the caravan is full of helpless Bionics who need us to hide them. Thinking of Agata, cowering behind Michela while the MPs tear through the hideout, I hope it's the latter. We're overcrowded, but I'll take that over being raided any day.

A sudden flash of movement catches my eye and I perk up, zooming in even closer with my binoculars. A cloud of dust is being kicked up by movement over the dusty ground, and among the haze, I spot something big and black.

"Incoming," I say into the COMM. "Not sure what we're working with here, but they've arrived."

"Copy, Bronson," Alec replies. *"Hold your position and assess."*

I keep staring into the binoculars, watching as the dust begins to clear, revealing large vehicles in their midst.

"Looks like a couple of big boys on wheels," I tell him. "Definitely being used for cargo of some kind … not moving very fast. I'm counting three."

"We've got guards on foot," Laura adds. *"Surrounding the big boys … at least eight to each vehicle. They're armed."*

I take count of the armed guards walking alongside the slow-moving trucks and realize Laura is right. Twenty-four of them on foot, each armed with a gun of some kind. As they come closer to where Laura and I lay hidden above, something about them strikes me as off.

"Do they look like MPs?" Alec asks over the line.

"No," I reply. "Or if they are, they're dressed in plain clothes."

But something tells me this doesn't feel like them, and I can't shake the premonition that blowing the canyon with them in the crossfire is a bad idea. Peering through the binoculars once again, I focus on the two guards at the front of the formation, large rifles slung over their shoulders. The first thing I notice is that both guards are women. The second thing I realize is that along with their plain clothes, titanium body parts cover different appendages on their bodies.

"We got hardware," I say into the COMM. "At least on the first two guards."

"He's right," says Laura from across the canyon. *"From my position, I'm counting about four others in the formation with hardware."*

"What do you say, Bronson?" Alec coaxes. *"Are we looking at some of our own, or something else?"*

I don't want to believe the 'something else' might be the Rejects, but when Laura speaks up, I become less certain.

"Son of a bitch ... it's the Rejects!"

They're coming closer now, so close they're almost underneath Laura and me ... which means in minutes, they'll be passing through the part of the canyon where Dax and his team set up the explosives. Sure enough, I notice the crude, black-market parts used by the Rejects, far different from the government-issue parts the rest of us have. Even my heart—given to me on my father's orders after my supposed death—is one of the best models there is. Nothing but the best for Daddy's boy.

"Janner, are you clear of the demo sight?" Alec asks over the frequency.

"We are clear and ready to blow this bitch as soon as you say the word," Dax replies.

Narrowing my eyes at the third woman in the first formation, my mouth drops open as the niggling of recognition begins.

"It's the Rejects ... like there's anything to discuss?" Laura says. *"Blow 'em up, Janner."*

"Wait!" I call out, way too loudly to be covert. But none of that matters, because I realize what's happening. "Don't blow it!"

Throwing the COMM into my bag, then slinging it over my shoulder, I roll off the side of the cliff and start descending, no longer afraid of being seen. The Rejects go into an uproar at the sight of me climbing swiftly down toward them in my camouflage. Guns point at me, and in my pack, I can hear Alec screaming at me through the COMM. He's probably thinking I've lost my mind, but as the girl I recognized pulls away from the others and comes forward, I know I'm doing the right thing.

She's got a scarf tied on the lower half of her face, but I swear I know her. She comes forward, lowering her weapon, her blue eyes boring into mine over the top of the fabric.

Narrowing her eyes, she inclines her head and studies me with a wrinkled brow while the women behind her continue leveling their weapons in my direction. I remember the hood I'm wearing and quickly snatch it off, revealing my face.

The wrinkled brow smooths out, and the girl's eyes get wide as she holds up a hand to urge her companions to lower their guns. As they do, she unwinds the scarf from around her nose and mouth, revealing a heart-shaped face and delicate features.

"Gage?" she whispers in disbelief.

The shock of seeing her again ripples through me, leaving me momentarily speechless. I fumble for my voice as she comes toward me, a smile breaking out across her features.

"Tamryn."

"Baron and the others abandoned us," Tamryn confesses an hour later.

An hour after she led me to one of the huge trucks, opening the door to the trailer to reveal her 'cargo'.

People ... dozens of them, crammed inside the dark space. The moment I laid eyes on them, it became clear they were in no condition to be turned away. Starving, ill, injured—they needed our help, Rejects or not.

Once I called the others on my COMM to let them know what was going on, they shimmied down the side of the canyon to come investigate. After a bit of back and forth with Alec and the senator over whether to take them in, it was decided the sick and injured would be taken to the infirmary, but handcuffed so they could not hurt anyone. All able-bodied among them were being held in the hovercraft hangar under heavy guard, also handcuffed so they could not overpower our soldiers.

Tamryn, we escorted to the conference room, where we waited for her to tell the story of how they came to be at our front door. Surrounding the conference table, Blythe, Dax, Laura, Olivia, Alec, Senator Davis, and the Professor stare at Tamryn as she takes a sip of the water someone gave her.

"Before going to Des Moines," she clarifies, her curious eyes taking in her surroundings. It's a far cry from the underground caves she lived in with the Rejects. "Baron said what was coming next would turn the tides in this war. He didn't want the weakest of us along—the women who couldn't fight, people with illnesses, those who had suffered serious injuries fighting for that asshole... He just *left* us."

Studying Tamryn, I believe what she's saying. She'd always been a tiny thing, but she's emaciated now, her cheeks caving in, her collarbones jutting out against the neckline of her top.

"We holed up in the old hideout in D.C. as long as we could," she goes on, leaning back in her chair and heaving a heavy sigh. "But they took almost all our food and supplies with them when they invaded Des Moines. We risked going out to scavenge for whatever we could find, but it was too risky inside the capital ... so we ran."

"Where did the vehicles and weapons come from?" Alec asks, studying Tamryn intently.

Everyone else is either suspicious of her, or feels sorry for her, based on their expressions, but I can't read Alec. He seems to be trying to figure her out, to determine whether to trust her.

"Some castoffs Baron left behind," she replies. "Old guns and trucks aren't as useful as the latest technology in weapons and hovercrafts."

At her disdainful tone, I wonder if she realizes those same weapons and crafts were likely provided by my father. Probably not. Those who followed Baron truly believed in him, having no idea he'd been manufactured by the very government they despised.

"We killed some MPs and stole their uniforms," she whispers, her eyes lowering as if in shame. "We used those as disguises to get out of the city, acting like we were transporting something. I don't know how we weren't caught, but no one seemed to care to check our cargo, so we skated by. From there, we stuck to abandoned areas, even camped out in some zones with heavy radiation... They seemed to be the only places we could be safe."

"So much for you guys not being strong enough," Laura chimes in with a grin. "You sure showed him!"

"Why did you come here?" Blythe asks, hands folded on the table in front of her. "You had to know it would be dangerous to approach us, after all the bad blood that has passed between us and the Rejects."

"We are no longer Rejects," Tamryn protests. "They abandoned us—after they took us in and promised us we would be protected, that we wouldn't be alone anymore. We realize now they never cared about us... Baron never cared. He just needed soldiers to march for him ... fight for him ... die for him."

Her voice cracks, but she doesn't shed a single tear, her blue eyes blazing with heat and rage. She's so different from the girl I used to know, yet in some ways still the same.

"Are you aware of what happened in Des Moines?" I ask, studying Tamryn more closely.

Her face is windblown, reddened along the cheekbones. Her lips are hopelessly chapped, and her short blonde hair streaked with black and red highlights is dry and matted. The rest of her crew had looked similarly bedraggled. They must have been on the run for a few months, cut off from the outside world.

She shrugs one shoulder, wrinkling her nose with a disdainful snort.

"What do I care what happened there?"

"Baron was killed," I state, raising one eyebrow. "We fought them off to stop the nuclear bomb, and wiped out most of them. Whatever was left of Baron's men were taken out in an explosion. Few escaped unscathed."

Her face transforms, becoming almost grotesque in the sneer twisting her mouth and the glee flaring in her gaze.

"Good," she snarls. "Are you sure he's really gone? No one restarted his stupid heart?"

I smirk, amused by this fire I'm witnessing in her. It's new, and I like it. "He was decapitated."

"Perfect," she says with a nod. "The bastard had it coming."

"So, we know *why* you came here," Olivia pipes up. "But you haven't mentioned *how* you knew where to go. I mean ... you came straight down this canyon. So you had to have known you'd find us here."

Her gaze cuts to me, and she narrows her eyes. I scowl, annoyed with her for the assumption I know she's making.

"He never said a word to me," Tamryn snaps, catching on to what Olivia is alluding to. "He spent weeks in Baron's clutches, and he never gave you guys away."

"Then how did you know where to find us?" the Professor asks, his voice low and raspy. He sounds as if he hasn't stopped crying since Jenica died.

Tamryn bites her lower lip, and her gaze snaps back to me. "I swear I didn't know until after you were gone, or I would have told you. You believe me, don't you?"

I can feel everyone staring at me, sense their curiosity and confusion over this exchange. But I have no idea what Tamryn's talking about.

"Whatever it is, just tell us," I reply, trying to understand what's happening. "We've already taken you and your people in. You have nothing to lose, but everything to gain by telling the truth."

"Baron was bragging about it to some of the guys right before Des Moines," she continues, her voice wavering as if she's losing the fight and will start sobbing any moment. "I think he planned to come here next...

Said this hideout would become the ultimate Reject den ... a haven for our people."

Slamming one hand down on the table, Dax rises to his feet, the vein in his neck pulsing. He's slowly losing his grip on patience, and I can't blame him. Tamryn can't know this, but if Baron knew where we were hiding, then my father likely knows.

"Goddamn it, just spit it out," he bellows.

Tamryn gazes at me, her tears finally spilling over, tracking a path through the grime staining her cheeks. "I'm so sorry for what they did to you, Gage... I'm so damn sorry!"

Dax looks like he's going to blow a gasket, but one touch of Blythe's hand on his arm keeps him in check.

"Young lady, drawing this out won't make it any easier," the senator speaks up, crossing her arms over her chest. "We need the information you have, and we need it now."

Swiping at her tears, she nods jerkily, her nose reddening as she looks at me. "They hid it ... with him."

Everyone's looking at me again, their eyes sweeping me from head to toe. Baffled, I wrinkle my brow and shake my head.

"I've been here for weeks, and spent just as much time on the road getting here," I protest. "I think I would have known if they slipped something on me."

Tamryn shakes her head and sniffles. "Not on you, Gage ... *in* you."

My body freezes in shock, my throat suddenly constricting. Blythe gasps, Dax swears under his breath, and the Professor slowly rises to his feet.

"Am I to believe there's a tracking device *inside* of him?" Hinkley asks, his face white as a sheet as he looks me in the eye.

"Yes," Tamryn replies. "They knew he'd eventually find his way back here. They were counting on it."

"How the hell did they get an implant inside of you?" Olivia asks incredulously.

I don't respond, my eyes still locked with the Professor's. He and I are experiencing the same realization. The skin around my surgical scar suddenly feels too tight, the organ in my chest heavy and foreign.

"It's in his chest," Blythe whispers from across the table, horror morphing her features. "Oh my God ... they attached it to the heart."

TWENTY-EIGHT

GAGE BRONSON, MICHELA ARLOTTI, AND BLYTHE SOL
RESTORATION RESISTANCE HEADQUARTERS
FEBRUARY 6, 4011
9:35 A.M.

"GAGE, SLOW DOWN FOR A SECOND, AND LET'S TALK ABOUT THIS," MICHELA PLEADS AS I move around my small room, throwing the bare necessities I'll need for travel into a large pack.

Thankfully, my niece has gone off to the schoolhouse to help tutor some of the little ones in math. I dread having to tell her I need to leave her ... yet again.

Shaking my head, I toss four pairs of my warmest socks into the open bag. "There is nothing to discuss here. My father turned me in to a goddamn homing beacon. Don't you get what that means?"

"That we need to figure out a way to get it out of you?" she ventures.

I pause halfway across the small space, a few rolled-up thermal tops held under one arm. Taking hold of Michela's wrist, I gaze down at her with my jaw clenched.

"It means," I say through clenched teeth, "the MPs could come crashing through our doors at any minute. It means if I stay here, I will be the death of every person inside this citadel."

For a long moment, Michela simply stares at me, not bothering to try to pull away from my hold. I'm not being as gentle as I should, but I need her to understand how dire this situation is. I need to get as far away from Headquarters as I can, as quickly as possible.

"Then I'm coming with you," she declares.

I shake my head. "No. I won't put you at risk, too. I can't leave without knowing someone will be here for Agata."

She draws her eyebrows together, her mouth turning down at the corners. "Agata barely knows me. She's likely going to want to go back to Blythe and Dax once you're gone, and I don't like your odds of survival if you go alone. I'm coming, Gage, and you can't stop me."

Yes, I can. I can physically restrain her, tie her to something. Hell, I could wrap a hand around her throat with just enough pressure for long enough to make her pass out. Then I could run like hell. But those things go against my nature, and my mind rebels at even the thought of hurting her in any way.

"If you leave alone, you will die," she argues. "And I don't know what I'm supposed to do without you."

My face begins to soften, my jaw unwinding as I release her. What the hell am I supposed to say to that? I might not love Michela, but I do care about her, and she has been here for me through my darkest time. Through the loss of both my sister, and Blythe, she has never left my side. She has never called me out for using her as an outlet for my pain.

I'm about to relent when someone knocks on the door. Michela goes to answer it, while I pull the shirts from beneath my arm and shove them down into the bag. It's Blythe I realize when Michela swings the door open, her mouth set in a thin line, her chin raised.

I know that look well. She's about to try to talk me out of it.

"Thank God," Michela grumbles. "Maybe he'll listen to *you*. He's got it in his head that he needs to leave alone."

"There's a chance he might not have to," Blythe replies.

Approaching the door, I stare incredulously at her. "You know as well as I do if Baron knew our location, then my father does, too. I can't stay here."

Blythe shakes her head. "Then it doesn't matter, does it? If he knows where we are, then he's coming. After you left the conference room, Alec and the senator started talking over plans we can implement to prepare for an attack. Running isn't an option with so many people here—out in the open, we're too big a target. At least here, we can hunker down and strategically fight off anyone who comes near us. They're coming ... and nothing can be done about that."

She has a point, but I still can't help the tremendous guilt washing through me at the thought of being the reason our haven is no longer safe.

"And what then?" I argue. "Let's say we fight, but eventually end up having to move. No matter where I go, my father is going to be able to keep tabs on me ... which means he'll always have a way to get to everyone else here ... a way to get to you."

My voice lowers on that last bit, becoming a bit rougher at the thought of my father anywhere near her. Agata, he might have mercy on because she's family. But Blythe ... he'll systematically destroy her, slowly and cruelly, just because he knows I love her.

"The Professor thinks he can remove the device inside you," she declares. "You'd have to come to the infirmary, so he can look inside to see what we're working with here. Then, he could do a procedure on the spot to take it out."

My chest begins to ache, bile rising in my throat at the thought of being cut open again. The memory of the two sides of my cracked sternum rubbing together makes me feel sick. But if it's what I have to endure to make sure my father can't get his hands on the people I care about, then I'll gladly endure it again.

"He's sure he can do it?" I hedge, not wanting to get my hopes up. If it turns out the device can't be removed, then I need to still be prepared to leave.

"You know the Professor," Blythe says. "He wouldn't say he could do it if he thought for one second he couldn't. Just give him a chance."

With a sigh, I run my hands through my hair. I have nothing to lose by giving this a shot, and everything to gain if it turns out I can stay with my people.

"Okay," I relent. "Let me finish pacing my bag. If it turns out that it can't be removed, I'm leaving immediately."

"Fair enough," Blythe replies with a nod. "When you're ready, the Professor will meet you in the infirmary, exam room four."

"Okay," I reply.

She falters in the doorway, fiddling with the fingers of her titanium hand with her human one. Her gaze darts everywhere but at me or Michela. It gives me a moment to study her, to soak her in for just a moment. She looks tired, with dark circles under her eyes and the pull of strain around her mouth. I want to ask her what's wrong—if something is going on with her and Dax, or if she's just worried about what this latest development could mean for the Resistance. But it's none of my business anymore ... as much as it hurts me to have to admit that.

"Well, I'll go now," she says after clearing her throat. "I hope the Professor can help you, Gage."

She leaves without a glance in my direction, pulling some deep-seated part of me with her. My legs are moving after her before my brain can catch up, my heart rate kicking up a notch at the sight of her walking away from me for what feels like the millionth time.

"I'm sorry," I blurt out, halting her in her tracks. When she turns to face me, we almost collide with each other, our noses brushing before she rears back with a sharp inhale. The impact of the near kiss ripples through me. Accidental it might have been, but now my stomach is churning and the overwhelming urge to make it purposeful grips me.

"What?" she murmurs, her voice breathy and strained.

"I'm sorry," I repeat. "You were right about my presence here. You were right to cast the vote to send me away—I see that now. I am and always will be a liability for the Resistance."

She frowns and shakes her head, her somber stare locked with mine. "If you're a liability, then so is Agata. None of us cares about that anymore. You are one of us now... Really, you've always been one of us. Don't apologize for being who you are—to me or anyone."

For some reason, having her forgiveness makes me feel lighter, as if I can accept any of the other repercussions of this if they don't include her being angry with me.

Lost in my own thoughts, I don't realize how long I've stood there until she mumbles a good-bye and then turns to leave. Even then, I can't move or breathe until she's almost out of sight, disappearing around the corner.

Exhaling, I turn to go back to my room, hoping to make quick work of my packing before heading to the infirmary.

When I enter the little chamber, Michela is sitting on the bed beside my pack, hands folded in her lap. She doesn't look up at me at first, but when she does, her eyes are as sad as Blythe's, causing the guilt to rear its ugly head again.

Following my instinct to trail after Blythe, I'd literally forgotten Michela had been in the room. She wasn't stupid enough to have missed it either, and that had to have stung. Apparently, disappointing the women in my life is something I'm becoming good at. Michela and I never really put a label one what we are—whatever this is—but everyone at Headquarters knows what went down between me and Blythe, and how I feel about her … about the whole fucked-up triangle thing she has going on with Dax and me.

Had, I remind myself. She's made her choice, and it wasn't me.

I go back to packing, trying to ignore the tension clogging the air. Relationship drama should be the last thing on my mind right now. The MPs could be gearing up for an invasion, and there's a damn GPS signal being emitted by the same organ that's keeping me alive.

Michela sits in silence while I finish, then stands once I've slung the loaded pack onto my shoulders. I meant what I said about leaving straight from the infirmary if I need to.

I reach out to her, but as she stands, she swats my hand away. She scowls at me, crossing her hands defensively over her chest.

"Let's get something straight here," she says, her tone clipped.

I raise my eyebrows. "Okay."

"I'm not her," she declares, inclining her head. "And I don't want to be."

Shit … I don't need this right now. Yet, I know I owe her this… I will stand here and let her say whatever she needs to say after the callous way I just acted.

"I don't want you to be," I reply.

She nods once, as if happy enough with that. "I understand there's a history that existed before I was in the picture. I also am aware you and I don't have any official labels, and we're basically just fuck buddies."

I frown, even though shame heats the back of neck, because that's exactly how I've been treating her. "Michela, you mean more to me than that."

I just can't love you. I don't need to say it out loud; we both know how true it is.

"Then act like it," she demands, now bracing her hands on her hips. "At least respect me enough not to forget I'm in the goddamn room just because she steps into it!"

Reaching up to cup her face, I sigh, lowering my head to give her a quick kiss. "You're right, okay? I'm a jackass, and I have no excuses. It's just ... it's complicated. You wanted to come here, to be part of the Resistance. This is how things are. Our lives are messy and dirty, and we're all just a little bit screwed up."

She laughs, and I'm relieved. I might not love Michela, but I don't want to hurt her—not even accidentally.

"I like it here," she says, raising up on her tiptoes to press herself against me. "With you."

"If we're lucky, the Professor will make it so I can stay," I reply, kissing her one more time before pulling away. "I have to go meet him now."

"Will you leave without saying good-bye?" she asks.

"Of course not," I reply. "I'll have someone come get you and bring you and Agata to me."

She nods in agreement, and then walks me to the door and out into the hall. We part ways, with me heading for the elevator, and her pausing in front of her door across the hall. She lingers, and I feel her eyes on me as I walk on. The heavy weight of her stare reminds me that she deserves so much better than me.

"THERE IT IS, RIGHT THERE," THE PROFESSOR SAYS A LITTLE WHILE LATER AS HE POINTS to the ultrasound screen. "It's a separate device that's been attached to the bionic heart."

Craning my neck to glance at the image of my mechanical heart on the screen, I find it hard to look away. This is my first look at the organ that was placed in my chest, and I can't help but notice how incredibly lifelike it looks. In the black-and-white image of the ultrasound, it could almost pass for a real heart.

Near the bottom, on the lower left valve, I see a white square with a blinking black dot in the center—the GPS chip.

"You said it's attached, not part of the actual heart, right?" I ask, glancing up at the Professor. "Does that mean it'll be easier to remove?"

He's bent over me with the camera pressed to my chest, his gaze intent upon the screen. Straightening, he pulls the thing away from me and the screen goes dark. Replacing his equipment, he closes the sides of the hospital gown over my chest.

"It definitely makes a quick removal that much easier," he replies. "I'll need to see how it attaches, so I'll know what tools are needed for removal. An imaging scan should give us a closer look. The good news is we won't have to completely crack your chest to get to it. This should be as simple as making a three-inch incision and going in between two ribs."

"Thank God," I mutter, pressing a hand to my old surgical scar. "What's the recovery time like for something that minor?"

"A few days," he informs me, removing his glasses and hanging them in the breast pocket of his lab coat. "You'll be groggy for at least the first day because of the anesthesia, and you'll have pain at the incision site, but nothing too serious."

Sitting up on the exam table, I nod. "Okay ... let's get this done. I want that thing out of me as soon as possible so I can get back into the fight."

"I'll need about twenty minutes to prepare," he says. "Until then, would you like me to send for anyone ... someone you want to see before surgery?"

"Agata," I reply.

The Professor nods. "Right away."

He slips out of the room, and I fall back onto the table, closing my eyes. Relief washes over me at the realization that I won't have to leave. After everything I fought through to get back here, being forced to just walk away would have been a crippling blow. Having to abandon Agata again would have been like ripping out my heart and leaving it behind.

She shows up a few minutes later, escorted by Blythe and Dax. Dressed in her combat practice gear, her hair is damp with sweat. I can see she's been working with Blythe, keeping her busy and distracted. I'm grateful for that.

"Hey, squirt," I say cheerily, sitting up to greet her.

"Uncle Gage, are you okay?" she asks, eyes wide as she takes in my attire—or lack thereof.

I smile and stand to hug her, picking her up and crushing her against my chest. "I'm fine."

And grateful she doesn't seem to know exactly what's going on. She might be smarter than most adults, but in many ways, she's still just a child. I don't want her to be frightened or paranoid because of this.

"It's just a little procedure for my new heart," I say, setting her back onto her feet. "It'll be over in a few minutes, and I'll be good as new."

"Can I stay?" she asks, clinging to my arm. "I won't get in the way, I promise."

I lock eyes with Dax, who gives me a nod to confirm what I already know—he and Blythe will stay with Agata while I undergo this procedure.

"No, squirt," I say, ruffling her messy hair. "But Blythe and Dax are going to sit with you until it's over, okay? And you can come see me after. Yours is the first face I want to see when I wake up."

She grins, revealing a mishmash of baby and adult teeth that never stops being adorable to me. "Okay, I will be."

"Good," I reply.

Dax folds his arms over his chest and gives me a once over with a little smirk. "Nice gown, man."

Smiling back, I shrug. "I thought it made my legs look good."

Blythe snorts, trying to choke back a chuckle, and Agata giggles.

The smiles fade when I ask my next question. "What's the plan? I hear preparations are being made for defense."

I don't mind discussing this in front of Agata. She's been training to fight, and we might even need her if the MPs come banging down our door.

"Alec is sending the drones on wider arcs over the canyon," Dax replies. "That should help us spot them further out, and give us more time to get ready if they come. Then there's the hideaway under the main training facility. It's a big space deeper underground where we can hide the kids and those who can't fight or aren't in the shape to."

"We're also stocking hovercrafts with supplies for travel in the event we have to evacuate in large numbers," Blythe adds solemnly.

I wince at the thought of what mass evacuation would look like. A slaughter, for one. The MPs would pick us off as we ran for our lives. With all the weapons that have been gathered over the past few months, I hope it'll be enough for us to be able to defend our home.

"Hopefully it won't come to that," I reply.

"Hopefully," she agrees.

The Professor returns then, another doctor on his heels. He clears the room, telling Blythe, Dax, and Agata they can wait in recovery room six around the corner from here. Dax wishes me luck, my niece kisses my cheek, and then the three of them leave.

"All right, let's get this over with," I say, climbing back onto the table.

I'm stuck with an IV, then given a sedative. As I lay back on the table and drift off to sleep, my mind turns to mush. Thoughts drift in and out so fast I can hardly hold onto one for more than a moment, then oblivion claims me completely.

When I open my eyes again, there's a nagging ache beneath my left armpit, the pulling of new stitches. My mouth is dry and my vision blurs, but the sweet blue eyes staring back at me are unmistakable.

"Heya, squirt," I croak, reaching out to her, my words slurred from the anesthesia.

She falls against my chest, and I hold her close, ignoring the flare of pain it causes in my side. Blythe and Dax are blurry shapes behind the Professor, who is fiddling with some controls on the panel housing my IV fluids and pain meds. He turns to me and smiles, a soft movement of his mouth with no teeth. It seems to be the best he can do these days.

"The procedure was a success," he informs me. "The GPS chip was destroyed... Your father can no longer find you."

Relief lowers my eyelids, and I let myself start to drift back off, my body relaxing now that my mind understands there's no need to run. I need to be rested up for the fight.

"Thank you," I murmur before falling back under.

TWENTY-NINE

I WAKE THE NEXT MORNING TO FIND TAMRYN SITTING BESIDE MY BED. THE DAY BEFORE, I drifted in and out of consciousness to find various visitors at my side. After Blythe and Dax left with Agata, Michela came and brought me soup from the chow hall. Then came Olivia and Alec, and Dax again with Agata, who'd wanted to say goodnight.

Finding Tamryn seated in the chair next to by bed this way is ironic, considering hers was the first face I saw upon waking up after my initial heart surgery. She tries to smile when our gazes meet, but it's a poor attempt. She still appears as haggard and exhausted as she did yesterday, the dark circles under her eyes and sunken cheeks making her look half-dead. I can't even imagine what all she's been through to get here.

"Hey," she murmurs, scooting a little closer to the bed. "How do you feel?"

Blinking to clear my vision, I take inventory of my various aches and pains. Aside from the soreness still lingering at my incision site, dry mouth, and the after-effects of the anesthesia still making me a bit tired, I feel fine.

"A little like I got stabbed in the ribs," I answer with a dry laugh. "But I feel better than yesterday, and I've been worse off."

She nods. "I know. Gage, I'm so sorry."

I fumble for her hand and squeeze it, shaking my head. "This wasn't your fault. You said you didn't know about the implant, and I believe you."

Lowering her eyes, she sniffs and seems to fight back tears. "I don't

261

just mean that. You tried to warn me about Baron and the Rejects, and I didn't listen. God, I was such a bitch to you."

"Yeah, kinda," I agree. When she glances back at me in shock, I laugh, and then groan at the pain it sends shooting through my side. "Look, we were both doing what we thought was right. When Baron found you, you were scared and being taken in by the MPs. He saved you, then brainwashed you to follow him, like he did with all his other followers. He was good at it … which is why my father chose him."

With a snort, she shakes her head, running a hand through her hair. "Yeah, that Alec guy told me all about it. Showed me the video you made spilling all of Daddy's little secrets. That asshole played us good."

"Not just you guys," I argue. "All of us got screwed. He's been in control from the beginning. And I know fighting him seems impossible—even stupid sometimes—but it's what we do. It's all we can do. The alternative is to lay down and accept it … accept death."

"I'm just grateful Senator Davis and the others have agreed to let us stay," she says. "After you left yesterday, they asked me to take a polygraph … me and the rest of the girls who helped get us here. We did it gladly … not like we can blame you guys for the mistrust."

"I take it you passed, and it was decided you guys aren't a threat?" I asked.

She nods. "The injured are being cared for, and they've set us up in the last few available beds. A few of us are having to lay on bedrolls on the floor, but it's better than what we've been doing."

The burning question I've been holding back falls off my tongue now, unrestrained. "What *have* you been doing, Tamryn? How did you survive?"

"We ran," she whispers, her eyes growing haunted. "Until there could be no more running. When we came across MPs, it was kill or be dragged in. So we killed … and we weren't always merciful about it. We ate through our supplies, and when those ran out, we had to scavenge." She pauses, covering her mouth with one hand and shuddering, a tear spilling down one cheek. "There were a few nights we … we had to catch and kill rats … dogs. Anything was better than starving. Ten women died along the way of starvation alone. Five others were taken or killed by MPs."

My chest aches for the girl I once thought I'd spend the rest of my life with. Our relationship during our high school years had been comfortable, a lot like the lives we led. Pampered, sheltered, rich ... privileged. I don't know about Tamryn, but I never saw a future like this one in the cards for us.

I struggle to sit up as she begins to sob, burying her face in her hands. Sweat breaks out over my brow and my ribs are throbbing, but I ignore all that as I throw my legs over the side of the bed. Reaching out to grab her, I pull her toward me. She comes without a fight, sitting on the bed on my good side and leaning in. I wrap an arm around her, holding her tight as shivers and sobs wrack her rail-thin body.

"It's okay," I croon, rocking her in a soothing motion. "You did what you had to do, Tam. You survived, and you made it here. I'm so damn proud of you. I always thought you were strong, but now ... you're one of the toughest chicks I know, and you're a survivor. Someday, this is all going to be over, and you'll be proud of yourself, too—for fighting, for seeing it through to the end, for not giving up."

Fixing me with a tearful stare, she sniffs, swiping at her eyes with the sleeve of her sweater. "Do you really think that'll happen? You think we can end this thing?"

"Of course I do," I reply with a reassuring smile. "Otherwise, what are we fighting for? And if nothing else, you saved all those women ... all those sick and injured people."

She leans back against me, seeming to take comfort in that. We sit together for a while, her continuing to cry on my shoulder, letting me take on all her fear and sadness. Eventually, she grows silent and still, a few sniffles coming here and there as she calms completely.

Sitting up with a sigh, she dries the last of her tears and takes a deep breath. "Okay, enough about that. I don't think I can take anymore crying."

"Okay, let's talk about something else," I agree.

She gives me a sly look and wiggles her eyebrows. "So ... you and Michela, huh? I thought you were with Blythe, but I hear she dumped you for the hot black guy."

I scowl, shifting my body so I can lie back against the pillows again. "Here less than twenty-four hours and you already know all the gossip. And for your information, she didn't dump me... She thought I was dead."

"News travels fast around here, and people talk," she replies, turning to sit facing me, her slender hip against my leg. "They talk about you three *a lot.*"

"I'm used to being talked about," I hedge, not wanting to know the details of what people are saying. What went on between the three of us is none of their business.

"Of course you are," she agrees. "President's son ... prep-school jock, golden boy ... The Patriot."

"Once this is all over, I look forward to a long life of being absolutely nobody to anyone," I grumble.

She inclines her head and gives me a confused look. "Really? You won't even consider getting involved in politics or activism—even after all you've been through?"

I shrug. "I'm tired, Tamryn. I can't even think past the next fight. Besides, being a politician is what my dad wanted for me. It isn't what I wanted."

"True," she agrees. "But imagine becoming one anyway ... but becoming an honest one ... a *good* one. A better one than he'll ever be. He doesn't win then, Gage ... you do."

She might be right, but I can't think about that now, not when our most pressing concern is the here and now. One thing I do know—The Patriot was and still is a freedom fighter. I speak out of weariness now, but I can't imagine a future in which I am not still a patriot in some form. Art is still my passion, but being a part of this fight has taught me that our passions and our destinies do not always align. For better or worse, my lot is thrown in with the Resistance ... until death, if need be.

I'M OUT OF BED THE DAY AFTER TAMRYN'S VISIT, ACCEPTING PAIN MEDS FROM THE Professor and leaping right into the fray. All available hovercrafts have been loaded with supplies, while every vehicle, down to the handful of hover bikes we own, have been fueled up. Dax leads a team out to the canyon, dressed in the desert camouflage suits and antigravity climbing gear. They place stronger explosives than the ones wet set up before, turning the entire canyon into a death trap. Alec has warned us that blowing them all will take out most of the canyon, the resulting collapse of the rock structures sealing off the entrance to Headquarters. As that entrance is the only way in or out, it means whoever is inside when we blow it will be sealed inside... The citadel itself might even collapse.

This makes the bombs our final resort—the trigger only being pulled if we end up having to run for our lives. Four pilots have been assigned to different hovercrafts in the event of a mass exodus, Blythe being one of them. I make a note to remember that she will be responsible for piloting *Icarus* should we have to flee. I would want to go wherever she and Dax are going.

Every available fighter is called in, and we are given our marching orders in the event of an attack. A schematic of the citadel on one of the Professor's large flat-panel screens shows us a color-coded map of where we are each supposed to be, armed and ready to defend our home.

The children are drilled over and over, their assigned protection working with them until they're able to make their way to the underground hiding space in a quick and orderly fashion. Agata is the only one treated differently. Her place will be by my side in case we need her for an EMP signal. It's risky, but the Professor worked with several of his lab techs to create miniature body armor for her. There aren't enough supplies for everyone to have armor here, but between the titanium vest and accompanying pieces, plus Agata's special helmet, she will be safe from any physical danger. She also has me as a literal human shield.

My niece doesn't seem very afraid of the possible pending attacks, which shouldn't surprise me. Training with Blythe has prepared her for every contingency, and she seems more resigned than anything else.

We've discussed the possibility of her having to fight for her life—to kill if necessary.

"If we don't fight, they'll kill us like they killed Mommy," she says in that sweet voice of hers. "I don't want to die, and I don't want you to die. So if we have to fight..."

"Yes, sweetheart," I say when she trails off. "We no longer have a choice."

She nods resolutely. "Then that's what we'll do."

The park is full of people each day, training and working to hone their skills. Even Tamryn and some of the women who arrived with her join in—eating like horses to try to gain some weight back in the chow hall, then going hard in the gym and at the range to prepare. Everyone seems aware of our dire situation, and that the MPs might have just been led right to our front door.

I try not to let guilt over being the reason our hideout is no longer a secret get to me. I'd been so desperate to get back to the place I've come to think of as home that I never stopped to ponder the lengths my father would go through to bring down the Resistance. No matter how many people try to reassure me, or tell me it isn't my fault, I lie awake at night with an unease sitting in my belly. Paranoia has me wanting to tear at my own skin, to pry into my joints and search for more hidden chips. The Professor has assured me three times now that nothing is there, but I can't help the sensation of my skin crawling, the feeling of being violated in some way one I find hard to forget.

As I think of Headquarters being destroyed—of the people I think of as my family decimated, forced to go into hiding—I also can't help but wish Blythe had succeeded in her mission in D.C. I wish that laser had hit its target. Maybe then, I would be able to sleep at night, hoping that perhaps my father's demise would mean the destruction of everything he has built.

I now understand why she was foolish enough to run off on her own and try to take him down, because aside from my worries over what's coming next, my only other thoughts are of his death. Of being the one to stand over his bloody, bruised body and pulling the trigger myself. Not just for me, but for every person I cared about who he's ever hurt. For Jenica and Sayer Strom. For Yasmine. For Blythe and Dax. For my sister.

It doesn't help that when we aren't prepping or training, we are gathered in the common room and dining hall around the television watching the news. His face is beamed through every airway, his lies and propaganda spewing like fetid garbage. Videos of people protesting and countering the Military Police end in bloodshed. Bionics are flushed out of hiding and executed, many of them shot right where they're found. The 'discovery' of more nuclear weapons caches allegedly in the hands of the Resistance is broadcasted far and wide, more justification for the president's guerilla tactics against us. But we are too busy preparing to defend our home to even think about what's being said about us on the media.

A few days after I leave the infirmary, Alec Kinnear approaches me, pulling me away from the common room where everyone's gathered around the television. His grave expression is sobering, and as he glances around to make sure we're out of earshot, I wonder what could be the matter.

"Everything okay?" I ask as he digs around in his pocket before coming out with a small cartridge.

"I need you to take this," he declares, dropping it into my hand.

It's a storage device, I realize, for information. It's got 'Plan B' printed on its side.

"Okay," I say slowly, wrinkling my brow as I glance from it up to him. "What is it?"

"Plan B," he says, looking at me like I'm an idiot.

"You don't say?" I drawl.

"Look," he whispers, stepping closer to me and dropping his voice. "In the event of an attack, there is information on there to back up everything you said in that video. Files, data, names and dates ... it's enough evidence to convict Drummond, along with everyone who had a hand in Project BioCrisis."

My stomach lurches, and my chest squeezes painfully as hope takes root once again. "How did you get all of this?"

"After we got your video, I started digging," he says. "It took a lot of time, and I had to be careful to cover my digital tracks... If I weren't already part of the Resistance, I could get life in prison for the databases I hacked to get all this."

I nod. "Okay, and what exactly am I supposed to do with it?"

"I've got an old Army buddy... Well, actually he was one of my superiors, an officer from my unit. If he receives this, I trust him to get it into the right hands. It has to be him—no one else. We can't even risk sending it to the media or broadcasting it online, or it can be shot down as just some conspiracy theory. This is everything we need to end Drummond, and we have it to get into the hands of someone who will ensure it gets investigated. His contact information is written on the back."

Turning the device over, I see a Washington D.C. address, along with an email address for a Captain Rourke.

Understanding the severity of what he just handed me, I shake my head in disbelief. "Why are you giving this to me?"

"Because you're a fucking survivor," he replies with conviction. "And because I have a copy, but I need someone else to have the backup, just in case..."

"Just in case you die," I fill in when he trails off. "You think they're going to attack."

He sighs. "I don't think they will; I *know* they will. I also know if your heart stops, you'll pop up like a goddamn daisy if someone gets to you with some blood or a defibrillator fast enough. I figure you're the best person to give it to."

Nodding, I close my fist around it and put it in my pocket. In my room, there's a silver ball chain necklace meant for dog tags. I intend to hang this device from it, and keep it on my person at all times.

"I've got it," I say, clapping him on the shoulder. "But for what it's worth, if a fight goes down, I think you've got a good a chance as anybody at survival."

Running a hand over his buzz-cut hair, he starts walking away. "Even if I were a betting man, I wouldn't take those odds, Bronson," he throws over his shoulder before disappearing.

His words strike me as true, but I still want to hold on to my hope. I want to believe we can all survive this thing. I want to believe Alec or I have a chance of delivering this evidence to Captain Rourke, and that it will tear down everything my father ever built. But as Alec pointed out, the odds aren't really in our favor.

That doesn't mean I won't fight until my last breath to try to make it happen.

THIRTY

A FEW DAYS LATER, I VISIT THE INFIRMARY FOR AN APPOINTMENT WITH ONE OF THE doctors who works under the Professor. After taking a bullet to the shoulder and being cut open for surgery, there are some concerns about infection and loss of mobility. While I've still got some soreness in my ribs and stiffness in my shoulder, I feel mostly as good as new. Still, I don't want to take any chances, so after a full day of helping with attack preparations, I hustle my ass over to the infirmary and head for my assigned exam room.

I spot Blythe and Dax in the hallway, heading toward a room across the hall from mine. Pausing near the door, I glance over at them.

"Hey, everything okay?"

Dax frowns at the sight of me—something I thought we were past, but apparently not—while Blythe lowers her gaze and looks as if she wants to sink into a hole in the floor and die.

Weird.

"Fine," Dax replies after clearing his throat. "Blythe hurt her wrist while working with the trainees today. We just want the Professor to look at it … make sure it's not broken."

We. Hearing him refer to them as a unit still stings, but I find seeing them together is starting to hurt less and less. It's clear she loves him— even if she also loves me—and I can't bring myself to get in the way of that if she's happy.

"Okay," I reply. "Hope it gets better."

Then, I push the door open to my own exam room, putting the awkward encounter behind me. The man who's waiting to inspect me—Dr. Wagner—greets me with a warm smile and prompts me to take my shirt off so he can get a look at my surgical incision first.

Tossing my thermal aside, I sink onto the exam table and lift my arm, so he can peel the bandage away and get a good look.

"Very nice," he murmurs, leaning in to get a closer look at my sutures. "I can see the incision is healing up well. The stitches should dissolve soon. Too bad we don't have a fully stocked facility here... the instant sealants are really so convenient."

It really would be easier for everyone involved if the Resistance had the kind of equipment used in the best hospitals across the country. But even as well-supplied as the Resistance is, we are still working with limited technology.

"I don't mind the sutures," I reply. "They itch a little, but it's tolerable."

"Hmm, good," Dr. Wagner mumbles, inspecting the bandage he'd just removed. "No oozing, pus, or blood... Very nice. No swelling. Let's keep it covered a little longer to protect it from being aggravated by your clothing. Come see me again in about a week, and we should be ready to get those stitches out."

"Sounds like a plan," I reply as he tapes a fresh bandage over the incision.

Tossing aside the old one, he removes his gloves, then starts inspecting my shoulder. A puckered circle where the bullet went in is still a bit tender to the touch, and I wince when he presses against it.

"Still feeling some pain?" he asks.

"Yeah," I grunt as he goes on prodding, then starts rotating my arm in different directions. "Mostly in the morning when I first wake up."

"Some stiffness is to be expected," the doctor says with a nod. "But the wound itself healed nicely, and as soon as your surgical scar has mended, you can begin light exercise to start rebuilding strength in the shoulder. Ease in to it... Don't push too hard, or you risk injuring yourself."

Releasing a sigh of relief once he stops torturing my shoulder, I nod.

"Sure, Doc. Light exercise ... got it."

"Now, I can also give you—"

The rest of his words are muffled by the sudden blare of an alarm. The loud noise throws me to my feet, my heart hammering as the overhead lights go dark, and white flashing ones begin pulsing in tandem with the alarm.

Dr. Wagner trembles, his eyes wide as they connect with mine. Now that I know about the alarm system and various warnings, there is no mistaking what we're facing here.

Code Black.

Reaching for my shirt, I pull it on and march toward the door, pulling it open. Doors open up and down the hallway, confused glances filling my vision as I glance in one direction, then the other. The siren is even louder in the hallway, the flashing lights causing tendrils of dread to coil in my stomach.

On the other side of the corridor, Dax barrels through the door with Blythe hot on his heels. Her head swivels to take in all that's happening. She's wearing nothing but a thin hospital gown, which confuses me considering she was only here to get her wrist examined.

But then, the sirens keep blaring and the lights keep flashing, and there's no time to wonder.

"Code Black!" Dax shouts, cupping his hands around his mouth to help his voice carry. "Evacuation protocol... Let's go, everybody, move!"

At the commanding tone of his deep, booming voice, the confusion in the hallway dissipates and everyone springs into action. Blythe darts back into the room—I assume to put on her clothes. I turn to Dr. Wagner, who's removing his lab coat and calmly pulling a leather medical bag from a cabinet.

"There are people on this floor who need to be evacuated, but can't walk on their own," he informs me. "The staff and I will get them to the hiding spot."

I nod. "As quickly as you can."

Then, I run from the room, my boots squeaking over the tiles. Dax is waving people toward the stairs, shouting for only people who can't walk or navigate stairs to use the elevator. A door swings open in front of me, and Tamryn appears, pushing one of her former Reject friends on a gurney.

"Gage!" she cries out, falling in step with me on the way toward the elevator and door to the stairs. "Do you know what's going on?"

"No clue!" I shout to be heard over the alarm. "Code Black means we're under attack. What's your zone?"

"Protecting the kids and the injured in the hideaway—zone four," she replies, out of breath as she slows near the elevator.

The doors slide closed, taking a full load of people in wheelchairs and on crutches down. Running a hand through my hair, I step aside just as a handful of lab techs and nurses come barreling past me for the stairs.

"Find your weapon, grab a COMM, and get this woman down to the hideaway," I tell her.

Before I can run off, she grabs my sleeve. Her eyes are wide as I turn back to look at her, her chin trembling.

"Be careful," she says.

I only have time to nod in response before rushing through the door of the stairwell, hot on the heels of Dax and Blythe, who squeezed through right before me.

"Where's Agata?" Blythe asks as we trot down the stairs.

The steel doors above us muffle the sound of the alarm, making it easier for me to hear her.

"With Michela," I reply. "They know what to do."

And as we burst through the stairwell door and dash for the building's entrance, I pray Michela and Agata have done what we went over countless times before this day. In the event of a Code Black, the two of them are to go to our room and equip Agata with her helmet and body armor before meeting me in the hangar—my defense zone for the attack. My weapons are already stored there, so I don't bother stopping by Hexley Hall.

I blow past Dax and Blythe as we run across the green, my bionic heart really kicking into high gear with so much open space in front of me. All around us, people scramble to get to their hiding spaces or battle stations, and pride lifts my chin as I realize no one is panicking or losing their shit. We've trained for this. We've prepared for this. We are ready.

Glancing over my shoulder, I spot Tamryn among those headed for the training building, relief sweeping through me that she'll be safe. She might know how to handle a gun now, but she's never been a fighter.

We reach the hangar and find it already half-full of the other soldiers assigned to this station. Only the strongest of us have been placed here—the first line of defense guarding the only entrance to our hideout. Our weapons are lined up in neat rows waiting for us to come claim them. I crouch to start strapping on my holsters, then quickly slip my guns into them. Picking up my knife, I hook it into a leather sheath on my belt.

Turning to look around, I find Blythe and Dax nearby, also armed to the teeth. Laura is a few feet away, her face hard and her movements efficient as she gears up. Soldiers are falling in line, and no one talks as we all face the sealed door of the hovercraft tunnel.

"All right, people, it's time!" Alec booms as he enters the hangar, drawing all our gazes to him.

He's dressed in old Army gear and combat boots, twin ARX shotguns resting in a double holster strapped over his shoulders, a CBX pistol sits at his hip. Olivia is at his side, a set of knives slid into a row of holsters attached to the leather vest she's wearing, and a handgun attached to her ankle.

"The drones spotted a unit of Military Police heading down the canyon," he continues as he strides toward the hatch, hands balled into fists at his sides, Olivia flanking him. "Our goal is to intercept them before they get a chance to breach the tunnel. Keeping them out is our best bet for survival, and the only way we can protect those people hiding underground in there. Where's my little EMP?"

"Right here," Michela calls out, shouldering her way through the growing mass of soldiers, one hand holding tight to Agata.

I smile and crouch down as Agata rushes toward me, her body covered in the titanium plate armor, the helmet held beneath one arm. I crush her in my arms for a moment, then set her back from me. Taking the helmet, I put it on over her pigtails and smile.

"Ready, squirt?"

She points at the small, low-caliber CBX attached her hip and grins. "Ready."

The little gun is probably equal to a .22 if compared to a weapon that shoots bullets. It won't hurt her with a harsh kickback, but it will hurt or kill anyone who gets too close to her—which I don't intend to allow to happen.

"Bronson, you remember the plan?"

Glancing over at the row of hover bikes fueled up and waiting in front of the hatch, I nod. "Stop the MP crafts at all costs."

"If we let them fly those things in here, we're dead," he replies. "I'm counting on you... You too, little EMP."

"I won't let you down," Agata reassures him with an adult-level of seriousness that brings a smile to my face.

Alec's COMM device goes off, and he answers it. Wes Graydon's voice comes over the line—the guy responsible for guarding the senator as the two of them monitor drone and camera feeds from the main control room.

"The MPs are within range," Wes calls out from the other side. *"I repeat, the MPs are within range."*

"Copy, Graydon," Alec replies before turning to me. "Go give 'em hell."

Grabbing Agata's hand, I stride toward the hover bikes, calling out over my shoulder, "Sky soldiers, move out!"

As I help Agata onto the seat, ten other armed fighters step forward and join me in mounting up. Laura is among them, a wide grin on her face as she straddles the bike next to mine and Agata's.

"Been a while since I took one of these babies for a spin," she quips. "But you know what they say about riding a bike."

"What? That it's a lot like fucking?" someone says from her other side.

"Shut your trap, there's a fucking kid here," she admonishes the guy with a shake of her head.

Agata giggles while I climb on behind her, and I chuckle. "Considering the circumstances, a little bad language is no big deal," I say.

"In that case, let's go fuck some shit up, little girl," Laura says, giving Agata a wink.

Someone opens the tunnel hatch, and while the heavy doors slide open, I arrange myself so my big body is enveloping most of Agata's. With my legs on either side of hers, my arms enfolding her to hold the handlebars, and her head against my chest, she's pretty safe from any gunfire. The phalanx of bikes surrounding us as we ascend and enter the tunnel will take care of the rest.

Our mission is simple: protect Agata while we get her in range to take out any MP crafts with her EMP range. If we force the MPs to come down the tunnel on foot, picking them off will be like shooting fish in a barrel … or rather, in a tunnel.

The drone of the engines echoes down the shaft as the end comes into sight. A moment later, the second hatch begins to slide open, revealing the red-orange walls of the canyon and the massive lead hovercraft at the front of the MP's formation.

"Okay, squirt, get ready!" I bellow, wrapping one arm around her waist while guiding the bike with one hand.

I give her a reassuring squeeze, then reach for the gun at my hip. The others follow suit, drawing their weapons as we near the first hovercraft.

Laser fire comes at us from the craft's guns, but we swivel and zigzag in our flight patterns, dodging it easily. We return fire, aiming for the craft's windows and the officers sticking their heads out of the side hatches to try to take aim at us.

As we draw close enough for me to see the pilot and his gunners at the helm, we all pull up, flying over the top of the hovercraft.

"Now, Agata!" I cry out, pointing my gun downward to shoot at the MPs sticking out of the top turrets.

As one of my lasers hits and drops a guy back into his hole, a shudder seems to vibrate the very air around us. In a heartbeat, the first craft is going down.

Whoops and cheers go up from our formation at the grating sound the first craft makes as it hits the ground and slides forward a few feet before stopping.

From this height, I can see the caravan of MP crafts, four more vehicles following this one. I estimate they're carrying almost a thousand officers total. A number we match a few times over now that we've taken in so many refugees. But with their technology, we are seriously outgunned.

"Let's go, squirt ... number two, you can do it!"

The bikes keep us blocked from laser fire while Agata concentrates on the second craft. It goes down just like the first, and we move on down the line. Three. Four. Five. They all go down, kicking up dust as they scrape the desert floor, a few of them even crashing into each other as they skid to a halt. With their engines and weapons systems down, they have no choice but to come at us on foot.

I raise my hand in the signal to return, and we swoop back around as one, putting our throttles at full speed as we begin the short ride back down the canyon. Below us, the MPs are piling out of the first hovercraft and beginning to form up, weapons ready. Every fiber of my being yearns to point my gun at them and start pulling the trigger as we fly over them. But it isn't our way to strike first. Even when they try to destroy our home and kill us, we take the defensive position. Besides, if I fire first, it could set them all off, and they'd easily shoot us down.

Instead, I speed up, the others keeping pace with me as we zip back through the tunnel hatch. Despite our cheers and celebration out there, we are silent as we travel back in, knowing we've only won a small toehold in what's going to be a long fight.

The hangar comes into sight, and I spot the other soldiers—hundreds of them ready to do battle with the MPs who will soon approach the tunnel.

Alec rushes forward to meet us as we land and begin to dismount. "Well?"

"Five crafts stuffed to the brim with officers," I inform him. "All of them grounded."

Alec whoops, and a cheer goes up from the formation. Dax rushes forward and snatches Agata off the bike, spinning her in circles and kissing her forehead.

"That's my little badass," he says affectionately.

She basks in the attention for a moment, before I hustle her toward one of our hovercrafts, which sits waiting to be filled in case we need to make a run for it.

"Get in and stay out of sight," I command, pointing toward the lowered gangplank. "If we need you again, I'll come for you, but until then, stay put. And if anyone who isn't with us comes onto this craft, shoot them in the face."

She nods and draws her little gun, running up the gangplank and disappearing inside. Pulling both my handguns, I run to the front of the formation, where Alec, Blythe, Laura, and Olivia stand, facing the tunnel.

"They murdered one of our leaders and have stolen our freedom," Alec calls out, his voice echoing through the hangar. "They force us to hide underground and kill us without cause. We've fought back every other way we know how ... now it's time to go for the jugular, to fight to kill. You got it?"

A collective roar rings out from us, rippling through the hangar and the tunnel beyond.

"They will not take prisoners!" Blythe adds, turning to look at everyone. "They will kill us, and then go after the innocents hidden below. Are you going to let them?"

"*No*," the hoard cries out, interspersed with additional cries of '*Fuck no!*'

"Then let's go fuck 'em up!" Dax yells, pointing the barrel of his shotgun at the tunnel.

Then, we are moving, converging on the tunnel and racing through the opening, five abreast. The grunts and pants of our exertions mingle with our boots beating over the steel floor, while outside, the marching of the MPs offers a responding drum beat.

The sunlit opening of the other end looms in front of us, and I raise my guns while Alec does the same on my left and Dax follows suit on my right. As we break out of the darkness and into the light, we open fire as one.

THIRTY-ONE

GAGE BRONSON, BLYTHE SOL, DAX JANNER, ALEC KINNEAR, OLIVIA
MCNABB, AND LAURA ROSENBERG
RESTORATION RESISTANCE HEADQUARTERS
FEBRUARY 10, 4011
7:00 P.M.

DUST FLIES UP FROM THE GROUND BENEATH HUNDREDS OF POUNDING FEET, MAKING MY eyes water and sting. But I blink away the moisture and focus on the officers within my sights. My fingers slam back on the triggers of my handguns at a steady rhythm, the one in my right firing first, then resting while I blast the second. It's hard to get a kill shot on an MP wearing full body armor, but it's not impossible.

The gap between their helmets and armor is the perfect target for a kill—the shoulder and knee joints as well. I move as if on autopilot, my body operating from muscle memory, my mind disengaged. An officer barrels toward me, and I smash his face shield in with the butt of my gun. As he falls back, stunned from the blow, I fire my other pistol right through the opening, throwing him to this back. Another grabs me from behind, and I drop to one knee, grabbing his arm and throwing him over my shoulder. His body hits the ground, kicking up even more dust. Lifting my foot, I smash his face in with it, his helmet and skull both giving way under the force of my heavy boots.

The sun beats down on us. Despite the chill in the air I felt earlier, I'm drenched with sweat, the press of too many bodies within the canyon causing the air to grow stifling.

Around me, soldiers of the Resistance fight—Dax alternating shots from his weapon with kicks from his titanium legs, barreling down anyone in his path; Alec double-palming his guns like me and firing without hesitation or mercy; Laura laughing as the officers try to take her hand to hand and discover she's a force to be reckoned with; Olivia darting at the speed of an eye's blink, her sharp knives drawing blood as she swipes them at throats and vulnerable joints.

Alec screams something into his COMM. A moment later, scores of our soldiers start climbing up the side of the canyon, the antigravity gear helping them adhere to the rock. Blythe is among them, her sniper rifle snapped to her back. Gunfire arcs upward toward them, and one soldier falls to his death.

Bodies litter the canyon—theirs and ours—blood mixing with the dirt. I point my gun at a man leveling his weapon up toward the climbers, and take him out before turning to defend myself from a guy coming at me from the left.

The MPs mostly have their face shields up, confronting us with the smooth, black fiberglass. Faceless, nameless, they show us nothing about them other than the fact that they want us dead.

Gunshots begin raining from above as Blythe and the other climbers start shooting from their new positions. More bodies fall, blood splattering everywhere. It coats my hands, my face, my clothing. But one thought of Agata hiding in the hovercraft renews my strength and purpose, and I know I cannot stop fighting until they are all dead.

We're beating them back, trampling over the bodies of the dead to push them toward the disabled hovercrafts. It is hard to believe, but we're actually gaining ground.

We compress in on them, our numbers quickly growing to match theirs—soon, we will outnumber them. Dax is on my left, Alec on my right, with Olivia and Laura completing our line. We fire without mercy, grunting, screaming, and roaring like savages, letting them taste every bit of the rage, fear, and pain we've experienced in the past few years.

And then, shockingly, the MPs begin to retreat, turning to run back the way they came, abandoning their vehicles in favor of getting out of the canyon. We pursue them, shooting them in the backs, taking down more of them in waves. They begin disappearing behind their destroyed hovercrafts, leaking out into the desert and leaving us, and our home, behind.

Instead of pursuing, we stop where we stand and watch them go. Then, we lower our weapons and wait for what might be coming next. From above, a few of the snipers are still picking officers off at a distance, while the others are gazing down at those of us at the front of the group as if to await instruction.

Alec holds his COMM up to his mouth and phones Wes. "Graydon, what do you see?"

"Nothing but a bunch of pussies, running scared," Wes replies a moment later. *"The drones are following, but they're literally running for their lives."*

Those close enough to have heard Wes send up a cheer, but Alec puts a pin in that.

"Don't get cocky," he says, sliding his pistol back into his holster. "You can bet your ass they didn't run away to stay away. They retreated in order to regroup. They'll be back."

The crowd parts for him as he begins heading back toward the tunnel, stepping over bodies and telling Wes to keep his eyes on the drone feed and report any movement. Glancing at the piles of corpses clogging the canyon, I cringe.

"We should probably move these bodies against the canyon walls," I say, kicking at an MP with my boot. "Clear the path."

"And make it easier for those assholes to march back up to our doors?" Olivia gripes.

"And prevent one of us from tripping over corpses and busting our faces open on the hard ground," Dax retorts, giving her a sharp look. "He's right. Everyone, pitch in."

We work quickly, trying not to examine our own losses too closely, although we do separate them since it is easy to tell the MPs in their armor from our people. Now isn't the time to mourn—not when the battle has only just begun. We efficiently stack the bodies of the MPs on one side of the canyon, clearing a path as far back as the stalled hovercrafts. Our dead soldiers are treated with more reverence, lined away from the MPs. Once this is over, hopefully we can come out here and find some way to honor our own.

The climbers come down off the ridge, and everyone goes back in through the tunnel. It closes behind us with a loud clang, sealing us in for the time being. Once inside the hangar, we find several crates of MREs have been opened, with canteens of water being passed around.

I happily accept one from Michela, who seems to have volunteered to hand them out. She hasn't fought yet—her group being responsible for the zones comprising the green stretch of grass in the middle of the citadel.

She frowns and reaches up toward my face. I wince when her fingers touch a scrape on my jaw I hadn't even realized was there.

"How are you holding up?" she asks. "How's your shoulder?"

"I'm trying not to think about it," I tell her, accepting a canteen and taking a huge gulp before passing it on to someone else. "When the adrenaline kicks in, I don't feel it, but it hurts like a bitch right now."

"Keep your head down out there," she says before I move on and let someone else approach to get their ration.

Agata is among those helping to hand out rations. When I check on her, she assures me she's already eaten and doesn't need to rest. So I leave her to it, proud of her for wanting to help. I find my friends grouped together, sitting against the wall near the parked hover bikes.

Wedging myself between Blythe and Laura, I sit and open my dinner. It's spaghetti and meatballs, and after going most of the afternoon and evening without eating, it smells like heaven.

We sit in a row and eat in silence for a while, passing a canteen of water back and forth—Laura on one end, then me, Blythe, Dax on her other side, then Olivia and Alec capping the other end.

"Do you think they'll be back tonight?" Blythe asks once we've stopped stuffing our faces long enough to breathe.

"Maybe, but not likely," Alec replies, leaning forward to look at us from his end of the row. "Makes more sense for them to attack when it's daylight

... but we'll hold our positions just in case. Wes and the senator will take turns watching the drone feeds, and will sound the alarm when it's go time again. In the meantime, I suggest everyone sleep if they can. This is far from over."

"What about the others?" Laura asks. "The ones hiding below, and the ones holding the other zones."

"They'll stay put, too," Alec says between bites of his own dinner. "They've got MREs, water, and bedrolls to sleep on... They'll be fine."

Silence falls again, and I polish off my spaghetti with a sigh, feeling much better now that I've filled my stomach and am no longer dehydrated. I lean my head back against the wall, willing my body to come down from the high caused by an excess of adrenaline.

"Do you think we're gonna die?" Olivia asks.

Dax snorts. "Probably."

"We should say stuff to each other," she suggests. "You know, whatever we need to say just in case one of us kicks the bucket."

Alec groans. "Baby, why you gotta be so morbid?"

"I'm just saying," she defends. "When someone you care about dies, you regret all those things you didn't say, right?"

She's right, of course, but we all fall silent, no one wanting to go first. Glancing around, Dax raises his eyebrows.

"No one? Fine, I guess I'll go first." He pauses before trading glances with Blythe. She gives him an encouraging smile, and he continues. "No one knows this but Blythe, but I used to sell drugs. As a matter of fact, it's what I was doing when the nukes hit, and I got buried under that semi-truck."

Shock ripples through me as I study him. Dax is rough around the edges, but I never would have pegged him for a drug dealer.

"Whatever," Laura says with a chuckle. "Heroine's legal in every state... Hell, so is coke."

"Which is why the Feds would have strung me up by my balls if they had caught me," he replies. "They didn't like it when we sold cheaper, synthetic versions of their products."

Alec leans forward now, glancing down at Dax. "I wanna hear about you getting destroyed from the waist down by a fucking truck, dude. Tell me ... did it fuck up *everything* below the belt? I mean ... can you still ... you know?"

Dax smirks. "Why don't you ask your girl?"

Blythe chokes on her last bite of food, while Olivia burst out laughing. Alec's face reddens as Laura teases him for putting his foot in his mouth and forgetting Dax and Olivia used to be an item.

"It works," Olivia says with a wink. "It works well... Blythe knows what I'm talking about."

Blythe lowers her eyes and shakes her head, a tiny smile pulling at the corners of her mouth. The moment is so lighthearted I don't even have it in me to get riled up over the reminder that Dax has had her in all the ways I once did.

"Gage, the first time I saw you, I wanted to mount you," Olivia says, shooting me a wicked glance. "I didn't, and I want to apologize for depriving you of the experience."

Laughter breaks out again, and I give Alec a sheepish smile. He's so red in the face I'm surprised he doesn't burst.

"Maybe in another life," I joke with a wink.

Olivia wraps her arms around Alec's neck. "I'm all yours, you loser ... forever."

He gives her a grudging kiss and grunts. "Fucking right you are."

Laura clears her throat, and we turn to look at her. Her face reddens. "I'm gay."

Silence falls over us again, and we exchange glances before replying in unison, "We know!"

She frowns. "Really?"

I nudge her with my elbow. "Only an idiot would see the parade of girls coming in and out of your dorm room and not draw that conclusion."

Laura laughs and lowers her head. "I always thought I was so discreet."

"Please," Olivia quips. "The only person around here who's a bigger slut than me is you."

"Hey!" Dax interjects. "I'm the resident man whore around here. Don't take that away from me."

"You're retired," Blythe reminds him, jabbing him in the side with her titanium hand. "At least, you better be."

"For you, I hung up my player hat for good," he murmurs, leaning in close to kiss her.

I glance away, giving them their moment. We go on this way for a while, our so-called secrets turning into fodder for jokes and ridicule. As it goes on, I notice Blythe falls silent, her head leaning against the wall, eyes closed. Resting my head beside hers, I reach out and take her human hand.

She flinches in surprise, opening her eyes, but then calms when she looks over and locks gazes with me. We sit there for what feels like forever, staring at each other. I stare at her so hard and for so long I discover new shades of brown within the dark depths of her eyes, amber hidden among the chocolate irises. Her bionic eye is almost a perfect match, only discernible if you stare hard enough and notice the machinery whirring in the pupil.

She interlaces our fingers with a shy smile. I smile back, and get my last words off my chest ... the only thing I need her to know if I die.

"I still love you," I whisper, my voice muffled by the laughter around us and heard only by her.

Moisture wells up in her human eye, but she blinks it away.

"I know," she whispers. "Me too."

A peace settles over me then, and I release her hand, content to sit and listen to the others rag on each other. We've had so few moments like this lately, and it's nice. After a while, the talk simmers down, and it goes silent. When it comes to Blythe, I've said my piece, and can die knowing she understands how unbreakable my love for her is. She had her reasons for choosing Dax, and I understand it, even if I don't like it. If I have to die tomorrow, I'll do it gladly knowing she never really stopped loving me. She just found what she needed when I wasn't around to give it to her. I can't blame her, and now that my anger has dissipated, I can no longer blame Dax.

Agata joins us, sinking onto the floor between my spread legs and resting her slender body against my chest. Surrounded by family, I nod off quickly, falling into a deep sleep.

WE ARE AWAKENED BY THE BLARE OF ALARMS. THE SUDDEN NOISE JOLTS ME AWAKE violently, and my head begins pounding. Agata balls up against me. Her eyes wide and frightened, she glances around for the source of the noise. Alec is on his feet in a heartbeat, while throughout the hangar, everyone else struggles to stand and shake off the fatigue. My shoulder screams in protest when I rotate it, breaking through the stiffness and forcing it into motion. Grunting at the pain, I move toward Alec, holding tight to Agata's hand as the noisy alarm dies away and Wes's voice comes over the COMM

"We've got incoming ... twice as many hovercrafts as before," he reports. *"They're surrounded by a swarm of hover bikes."*

"Fuck," Alec spits, his jaw tight. "All right. Alert zones two and three that they might have incoming soon. We're going to do everything we can to fight them back, but they're our next line of defense."

"Copy," Wes replies.

"And Graydon?" Alec adds.

"Yeah, boss?"

"Should the MPs make it as far as zone three, get the senator into hiding. Do you understand? Under no circumstances can she or the Professor fall into enemy hands."

"She's in good hands, Kinnear."

Clipping the COMM back onto his belt, he turns to me. "You and Little Asskicker up for round two?"

Agata pulls on her helmet and nods, the only confirmation we need. My team of ten accompanies me to the bikes, but Blythe is trailing behind, her mouth pinched with worry.

"You'll have the other hover bikes to contend with," she says, placing a hand on my arm. "Let me and the other climbers go out first and get in position... We can pick them off and give you a better chance."

"Good idea," I tell her, turning to help Agata onto our bike. "I'll give you a five-minute head start."

"That's more than enough time," she confirms, before signaling to the climbing team.

They rush through the tunnel, rifles strapped to their backs, and I slip onto the seat behind Agata. The five-minute wait is killing me, but I know once she's in position, Blythe can be trusted to have our backs.

"Listen, squirt," I tell her. "There are twice as many crafts now, which means you have to be as fast as possible in taking these down, okay? I know it can tire you out after a while, but I need you to dig deep."

"I can do it," she assures me, so calm in this situation that it's eerie.

Has she gotten so used to death and destruction that it doesn't faze her anymore? It hurts a little, to see her so accepting of such an environment, when all I ever wanted was for her to be like a normal little girl. I make a promise to her in my mind. I'll fight for her chance to be normal ... to not be used as a walking weapon for the rest of her life.

And by the time that's done, my five minutes is up. I guide my bike toward the tunnel again, Laura and the others on my tail. We speed out toward the exit, the open doors revealing the first glimmer of sunrise. The dark blue of the night is melting away, as orange and pink spread upward on the horizon. I hear the crafts before I see them, then the low drone of engines.

A rifle goes off somewhere along the canyon, and I see a gleaming bike falling out of the sky, its armored rider thrown from his seat. There are dozens of them, surrounding the first craft, zipping side to side and dipping up and down to avoid more of the laser fire coming from the ridge. I draw one of my pistols and add my own fire into the mix, aiming for one of the bikes to the left of the craft. It goes down, and then someone else shoots another, sending it spiraling.

"Okay, Agata, let's do this!" I say in her ear, concentrating on steering and shooting so she can do what she needs to.

The first hovercraft goes down just as the other bikes swarm us, surrounding us in laser fire. Blythe's team shoots back from the ridge, and I swerve to avoid being hit or colliding with another bike. Agata concentrates on the next craft, but an MP bike appears beside us, trying to knock into us from the side, and throw us off. I swerve to avoid him, but he follows, still trying to sway into us.

Shooting has gotten too dangerous now with so many of them mixing with so many of us. Meanwhile, the huge hovercrafts bearing thousands of officers are getting closer and closer to the tunnel.

I lean over, keeping a tight hold on Agata, who shrieks as we go almost sideways. Gripping the collar of the man's armor, I give him a rough shove and topple him from the bike. He falls into another MP, throwing him from his bike as well, and the two go screaming to the bottom of the canyon together.

"Come on, squirt," I encourage as we go upright again. "We've got more work to do."

She nods. I point to the next craft in the convoy, flying over the first one she grounded. It goes down quick—so quick it falls on top of the first one, producing the crunch of metal and cries of the officers inside.

The laser fire continues around us in a hailstorm of red streaks as the sun starts to climb, bathing the canyon with orange light. Suddenly, the third craft stops, a few hatches in the sides opening and releasing another swarm of MPs mounted on hover bikes.

"Shit!" Laura cries out from just in front of me, firing her automatic ARX at them as fast as her trigger finger will allow.

Then, from behind the third craft, a fourth one shoots up like a rocket, a long, cone-shaped mechanism fixed to its front. I realize what it's for in an instant, and a string of curses falls from my mouth as I swerve to avoid another gunshot.

"That one, Agata!" I scream to be heard over the racket of engines and the clash of bodies below.

Alec and the others have come from inside to hold off the officers spilling out of the first two hovercrafts, but I don't have time to think about it with that ominous, cone-shaped craft heading right toward us.

Agata focuses on it, and I breathe a sigh of relief when it does a sudden nosedive, the sharp front of it penetrating the top of the stacked hovercrafts below it. They're piled on top of each other now, effectively clogging the canyon and blocking the rest of the caravan from moving forward.

A hover bike descends on us from out of nowhere, the officer seated on it making a grab for Agata. She kicks me in the face, and then pulls Agata out of my lap by her helmet.

"No!" I shout, reaching out to grab the edge of the MP's bike just before I can fall to my death. Mine stalls out and plummets as I hold on to the footrest of the MP vehicle with one hand, making a grab for Agata with the other.

Legs and arms flailing, she screams as she slips out of the helmet and plunges downward. I swipe with my free arm, grunting as her little body makes contact with my forearm. I curl it inward, scooping her against me, and try to hold on with my other arm. The officer throws Agata's helmet aside and takes aim at me with her CBX. I'm helpless, my injured shoulder screaming in protest as I try to decide between holding on for dear life or being shot in the face.

A laser comes out of nowhere and kills the officer, throwing her from the bike. Laura comes hurtling at us and pulls up short, reaching out to take Agata from me.

"I gotcha, sweetheart," she assures Agata, pulling her onto the seat in front of her.

I groan and grit my teeth as I grab hold of the bike with my other arm and start to pull myself up. Laura covers me, keeping a hold on Agata while firing sporadically at passing hover bikes. Another laser zips toward me, narrowly missing. Taking a deep breath and letting it out on a hiss, I force myself to power through and muscle my way onto the seat. One of my pistols is gone, I realize as I right myself, but I still have a backup, plus my knife.

Above us on the ridge, another one of the cone-shaped hovercrafts has landed ... and the triangular-shaped end is now spinning rapidly, chipping away at the rocky canyon. Burrowing its way in.

"Agata, honey," I cry out, glancing over to where she sits in front of Laura. "That one ... take out that one!"

Laura guns the bike and tries to get her closer. I follow, firing my pistol at anything that comes at them. But then, Agata cries out and claps her hands over her ears, her body bowing as if someone has jammed something sharp against her spine.

It's exactly what happened at the Stonehead rescue mission, the one where we lost Olivia. Some frequency we can't hear disturbs Agata's bionic left brain, rendering her abilities useless, and, apparently, causing her quite a bit of pain.

"Shit!" I roar as she slumps back into Laura, whimpering as it seems to have let up for now.

She tries again, her eyes narrowing and her body going rigid as she focuses on the large drilling craft. It's hammering away at the canyon, sending chunks of rock flying through the air.

Then, she cries out again. This time, a drop of blood runs from one nostril and then another. Laura gasps, trying to still Agata's body as it begins to convulse. Then, she passes out, slumping forward in the seat.

"We have to get her out of here!" I call out, unable to think past any objective other than getting Agata to a safe place.

And as we turn tail and zoom back toward the tunnel, I realize it doesn't matter anyway. Just before the passageway swallows us back up, I glance over my shoulder and watch the drill shudder to a stop, before the craft operating it descends into the hole.

Resistance Headquarters has just been breached.

THIRTY-TWO

GAGE BRONSON, BLYTHE SOL, DAX JANNER, ALEC KINNEAR, OLIVIA
MCNABB, AND LAURA ROSENBERG
RESTORATION RESISTANCE HEADQUARTERS
FEBRUARY 11, 4011
5:45 A.M.

CARRYING AGATA IN MY ARMS, I RUN AS FAST I CAN THROUGH THE HANGAR, DODGING the hundreds of bodies surging in the same direction as me. Those who did not go out into the canyon to fight are now turning to enter the citadel as word of the breach begins to spread. COMM devices buzz, the wine of laser weapons being fired up interspersing with the pounding of boots.

I can't think past getting Agata out of dodge—of hiding her in the safest place in Headquarters right now so I can rejoin the fight. The drilling craft drifts down toward the formed-up soldiers who have been waiting their turn in zone two—the area housing our playground and outdoor training area. Behind it, the sound of other vehicles pouring through the opening kicks my heart rate up a notch, fear settling in my gut as I realize there is no escape. The only way out of this is to kill them all and hope more of them don't come.

Michela lifts a humongous grenade launcher over her shoulder as I run past with Agata, and aims it at the drill. My back is to her when it fires, but I hear the hiss of the grenade leaving the weapon, the resulting explosion as it makes impact.

I pass zone three, where the next line of defense waits their turn, eyes wide as they watch the spectacle. Nearing the gym and training building, I glance down at Agata. She's starting to stir awake, but she's nowhere near strong enough to be of any use, and without her helmet, she's a sitting duck.

Bursting through one of the side doors, I take the stairs down to the basement and trapdoor leading to the underground hideout. Gasps resound through the space as I thunder down the stairs with Agata in my arms. I spot the Professor in one corner of the room, his eyes filled with concern for my niece.

Children huddle on bedrolls, staring at me with wide eyes as a few of the women come forward to meet me, Tamryn among them.

"What happened to her?" she asks, brow furrowed as she accepts Agata's light weight from my arms.

"No time to explain; we've been breached," I reply.

More gasps and some cries of alarm ring out through the crowd, but I hold my hand up for silence. "Don't panic. They haven't gotten past zone two yet ... but you guys have a protocol, right?"

Tamryn nods, handing Agata off to one of the nurses from the infirmary. "Alec set up his perimeter barrier thingy. Once you're clear, I'll push a remote and the protective dome will surround the building. Nothing can get in or out."

Unless something or someone destroys one of the mechanisms controlling the barrier, but I can't think about that now. Used to keep protesters safe in D.C., Alec's invention is their best bet for survival.

"Follow me up, and employ that thing the second I'm out of range," I tell her. "Don't come out until someone calls for you. Keep your COMM on."

"I will," she agrees, then follows me as I barrel up the stairs.

I hardly have time to look back as I exit through the side door I entered and take off toward the green. Swarms of hover bikes have come through the hole in the roof, and while one hovercraft has been shot down by rocket launchers, two others have managed to get in and avoid being shot down. Zones two and three become one as they join forces to converge on the invading MPs, weapons raised.

As I draw my remaining gun with one hand and take my knife in the other, I see more fighting going down in the hangar and my heart sinks. They've breached us from two different areas, and now they're flooding our home, spilling through the ceiling and swooping in through our tunnel with deadly intent.

I throw myself into the fray, spotting Michela and fighting my way toward her. She's a competent fighter, but I'll feel better if I'm close enough to protect her. I don't even want to think about our odds right now; I simply fire at the first MP who comes within range of my gun, then duck when another one takes a swing at me. Autopilot kicks back on, and I'm fighting without thinking, violently taking down anyone wearing white body armor.

An armored fist crashes into my jaw, throwing me onto the ground. I roll onto my back and then to my side just before the officer's boot can crush my head. A swarm of fighters closes in around me, and I scramble to get my bearings, my hands and feet lashing out against fallen bodies. A burst of pain at my temple follows someone's boot connecting with my head, and a trickle of blood runs down my face.

I'm being trampled, my body pressing down among the dead ones as the fight rages around me. Someone steps on my chest, and someone else crushes my ankle under their boot. Each trample hurts, but I can barely draw breath, let alone spare enough to cry out.

I don't know how long I lay there, fighting to breathe and not be suffocated in the crush, but then the fight seems to shift, opening some space for me to climb from among the twisting pile of bodies. But as soon as I'm on my feet, something slams into me from behind, throwing me onto a patch of grass belly-down.

"Gage!"

It's Michela calling my name from among the chaos, sounding far away and panicked as the barrel of a gun presses against the back of my head.

I struggle against inevitable death, but a foot holds me down, applying heavy pressure between my shoulder blades.

But then, another voice comes at me, this one much closer and mechanical, warbled by a helmet.

"Not this one... Can't you see he's the president's boy? He goes with the high-profile arrests."

Relief sweeps through me as I'm hauled to my feet, my wrists imprisoned in ionized handcuffs. It's a shitty place to be, but it's better than being dead.

A group of them surround me. Over their heads, I can see the fight raging on. Michela has disappeared, swallowed up by the mass of bodies battling it out. I have no idea whether she's alive or dead.

I'm shoved along the perimeter of the citadel, my heart sinking as I watch our soldiers falling by the tens, outnumbered and outgunned by the torrential force of the Military Police. My ankle throbs, my tightly laced combat boot the only thing allowing me to put weight on it without collapsing. I'm being led to a hovercraft, one idling directly beneath the massive hole in the roof. The gangplank is down. Ahead of me, someone else is being pushed up the incline in handcuffs. One of the hands is bionic.

My gut clenches as I spot the Resistance symbol tattooed onto the back of her neck, just beneath messy strands of dark hair come loose from her ponytail.

"Blythe!" I call out in shock.

She twists between the two men holding her arms and glances back at me, her eyes wide and wild, a nasty bruise beginning to swell beneath one eye and a trickle of blood drying on her chin. One of my escorts reaches out and shoves her, causing her to stumble and almost fall. The sight of his hands on her makes me see red, and a low growl rumbles in my chest as I lunge toward him. My body collides with his, the force of my rage enough to throw him off balance and onto the gangplank, his armor clanging loudly. Two men struggle to get me under control, but I manage to stomp on his helmet a few times, shattering his face shield to reveal a bruised and bleeding forehead.

"Keep your hands off her!" I yell, fighting against the hands trying to hold me down, my chest heaving with the force of my need to maim and kill these assholes.

Another blow to the back of the head subdues me, and my vision blurs as I'm dragged along, into the back of what appears to be a prisoner transport craft. Rows of seats with shackles attached to them line each side of the vehicle. In one of those, Olivia has been bound and gagged. Her nose is bloodied and crooked, likely broken, blood staining the scrap of cloth shoved between her lips. Her eyes are blue slits of rage, narrowed and fixated on the men who captured her. She moves slightly, and blue lines of electricity crackle over her body, forcing a scream from deep in her throat. That must be how they managed to keep someone as fast as her subdued.

They're shoving Blythe into the seat next to her. The moment her ass hits the leather, she starts fighting, screaming like banshee as she kicks out at the men trying to chain her to the chair. One of them takes her boot to the face, falling back and crashing into the officer behind him. The second grabs her foot and shoves it aside before punching her in the stomach. She doubles over with a groan, and the familiar rage is on me again, propelling me forward despite my shackled hands.

Something jolts me, pricking every surface of my skin with heat and a stinging sensation. My body convulses. I drop to the hard ground of the craft, causing my head wound to gush even more blood. I can't see the weapon used to subdue me, but if I had to guess, I'd say it was an electrified baton.

"Get that one under control!" someone shouts, before I'm hauled to my feet again and thrown into a chair.

My head lolls forward, blood seeping into one of my eyes. I'm too weak to fight back as they secure me with so many chains the only thing I can move is my head. I turn it to glance at Olivia, who has tears mixing with the blood on her face, though she seems to be trying to hold as still as possible now to keep from being shocked again. Looking over at Blythe, I find her staring blankly ahead, her jaw clenched. If I know her, she's mentally tearing each of these guys apart in her head.

The officers come and go, some barking into COMMs, the discordant jumble of voices too much for me to discern. Then, they all part to make room for someone who walks onto the craft like he owns it. He strides confidently toward us, pausing when he stands just in front of Olivia. Removing his helmet, he reveals himself to be one of the Resistance's most hated foes.

Captain Rodney Jones of the Restoration Enforcers.

His steel-gray eyes glitter in his dark face, the dark skin etched with cruel lines. He glances down at Olivia and grins like a cat cornering a mouse, while she stares up at him with wide eyes.

"Remember me, sweetheart?" he says with a sneer, his mustached upper lip pulling back from his teeth.

She screams around her gag and lunges, the chains holding her back and the collar electrocuting her again. Still howling her fury, she jerks against her restraints, her gaze murderously fixed on the man who destroyed her at Stonehead. I only heard bits and pieces, but everyone knows rape, beatings, and torture were all on the menu—Jones and his men at the prison all taking part in violating Olivia.

Jones chuckles and approaches Blythe, bending down until they're almost nose to nose. "Zion Sol's little girl. How long's it been now ... two, three years?"

Blythe growls and spits right in his face, her mouth curving in a satisfied smile as he rears back, cringing in disgust. He removes one of his armored gauntlets and uses a gloved hand to wipe his face.

Turning away from her, he moves on to me. I know what this man did to Olivia, and that he is the one who pointed a gun at Zion Sol's head and pulled the trigger. So, even though he's never done anything to me, personally, I'm still wishing for him to get close enough for me to head butt him.

No such luck. He keeps his distance, but still looks at me with a healthy amount of amusement. "Gage Drummond ... or is it Bronson? Or ... The Patriot, right? Talk about an identity crisis."

I don't respond, merely keeping my eyes narrowed and fixed on him. If there's any chance I can get free and make a dent in their numbers, he'll be the first I go after—if for no other reason than to avenge the two women sitting beside me.

"Your daddy is going to be very pleased when we return to D.C. with the three of you in tow," he says before turning to one of his subordinates.

"What about the others? Any sign of the Professor or the senator?"

"Not yet, Captain," the officer, a woman, replies. "Those who are not engaged in the fight are searching every available building, though there is one particular structure that's been shielded in some way. We're trying to figure out how to get in right now."

Jones nods, seeming satisfied with these updates. It was only a matter of time before they figure out that the protective dome is hiding something or someone important. By now, I imagine Wes has gotten the senator inside the hideaway, along with the Professor and the others taking shelter there. Hopefully, Alec's technology will hold up long enough for us to figure out a way to save them.

"Good, it won't be long now," Jones says. "Once we start dropping the fire bombs, everyone who's in hiding will be smoked out. In the meantime, I want to get these three on their way to D.C. Better to turn in a partial prize than nothing. If we recover more of the high-profile targets, another transport can be arranged. In the meantime, anyone not on the list is useless. Leave none alive."

With a swift nod, the woman turns on her heels and leaves to deliver his orders. "Yes, Captain."

After trading words with a fellow officer, the woman leaves, and Captain Jones disappears into the cockpit.

Fire bombs? The MPs came prepared to decimate us. When Blythe glances past Olivia at me, her desolate gaze echoes my sense of helplessness. They are about to incinerate our home, and there is nothing we can do to stop them. Agata, Michela, Dax, and the others ... all of them will be lost.

A moment later, the gangplank begins to close. With a shudder, the hovercraft engine fires up and we begin to ascend. Jones reappears, motioning for an officer to help him begin removing his armor.

"Fucking heavy stuff," he complains as the various pieces begin falling away, revealing the black flight suit he wears underneath. "No need for it where we're going ... at least not until we land."

The other officers take this as their cue to follow suit. Eventually the pieces are stored out of sight, the MPs seeming more human and less intimidating without them. I count them as we ascend through the hole in the dome, and estimate about ten, plus the pilot. If we could get free somehow, the three of us could likely take them out. We've certainly faced worse odds.

I've just started trying to calculate a way to loosen the shackles around my feet when the drone of hover bikes kicks up outside. I perk up, glancing through one of the round windows just in time to see a familiar face grinning at me through the glass. I chuckle as Dax pushes the bike upward, disappearing out of sight. There are others—at least two of them, but I can't see who's riding them. It doesn't matter... All I know is we're about to get rescued.

A moment later, something drops onto the roof of the craft, jolting all the MPs into action. They reach for their weapons, three of them aiming up toward the round hatch in the roof, the others targeting various windows. Jones holds one hand up to still them, cocking his head to the side as if listening for something, his eyes narrowed.

A hunk of metal comes flying into the craft, its force and speed taking down one of the officers. It's the door of the hatch, I realize as I stare up at the hole left by its destruction. Jones orders his men to fire, but before they can pull the trigger, Dax drops through the hole. He kicks one MP in the chest, sending him flying across the craft, before turning to knock a gun pointing right at his face sideways. As he goes toe to toe with two MPs at a time, another body falls through the open hatch—Laura this time.

She has a piece of metal in her hand, a broken hunk of something that makes for a nice bludgeon. She slams it across the head of the nearest officer, whipping him around and sending blood and gore flying. A second officer tries to grab her from behind, but she slams her elbow back into his middle, then spins and lashes out with her bludgeon. He goes down next to the first guy, his face destroyed by the weapon.

A third body drops into the midst of the fray, and Alec rises from a crouched position to join the fight. He's all raw anger at the sight of Olivia chained and bloodied, his enraged roar filling the craft as he goes after the

MPs with his bare hands.

Jones has retreated to the cockpit, leaving his officers to fend for themselves. Our three rescuers make quick work of them, leaving them in bloody heaps and stepping over the carnage to get to us. Relief sags my shoulders as Alec approaches, pulling an object from one of the many pockets in his cargo pants. Bending in front of Olivia first, he begins using it to pick the locks, while Dax and Laura approach the cockpit.

I crane my neck to watch as Dax meets Jones head-on, while Laura battles the copilot. Fists fly, blood splattering the floor and walls of the craft as Jones and his fellow soldier give as good as they get—Jones' freakishly juiced-up muscles making him a match for Dax in size, and superior to him in strength.

The moment Olivia is free, Alec tries to grab on to her, to assess her injuries, but she lunges from the chair and out of his hold, heading straight for Jones.

"Olivia, no!"

But Alec's warning comes too late; Olivia draws two knives from the sheaths lining her vest and goes after Jones, joining Dax in fighting him back.

"Shit!" Alec grumbles, kneeling in front of Blythe to free her next.

Olivia seems to be holding her own, despite her injuries. I think she's driven by pure fury, her superhuman speed helping her get quite a few blows to Jones with her knives. He's bleeding from cuts on his chest, back, and biceps, roaring in rage and pain every time Olivia manages to get another piece of him. He concentrates on fighting Dax, unable to handle both him and Olivia at the same time.

Blythe springs free of her bonds and rushes toward the cockpit, sidestepping the fighters and coming up behind the pilot, who has navigated our craft out through the hole and over the canyon. He grunts and tries to fight back when she swings her titanium fist at him, throwing him out of the pilot's chair. While Alec crouches to free me, Blythe knocks the pilot unconscious and takes over the controls.

The copilot falls dead at Laura's feet with one last swipe of her weapon, and she turns to swing it at Jones. She catches his shoulder blades, but he barely even flinches, remaining on his feet and smashing Dax in the jaw with a powerful right hook. When Dax stumbles away from him, tripping over the copilot's dead body and slamming to the floor, Olivia rises in his place, lunging at Jones.

He grabs her in a vicious bear hug, wrapping his massive arms around her body and squeezing so hard I'm surprised she doesn't snap in half. Then, he throws her to the ground with a vicious body slam.

"Alec, hurry up," I urge, keeping my gaze on Olivia and Jones.

"I'm trying," he gripes. "They put five times more locks and shit on you."

His head is lowered as he works to free me, so he doesn't see Jones straddling Olivia, fist raised to strike her again. But Laura is on him in an instant, wrapping her arms around his neck and trying to haul him off. He throws her aside as if she weighs no more than a rag doll, and when Dax tries the same thing, he gets thrown aside, too.

Jones turns back to Olivia just as she pulls another knife from her vest and jams it into his gut with a savage snarl. A twisted smile of satisfaction pulls at her mouth as she yanks it free, gleefully watching as blood begins soaking his flight suit.

"You fucking bitch," Jones rasps, his eyes wide with shock.

She stabs him again and again, her movements a blur as anger and adrenaline fuel her superhuman speed. Jones falls from on top of her, his eyes glassy as blood pools around him, spreading outward in a rush too fast to staunch. Olivia throws his body aside with a grunt, then struggles to her feet. The lock around my last set of shackles clicks open, freeing me to stand. Alec turns to watch, along with the rest of us, as Olivia stands over Jones' prone body, the bloody knife still clenched in one fist, her fingers and knuckles stained crimson.

"You stick me, I stick back, bitch," she growls, drawing one foot back and kicking him in the face for good measure. His head snaps to the side, and his eyes close as a few teeth go skittering across the floor.

She drops the knife and stumbles back from Jones' body, her chest heaving with labored breaths. Alec rushes her, sidestepping the dead bodies to take her into his arms. Cupping her face, he kisses her full on the mouth, then pulls back and gives her a wide smile.

"That's my girl," he declares proudly. "You said you would do it, and you fucking did it. You killed that son of a bitch."

Still gazing at Jones over Alec's shoulder, Olivia seems to be in her own world, fixated on the object of her torment. I wonder if killing him with her own two hands will bring her any kind of peace or relief.

Dax and I join Blythe in the cockpit, with Laura hot on our heels. Below us, the canyon stretches, filled with more MPs preparing to march into the tunnel. Those of our people who were still outside are now dead, their bodies littering the dusty ground by the hundreds. Those of us that remain are now trapped inside with firebombs about to be rained on them.

"I think it's safe to say defense is now off the table," Blythe says as she stalls the hovercraft so we float just above the canyon. "It's time to implement the escape plan."

"Agreed," Alec says, keeping a tight hold on Olivia as they enter behind us. "But we can't get into the hangar this way ... not with all those MPs blocking the entrance. And if we go back the way we came, we could get into the hangar, but we still wouldn't have a clear path out."

"We *have* to get in there," I state, glancing from the scene below us to Alec. "All our supplies and vehicles are in the hangar. Without them, we stand no chance of survival."

Running a hand through his hair, he sighs. "Blythe, what's our artillery looking like?"

"The guns on this craft are automatic laser fire," she replies. "No heavy artillery ... it'd take us too long to shoot them all down. By the time we did that, they'd find some way to bomb us out of the sky."

"How much fuel is in this thing?" Laura asks, peering over Blythe's shoulder at the various meters and gauges.

"It's almost completely full," she replies. "Why?"

Laura nods decisively and turns to face us, her face determined. "This entire vehicle is a flying bomb ... it crashes in the canyon, the fuel will ignite and explode. Aim it right at the tunnel, it'll block the opening and kill anything standing too close. Any MPs left alive will be shit out of luck, unable to get inside without a hovercraft. Aside from this one and the ones Agata destroyed, there aren't any left on the outside. It'll buy enough time to get inside to the hangar, and start evacuation."

I frown. "The explosion would kill us."

"Not us," she argues, hands folded over her chest. "Just me."

Blythe sucks in a sharp breath, and Dax flinches as if someone just slapped him.

"No," he grinds out from between clenched teeth. "Fuck that. No one dies ... not like this."

"The hover bikes are still on the roof of the craft where we left them," she argues. "You guys take those and fly back the way we came... Let me handle the rest."

"Absolutely not," Blythe argues. "We aren't running away while you kill yourself. Besides, won't the hovercraft explosion set off the explosives we lined the canyon with? That would make the whole citadel cave in on itself!"

"No," Alec replies, his pensive gaze never leaving Laura. "The ones lining the canyon are very stable, and set far enough away from the tunnel that they shouldn't go off unless I detonate them."

"You aren't suggesting she do this?" I argue, turning to Alec. "It's insane."

"It would work," Laura counters.

Grabbing her arm, Dax leans over her, his face all hard lines and planes. "You're one of my best friends. No way in hell I'm leaving you behind to take the fall for us. You get that? We go down together, or not at all."

"That's ridiculous," Laura argues. "You're all needed."

"So are you," I say softly. "I'm with Dax... We won't let you do this."

"Agreed," says Blythe, stepping up between Dax and me and folding her arms defiantly over her chest.

"Then it's settled," Alec says, still holding Laura's gaze. "We all leave together and fight our way back in. We go back in through the ceiling hole, retrieve our people, escape out the same way, then blow the canyon.

Agreed?"

Everyone agrees verbally except Laura. She's still looking at us in that stubborn way of hers, as if she thinks we're nuts. But we've tolerated enough loss, and the night isn't even over yet. None of us wants to willingly let her go to her death.

"Fine," she grumbles after a moment. "Let's go then."

We head to the center of the craft, where the opening of the roof hatch is located. Dax pulls himself up and through it first, then reaches down for Blythe. She puts a hand in his, and he pulls her up to join him. Olivia follows, then, me, then Alec.

He crouches and lowers his hand for Laura, but she doesn't reach back. Instead, she takes a step away from the hatch, then another.

"What is she doing?" Olivia asks from Alec's side, brow furrowed as she peers into the hole.

"Rosenberg, get your ass up here!" Dax roars, leaving Blythe on the bike they will share and stomping over to the hatch.

Giving us an apologetic look, she shakes her head. "I told you ... it's better this way. Now, get the fuck out of here. You've got thirty seconds before I take this thing down."

"No!" Olivia cries out, lunging as if to climb back down into the hole and go after her.

Alec catches her around the waist and pulls her back. "Do what you have to do, soldier," he says, saluting her with his free hand while holding Olivia back with the other.

Laura salutes him with a grin. "It's been an honor, Corporal."

"Same here, Sergeant," he replies, reminding us all that she used to be his superior officer in the army. The two have a history that makes it easier for Alec to accept what's happening. I have a feeling if Laura hadn't stepped up first, he might have volunteered to do it himself.

"Don't do this," Dax pleads as he continues backing away from the cockpit. "Please, Laura. Please."

"Come on, Janner," she says with a wink. "Don't turn into a pussy on me now... I figure I've cheated death enough... It's time for me to let him win this round."

Then, she disappears into the cockpit, the sliding door slamming shut behind her, the sound of the lock clicking echoing through the craft. We couldn't get her out of there if we tried.

I rush to the bike and climb on alone, while Alec drags Olivia kicking and screaming to theirs. Dax is the last to leave, casting one last mournful look down into the hatch before running to his waiting bike and climbing on in front of Blythe. We take off as one, leaving the hovercraft behind and soaring up into the night. I glance back over my shoulder and into the hovercraft's front window. Laura sits in the cockpit, her face a mask of determination as she takes hold of the controls. She meets my gaze and gives me a reassuring nod, her expression one of serene acceptance.

It's the last glimpse of her I get before the vehicle begins to plummet, its twin guns blazing with red lasers as it careens into the canyon. The lasers tear through the MPs on the ground like a knife through butter, throwing them to the ground one by one as Laura increases speed and heads straight for the tunnel. Seconds later, it makes impact, the entire thing going up in flames that spread and consume everything in their path.

THIRTY-TWO

GAGE BRONSON, BLYTHE SOL, DAX JANNER, ALEC KINNEAR,
OLIVIA MCNABB
RESTORATION RESISTANCE HEADQUARTERS
FEBRUARY 11, 4011
6:55 A.M.

THERE IS NO TIME TO MOURN LAURA'S LOSS. THE MOMENT THAT HOVERCRAFT EXPLODES, we are speeding for the open hole above the citadel, prepared to go back in and fight to get as many of our people to safety as possible.

Flying over the carnage made of our home, we find both Hexley and Mosley halls on fire, flames spreading to consume them floor by floor.

"Graydon, this is Kinnear, do you copy?" Alec bellows into his COMM as we approach the hangar opening.

"I'm here, Kinnear," Wes answers a moment later.

"Prepare for evacuation," Alec replies. "I repeat, prepare for evacuation! We're bringing hovercrafts to you shortly. Stand by!"

"Copy, Kinnear ... ready for evacuation on your command."

On the green below, the last of our forces battle it out with the hundreds of MPs still inside. The way to the hangar is clear, so we go for it full throttle, entering the cavernous space without incident. Throwing herself off the bike, Blythe makes a run for *Icarus*, Dax hot on her heels. I'm right behind them, while Alec and Olivia dart toward the *Neville I*.

By the time Dax and I step onto the craft, Blythe has it fired up and ready to fly. The gangplank comes up behind us. We dash down the center aisle between rows and rows of seats, to where she sits in the cockpit.

"Man the guns," she commands, her gaze focused on the opening of the hangar leading out into the citadel.

I drop into the chair on her left, while Dax takes the one on the right—his area controlling the light fire weapons, while mine mans the heavy artillery.

Alec and Olivia are right behind us as we come out into the citadel, arcing left to avoid the burning dorm buildings and heading toward the green. The entire citadel shakes, our craft thrown off course momentarily as an explosion rocks the world around us. The building housing our chow hall goes up in flames, as the MP crafts carrying the fire bombs hit another target.

Ahead of us, the protective barrier is still erected around the training building, but it has to come down for the occupants of the hideaway to be able to get to us. Blythe turns the craft so the back gangplank is facing the building, while beside us, Alec does the same. Across the green, a fresh batch of MPs are coming at us, guns drawn.

"You hold them off with the hovercraft guns, while me and Gage go help guide people in," Dax says, standing and reaching for a pair of automatic CBX handguns from beneath the control panel.

He rises from his station and tosses one of the weapons to me. Blythe stands and scowls.

"But—"

Dax closes the distance between them, the gun held behind his back, the other grasping her arm tight. Lowering his head, he whispers something in her ear. I can't hear what's being said, but whatever it is convinces Blythe to deflate with a sigh.

"You're right," she relents. "I'll stay here and man the guns."

Giving her a swift kiss, he leaves the cockpit. I follow him, uncertain why Blythe complied so easily when I know she'd rather be in the fight. Still, I can't help but feel relieved that she's on board the craft, safe.

Dax and I barrel down the center aisle and out through the gangplank just as Alec presses the button on his little remote to lower the clear protective dome. Behind us, the MPs come within range of the hovercraft guns. A moment later, Dax and Olivia both open fire.

Alec falls in with us, easily keeping pace with our longer strides as he holds his COMM up to his device and screams into it.

"Graydon, let's rock and roll! All bodies to the surface and running to the hovercrafts as fast as possible. Those with weapons be prepared to use them. We got company!"

Wes responds, but my blood is rushing in my ears and I can't hear a thing anymore. The need to protect these people—among them, the Professor, the senator, Agata, and Tamryn—makes my hands shake. I will do whatever it takes to get them safely out of the citadel.

Wes comes barreling through the side door first, Agata held in one arm and balanced on his hip. He holds a pistol in the other. I'm relieved to see she's awake and alert now, though she looks exhausted and haggard.

"Everything's going to be okay, squirt," I call out. "Everything's fine!"

There isn't time for much else, as Wes is followed by dozens of others. They trail him across the stretch of grass between us and the hovercrafts, while Dax, Alec, and I follow along to provide cover fire. I recognize a few medics and nurses from the infirmary, their faces determined as they push the non-ambulatory patients with one hand, while clinging to guns with the other.

Beyond the crafts, the MPs who aren't taken out by the guns are headed straight for us, weapons blazing. On the other side of the rushing formation, those of our people who fought to defend zones two and three are coming at them from behind.

Once Wes has stashed Agata safely onboard *Icarus*, I rush past it and start firing at the MPs, picking them off in twos and threes thanks to my weapon's automatic feature. Spotting Michela in the thick of the fight, I work my way toward her, alternating between shooting and fighting hand to hand with whoever gets in my way.

Glancing over my shoulder, I notice the *Neville I* is almost completely full, but there is still a steady stream of people coming out of the hideaway. We need every available vehicle we can get.

"Michela," I call, punching through the open face shield of an officer and knocking him unconscious before throwing his body aside.

"Gage," she shouts, fatigue heavy in her voice. Even still, she fights as if her life depends on it—which it does.

"Can you fly a large hovercraft?" I ask, turning back to back with her and raising my gun to fire at the nearest MPs

"Not well," she replies with a grunt. "Why?

"We need the *Neville II*, but it's still in the hangar," I reply. "We need to get it over here."

Glancing at her over my shoulder, I see her jaw is clenched in determination, her eyes wide and wild as she ducks to avoid a flying fist. Before she can react, I leap over her bent body and kick the guy in the face, whipping his head around and knocking him out.

"I can do it," she declares, before grabbing the nearest soldier by the arm. "You, come with me!"

Before I can tell her to be careful, the two are swallowed into the crowd, shooting their way back toward the hangar. Confident Michela can handle herself, I work my way back through the fight, shouting for all Resistance soldiers to retreat to the hovercrafts for evacuation.

Those who can follow me, and we move toward the crafts while firing at our pursuers. Arriving at the hovercrafts, I find the *Neville I* already completely full, its gangplank sliding up and into place as Dax and Alec provide cover fire along with the big guns being operated by Olivia and Blythe. Senator Davis and the Professor direct people onto *Icarus*, urging them to move quickly and not panic. The inside is more than half-full, even with children sitting on laps.

"We've got another vehicle coming," I say, skidding to a stop beside the Professor.

He nods in acknowledgement, then goes back to directing people on the craft. I join in, shoving my gun into my holster and picking up children two at a time to get them on board faster, stooping to lift an elderly woman gingerly into my arms before finding her a seat, barking at the able-bodied to move faster and find a place in the hovercraft as quickly as they can. One of the older kids comes running, Dog on a leash with him, and I'm glad to see that someone thought to bring him to the hideaway. He's as much everyone's pet as he is Blythe and Dax's.

Tamryn appears among those emerging from underground, pausing as the line stalls—*Icarus* is almost full. She's still pushing the gurney of her friend, the same one she helped get away from the infirmary. She looks worried, glancing around at the death and carnage taking place just beyond the hovercrafts, her bottom lip red and swollen from her nervous chewing.

The drone of a hovercraft engine draws my gaze in the other direction, and my hopes lift when I see that Michela has followed through. The *Neville II* approaches us, along with a surrounding convoy of smaller vehicles.

But MPs on the ground have noticed them and turn their guns upward, opening fire on the approaching vehicles.

"Shit!" I bellow before starting in that direction, drawing my gun again. If any of the MPs hit home, the vehicles will crash, causing us to lose lives as well as modes of transportation.

"Gage, what's going on?" a voice calls from my side.

It's Tamryn, who has run to catch up with me easily, her double bionic legs making her quick.

"They can't approach without cover fire," I say, pointing toward the formation of vehicles flying our way.

A laser hits one of the smaller crafts, and then another. After a moment, it drops from the air, crashing to the ground and exploding into a ball of fire.

"You can't do it alone," she says.

I am about to tell her Dax and Alec have already noticed and begun targeting the MPs who are shooting at our crafts, but Tamryn has turned back and dashed toward the building. Before I can even fathom what's happening, she appears again, this time pushing her friend on the gurney.

"Tamryn, what are you doing," I scream as they blow past me.

I kick it into high gear, my heart thudding in a rapid drum beat as I try to catch up to her. She pulls a gun from the back waistband of her pants and points it out in front of them, while the woman on the gurney whips the blanket covering her lower body aside to reveal a set of double bionic legs with guns mounted on each one. Cartridge belts full of ammunition are fed into them. My mouth drops open as she pulls a lever on each leg, loading the ammo with a 'click'.

"Ready, Jay?" Tamryn asks, out of breath but still steadily running beside me.

"Let's go," Jay answers, before lifting one of her legs and opening fire.

I join them, adding my laser fire as we come up beside Alec and Dax. Jay's legs vibrate from the kickback of each shot, her ammo feeding through the gun swiftly. MPs drop like flies, while we lose two more smaller vehicles. Tamryn opens her mouth and lets out a long, high-pitched scream as her index finger slams on the trigger again and again, every ounce of the helplessness and anxiety that plagued her falling away until a fierce warrior stands in her place.

And to think Baron abandoned her for not being 'strong enough' to fight.

The remaining crafts fly over our heads, safely landing in front of the building. While those in hiding can safely get on board, we still have soldiers out there who need cover fire to reach us.

"We need to get the others safely to the hovercrafts," I say, turning to glance at Dax and Alec on my left, then Tamryn and Jay on my right. "You guys ready?"

"Fuck yeah," Alec declares while Dax nods.

Jay pushes her empty cartridge belt aside and feeds a new one into her right leg before giving me a thumbs-up. "Locked and loaded."

We take off toward the remaining fighters, their numbers greatly diminished—the living battling it out in a seat of fallen bodies. Our guns go off in a chorus of laser fire and bullets, tearing down the remaining MP force while our last surviving soldiers join us in fighting them off. Within minutes, the last officers fall, and a cheer goes up from our force. The celebration is short-lived, however, since our window of escape is narrow. A small unit of about fifty MPs comes running toward us from behind a fallen craft—a troop that fell back to regroup as we took the others out. There are half as many of us, but we can take them.

However, before any of us can make a move, Tamryn rushes forward, pushing Jay's gurney toward them.

"Run!" she calls over her shoulder before continuing toward them.

"Tamryn, *no*," I roar, even as Dax grabs my arm and hauls me in the other direction.

The others are moving, running toward the hovercrafts. The *Neville I* is already in the air, along with several other smaller crafts. The sound of Jay's legs firing in tandem fills the now-quieted dome, mingling with the return laser fire of the MPs. I run at the back of the pack, glancing over my shoulder to watch Tamryn, praying all the while that she will make it out of this alive. I cannot bear for yet another person to die trying to help me get away.

"Dude, come *on!*" Dax yells, giving me a yank toward *Icarus*.

"I'm not leaving without her," I counter, yanking my arm out of his hold and taking another look back at Tamryn.

They're surrounded now, about half the MPs down, while the others close in on her and Jay, guns raised. My entire body tenses with the need to run over there, to help her, but Dax has got a strong grip and he isn't letting me go.

Tamryn lets out another long scream, raising her gun and beginning to fire at the same time Jay leans back and lifts both legs, joining her friend's battle cry. Tamryn shoots while turning the gurney in a circle. Before long, they're spinning on the gurney's wheels, bullets and laser fire tearing through the surrounding MPs

The officers return laser fire, but drop like bricks, their bodies jolted by Jay's ammunition or shot through with Tamryn's lasers. But as the last of the MPs falls, so do both women, their bodies riddled with smoking holes from the heated laser fire.

Tamryn falls sideways, pulling the gurney with her and causing Jay to pitch to the ground. Neither of them gets back up.

"No," I whisper, tears filling my eyes... I can't take them off Tamryn's crumpled body. Unmoving. Dead. "No, goddamn it!"

Dax's hand on my shoulder becomes comforting, but he's still steadily trying to pull me toward *Icarus*. "I'm sorry, man... I'm so sorry. But we have to go. Now."

Nodding, I let my mind go blank and my body take over. My feet move—one in front of the other—while I use the back of one hand to dash the tears from my eyes. I had mourned Tamryn before, the loss of the girl I had once known as she'd sunk into the dark hold of Baron and the Rejects. Now, I mourn the future she could have had now that she'd seen the light. I suppose in time, I'll come to think of her as a hero ... the fighter who saved the lives of our last remaining soldiers with one daring act. And Jay as well. I hadn't known her for long, but damn that girl had been spectacular.

I register Dax shoving me down onto the chair on Blythe's left, in front of the controls for the big guns, then Blythe's hand on top of mine. I turn to stare at her, my mind whirling chaotically as I try to process everything that just happened. Her eyes are sad as she holds my gaze and gives me a pitying look.

"I'm sorry," she whispers.

I nod to acknowledge her words, but cannot speak. Agata appears at my side from the passenger area and sinks into my lap, curling into my chest. I strap my seatbelt around both of us as *Icarus* rises from the ground, waiting its turn to exit through the hole. The smaller crafts go out first, followed by *Neville I*, then *Neville II*.

As we exit last, Alec's voice comes over the radio.

"Kinnear here. Final check to ensure everyone is clear before we blow this thing."

Pressing a button near her own controls, Blythe responds, "Clear."

Wes replies next from the helm of the *Neville II*, then Michela from one of the smaller crafts—which she handles with more skill than the larger ones. One by one, the others respond, and as we float higher, seeking coverage among the clouds until nightfall, what's left of Restoration Resistance Headquarters is torn apart. The explosives along the canyon ignite, the rock caving in and sending up clouds of dust and a huge ball of fire.

Holding Agata close, I close my eyes, even though I know I need to watch the radar screen for any approaching MP crafts. Yet, the comfort of having her safe with me is one I'm not ready to put aside yet. I draw strength from her little body, this girl who is so much wiser and braver than most of us could ever be.

"I'm so proud of you," I murmur, kissing the top of her head. "You were a big help today."

When she glances at me, she has tears in her eyes, her cheeks reddened. "But I couldn't get them all. They breached the hideout because of me... This is all my fault."

My chest aches at the look in her eyes, the rough sound of grief in her voice. "No, squirt ... none of this is your fault. You did the best you could today... Everyone did. There were just too many of them."

Sniffing, she lays her head on my shoulder and sags against me, closing her eyes. "Our home is gone. Where will we go now?"

As Agata's guardian, I am used to being prepared to answer her questions, to always know what to say. But this time, there are no words of comfort or useless platitudes. Agata is too smart to believe them anyway.

So, I say the only thing I can in a situation like this. "I don't know, squirt... I really don't know."

THIRTY-FOUR

GAGE BRONSON, BLYTHE SOL, DAX JANNER, ALEC KINNEAR, OLIVIA
MCNABB, MICHELA ARLOTTI, WES GRAYDON, SENATOR ALEXIS DAVIS, AND
PROFESSOR NEVILLE HINKLEY
UNKNOWN LOCATION
FEBRUARY 25, 4011
9:10 P.M.

FOR TWO WEEKS, WHAT'S LEFT OF THE RESISTANCE BECOMES TRANSIENT, OUR hovercrafts taking to the sky during the day, hiding among the clouds. At night, we search for places to make camp and sleep. Abandoned buildings, radiation zones, thick forests ... no place is off limits as we do what we can to feed, clothe, shelter, and protect hundreds of Bionics, their families, and the ex-Rejects Tamryn brought to Headquarters.

Thanks to Alec and the senator's careful planning, our cargo holds are brimming with essential medical supplies, food, clothing, tents and blankets, weapons, and drums of fuel and water. A rationing system ensures everyone gets what they need, while guaranteeing we don't burn through our supplies too quickly.

On the first night, we camped out in an old burned-out warehouse, the remaining leadership of the Resistance sitting around one of many campfires. Someone suggested talking strategy—figuring out what our next move should be. Yet, we were all too shell-shocked to do anything more than sit there, staring listlessly into the fire. Those of us who fought looked like hell—bruised faces, grimy clothes ... bloodstained hands.

But as the days pass, we step up like we always do and lead. We make sure everyone is fed, and those who need new clothing get some from the crate holding various articles in assorted sizes. We arrange guard patrols wherever we've stopped to sleep, and we break up fights that start among people who are just lashing out because they're afraid.

At night, we sit around the campfire and plan. We try to decide if the place we've hunkered down for the night might be a safe area to set up shop—to rebuild and put down roots. But none of them are good enough, our campsites either too exposed, too dangerous due to radiation, or just plain too small. As well, it is difficult to make plans or decide what to do next, when we have no eye into the outside world—no television, no internet, no twenty-four-hour news cycle to let us know what the president might be up to.

I share a tent with Agata, Michela, and two small children who lost their parents in the attack. We are squeezed tight into the space, but I enjoy the closeness with Agata—take comfort in knowing she's close enough to protect if something should happen. Despite it being February, the temperatures remain mild at best, a good side effect of global warming … at least for us at this time. I couldn't imagine trying to do this while entrenched in snow and lashed by frigid winds.

Just as he was during the battle, Dax watches Blythe like a hawk, his protective nature in overdrive. It's gotten so bad that she's grown irritated by it, insisting she's fine when he tries to stop her from taking late-night guard patrols, or pitching in with tasks requiring heavy lifting. Maybe it's the fear of being out in the elements, an easy target for my father, that has him rattled. I can't blame him for wanting to keep her safe. With him being so overbearing about it, I try to stay out of her way, even though I can't help but be aware of where she is at any given time. It's part of the thread tying us together, the pull I can't resist. Mine and Michela's odd relationship seems to be on hold out here, with everyone grieving for our lost friends and the lack of privacy. Which is probably a good thing considering the confessions Blythe and I made to each other when we thought we might die. I'm not sure I can continue to treat Michela as nothing but a way to forget my pain … not when the knowledge that Blythe still has feelings for me is never far from my mind.

But for now, I try to concentrate on the future … whatever that might bring. As I told Agata on the night we left Headquarters, I honestly don't know what we are going to do or where we will go. All I know is that if even a piece of the Resistance still exists, I will fight to preserve it, to be a part of it.

WE ARE FOUND ALMOST THREE WEEKS TO THE DAY AFTER OUR ESCAPE. HIDDEN INSIDE an old church, we are eating our rationed dinner before turning in for the night when one of the guards we put on patrol comes running inside, rifle swinging from its strap around his body.

"Incoming!" he shouts, alerting everyone in the room. "MP hovercrafts closing in!"

Screams and gasps of shock ripple through the room, and I am on my feet in an instant, my dinner falling to the floor, forgotten. Those of us who are armed and can fight rush for the church's only doors, leaving Senator Davis and the Professor to calm the others.

"How many?" Alec asks as we approach the guard, a young man who'd been a fresh recruit before the attacks.

"Three, at least that we can see," the boy responds as we exit the church and rush down the front steps.

Near the open double doors, Dax tries to convince Blythe to go back inside, while she stands there with her rifle, calling him every foul name in the book and telling him to back off and let her fight. Dog sits at her feet, watching his parents fight with his ears perked up and his tongue hanging out.

But as two of the crafts land and open, unleashing dozens of MPs, I know there can be no fighting. There are too many of them, and not enough of us who can fight. We escaped with more women, children, elderly, and injured than anything else.

"We have to make a run for it," Alec says, raising his gun to open fire as the MPs start toward us. "Blythe, Wes, get to your crafts and fire them up. We'll provide cover and evacuate."

The young guard runs inside to spread the news as we rush forward to fight the officers back. Our crafts are parked out back of the church, hidden among the trees, which means our people have to follow the path that Blythe and Wes take now as we provide cover fire—around the side of the building. Dog ambles along behind them, follow Blythe to *Icarus.*

We spread out to form a protective half-circle around the front of the church, trading fire with the MPs as people come pouring out of the building, rushing down the steps. Some of the laser fire shoots past us, and I hear cries of alarm and screams of devastation as bodies hit the stairs behind me. But I cannot turn around… I cannot allow myself to be afraid or saddened by what I've seen. Because if one of those bodies is Agata's, I would lay down beside her and wish for death.

"Stay low," I shout over the gunfire. "Stay low and move! Get to a ship!"

The officers rush us, trying to push us back, so we meet them with equal force, all bets now off as we go toe to toe, hand to hand. I crouch and pick up a large rock as an officer comes at me, using it to bash his wrist and knock his gun out of his hand. Then, I pull it back and crash it into his face shield. I keep swinging until I've broken through and smashed skin, cartilage, and bone, leaving him an unconscious, bloodied heap on the ground.

We fight without scruples, disabling and killing with an ease I think most of us fear. But we are like cornered animals, willing to scrap and fight for survival.

The MPs break our line and try to rush the church, but we pursue them, gunning many of them down from behind before they can even step foot inside. I don't see Agata among the last of those to leave the church, so I have to assume she's safe on board *Icarus*, which is where I head now as I follow the others, running around the corner and turning back to shoot at any remaining MPs. The bodies of our own litter my path—medics and nurses, children, an old lady who liked to tell the little ones campfire tales each night to keep their spirits up. All of them gone in the blink of an eye.

The *Neville I* is already taking to the sky with Wes Graydon at the helm, and I spot Alec, Olivia, Blythe, Dax, Michela, and the Professor on the ground, still ushering people onto the last remaining crafts.

"Wait!" a woman's voice cries out, her high-pitched voice a dagger in my heart as I turn to find her running toward us with a child in her arms, her eyes wide with desperation. They must have fallen back somehow, left behind in the heat of the fight and the ensuing panic.

Dozens of MPs are on her trail, guns leveled at her back. Three of them fire at once, but it only takes one laser to hit home. It hits the woman's back. She lurches forward with a cry before dropping face-first onto the ground, the child pinned beneath her.

As the last few people run onto *Icarus*, the Professor steps forward, his hands shaking as he pulls out the gun he's been keeping in a shoulder holster someone gave him. I've never seen him use it, but he raises it now as he takes a step forward.

"What are you doing?" I ask, pulling him back toward *Icarus*. "We have to go!"

"That child is still alive!" he declares before ducking under my arm and rushing forward.

Raising his gun, he sprints across the space separating us from the remaining MPs. Another wave of them is coming, and he's running at them alone.

"Dad, no," Dax cries out, horror coating his words as he darts past me to follow the man.

From there, everything happens so quickly I hardly know if I'll remember it all in the days to come. Olivia, Alec, and I jump into action, guns blazing as we provide cover for the Professor. He stoops and gingerly pushes the woman's body aside, reaching down to pick up the child. Standing, he turns to run back to us, child in both hands, his gun forgotten on the ground. The child—a little boy—is wailing, his arms stretched back to the woman lying in the dirt and now being trampled on by the man who shot her.

The new wave of officers pursues, none of them shooting now—probably because they recognize the Professor as a high-value prisoner.

Instead, one of them ignites an electrified baton and breaks away from the others.

I allow myself an extra burst of speed, breaking away from the others and trying to intercept the Professor and the boy before they do. Hinkley and I meet in the middle, and he shoves the child into my arms just before the baton cracks down on his back. I retreat with the boy held close, my mouth open in horror as the Professor goes down with a cry of pain, his body contorting and convulsing as blue lines of electricity dance over his skin.

Choosing to save the boy he risked himself to rescue, I turn and run, passing Dax and Alec and heading back for *Icarus*. The *Neville II* is going airborne, leaving only *Icarus*. Blythe snatches the boy from my arms and turns to the gangplank, leaving me free to return to the fray.

Olivia, Dax, and Alec fight the MPs surrounding them, while the Professor is dragged away, his wrists secured behind his back in ionized cuffs. Panic flares in my chest as I realize we could lose them all in an instant.

I pull my gun and fire, taking down one of the MPs holding the Professor. But the one with the baton just strikes him again to keep him subdued and shoves him toward a waiting craft, out of sight.

"Shit, shit, shit," I shout before taking my rage out on the nearest officer. He gets lifted and thrown against a tree, his body breaking on the trunk despite his protective armor.

Olivia screams, the prodding of another electrified baton sending her shuddering to the ground. As MPs surround her, one opens an electric collar to keep her in check. Alec flies into a rage, trying to fight his way to her. But there are at least five MPs between him and her, and they seem to converge on him at once, pushing him back.

Another gang of them is on Dax next, three guys wrestling to keep him down as he struggles and roars, still strong as an ox despite being shocked several times. Another group advances on me, but I open fire again, taking down the one with the baton first, then the one holding a collar similar to the one around Olivia's neck.

Then, suddenly, more gunfire comes from behind me. Before long, Blythe and Senator Davis are at my side, weapons raised as they help me take them down one by one. Alec is running after the men dragging Olivia to the same craft the Professor was taken to, but is caught by the arms by two MPs, who throw him to the ground and wrestle to try to cuff him. The Senator picks them both off with her rifle, while Blythe and I pursue the four men carrying Dax's heavy body by the arms and legs. He thrashes in their hold, but he's been burned badly from the baton. One of his shoulders looks like it's dislocated. He's in pain and weakened, unable to get them to drop him.

Blythe shoots one, and he goes down while the other three struggle to keep their hold on Dax. I shoot another, then drop my gun and tackle the third, causing both he and the fourth guy to drop Dax. As the MP and I wrestle on the ground, Blythe knocks the fourth guy out with her titanium hand, then kneels to try to help Dax up.

I break my opponent's neck before struggling to my feet, just as another wave of them come around the corner. They swallow up Olivia, who's dragged through the middle of their swarm and onto the craft. We open fire on them, but it's no use. There are five of us—four, actually, since Dax can't be counted in his present state—and far too many of them.

"We have to run," the senator cries, gasping when a red laser nicks her shoulder, cutting through her sweater and burning the skin.

Dax is on his feet, but stumbles again, so I grab him and loop one arm over my shoulders, while Blythe does the same on the other side. While Alec and the senator cover us with gunfire, we rush toward *Icarus*. Dax stumbles along between us, his head lolling on his shoulders as he groans in pain.

"Leave me behind," he manages. "I'll just hold you back."

"Not a chance," I grunt, holding him tighter and trying to pick up the pace.

He grows heavier, one of his legs going out as a laser tears through his knee, ripping off one of his bionic prosthetics. Blythe screams as he falls, dragging her down with him and throwing me off balance.

I crouch to help him up, but he lifts his head and looks at me with pleading eyes.

"Run," he whispers, his voice hoarse. "Promise me you'll take care of them."

My response is a grim nod as I release him and reach for Blythe, prying her off the ground and to her feet.

"*No*," she screams, flailing against my hold.

Alec grabs her other arm, helping me drag her as the officers fall back, seeming content enough with Dax that they feel no need to pursue us.

"*Please*," she cries, even once we're up the gangplank. "Please don't leave him! We have to go back!"

"We can't save him if we stay," I try to assure her as we make it inside the hovercraft. "If we run now, we can go back for him later."

Alec releases her and rushes up the center aisle toward the cockpit, the senator hot on his heels. Blythe pummels me with both fists, the fall of her titanium hand nowhere near as painful as turning back to watch them drag Dax away is, his destroyed bionic leg left lying in the dirt.

Our gangplank goes up, and Alec gets us airborne within seconds. Blythe collapses against me, sobbing and shaking her head as I sink to one knee on the floor and hold her against my chest.

"I'm sorry," I whisper, my entire body shuddering as I try to get a hold on my own emotions for her sake. "Blythe, I'm so sorry."

Glancing up, she continues to shake her head. "How could you leave him behind? They'll kill him!"

Taking a deep breath, I muscle my way past the urge to cry, the sight of her flushed cheeks and the tears running down her face ripping through me like a knife. "If they wanted to kill him, they would have. Him, the Professor, Olivia ... they'll keep them prisoner until..."

I trail off, realizing my words can bring her no comfort. Remembering Olivia's time in captivity, I know if we don't rescue them, those three are going to wish they were dead.

"I need him, Gage," she whispers, her voice broken and her body limp in my arms. "I need him."

And because I would move heaven and earth to give her whatever she needs, I make her a promise. "We will save him, okay? All three of them. I promise, we will get to them in time. Do you trust me?"

Swallowing a sob, she trembles, but nods her head. "I do... I trust you with my life. And his."

I nod, gathering the resolve I know I'll need for what will come next. Rescue missions were impossible before, but they are even more so now. "Then trust me when I say that I will die to bring him back if that's what it takes. For you ... I *will* bring him back."

Nodding again, she holds my gaze for another moment before allowing me to help her to her feet. I lead her to the cockpit and sit her in one of the gunner's chairs, knowing she's in no condition to drive. Peering back into the passenger area, I find Michela and Agata sitting together near the middle of the craft, the senator in a window seat, her eyes glassy as she gazes out over the passing clouds. Does she feel the same guilt I do, over being helpless to do anything while three members of our family were dragged away before our very eyes?

I can't dwell on that now, or my own guilt over what just transpired. I sink into the other gunner's chair and glance over at Alec, who glares angrily out the front window, his hands tight on the controls.

"Can we follow them?" I ask, glancing at the radar screen that shows the MP crafts heading in a different direction from us, as well as the *Neville I* and *Neville II* just ahead. We should catch up to them in no time.

Alec shakes his head. "We could, but with a craft full of women, children, elderly, and injured, it would be suicide. Besides, we already know where they're going... The same place they always do before executing us in front of the world."

Stonehead.

The place where Olivia was brutalized and tortured, where Bionics go in, but never come out. I run a hand over my face. I want to ask what the hell we're supposed to do now, but with Blythe sitting so close by, I won't. I need her to continue to trust me, to be confident in me. Otherwise, she might do something rash on her own, which I can't allow. To lose her after everything else that's happened would end us all. The Resistance needs her. *I* need her.

Instead, I keep quiet and allow myself to mull over all the different possibilities. There's no time for planning or talk right now, while we are simply in survival mode, escaping the enemy to live, to run and fight another day. I know that once we land someplace for the night, we will get together with the senator to talk things over, to figure out some sort of plan.

So I think, I plan, and I pray with all my might that Dax and the others are strong enough to withstand what awaits them at Stonehead.

THIRTY-FIVE

GAGE BRONSON, BLYTHE SOL, ALEC KINNEAR, MICHELA ARLOTTI,
WES GRAYDON, AND SENATOR ALEXIS DAVIS
UNKNOWN LOCATION
MARCH 2, 4011
11:05 P.M.

ANOTHER WEEK OF TRANSIENCE PASSES US BY, AND WE'RE NO CLOSER TO COMING UP with a plan than we were the day the Military Police came and dragged Dax, the Professor, and Olivia away from us. We stick to our patterns of flying during the day, and making camp at night. Alec has become far choosier in deciding where to land each day, sticking mostly to radiation zones, despite the health risks they pose.

Each night, we get reports of people becoming ill, vomiting, and suffering the effects of limited exposure. I'm not sure how much longer we can withstand it before we're all eventually poisoned. We try to stay to levels with less than two hundred millirems, but even that is enough to make people sick for a day or more. I've noticed Blythe vomiting from time to time, and she isn't eating much, exacerbating the guilt gnawing away at me over what went down at that church. And for each day that passes, I can't help but wonder what horrors the Enforcers might be visiting on our friends—what new methods of torture they've come up with since our last visit to Stonehead.

Our supplies begin to run low. With no way to scavenge or gather more, we run the risk of not being able to feed anyone once our food runs out.

On the seventh night, we sit around our campfire as usual, our much smaller group of leaders—Blythe, Alec, Wes, Senator Davis, and me. Michela comes and goes as we talk, bringing bowls of a thin soup someone put together for a late dinner.

"If we don't find a place to settle soon, we're going to die out here," the senator declares between bites.

"What exactly do you suggest?" Wes asks. "No place is as safe as Headquarters was."

"Headquarters is gone," Alec mutters, accepting his portion from Michela with a curt nod. "And we'll probably *never* find a place that safe, or with the same technology, so stop bringing it up. The senator is right ... we need a solution, and fast. We're sitting ducks out here, and we can't even think about running off to save Dax, Olivia, and the Professor until we have a safe place to put everyone counting on us to keep them alive."

He says this in an abrupt, clipped tone, but there's no disguising his worry for Olivia. His face has grown harder and harder by the day, and his mouth is always pulled into a thin, harsh line.

Michela approaches Blythe, offering a bowl of soup, but she declines with a shake of her head. Before Michela can walk away with the bowl, I stand and take it from her. Approaching Blythe, I hold both mine and her portion.

"Blythe, you need to eat," I say softly, sinking down onto the ground beside her. "To keep your strength up."

Shaking her head again, she avoids my gaze, drawing her knees up to her chest and hugging them. She's hardly spoken since Dax and the others were taken, and barely participates in these meetings. It's as if she exists on autopilot now, only eating or drinking when necessary, no longer engaging with the people around her. She has withdrawn the way she always does when bad things happen. It's the only way she knows how to survive.

Still, I can't let it continue, not when there are so few of us who can fight and lead. Not with everyone watching her—the walking, talking symbol of our Resistance.

"Listen," I say, my voice soft. "We need you, okay? We need you healthy and here with us. Don't you want to be strong enough to be able to go after Dax when we come up with a plan? You can't do that if you starve yourself to death."

Setting my bowl down, I grab her spoon and dig in for a healthy amount of the soup before holding it up to her lips.

"I will feed you like a baby if I have to, Blythe... Don't try me."

That gets the smallest of smiles from her and some eye contact. When those eyes meet mine, so full of sadness and pain, I want to find some way to banish it all.

"You're right," she croaks, her voice hoarse from underuse. She clears her throat. "I'm sorry... I'll eat."

Accepting her bowl from me, she starts to dig in, taking big, hearty bites. Satisfied, I reach for my own bowl. I have the spoon halfway up to my mouth when a derisive voice whispers in the darkness.

"*Pitiful.*"

I pause when I recognize the voice, my mouth falling open as I turn my head to glare at Michela, who has just delivered her last bowl of soup and stands nearby, watching Blythe with a sneer on her face.

Blythe stiffens and swallows, having heard, too. She slowly turns to look at Michela, her nostrils flaring with barely contained rage.

"What the fuck did you just say?" she challenges.

Michela looks away for a moment, as if she hadn't meant to be overheard. But then, she approaches Blythe, hands on her hips, chin defiantly raised.

"I said you're *pitiful*," she fires back, venom lacing her tone.

Setting the bowl aside, Blythe slowly rises to her feet, hands balled into fists at her sides. "Excuse me, what the hell is your problem? In case you hadn't noticed, this is a *leadership* meeting. So you need to take your smartass mouth over there by the soup kettle and go back to playing waitress."

Michela scoffs. "Better than playing victim. Sitting around here pouting because the Military Police took your man. If it were *my* man who'd been taken, I'd be in the fight with everyone else, trying to figure out a way to get him back ... not moping around and being spoon fed like a fucking toddler!"

"Michela, that's enough," I interject, rising to my feet.

"If it were *your* man?" Blythe counters with a smirk. "I'm sorry, but *where* is this mythical man you speak of? Oh, that's right—you don't have one because you're an annoying, clingy, attention-seeking bitch! Maybe instead of wasting energy worrying about me, you should be worried about yourself and the fact you're chasing a guy who doesn't even want you."

Michela crosses her arms over her chest, looking smug. "He certainly seemed to want me back at Headquarters... Not that you would know anything about what he was up to while you were using Dax to make him jealous."

"Ladies, this is ridiculous," the senator declares, rising and coming to stand between them. "Settle down."

"Fuck you," Blythe explodes, blowing past her and getting right in Michela's face. "You don't know shit about Dax and me. As for Gage ... you barely know him."

"Oh honey, I know Gage far better than you do," Michela hisses, leaving no room to mistake her innuendo.

Blythe growls, putting her hands against Michela's chest and shoving her hard. "Slut!"

Michela recovers and advances on her, returning the shove. "Bitch!"

"Cunt," Blythe retorts.

She counters quickly with a swift slap to Blythe's left cheek, the sound echoing throughout camp. Everyone has fallen silent now, watching the argument with slack jaws and stares of disbelief. A growl unfurls from Blythe's chest as she lunges at Michela, tackling her to the ground.

"Hey," Alec growls, coming toward them with a glare. "That's enough... Cut the shit!"

The two roll back and forth, wrestling in a tangle of arms and legs before Blythe gains the upper hand, straddling Michela and curling her human hand into a fist before delivering a blow. Michela grunts as the fist strikes her cheekbone, then counters with a shot to Blythe's ribs.

By the time Alec and I get to them, Blythe has punched her again, busting her lip. Michela screams and claws as I pull Blythe off her, succeeding in leaving a few gouge marks down the side of Blythe's neck. Alec hauls Michela up by her arm and shakes her.

"*Enough*," he roars, silencing both girls and halting them before they can go after each other again. "Are you two fucking kidding me? We're on the run right now, three of our people have been taken prisoner, and you're fighting over a *guy*?"

Blythe yanks out of my hold, pointing an accusing finger at Michela. "That bitch came at me first."

"I don't care," Alec snaps. "You two think you're the only ones hurting over this? That I don't want to go after them in a murderous rage?" he says, glaring at Michela when he spits those words out. "Or that I don't want to retreat into myself and disconnect from it all?" he adds, turning back to Blythe. "But I *can't*, because these people need us to lead them. The woman I love was snatched up right in front of me, and I'm fucking dying without her! But goddamn it, if I can keep my shit together, so can the two of you. You don't have to like each other, but this petty bullshit won't happen again."

For a long while, everyone falls silent, staring off into different directions. It's the first time Alec has let any of us know how he's feeling after losing Olivia, giving us a glimpse of his own inner pain.

Blythe breaks the silence first, turning to glare at Michela. "Keep her away from me, or I'll shove my fist through that big mouth of hers and leave her with a few less teeth," she hisses before turning to stomp toward the tent she shares with the senator and two other women.

Michela opens her mouth as if to retort, but I'm on her in a heartbeat, grasping her upper arms and lifting her clear off the ground.

"What the hell?" she protests, squirming in my hold as I walk her away from camp and toward the edge of the clearing.

We disappear into the trees, but I keep going, past the patrolling guards and out of earshot of camp. Michela stops fighting, but through the meager light coming from our campfires, I can see her deep scowl.

I set her on her feet, crossing my arms over my chest. "That was out of line."

She rears back as if I've slapped her, confusion and hurt slashing across her face. "*I'm* out of line? Look what that bitch did to my face!"

"Don't call her that," I snap. "You hit her first, and the things you said… You owe her an apology, Michela."

Rolling her eyes, she shakes her head in disbelief. "God, you're just as pitiful as she is. What—you think since Dax is gone, you can swoop in and take her for yourself?"

If she were a man, I'd punch her in the face, but because she's not, I keep my hands to myself.

"Dax is my friend," I state between clenched teeth. "I'm going to do everything in my power to bring him home … for *her*. So they can be together again."

"And meanwhile, you'll indulge in your sick little fantasy of being there for her in hopes that maybe she'll choose you over him this time?"

"Michela—"

"No," she interrupts, ignoring the clear warning in my tone. "I've had enough of watching you fawn over her, handling her like she's some kind of precious piece of glass. *She's* the symbol you all rally around? That hollow shell of a person who falls apart when shit gets rough?"

"Blythe Sol is braver than any other woman I know," I say, irritation making my tone sharp. "You—the girl who got to stay in her cozy little hideout beneath a pizza parlor—can never truly know what it was like for her to be on the front lines of it all from day one."

Her chin trembles as the first spark of remorse creeps into her expression. "I lost my father—"

"And her entire family was gunned down right in front of her," I cut in. "Through all of this, you've had your sister and your cousin. She lost *everyone*. And now that she has a family again with the Resistance, the people she loves keep dying. Jenica, Laura, even me. But after she's done retreating and licking her wounds, she always comes back swinging, stronger and more full of fire than ever … and *that* is why she is our symbol."

Michela stares at me in openmouthed shock for a while before recovering, lowering her gaze to her feet. "God, I'm an idiot. All this time,

I thought maybe you were just obsessed with her ... maybe only wanted her because someone else had her. But you really do love her, don't you?"

"I do," I reply without hesitation. Because it's simply an element of my existence, no longer something that needs to be questioned or explained.

She nods, glancing toward camp. "I wasn't trying to start anything... My irritation and fatigue got the best of me, and I didn't think she'd hear me."

"But she did," I say. "Alec was right—we don't need this right now. There are too few fighters left for us to start trying to kill each other."

"So I guess you want me to apologize," she says with a frown.

"Maybe not right this second," I say with a wince. "Blythe has a temper, and the best thing you can do after she's been set off is give her some space. If you go to her now, I won't promise you'll come back with all of your teeth."

"I can handle her, you know," she says before brushing past me to return to camp. "I didn't need you getting in the way."

It sits on the tip of my tongue to remind her that one blow from Blythe's titanium hand is all it would take to knock her out cold, but I bite back my retort and let her go, taking a moment to get myself together. While what just happened between Michela and Blythe seemed like no more than a cat fight, I can't help but wonder if there hadn't been more to it on Blythe's end. Could she dislike Michela because of what went on between us at Headquarters? Was she jealous, like Michela claimed?

Running a hand over my hair, I sigh. Of course she's jealous ... just like seeing her with Dax sometimes makes me want to put a hole through a wall with my fist. This sick, twisted connection between us won't let up, even when we have attached ourselves to different people. The only difference is that I know Blythe loves Dax, while my feelings for Michela don't go beyond admiration and physical attraction.

"God, what a clusterfuck," I mutter.

But it was the clusterfuck making up my life, for better or worse. Deciding I can't avoid the tension at camp forever, I come away from the tree I've been leaning on and start toward camp.

Without warning, something shoves me from behind, and I fall facedown onto the ground. A heavy weight compresses my back and my head is yanked up by the hair, a rough gag forced between my lips. Then, a cloth falls over my head, turning my vision black.

WHEN THE SACK IS PULLED OFF, I FIND MYSELF IN THE LAST PLACE I WOULD EXPECT. I'M still gagged, but as my eyes adjust to the change in light, I can see my surroundings just fine.

A dimly lit room with nothing more than a yellow bulb illuminating it closes me in—a tight space. There is no furniture in this rough room with its floor, ceiling, and walls made from concrete ... only the chair I'm sitting in, my ankles tied to the legs, my hands still secured behind my back.

Standing just before me are three people—two men and one woman. Dressed in all black, their faces and clothing are covered in green and brown camouflage paint, their hair covered in black skull caps, weapons resting in holsters at their hips, shoulders, and ankles. One of the men steps forward, his eyes a shocking electric blue amid all the face paint. He pauses right in front of me, hands folded behind his back.

"I'm Davian," he says, his voice gravelly, his tone light and casual. "Who are you?"

I narrow my eyes, trying to figure out where I might be, and why I was taken from camp. These guys clearly aren't MPs, but the government could have some new faction of enforcement I know nothing about. I clamp my lips together, determined not to give him any information until I know more about what's going on.

Davian sighs and inclines his head at me. "Look, man, you're trapped here. We searched you and took your gun, you're tied to a chair, and you're a big guy, but the three of us could probably take you down if you managed to break loose. We saw your people at camp, but didn't want to invade without knowing what we're dealing with here. So either start talking, or we go into that clearing, guns blazing to take down whoever is there."

A threat, one that terrifies me to my core. Still, I keep silent, glaring at Davian without flinching.

"Fine, just answer me this one question," Davian relents. "Are you, and the people at that camp, Bionics?"

Despite wanting to hold my ground, I need to know where this is going ... who Davian is and what he wants. Lifting my chin, I decide to take a chance that giving him one piece of information will either doom me, or save me.

"Yes," I reply.

He waves the woman forward. "Sabra, check him."

She produces a wand from her belt, one I recognize as a scanner for bionic hardware. Sweeping my body with the instrument, she pauses over my chest once it starts beeping, then continues down to my feet.

"Bionic organ in his chest," she reports. "Heart or lungs ... no other prosthetics."

"One of us," Davian confirms with a nod. "Judging by the size of your camp, I'm going to assume you're with the Resistance?"

I eye Davian incredulously, still not certain about trusting him. Rolling his eyes and huffing in irritation, he yanks up one pant leg to reveal a titanium leg, while Sabra leans closer so the meager light can show me the truth of what's in the depth of her stare. Both her eyes are Bionic, the whir of machinery just visible in her pupils when she gets up close.

Glancing toward the third person, I raise my eyebrows. "And you?"

"All mine are internal," the man replies.

I nod, deciding to believe him since he's with two other Bios.

"So, answer the question," Davian prods. "Are you with the Resistance?"

"Who wants to know?" I counter.

"Just the leader of an organization with the means and supplies to take you in if need be," he replies with a shrug. "But you don't have to take me up on my offer."

Once again, he's got me second guessing myself, wondering if the next thing I say will save everyone I care about, or doom us all.

"What organization?" I hedge.

Backing toward the door, Davian gives me a smug grin. "You didn't think the Resistance was the only Bionics movement out there, did you?"

He swings the door open while Sabra kneels to untie my feet. She leaves my wrists bound behind my back, and gives me a little push forward. My mouth falls open as I stumble toward the doorway, beyond which lays a large cavern lined with walkways. Behind those walkways are doors, which open and close as people—Bionics—come and go using metal stairs to move between the various floors. It all descends into an enormous pit, half which seems to serve as a dining hall, while the other is filled with furniture where several more people lounge and talk.

Glancing back to Davian, I am unable to find words as I soak in the truth of what he's just revealed. There is another faction of Bionics hiding right here in America … and by the looks of things, they have been for a very long time.

"Welcome," Davian says, sweeping his arm out over it all with pride, "to The Underground."

THIRTY-SEVEN

GAGE BRONSON, BLYTHE SOL, ALEC KINNEAR, WES GRAYDON, AND
SENATOR ALEXIS DAVIS
THE UNDERGROUND
MARCH 3, 4011
12:20 A.M.

HALF AN HOUR LATER, WE SIT AROUND OUR CAMPFIRE—OUR REMAINING RESISTANCE leadership, with Davian, Sabra, and the third guy, whose name is Zander, mixed in. After relenting and telling them I was, in fact, with the Resistance, along with my identity as The Patriot, Davian asked me to arrange a meeting. So, here we sit after a quick round of introductions and everyone getting over the shocking revelation that there has been another Bionics organization under our noses without our knowledge all this time.

"I have to say," Davian begins once tin mugs of strong, black coffee have been poured from the insulated container he brought as a peace offering. "It's an honor to meet so many key players of the Resistance. We don't have TV or internet in The Underground, but we get snatches of news from time to time. Senator Davis ... or should I call you President Davis?"

She smiles graciously. "Senator will do for now, thank you."

He nods and smiles, the motion kind of charming even with all the face paint. "And The Patriot himself... If I had known who you were, we would have been gentler with you, man. Sorry."

I shrug. "It's no problem."

"And you, Ms. Sol... Wow, what a privilege. We've all been so proud of you."

Blythe nods and murmurs her thanks, but mostly studies the trio in silence, likely trying to decide, just as I had to, whether we should trust them.

"We were awfully sorry to hear about what happened to your main hideout," Davian continues. "Gage told us the bare bones of the story, and we hate to see your women and children ... your elderly, displaced like this. Which is why we are prepared to take you in, if you need a safe place. The Underground has gone undetected since the Bionics were first forced into hiding."

"I can't believe you've been here this entire time," Alec says, shaking his head in disbelief. "How have you managed to fly under the radar for so long?"

"Our home is actually an old underground bunker—one built by the government to be used for sheltering soldiers underground in times of war," Sabra speaks up. "But it's been long abandoned and forgotten."

"And you have the space for all of us?" the senator asks. "Even after all that's happened, we still have hundreds."

Davian nods. "The bunker is huge, and each room capable of holding up to six—bunk beds built into the walls, you see."

"How have you gone unnoticed for so long?" Blythe chimes in. "I find it kind of hard to believe."

"It's simple, really," he replies. "Most of our people stay in the bunker, with only our patrols and scavenging teams leaving The Underground. Patrolling the area for MPs is how we found your camp, and Gage here... Our scavenging teams are responsible for making sure we never run out of food, water, or other vital supplies. It's a small community compared to what the Resistance was, but we keep to ourselves and don't stir up trouble... It's kept us safe so far."

I exchange a glance with Alec, and wonder if he's thinking the same thing I am—that the Resistance is known for stirring up trouble to get what we want and fight for our place in the world.

"I think I can speak for us all when I say we'd be happy to shelter our people with you," the senator says, to which we all nod in agreement. "We are also capable of pitching in—adding our resources to yours, joining your patrol and scavenging teams, or whatever else is needed."

Davian grins. "Great! We should probably get moving. You've got a lot of bodies and cargo to move, but with our people pitching in, we can help make it go smoothly."

"There's just one other thing," Alec cuts in before Davian can get to his feet.

"I'm all ears," he replies, inclining his head.

"We have three people who have been captured by the Military Police," Alec replies. "Among them is Professor Neville Hinkley himself."

Sabra gasped. "The man who created the technology that saved our lives?"

"The very same," Alec confirms. "The Resistance's next mission is to rescue the Professor and two other prisoners, so a group of us will need to set out as soon as possible. Any weapons, supplies, or smaller aircrafts you could supply us with would be greatly appreciated. I can guarantee we'll return with items more valuable to replace them, as well as more food or fuel to store. We just ... we need to get them back. It's imperative that we not allow the government to execute them—or worse, torture them for information."

Davian falls silent, trading glances with his two companions before looking at Alec. "I'm sorry to hear about Professor Hinkley. We all owe him our lives. I cannot imagine how hard it must have been for you to see him, and your friends, taken captive. However, I have to let you know one other thing about The Underground before you join us. Unlike the Resistance, we are not a fighting movement... We are a shelter for people of our kind who need a place to hide."

"We understand that," Alec says with a frown. "We aren't asking for you to fight; we just need supplies—"

"Hear me out," Davian cuts in. "We firmly believe the Bionics can never have a place in society ... not after all that's happened. We believe in a separate civilization, one where we can live in peace without the invasion of the American government or those it deems 'normal.' It is for that reason, and for the safety of the people we govern, that we stick by this rule—if you leave and engage in conflict with the Military Police or any other faction of the government, you cannot return to The Underground."

My mouth falls open at what I'm hearing, and I trade disbelieving glances with Blythe. "Are you serious?"

Davian pierces me with his sharp eyes, his expression grim beneath the camouflage paint. "It is necessary to keep our people safe. Confrontation with MPs is only allowed if we encounter them on patrols or while scavenging and must fight for our own lives or to protect our home. We don't bother them, and they don't bother us... It's how we've survived here for so long."

"Our friends need help," I argue. "The Professor needs help!"

"And we will do nothing to stop you from going to deliver that help," Davian replies, his voice remaining even and amiable. "We will even help out with whatever supplies you might need for such a mission. But once you have left on this mission, you cannot come back. I'm sorry, but you have to understand ... we have people to protect, too, and can't risk you being followed back here."

Looking around at the Resistance leadership, I find varying degrees of disbelief, shock, and despair on each of their faces.

But then, Alec turns to me with an expectant gaze. "Bronson, you saw the place from the inside. What's it like?"

"Big," I answer honestly. "Hidden so well we would probably never be found. Well supplied and organized."

Alec glances over at the senator, and the two seem to communicate without speaking. After working together within Headquarters while the rest of us went off on missions, I can see how they'd form such a relationship.

"Davian, we accept your offer and thank you for your kindness," the senator replies, extending a hand to him.

"What are you doing?" Blythe asks. "Didn't you hear what he said? Once we go in, there's no coming out if we want to continue having a place to live."

"An issue to deal with once those we must protect are safe," Alec points out. "We can't keep them out in the open like this ... not unless we want a repeat of what happened at that church. Those who want in on the mission can choose to leave with the full knowledge that they can't come back. It's a risk we have to take if we want to save them, while protecting the innocents among us."

He's right, even though I'm not happy about the terms of Davian's offer. If we leave to rescue Dax and the others, we run the risk of not having anywhere to take them once they've been freed. And what kind of shape will they be in after days—or by the time we find them, weeks—of mistreatment and torture? But I don't intend to keep my mouth shut on this. Once all our people are safe and secured, I intend to try to change Davian's mind. The future depends on it. My promise to Blythe depends on it.

"Come on," Davian says, rising to his feet after shaking the senator's hand. "Let's get you guys settled in."

HOURS LATER, WE ARE MOVED INTO THE UNDERGROUND. OUR HOVERCRAFTS HAVE been hidden in the woods, covered by foliage to camouflage them as best we can. All our food, water, medical supplies, and fuel have been combined with theirs, and Davian assures us that after we've had a chance to rest, we will all be given responsibilities and jobs to perform as part of The Underground.

The setup isn't as comfortable as Headquarters, but it's better than we've had these past few weeks. The food in the dining area is plain, but hot and filling. I sit across from Blythe with Agata at my side and clean my plate, encouraging her to try to get something in her stomach. She takes a few bites of everything, but mostly sits and observes our new home. After dinner, we are allowed to choose rooms from among those that haven't been filled, most of which are on the top three floors of the place.

Opening the door to one of the little chambers, I find six bunk beds built into the left and right walls, and a desk in the space between them. Flanking it are dressers for holding clothes, and a small closet sits open near the door. There isn't a lot of space, but it looks like most of us can spread out with so many rooms available. As Agata bounces into the room, claiming one of the top bunks for herself, I linger in the doorway, glancing out at the walkway to make sure our people are settling in okay. Below us, The Underground buzzes with activity, every person doing their part to help run the place efficiently.

I spot Blythe standing in front of the door to an empty room a few units down, a bag slung over one shoulder. She stares blankly into the space, unmoving as people walk around her, toting their own belongings to their destinations. She looks so heartbreakingly dejected, so alone, that I can't help the pull I feel toward her. My feet are moving before I realize it, and I'm at her side in an instant.

"Hey," I say, peering down into her haggard face. "You okay?"

She blinks, looking up at me as if she hadn't even registered my presence until I spoke. That's how things are between us; my existence means nothing until she acknowledges it. And I'm so pitiful that I will stand here for as long as it takes to get her to look at me, to notice me, to see the love in my eyes when I look at her.

"I ..." She sighs. "It's so stupid. All this time we've been out on the road and I've been sharing a tent with a bunch of other women ... I thought I wanted a space to myself. A room where I could be alone. But here I am, and I can't go inside."

Peering into the room, I find it empty just like she said, all six beds still neatly made, the closet vacant. My chest aches as I realize that if things had gone differently, she'd be bunking with Dax, maybe trying to figure out a way they could share one of the narrow beds.

I take her hand and squeeze it. "Me and Agata need another roommate anyway. Come on."

She doesn't resist when I pull her along, toward our open door. When we come into the room and Agata sees Blythe, her face lights up and she rushes forward. Blythe bends down to hug her tight, closing her eyes and hanging on for a long time.

"Are you moving in with us?" she asks when they pull apart.

"Seems like it," Blythe says with a forced smile.

"I took the top bunk over there, but you can have the other top one if you want," Agata declares before climbing into the bunk. She's changed into shorts and a t-shirt for sleeping, and I predict she'll be conked out in no time.

Closing the door, I gesture toward the beds. "Choose whichever one you want ... I'm not picky."

Glancing around, she selects the bottom bunk on the left side of the room. So, I take the bottom on the right, sitting on it while I bend over to take off my boots. Blythe follows suit, pushing her shoes neatly under the bed before starting to unbutton her jacket. I open the bag I stashed on the bed—the meager belongings I packed and stowed on board *Icarus* during our preparations for the invasion, and pull out a clean pair of sweatpants.

Blythe gathers clothes from her pack, and we stand at the same time, facing each other in the cramped room. Awareness of her floods my entire being, her scent permeating my nostrils, the heat of her body kicking my temperature up a few degrees.

Swallowing convulsively, I tear my gaze away from the tank top hugging her body and turn my back. I can hear her moving around, and glance over my shoulder to find she's turned, too, giving me privacy. She pulls her hair up and winds it into a bun, revealing the black ink of the Resistance tattoo on the back of her neck. I turn away before she can unhook her bra, and concentrate on changing. I'm exhausted, and tomorrow will bring a host of new problems to be solved.

Once I'm in my sweatpants, I push my bag under the bed beside my boots and climb onto my bunk. Blythe follows suit, now dressed in a clean tank and pair of shorts.

After we lay there for what seems like a long time, she turns her head to look at me. "Still awake, too?"

I nod, propping my head up with one hand. "Yeah. Kind of hard to rest now. I still feel like the walls are going to come crashing in on us any second now."

"I know what you mean," she replies. "It's hard to feel safe after all that's happen."

"But we are safe," I remind her. "And I'm here. Try to sleep, okay? I'll lay awake a little while longer if it makes you feel better."

Turning onto her side so she's facing me, she pulls the blankets over her shoulder and nods. "It would, actually."

So, we lay there, with Blythe staring at me, holding my gaze as if assuring herself I'm still awake. It's hard to look into those beautiful brown eyes—and not to want to cross the room and take her into my arms, pull her into my bed and hold her.

But it's not my place to do any of those things. It is Dax's—and I have promised to bring him back to her. As I watch her finally drift off to sleep, I resolve myself to hold true to that promise. No matter what it might cost me.

I'M AWAKENED HOURS LATER BY BLYTHE'S MURMURING AND MOANING—THE SOUNDS OF a nightmare coming from the other side of the room. I sit up and rub my eyes as she begins to thrash on the bed, the covers tangled around her legs. Her eyes are squeezed shut, and tears run down her face as she fights something in her sleep, her body convulsing and her limbs flailing.

"Dax," she whispers, her voice broken ... afraid. "Dax, no."

Pity lances through me, and I'm on my feet in a heartbeat, crossing the room to kneel beside her bunk. I reach out to touch her, bracing a hand against her forehead and smoothing it through her tousled hair. She struggles for a bit more, but stills when she hears my voice.

"Blythe," I murmur, leaning close and pressing my mouth to her ear. "It's me... It's Gage. You're safe, remember? It's over. I'm here."

She opens her eyes slowly and looks at me, more tears shimmering in the depths of her human eye. "Gage?"

I nod and try to smile for her, to put on a brave face. "Yeah, sweetheart, it's me. You had a nightmare about Dax?"

She nods, closing her eyes and sobbing. She tries to curl in on herself, but I haul her from the bed, blankets and all. Taking a seat at the desk, I settle her in my lap and cling to her. Fuck what is or isn't my place. Dax isn't here, and I know if our roles were reversed, he would comfort her this way, too—he likely did after my supposed death.

"Hey, it's okay," I murmur, shifting her weight so she's more evenly settled across my thighs.

"They could be torturing him right now," she whispers, swiping at her wet face with her human hand. "They could have killed him by now."

Taking her face in my hands, I force her to look at me. "He isn't dead. I refuse to believe that. And Dax is strong... Come on, he's one of the strongest people we know. Did you see how many men it took to bring him down? He can handle whatever they do to him, and he'll still tell them to fuck off and kiss his black ass."

She chuckles at that, the sound still heavy with grief. "You're right. I just ... I need him to come back to me in one piece. I need him... *We* need him."

I nod. "I know... I understand."

"No," she says, shaking her head. "You don't. But I need to tell you something, and I need you to promise not to tell. No one else can know."

I frown, studying her face for any clue as to what this could be about. "You can tell me anything, Blythe. You know that."

She nods and sniffles, wiping away the last of her tears. "That day, before the Military Police attacked, you saw Dax and me in the infirmary."

"Sure," I replied. "You were getting your wrist checked out."

She shakes her head at me, her eyes wide ... and I remember the hospital gown. I remember thinking it odd that she'd need to disrobe to have her wrist looked at. Dread unfurls in my gut.

"What's wrong with you? Are you sick? What happened?"

"A few weeks before that day, the Professor took a blood sample to run a test," she says, her voice low as she avoids my gaze. "It came back positive."

"For what?" I prod, trying not to be impatient. But she has me worried, my mind running through all the possibilities, everything that could be wrong with her.

"I was at the infirmary for an abortion," she says, meeting my eyes again, her own haunted and shimmering with unshed tears. "Dax and I couldn't bring a baby into the world ... into *this* world. So we asked the Professor to perform the procedure. It was supposed to be done the day Tamryn arrived with her friends, but got postponed once we realized we might be attacked. Days went by with us trying to fit it in, but there was so much going on, too many things we had to do to prepare for an attack, and..."

She stops and my throat seizes, the realization of what she's trying to say slamming into me like a ton of bricks. My head spins as I try to grab hold to one thought, my heart pounding while I attempt to latch on to a single emotion. But there are too many thoughts, too many feelings brought on by this news.

But it all boils down to the woman I love being impregnated by the man she chose over me. A man I love like a brother, but hate for the split second that my mind and heart settle on envy—envy for the life she created with someone else, anger it isn't mine, that she didn't choose me.

"I was on the table when the alarms went off," she says, her voice tinged with incredulity, as if she still can't believe it. "We were about to begin..."

"Blythe," I whisper hoarsely, anger melting away and shock taking over, followed by fear. "Are you ... you're saying..."

Take care of them, Dax had said to me just before they dragged him off.

I'd misunderstood, thinking 'them' referred to her and Agata, or maybe her and the entire Resistance family. But now, I realize his meaning, what Dax has placed on my shoulders.

Nodding solemnly, she places a hand over her belly. "Yes ... I'm still pregnant with Dax's baby."

EPILOGUE

(Dax Janner)

THE ROOM I AM IN IS COLD—FOUR WALLS OF SOLID CONCRETE THAT EVEN I AM NOT strong enough to fight through. And even if I was, I'm not at my full capabilities right now, my body broken, my skin still throbbing from the burns created by electrified batons striking me over and over again. There's a cot against the wall so narrow and short I can barely fit on it. A toilet in the corner that doesn't flush right every time, and makes the room stink to high heaven. I suspect they leave it that way on purpose—yet another fucked-up, twisted thing they can do to try to break me.

There's nothing else in the room—no cellmate, nothing I can use to amuse myself, no way out except the steel door that's always locked. A hatch and small shelf built in the door are for them to slip me my meager meals—just enough to keep me from dying. The first two days, I refused to eat anything they gave me, afraid they might poison me or give me some sort of serum to make me talk. I hurled the metal trays against the wall, sending the broth and water splattering everywhere, the hunks of stale bread to the floor.

On day three, they forced a tube down my throat—but only after they'd beaten me into submission and strapped me to a table. With one of my titanium prosthetics gone—replaced by a heavy fiberglass one that is utterly useless—I'm slow and unsteady on my feet, my gait uneven. It's good enough to get me to the toilet and to the door to grab my food, but not for much else.

So far, no one has told me what's to be done with me, but it's not like I don't already have a clue. I'm sure they're just trying to think of a clever way to kill me first ... the most effective way to murder me on live TV to drive home their message.

Lying back on my narrow cot, I close my eyes and think of Blythe—of my child growing inside her even now. Or is it? Is anybody even still alive? Did they get away safely after I was dragged onto that hovercraft, legless and in chains?

Blythe's alive ... she has to be. Gage would never allow anything to happen to her. I can't help but chuckle at the irony of it. Most guys would be afraid to leave their woman with the guy who wants to steal her away. But not me. I know 'the other guy' will do everything in his power to make sure my girl and my baby are safe.

It's enough to get me through each day, closing my eyes and imagining what she might be doing. Maybe helping set up camp somewhere, or meeting with the senator and the others to find a safe place to settle. I hope she's eating enough. Nausea has kept her from taking in as many calories as I'd like, and I'm worried she's become too thin this early in her pregnancy. Once our chance for an abortion was snatched away, my concerns turned toward a healthy baby and a healthy mother, because—ready or not—Baby Janner is coming in about seven months

I imagine her crying, angry and sad over watching us get captured. But Gage will comfort her—he'll take her into his arms, hold her and tell her everything will be okay. I need that from him, just as much as Blythe will. I need someone to be there for her, because I know how easily she can be shattered. Gage will hold her together.

I daydream about being rescued, about *Icarus* busting through the wall of my cell—wherever the hell this cell happens to be—and bailing me out, taking me home. Wherever home happens to be these days. Blythe—she is home. Where she is, that is home to me.

The door opens suddenly, jarring me out of my fantasy. Four MPs with riot gear on and heavy shields raised approach, one of them carrying the dreaded electrified baton. I'm hauled to my feet and slammed to the floor, my vision blurring slightly when my head hits the cement hard. I'm shackled hand and foot, the chains between my ankle cuffs so narrow I can only take small steps. Not that I'm going anywhere fast on a bum leg.

My heart rate accelerates as I realize I'm being taken down the hallway, away from the other cells. More steel doors pass me on either side, and I wonder which ones hold Olivia and the Professor. Have they been treated badly? Tortured? Killed?

I clench my jaw and force myself to concentrate on the present. I can't think about what my friend and the man I call my father might be going through right now, because it'll just make me angry. And if I get angry and do something stupid, I could make things worse for myself, and them.

I'm ushered into a larger room, this one boasting shelves and shelves of what appear to be tools and surgical instruments. A steel table with straps and buckles is elevated vertically, a mechanism beneath it used to control it. In that room, I find several men in starched black uniforms, white earpieces inside their ears. I stumble as I'm pushed forward, and the men part to reveal the one in their midst—the last man I expected to see down here.

He's dressed impeccably as always, in a navy-blue suit and red tie, his brown hair combed tediously back from his face. His blue eyes assess me with equal parts disgust and curiosity as he pauses just in front of me, waving the MPs away. They scurry out the door, but the men in black stay—men I realize must be Secret Service.

"Dax Janner," he says in a light voice, his perfect diction even more annoying in person than on TV.

"Drummond," I say, curling my upper lip as if the name tastes rancid on my tongue.

"That's *Mr. President* to you," he snaps, his eyes flashing like strikes of lightning.

Pursing my lips, I reach for the drawstring at the waist of the white pants they gave me, matching the rough white shirt on my back. Loosening it, I pull my dick free and—while still holding his gaze—proceed to piss all over his shoes. I can't help a cocky grin as he blinks in shock, his mouth falling open as my urine splatters his expensive shoes and pant legs. His agents move forward, but Drummond stills them with one hand, holding my gaze and actually waiting for me to finish.

I empty myself and make sure he gets every drop before pulling my pants back up. "That's what I think of you ... *Mr. President*," I snarl.

Drummond smiles, the motion cold and humorless as he takes a step away from me and begins unbuttoning his suit jacket. He takes his time, acting like he doesn't know he's standing in a puddle of my piss. Rolling up his shirt sleeves and loosening his tie, he approaches me again, hands braced on his hips.

"Did you know I used to be the general of the Military Police? Before I got into politics," he says conversationally, as if we're talking about the weather.

I shrug one shoulder. "And?"

He chuckles. "I just wanted you to remember that the next time you think to disrespect me. I'm not the sort of politician who makes others do his dirty work."

The second the last word has left his mouth, he takes a swing at me, his fist flying with a speed I can't dodge at this proximity. He throws me against the wall, my jaw throbbing as I struggle to stay on my feet.

Turning toward the table, he waves a hand at his agents. "Strip him ... and someone clean this mess up."

Four men come toward me, and I attack, head-butting the first, and slamming my shoulder into the second one's torso. Whatever Drummond has planned, it can't be good, but I'll be damned if I'm just going to lie down and take it.

I kick, flail, and even bite while they cut my clothes away and hurl me across the room toward the elevated table. They strap me down, the strips of leather holding my head motionless, then crossing my chest, stomach, and legs, effectively pinning me flat.

Coming up beside me, Drummond pulls a lever, and the table begins to move, floating up and back until I'm horizontal, then continuing until my feet are elevated, my blood rushing to my head.

He crouches beside me, his cold smile still in place. "Now ... how much of this you have to endure is up to you, Mr. Janner. I will stop when

I hear what I want from you. Got it?"

I spit in his face, satisfied at his disgusted expression as he wipes my saliva away with his forearm. "You know what you can do? You can take one of those electrified batons and shove it right up your ass."

Drummond nods, as if he was expecting this. "Very well. Shall we begin?"

An agent approaches and drops something over my eyes and nose, blotting out the room. I register its feel—some kind of cloth. Panic wells up in me as I realize what's about to happen just before the water comes, streaming over my eyes and forehead in a slow trickle, then becoming a deluge running over my nose and mouth.

I try to remember that it's a mind trick, a form of torture meant to create the sensation of drowning.

But my rational mind loses out and my body takes over, flailing as I sputter and gasp for air, my body shaking the table. It seems to go on forever as my lungs burn and I fight to breathe, to survive, to make it through until the water stops.

Once it does, I suck in mouthfuls of air, my chest heaving against the straps holding me down. Drummond's voice comes next, close to my ear.

"Where are the rest of the Resistance? Where are they going?"

Still working to breathe while I still can, I manage to grind out, "Fuck. You."

Drummond moves away. "Let's go again."

More water pouring over me in waves—drowning me, suffocating me as I convulse and writhe. The questions come between rounds, but when he dares to ask me Blythe's location, I clench my fists and tell him to bring it on. Waterboarding, beatings, starvation ... I will go through it all if it means he never finds her. I will do whatever it takes to make sure he never lays a hand on her.

And so, I keep her face in the forefront of my mind, trying to imagine what our baby will look like when he or she is born. By the time the waterboarding session ends with Drummond frustrated at me for not talking, I've given up hope that I will ever get to find out.

ABOUT THE AUTHOR

EVER SINCE SHE FIRST READ BOOKS LIKE *CHRONICLES OF NARNIA* OR *GOOSEBUMPS*, Alicia has been a lover of mind-bending fiction. Wherever imagination takes her, she is more than happy to call that place her home. With seven Fantasy and Science Fiction titles under her belt, Alicia strives to write multicultural characters and stories that touch the heart.

The mother of three and wife to a soldier, she loves chocolate, coffee, and of course good books. When not writing, you can usually find her with her nose in a book, shopping for shoes and fabulous jewelry, or spending time with her loving family.

CPSIA information can be obtained
at www.ICGtesting.com
Printed in the USA
LVOW11s0329130218
566354LV00001B/8/P